UNNATURAL CREATURES

"A refreshing spin on the original Gothic tale, rounding out the backstory of Frankenstein's monster with insights . . . This book has it all. *Unnatural Creatures* is an atmospheric, reimagined classic about the lines we cross for loyalty and love."
— *Foreword Reviews*

"Lushly atmospheric and rich with historical authenticity, *Unnatural Creatures* is a riveting Gothic tale that I devoured in one sitting . . . An inspired reimagining that was impossible to put down."
–MIMI MATTHEWS, *USA Today* bestselling author of
The Siren of Sussex and *John Eyre*

"Deftly uses the political climate of late 18th-century Geneva to add depth and nuance to one of literature's best-known stories of one man's folly, but it is her choice of protagonists—the three women closest to Victor Frankenstein—that truly elevates her work . . . *Unnatural Creatures*, like the novel that inspired it, is a richly atmospheric work of Gothic wonder."
—MOLLY GREELEY, author of *The Heiress: The Revelations of Anne de Bourgh* and *The Clergyman's Wife*

"This is the feminist reimagining of *Frankenstein* you didn't know you needed . . . A tribute to the strength and resilience of women that would make Mary Shelley proud."
—CLARISSA HARWOOD, author of *The Curse of Morton Abbey* and *Impossible Saints*

"Whether you're a devoted Mary Shelley fan or have never read *Frankenstein*, don't miss this masterful retelling. It's the kind of book that traps you within its pages and won't let go."

— ALYSSA PALOMBO, author of *The Spellbook of Katrina Van Tassel*

"Written by a true artist who understands that enlightenment can come from darkness. Waldherr's latest is a rich feast for fans of the gothic novel."

—LIBBIE GRANT, author of *The Prophet's Wife*

"A sensuous and empathetic look at the three women who knew Victor Frankenstein best . . . A veritable tour de force!"

—PAULETTE KENNEDY, author of *Parting the Veil*

"Waldherr transforms the women of Mary Shelley's *Frankenstein* from victims into protagonists . . . She sheds new light on one of literature's most famous stories."

—FINOLA AUSTIN, author of *Brontë's Mistress*

"In a masterful Gothic rendering, *Unnatural Creatures* reimagines the classic tale of *Frankenstein* through the eyes of the story's hitherto silent women. With its heartbreaking plot twists and stark sense of impending doom, Mary Shelley herself would be deeply moved by this dark tale of revenge and redemption."

—STEPHANIE MARIE THORNTON, *USA Today* bestselling author of *And They Called It Camelot*

"Waldherr skillfully weaves together the lives of the Frankenstein women in a feminist retelling of the classic tale of men and their monsters. This is a book that will seep into your bones and chill your heart in the best possible way."

—HESTER FOX, author of *A Lullaby for Witches*

UNNATURAL
CREATURES

A NOVEL OF
THE FRANKENSTEIN WOMEN

UNNATURAL CREATURES

* * *

KRIS WALDHERR

MUSE
PUBLICATIONS
NEW YORK

M🌿SE

Books *that make you think.*
Books *that make you feel.*
Books *that inspire.*

First trade paperback edition October 2022.

For inquiries on bulk purchases, contact Muse Publications Special Sales: sales@readmuse.com

Library of Congress Control Number: 2022902182

Cover and interior design: Kris Waldherr

Copyediting and research assistance: Thomas Ross Miller

Cover and interior photography and art: Rekha Garton/Trevillion Images; Adobe Stock/Sergey Nivens; Adobe Stock/Mannagia; Adobe Stock/Mark Carrel; Adobe Stock/DrObjektiff; Shutterstock/Edgars Butans; Shutterstock/Brandt Bolding

Epigraph and excerpts at the start of each chapter are from the 1831 edition of *Frankenstein, or The Modern Prometheus* by Mary Shelley.

Trade softcover: ISBN 979-8-9853512-0-0
Library hardcover: ISBN 979-8-9853512-2-4
E-book: ISBN 979-8-9853512-1-7
Audiobook: ISBN 979-8-9853512-3-1

For M.W.S.
Mother of Monsters
In Gratitude

"*I am an unfortunate and deserted creature; I look around, and I have no relation or friend upon earth . . . I am full of fears, for if I fail there, I am an outcast in the world forever.*"

— MARY SHELLEY
FRANKENSTEIN, OR THE MODERN PROMETHEUS

December 1799
North of Archangel, Russia

THIS WILL BE HER THIRD death since she became a monster.

So far, she has survived a death at the end of a rope, a second born of bullets. Now, as she stares out at the wide frozen sea stretching before her, she'll survive a death of ice—or so she hopes after months of traveling north. For at this stage of her journey, hope is all that remains. She carries it close, inside the satchel she clutches against her breast even in sleep. The satchel has grown so light that she no longer notes its weight. Though it is emptied of the dry tack and dried beef that filled it when she left Archangel, the satchel contains a collapsible telescope and a smashed compass. Finally, there's a locket containing a gentlewoman's portrait, whose provenance she refuses to recall.

Useless as the satchel's contents may be, she cannot bear to lose them, for this would be acknowledgement that she is truly without possessions in this world.

Without hope.

She halts to gather strength. The wind is especially bitter this morning; satchel or no, how shall she go on? She'd begun her journey intending to save others from death. Now she can't even save herself. She tells herself not all is lost. After all, she's resilient. She's learned to subsist on melted ice and hazelnuts gathered long ago, punctuated by unexpected gifts of meat. As a result, she's grown so slight she weighs less than a full-grown wolf. She appears a girl, not a grown woman. Nor does she appear a monster—but she knows better.

She circles and stares. No matter which way she turns, a bowl of white surrounds her. It's so different from the Mer de Glace, whose sea of ice fed into mountains tall enough to scrape the clouds. This snow-scape before her is flat. Affectless. Worse, the snow has hardened into a slick surface.

The muscles of her thighs burn. Her toenails peel from their beds of flesh. Her arms ache from holding them aloft for balance. Her stomach churns with air. Frostbite is a certainty though she's protected her eyes with goggles, her body with reindeer fur and trousers. She'd been warned to expect such ordeals when she'd left Archangel to trek north with her dogs and sled, fully provisioned for what may come. But now with a broken compass and cracked telescope, legs stinging, arms heavy, feet limping, and stomach emptied, she has no choice. Time to face her third death.

She lies down upon the ice, praying she'll somehow survive again like the miracle she is. Her eyes grow heavy. Hands numb. And then her mind returns to Geneva. To a time before it all began, when the three of them still lived. Before she knew of the curses plaguing them and so many others.

She envisions herself inside a snowy garden that appears to be Eden. The garden is set a league east of Geneva, by a mansion with a candle-lit tower. However, neither the garden nor the mansion were Eden—she knows this now. Still, if it were possible to go back to those days, she would.

She can never go back. But she can remember.

And so she remembers it all. She watches it all. It all unfolds like a tale as the snow begins anew.

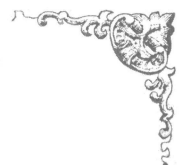

VOLUME ONE

THE MOTHER

* * *

Sixteen years earlier

CHAPTER I.

"But Caroline Beaufort possessed a mind of an uncommon mould; and her courage rose to support her in her adversity. She procured plain work; she plaited straw; and by various means contrived to earn a pittance scarcely sufficient to support life."

* * *

SOME TALES AREN'T what you think. Nor do they begin when you expect, such as at the stroke of midnight. Instead, this tale starts with a clock chiming five of the morning inside that mansion with the candle-lit tower, the one overlooking the snowy garden a league east of Geneva. It's two weeks before Christmas.

As the grandfather clock completed its final toll, the mansion's inhabitants remained asleep, though some would soon need to wake. The youngest maid, Sophie, curled like a hedgehog around her solitary pillow in an attic dormer, resisting the pull of a winter morning. In the same bed, the scullery maid snored beside her. Though she was only a year older than Sophie's thirteen, her stockinged toes poked out beneath the hem of the blanket; every so often, she wiggled them. Beyond their dormer, three other rooms equally spare, which sheltered the cook, butler, footman, and gardener. A floor below, Victor, the eldest son of the house, and Elizabeth, the adopted ward, lay in their far grander chambers, enjoying the oblivious slumber of the wealthy. In a room down the hall, the master, who'd dozed off while rereading the philosophical works of Rousseau.

None in the house stirred save for the mistress, Caroline Frankenstein, who occupied the solitary room in the candle-lit tower.

Caroline's eyes twitched as she shifted in her bed, revealing she was dreaming unhappily. It was a nightmare she'd suffered regularly since becoming a bride two decades earlier. In it, she was a girl of nineteen again, cursed by her father's ineptitude and pride. To support them, she was trapped plaiting straw for hats in a cold dark hut—a humbler labor than any of her servants ever experienced. Caroline's blistered fingers seeped blood at their tips. *"Faster, faster,"* she heard inside her dream. *"More, more."* As she dropped each straw plait into the basket beside her, the window shutters juddered against a persistent wind. Yet all she sensed was pain, for her mouth ached from a tooth extraction. Aching gums or no, she'd no choice but to keep her fingers flying or all would be lost.

Suddenly, the shutters snapped open. Piles of straw flew about Caroline's head, prickling her eyes and ears. She leapt from her stool to harvest straw from the wind. To begin anew just as her father arrived to urge her.

Faster, faster. More, more.

Caroline awoke gasping for air, deeply thirsty, and most importantly, alone. Morning had arrived, though so early that the sky appeared watery with a purple luminance. The snow had ceased. So had the thunder. Her candle, which she insisted on keeping lit while she slept, had devolved into a puddle of beeswax.

These days, her husband Alphonse never joined her in her bed. After suffering two miscarriages and a stillborn since the birth of their youngest son Ernest seven years earlier, Caroline was eager for her body to settle into complacency. Her heart couldn't suffer more loss. If that wasn't cause enough, Ernest's health was delicate as a milkweed. They'd had to send him to the Alps for his lungs; her doctor whispered this was due to Alphonse's age, for he was nearing sixty-five. Ernest wasn't sturdy like Victor, their eldest, or exquisite, like Elizabeth, their ward.

But now, after that dream, she wished Alphonse was there. He'd understand. He'd hold her, promise she was safe. He'd light a new candle for her, as many as she wanted without scolding for the waste.

Though he'd never been the dashing young nobleman she'd yearned for as a maiden, he'd proven the loyal companion life required. No woman's life was truly her own, but hers had been saved by Alphonse, who'd remained her father's only loyal friend after their ruin.

Caroline pulled herself up against her pillows. She rang for Sophie to bring her morning tea.

And then she recalled what spurred her nightmare. The pamphlet she'd found near her garden before the snow.

The Private History of Marie-Antoinette the cover said, accompanied by pornographic illustrations that made Caroline flush. The cover was ridged with mud, probably trampled beneath a rushing coach. Fearful of someone finding it, Caroline had brought the pamphlet home to burn, but the paper had proven too damp. She'd settled for hiding it under her bed, hoping no servant would dust there. She'd burn it later, though an important question prodded her: who'd brought the pamphlet so close to her home? Could it have been a university student, a traveler? Or even a disgruntled soldier? She prayed it wasn't one of her servants.

Though Caroline bore little interest in the French queen, there was no mistaking the pamphlet's dangerous rhetoric. Pamphlets encouraged violence. Pamphlets seeded rebellion beyond borders. France was not Geneva, but as a city-state republic without an army Geneva was dependent on France—especially after the Genevan Revolution the previous year, which had been incited by similar pamphlets. French troops had helped end the uprising, and made it possible for the Frankensteins to flee to the safety of their country house in Belrive— but not before armed rebels had closed the city gates and taken Alphonse and other aristocrats hostage. She'd truly feared he'd be murdered.

What happened then can no longer harm us. We're safe.

She wished she could believe this.

Another rush of anxiety rose, wrapping itself around Caroline's throat. Such emotions were unworthy of her position. She was the wife of a syndic, which was as close to nobility as Geneva possessed; syndics ruled akin to magistrates. The girl she'd been with the plaited straw, the blistered fingers, was long gone. Though she would soon turn forty, her chestnut hair revealed only a few strands of grey. Her face bore faint wrinkles on the corners of her mouth and dark eyes, which flashed with brilliance under sunlight. She appeared as she wished to be seen: the grace-filled wife and loving mother of two children and one much-adored ward. Not that it mattered to her dreams.

Without thinking, she tapped her fingers against her slim thigh beneath the bed linens. Ten times. One for each finger. Only that, nothing more. Her anxiety receded. Where was Sophie? She rang her bell again, welcoming the arrival of irritation over fear.

"Late as usual," Caroline murmured.

At last Sophie arrived. No apology, no smile.

"Madame," she greeted, dipping a quick curtsey. (Hadn't her curtsey been deeper a year earlier?) She set a painted tray bearing a silver pot, pitcher of milk, and accoutrements onto the nightstand. As she poured the thin amber stream into a china cup, a strand of auburn hair fell across the saucer. Sophie's hair.

Instead of an apology, the maid brazenly met Caroline's eyes before she blew the strand away.

Caroline bit back a retort, horrified. *It couldn't be her with the pamphlet.* She'd never have considered Sophie capable of such. But then again . . .

Faster, faster. More, more.

Just as Sophie curtseyed and turned for the door, Caroline coughed delicately.

"Madame?"

"Open the shutters, if you please." Caroline flushed as the words emerged from her mouth slurred. Her teeth had been so pretty once, so perfect, but they'd been affected by malnourishment: she'd never been able to conquer the lisp they caused. Alphonse said her lisp was charming, like the lilt of a song.

Sophie obeyed.

"Wake Mademoiselle Elizabeth and bring her to me. Afterward, I've a gown that no longer suits. You may have it, if it pleases you. The yellow *indienne.*"

A show of benevolent generosity cultivated loyalty from servants. Wasn't that what Alphonse advised?

Once Sophie left the room, Caroline set down her teacup, her hand shaking. She'd feel better once Elizabeth was there. Elizabeth, who knew how to soothe her worries.

Caroline glanced toward the window overlooking the lake. It was a fine December day, bright with the promise of a clear sky after last night's snow. Perhaps she'd take Elizabeth and Victor for a carriage ride toward Cologny, where the coast rounded. Now that Elizabeth was twelve, the girl was starting to appear more grown than not. Her beauty drew admiration wherever they went—but the real question was whether Victor admired Elizabeth too. Caroline suspected he did, judging by the lingering looks he stole when Elizabeth was unaware. His thoughtful manners made him seem mature beyond his nearly thirteen years. He was a gifted student. A devoted son. She adored him.

All is well. You just need to remain calm.

A knock sounded, giving Caroline a start. Sophie was alone, face taut like she'd broken a plate.

"Madame? I beg your forgiveness . . ."

Caroline's heart tripped. "What's happened?"

"Mademoiselle Elizabeth is gone."

* * *

"What do you mean, *gone?*" Caroline hissed as she rushed down the marble stairs, nearly tripping on the Alençon lace hem of her dressing robe. Such was the clamor of her steps that Alphonse bolted from his room, and Victor had thrown his arms around his mother's waist like he was still a child. "How can Elizabeth be *gone* without anyone's notice? Didn't you bring her breakfast?"

"Mademoiselle's door was closed," Sophie said, avoiding Caroline's glare. "I thought she was sleeping. I did not wish to wake her. Then I noticed her bed hadn't been slept in."

"You mean you did not wish to bring her breakfast," Caroline snapped.

That pamphlet. What if her disappearance had to do with it?

Caroline's panic rose as she imagined a revolutionary stealing into their home, coming across Elizabeth alone in bed, thinking her older than her years. Caroline's fingers clenched against her thigh. *One. Two. Three . . .*

"She's not downstairs," Alphonse reported, gasping for breath. "I'm sure she's fine, darling. I suspect she's outside. She probably made her bed herself." How vulnerable he appeared with his nightcap askew, his beard stubble. His face was especially pallid that morning too. "You remain here. I'll look in the garden."

"No, no. I'll come with you."

Faster, faster. More, more.

Out into the walled gardens they rushed, Caroline shivering in her too-thin silk robe and her soaked embroidered slippers; the soil was muddy beneath the snow. At this time of the year, the gardens were a scant shadow of their summer glory, when they'd spilled roses of every hue looping with bees and dragonflies, scented with honeysuckle and lilacs and lavender. The arrival of the first frost had brought the water in the tiered fountain to a frozen hush, along with the lily pond, which wasn't much bigger than the long mahogany table they used for formal dinners. Knowing Elizabeth, she'd probably given way to an impulse of inspiration, for she was a dreamy child unlike Victor who was bookish, or Ernest, who was frail. Still, they had to find her.

Once Caroline reached the terrace's first step, her eyes strained into the lily pond's dark waters. The icy surface remained unbroken. Anyway, Elizabeth knew not to fall into a lily pond. Still, Caroline's heart pounded as though it would leap from her body.

"Do you see her?" she called out.

"I see footsteps," Victor shouted from across the garden.

"One set? Or two?"

Sophie answered, "I can't tell if they're from last night. So muddy!"

"She couldn't have gone far," Alphonse assured. "When did you last see her, dearest?"

"After supper."

"You didn't check on her in bed?" Alphonse asked.

"It was late . . ." And she'd been too distressed by that pamphlet—so troubled she'd found herself unwilling to confide in him, though what could she have said? That she still feared loss though it had been years since her last miscarriage and months since the revolution? That she still had nightmares? That she feared one of their servants might be a revolutionary?

Just then a fox dashed before Caroline's feet before it dissolved into fog. White furred. Pink-eyed. It looked freakish. Where had it come from?

Sophie kneeled on the ground. "Breadcrumbs. They appear fresh."

"Look!" Victor pointed toward the large oak that lay in the center of the garden. "Over there."

"What do you see?" Alphonse's voice quavered.

"Something red beneath the oak, Father. I can't tell what."

Caroline's heart pounded in her ears as Victor ran toward the oak, outpacing Sophie.

And then Caroline saw it. Or, rather, *her*.

Half-hidden under muddy leaves, much like that pamphlet had been, a pair of thin grey legs protruded. A torn petticoat. A girl smaller than Elizabeth. A child really, perhaps ten years of age, with hair of an indiscriminate color. She was so pale, like snow. As for the red Victor spied, it wasn't blood. It was a painted bucket; presumably it belonged to the girl. The red bucket laid beside her tangled in ivy. Abandoned.

Caroline drew closer.

The girl was curled into a tight ball. Her mouth gaped like a crack in a wall. Her lips were chalky. Silent. She was thin, boney. Her clothing, sewn of a rough linen, was torn in places and mended in others. Her flesh was colorless, more akin to a coating of wax than a substance bearing blood and nerves. Her blanched cheeks wore the yellowed remains of a bruise. Her forehead scratched by random scars. A burned hand. Her lank silvery hair loose from its plaits. Worst of all, the girl's torso twisted abnormally. Someone, or something, had snapped her like a twig. Someone unimaginably strong and cruel.

Such was Caroline's shock that it took her a moment to realize the snow girl wasn't alone. Elizabeth lay beside her, her arms curled around the child's waist.

Her ward's eyes snapped open at Caroline's approach, pupils dilating.

Praise God, she lives. Caroline grabbed Elizabeth from beneath the oak, and embraced her so hard that she squeaked.

As for the snow girl, Victor spoke first. "Dead. She must be."

"The poor child . . ." Caroline breathed.

Her arms tightened around Elizabeth, imagining her in the snow girl's stead. Where had she come from? Who'd killed her? She couldn't be alive. Not with such injuries. Caroline's eyes filled. It was all her fault. She should have told Alphonse about the pamphlet. Should have warned everyone. Now it was too late.

"Look!" Victor pointed toward the snow girl.

Her chest rose and fell, shallow but true.

CHAPTER II.

"They consulted their village priest, and the result was, that Elizabeth Lavenza became the inmate of my parents' house—my more than sister—the beautiful and adored companion of all my occupations and my pleasures."

* * *

INSIDE THE KITCHEN, the Frankensteins and their servants laid both girls before the fire after displacing the kittens sleeping there in a box. Elizabeth shuddered from the heat, muzzy from shock. As for the snow girl, Caroline's heart tripped as she considered her limp body, which Victor had carried inside. Caroline pressed her fingers against the girl's icy wrist.

The snow girl's pulse was so faint. Slow, like a clock winding down.

"She's alive," Caroline announced. "Let's get her a hot bath."

"I'm so sorry!" Elizabeth blinked rapidly, bunching her dressing gown in her fists. "It's my fault! I woke early. I'd gone outside to feed the swans. I found her there under the oak. I-I thought to save her. Comfort her."

"The best comfort is a full belly and a warm fire, not a hug in the snow," Sophie accused as she gathered hot water for the tub, which Alphonse had set before the fireplace. "How could you lay with her there like an idiot? Why would you let her freeze instead of calling for help?"

"Hush!" Caroline snapped. "Don't speak like that to her or—"

"No, Sophie's right." Elizabeth's words were muffled by sobs. "I should have run for help, especially once I saw her spine was broken."

"Her spine isn't broken," Victor explained. "She's a hunchback. Scoliosis."

Scoliosis. Was that the scientific term? Caroline hadn't known. Whatever her illness, the girl remained pale as frost and as peculiar of stature even out of the cold. Pale hair. Even paler skin. Otherworldly. An unnatural creature. Hunchback or no, she was as ugly as Elizabeth was exquisite. The girl's face was wide as a moon, her eyes deeply shadowed. Her lashes were long and grey-pale, akin to torn cobwebs. Mud and dead leaves matted her hair. She stank like she'd been dunked in a chamber pot.

"I don't recognize her from the village," Alphonse said.

"Nor do I," Caroline agreed.

"Out of the way!" Sophie ordered, struggling with a bucket of steamy water.

"I'll take that," Victor offered. Caroline smiled; her son appeared a knight from a fairy tale, a prince in waiting. But then her attention returned to the hunchbacked girl, who'd let out a whimper. Perhaps they should call for a doctor. She'd decide after the bath.

"My dear, you should return to bed," Alphonse said. "Sophie will take care of her."

Caroline waved away her husband. "No, I'll bathe her."

"I'll help," Victor said, his brown eyes bright. "I'd like to look at her spine."

Caroline's brow crinkled. "The poor child requires privacy, not an examination." To Sophie: "Tell Cook breakfast can wait."

Now alone with the hunchbacked girl, Caroline set to preparing her for her bath. First, she dosed the girl with laudanum in case she was in pain. (She'd assumed it was pain causing her to whimper. Or was she calling for her mother?) The girl's color had improved, but her fine-boned hands were ruddy, hopefully not from frostbite.

Caroline tested the bath water. Not too hot. Not too cold. An unconscious smile rose across her lips, one she hadn't forced for once. Children loved Caroline. Caroline loved children. Fate had brought the girl to her much as it had Elizabeth. That must be it.

Though it was nearly a decade since Caroline had welcomed Elizabeth as her own, the details of that autumn day had never faded. She and Alphonse had been traveling by carriage near Lake Como, accompanied by Victor, who was then only four; after his birth, she'd remained barren of womb. She'd been weeping, for that morning another cycle had arrived to dash hope, when a glimmer of gold curls caught her attention. A set of large, inquisitive eyes as blue as the Alpine sky. A small girl. The most beautiful child she'd ever seen. She resembled an angel from a Renaissance fresco.

The beggar woman accompanying the golden-haired girl had explained she was an orphan with no worldly possessions save a noble name. "She's meant to be ours," Caroline whispered to Alphonse. "We'll save her. Offer her a home." In the end, Elizabeth accompanied the Frankensteins back to Geneva as the daughter of Caroline's heart, if not her blood, though she addressed Caroline as aunt rather than mother.

Caroline's memory faded as her thoughts returned to the hunchbacked girl in her lap. Perhaps Caroline could save her too.

Caroline asked in her gentlest voice, "What is your name, child?"

The girl flopped in her lap; the laudanum had affected her.

"I'm going to bathe you. I promise I won't hurt you . . ."

Caroline carefully unbuttoned the girl's collar and let out a yelp. Lice crawled along her nape.

"Is everything all right, my dear?" Alphonse called from outside the kitchen door.

"All's fine." A nervous laugh.

Lice won't harm you. It's nothing you haven't seen before. There'd been plenty of vermin in that cottage with her father. Caroline sucked in her lip and flicked lice from her wrist.

The girl moaned softly as Caroline unbuttoned her shabby canvas smock. Beneath the smock, her chemise was stained with what appeared to be dirt. *Not dirt. Worse.* The girl had fallen in horse dung—that's what Sophie had smelled. Caroline glanced inside the girl's drawers. They were clean. She was also older than Caroline expected; soft down crested the cleft of her sex.

Caroline threw her clothes into the fire. The girl snored gently, unaware of her nudity.

By then the sun had broken through, flooding the kitchen in morning light. It revealed the girl's flesh to be laced with bruises and scars. Burns, some pale from age, others raw and new. Either the girl was clumsy or she'd won someone's acrimony. As for the scoliosis, her spine twisted like a tree, granting her right shoulder an unusual height. She was perhaps the ugliest child Caroline had ever beheld, but it wasn't because of her hunchback. It was because of neglect.

Caroline's eyes filled. *How could someone be so cruel?* She couldn't comprehend it.

The girl didn't resist as Caroline settled her into the bath; the laudanum had done its job. She met Caroline's stare. Her eyes were a strange colorless hue, akin to trout beneath a stream. Laudanum or no, she bore an intelligence in her gaze. An awareness. She shuddered as the heat of the water rose up her bony limbs, crossed her arms over her breast buds.

"What's your name?" Caroline asked anew. "Where did you come from?"

The girl blinked, eyes tearing. Her mouth opened, shut. She bit her lip. What if she was a mute? Caroline hadn't considered this.

It took Caroline a half-hour to wash and comb out her matted hair; the girl dozed and woke, shivering as though she'd couldn't recall how she'd arrived naked in a tub of water. Caroline carefully drowned each louse, smashing the corpses inside a rag.

"Shall I keep you?" Caroline asked as she toweled the girl's hair. Her clean hair was a silvery hue, like moonbeams. Straight, without a hint of curl. "You'd like that, wouldn't you?"

As would I.

The girl forced an ungainly smile before her eyelids flagged anew. She wasn't ugly. Not really—all it took was some soap and care. As for the scars and bruises, those would heal in time.

Humming, Caroline plaited the girl's hair into a crown and dressed her in one of Elizabeth's cast-offs. It fit her perfectly. Like a doll. Again, that strange hope rose. *It's a sign she's here. Fate.*

"There! Better?"

The girl's mouth twisted slowly. She could talk. She would talk.

"What is it?" Caroline pressed.

Tears filled the girl's eyes. A sob.

Before Caroline could comfort her, a knock sounded.

"Madame?" Cook's voice came from outside the kitchen door. "I know whose child she is. She's the daughter of the gravedigger,

Monsieur Moritz. He died two days ago. Her name is Justine—I'll fetch her mother."

* * *

"She ran away," Madame Moritz announced an hour later; she'd arrived at the Frankensteins' door clutching the hands of two children, both as colorful as Justine was pale. A boy and a girl. Rosy-cheeked cherubs with brown curls, blue eyes. Oil paintings beside a silverpoint. "I'd sent Justine out to fetch water, and had no idea where she'd gone. Certainly not trespassing in your garden!"

Madame Moritz's low tone belied the ruddiness of her face—Caroline sensed she was fighting her temper. She was also, from the looks of it, about six months with child, belying the grey hair peeking from her linen cap. She perched on the only chair large enough in Caroline's morning room to contain her bulk, children clutched against her swollen belly, which her black wool cloak barely covered. Caroline rushed with envy at Madame Moritz's fertile state—three children including Justine, a new baby underway—before reminding herself that her husband had just died.

Madame Moritz scowled at Justine. "I apologize for the disturbance she's brought, Madame—forgive me, what's your name? Your servant never told me."

"Frankenstein," Caroline said, her tone hollow. "I'm the syndic's wife."

"I'd been the gravedigger's wife myself." Madame Moritz's tart tone was at odds with her swollen eyes.

Caroline was uncertain how to respond. Nothing about the morning had gone as expected; at least Elizabeth was safe. As for Justine, Cook explained the girl had been a favorite of her father, whose doting had annoyed his wife. Hence, the bruises and scars. She was also older than expected—twelve, which made her close in age to Elizabeth and Victor. The girl still dozed, eyelids fluttering with laudanum-induced dreams. Justine's situation was sad, tragic even. But children were misused all the time—Caroline couldn't save all of them. Though at least she'd saved one . . .

She glanced at Elizabeth, who was seated beside her on the chaise. Angelic Elizabeth. Adored Elizabeth.

"Mama, what did Justine do now?" Madame Moritz's other daughter mewed. "Why is she here?"

"It's our fault, Madame Moritz," Caroline said, careful to enunciate each word to avoid lisping due to her bad teeth. "Forgive us the delay in returning your daughter. My cook recognized Justine, but this took longer than I wish."

"Has your daughter done this before?" Elizabeth asked, a nervous giggle marring her question. Her gaze slid between Madame Moritz and Caroline as though she was watching a game no one wanted to play. "Run away, that is?"

Madame Moritz turned her glare toward Elizabeth. "You're cheeky, aren't you?"

Elizabeth appeared set to cry when Caroline rose from the chaise. She flushed as she grabbed a glimpse of herself in the mirror over the mantel. With all the turmoil that morning, her hair still spilled in chestnut-hued curls around her shoulders, like she'd just risen from bed; she remained dressed in the French-style chemise gown she favored for mornings. She looked half-dressed, frivolous compared to mourning garb. Still, Caroline would do what she could.

She clasped Madame Moritz's hands. "Again, I am so sorry for your loss. I've been told Monsieur Moritz was a good man from those who required his—" she searched for an appropriate word "—services. If we can help your family . . ."

Madame Moritz sniffed at Justine. "I'll take her and trouble you no more."

"She still sleeps," Elizabeth said eagerly. "We can bring her home once she wakes. Your other children are invited to remain as our guests. We'll amuse them for you."

Caroline said, "As for Justine, I can fetch a physician, for which I'll bear responsibility. For her spine. Please."

"You'd be wasting your time." Madame Moritz's voice broke. "She'll never improve—believe me, I know! The girl's a half-wit. No doubt she made up some story about how she ended in your garden." She tapped Justine's arm. "Wake! We must return home!"

As Caroline watched Madame Moritz lead Justine and her sisters from the morning room, Elizabeth stood beside her aunt.

"Her father's dead," Elizabeth said in a restrained tone. "And a new baby soon. They'll starve."

"The mother seems the sort to refuse charity," Caroline answered. Anyway, having a father was no guarantee against starvation—this she understood too well.

The front door shuddered. Slammed. Through the window, Caroline and Elizabeth watched Madame Moritz drag Justine toward the gate, the other children skipping ahead. Justine's feet shuffled against the gravel walk. "Hurry, girl!" Her mother slapped the side of her face.

Caroline cringed. Was the girl crying? She was.

Caroline's eyes stung in response. She recalled how trusting Justine had been while she'd bathed her, the improbable hope that had bubbled. Her mind returned to that seditious pamphlet hidden beneath her bed. She'd actually forgotten about it in the turmoil. Strange how hope and fear could dwell together, like nettles beside lilies.

Caroline turned from the window. Time to get on with the day. Time to do something—anything—besides stare at a girl she hadn't known existed until hours earlier. The world was full of sorrows. There was nothing to do but endure.

Or was there?

Caroline spoke quickly. "What if there was another way to keep the girl? One that wouldn't wound her mother's pride?"

Elizabeth immediately understood. "Don't we have need for another servant, Aunt?"

"Yes. Yes, we do."

And like that, hope returned.

"Hurry!" Caroline called. The door. Her shawl. They rushed outside in the cold, breath pluming, just as Justine and her mother reached the iron gate.

"Stop, Madame! I've a proposal for you!" Caroline cried.

Madame Moritz glared over her shoulder. "Haven't you done enough, Madame Frankenstein?"

"I've use for your daughter. Employment."

Madame Moritz shook her head. "We've no need of your charity. No need!"

"Not charity, Madame Moritz. I've use for a maid!"

"A maid? Really?" Madame Moritz advanced toward Caroline, Justine dangling from her grasp. "You're too good for her. Look at her— she's a monster! You should take my other daughter."

"Only Justine will do."

Madame Moritz offered a bitter laugh. "Why her?"

Caroline flailed for words. "Because she'd work hard. Because she's close in age to my niece. I'll send you her pay."

Madame Moritz shoved the girl Caroline's way. "Take her then."

* * *

Midnight. One house. Three beds.

Upstairs in her solitary bed, Caroline said her prayers and crawled beneath the blankets after burning the pamphlet, which had finally dried out. Her chest released as the threatening pages flared then blackened into ash; she'd soon forget that shocking drawing of Marie Antoinette's half-clad figure. As for Sophie, Caroline decided she'd had nothing to do with the pamphlet. For whatever reason, rescuing Justine had eased Caroline's fears, though she still questioned how the girl came to be in their garden.

Fate, she told herself again. It was fate Justine ended up in her garden. Fate Elizabeth had found her. The girl was fatherless. The mother abusive. Who could blame Justine for running away?

Already, Caroline's spirit was lighter. Once she'd rescued Justine from her mother, the girl had pressed against Caroline's hand like a cat. And then at last, Caroline heard the girl's voice for the first time. Her voice was high-pitched, broad-voweled. Fated.

"Madame, anything you need of me, I shall do for you. This I promise."

Which was exactly what Caroline yearned to hear. After all, what was more useful than a loyal child?

Smiling, Caroline wrapped her arms around herself beneath the covers. For the first time in months, she didn't light a candle before sleep or think of curses. Her hands relaxed. Instead of tapping, she counted blessings.

Before she reached ten, her eyelids grew heavy. Therefore, she didn't hear an owl swoop toward the white fox hidden beneath the great oak, where they'd discovered Justine that morning. Nor did Caroline hear Elizabeth, who couldn't sleep, abandon her bedroom to seek Victor.

As Elizabeth strode through the darkened house, the long hallways were shadowed save for the shimmer of moonlight reflecting the lake. Once she reached Victor's room, she crawled into his soft warm bed beside him, like they were still children as when they'd met. Without awareness they lived in a world different than the one they'd grown up in . . . a world that now judged them for their rank and privilege.

Elizabeth inhaled deeply, pressing her nose against Victor's neck. One of the kittens from the kitchen slept beside him in a haze of grey-striped fur. A leather-bound book rested on Victor's chest. Agrippa's *De occulta philosophia libri tres*—he'd fallen asleep reading it. A candle burned on the table beside his bed, spilling gold across his features. He was so good. So kind. So smart. How she loved him.

He cracked an eye open. "Sleep, dearest friend."

And Elizabeth did, but only after she blew out the candle.

Her breath sent the thin scent of beeswax drifting toward the attic where, in a third and final bed, Justine lay beside Sophie in a dormer room; the scullery maid had been moved downstairs next to the kitchen. Once Sophie's shoulders rose and fell with sleep, Justine's eyes blinked open. She abandoned the bed to silently pad downstairs in the dark.

Justine reached the third floor, then the second, which bore the unexpected comfort of carpeting. Past Caroline and Victor's room, where Elizabeth still slept in his arms. Down hallways and past doorways; anyone watching would say the girl possessed a distinctive limp, one different than a sprained ankle.

As Justine explored the house, her hands trailed along the wood, the wallpaper. She paused every few steps to stare. The gilded mirrors. The Persian rugs. The damask curtains. She wiped her cheeks, which were wet. Happiness and sorrow. Loss and gain.

She continued her solitary tour toward the stairway that curled into the entry hall, where carpeting returned to cold white marble. She halted in front of a life-sized painting, which hung over the mantle there. A portrait of Caroline.

The oil painting was the first thing everyone noticed as soon as they entered the Frankenstein mansion. Its style was darkly florid, like something from a century earlier. Everyone knew Alphonse had commissioned the portrait soon after he'd wed Caroline. The painting depicted a mournful girl in rustic dress kneeling beside a pine coffin, which was surrounded by piles of straw. Caroline at her father's funeral. Some gossiped it would have been more respectful to portray her wearing court clothes, but Alphonse disagreed. He claimed the painting revealed the nobility of Caroline's soul.

But Justine did not know this then. She only knew it was a portrait of the woman who'd rescued her.

"Anything you want of me," she whispered, "I will do for you."

A long moment later, she backed away. She returned upstairs.

CHAPTER III.

"Do you remember on what occasion Justine Moritz entered our family? . . . Madame Moritz, her mother, was a widow with four children, of whom Justine was the third. This girl had always been the favourite of her father; but, through a strange perversity, her mother could not endure her, and, after the death of M. Moritz, treated her very ill."

* * *

LATER, when all was said and done, Caroline would consider Justine's entrance into their household as the moment when change arrived for the Frankensteins. It wasn't the usual change a new servant brought. Nor was it what Caroline expected. Though this change was imperceptible at first, it was like a stone wedged in a wall before the cement set. While the wall remained functional, it appeared ever so slightly off. Not that this was bad, mind.

For starters, as a result of Justine sharing a dormer with Sophie, Sophie began to oversleep; before then, the scullery maid always awakened Sophie, who was responsible for Caroline's breakfast and hair. Therefore, when Justine shyly offered her services to Caroline, Caroline accepted. *She'll learn from this*, Caroline told herself; it remained unclear whether she meant Sophie or Justine.

Such was the change confronting Sophie when she appeared a half-hour late one morning nearly two weeks after Justine's arrival, just before Christmas: Caroline's bedroom was already fragrant with coffee and freshly baked bread. A fire already blazed in the grate, which Justine had started. Caroline was already seated before her vanity wearing her favorite gown, a periwinkle blue *robe à l'anglaise*, with her hair dressed. It was a complicated coiffure too, one involving curls and interwoven plaits. Justine had done well—and then Sophie arrived.

Caroline watched Sophie's eyes widen at Justine's unexpected presence. The girl stood on the bench beside Caroline, setting a silk flower into a curl. Victor slouched in a chair across the room reading a book and drinking coffee; he'd knocked at his mother's door soon after she'd dressed, stating he'd had a nightmare. Caroline's mood was such that, for once, this didn't seem a sign of impending disasters or curses.

Sophie offered an awkward curtsey. "Madame."

Not so bold now, are we? Instead of clenching her fingers, Caroline suppressed a smile. "Ah, there you are at last!"

Victor closed his book. "Shall I leave, Mother?"

"No, it's fine, darling." He looked particularly grown-up that morning, Caroline decided. How broad his shoulders had become! His voice was starting to settle, and he was taller than she now.

He bent to kiss her cheek, the sour aroma of coffee lingering on his breath. "I'm a distraction. I know today's an important day."

Yes, an important day. Caroline tried to ignore the rise of nerves his words provoked.

Once Victor left, Sophie dropped another curtsey, this one deeper. "I'm sorry for my tardiness, Madame. It won't happen again."

"It matters not. Justine did my hair. I never have expected this—how clever she is!"

Justine beamed at Caroline as though she was the Virgin Mary come to life. "My father taught me. He'd help my mother with her hair. Well, and others' hair as well—Papa had so many talents."

"Well, you've certainly a gift." Caroline admired herself in her mirror. "Don't you agree, Sophie? Oh, Justine also sews. I've a gown that requires hemming—you know the one."

Sophie said eagerly, "The floral sack gown. I can do it, Madame."

Caroline waved a hand. "Ah, but look at how late you were! Let Justine assist you. Today is an important day. Or have you forgotten?"

"The Christmas soirée—I know." Sophie flushed. "I can hem the gown, Madame."

It was the Frankensteins' first time holding an event since the Geneva revolution. It had been Alphonse's idea. He'd pushed for the soirée despite Caroline's reluctance. A way to mark all had returned to as it should be.

"You should be helping Cook in the kitchen."

"I can do both, Madame." And then Sophie actually smiled as she departed.

Now alone with Justine, Caroline stole a glance at her. The girl had cleaned up nicely, though she still appeared more fey than human—perhaps that's what came of having a gravedigger as a father. That morning, she was wearing another one of Elizabeth's castoffs, which fit her perfectly, a Turkish red shortgown over a linen petticoat. Justine hummed tunelessly as she arranged Caroline's brushes, comb, and toiletries across her vanity. It was deeply reassuring.

Caroline's mind would be even more eased once she presented the proposition she'd mulled since the girl's arrival. It was a simple proposition, one that should be easy to agree to. *"Madame, anything you need of me, I shall do for you,"* Justine had vowed; this had spurred Caroline's plan.

Caroline cleared her throat to gain Justine's attention. The girl dropped a brush, which dislodged a small porcelain shepherdess on the edge of the vanity. The figurine shattered in a hail of white shards.

The girl curled herself beneath the vanity. "I'm sorry, Madame! So very sorry!"

Caroline fell to her knees next to the girl. "Come out! You needn't hide from me."

Justine untucked her head; her eyes brimmed with tears. "You're going to send me back, aren't you?"

"No, no—I never cared for that piece anyway. And I startled you, didn't I?"

"Did you?"

Caroline nodded. "It was my fault it broke, not yours."

The girl ceased rocking herself. "You're not angry?"

Caroline offered what she hoped was a beatific smile. "You will find our family is not like those in France. We treat our servants as our equals." She stretched a hand toward the girl. "Will you come out? Please?"

After a long moment, Justine accepted Caroline's hand. How sweet the girl was yet feral, like a dog who'd been scolded so often it no longer trusted its instincts.

Once Justine stood, Caroline tucked a strand of Justine's strange, colorless hair into her plaits. "There. Now you're settled."

Justine drew a shuddering breath. "I'm very grateful to you, Madame!"

"That makes me very happy, Justine." Caroline's pulse picked up. *Ask her now.* "Once I understood what happened with your father," she continued in a careful tone, "I knew I had to help your family. You, in particular."

"Because you found me in your garden?" Justine had yet to explain how she'd arrived there; Caroline hadn't pressed her. Who could blame her for running away from such a mother, especially now that her father was dead?

"More than that, Justine . . ."

And then there it was, the opportunity to present Caroline's proposition.

"I have a favor to ask of you. While you are here, I hope you will tell me if you notice anything untoward in my household."

The girl's sallow cheeks flared with color. "Untoward? What does that mean?"

"Unusual. Alarming." Though Caroline hadn't found another pamphlet since that one time, she remained vigilant.

Justine cocked her head like an anxious dog. "What should I look for, Madame?"

"Listen to what others say. Anything you hear. Or if you see someone visiting who seems out of place."

"Someone visiting your servants? Or your children?"

Caroline offered a tinkling laugh accompanied by a vague gesture. "Anything you notice. I can check on my children myself."

"I did see someone that night, right before you found me," the girl whimpered. "That's what chased me into your garden."

Chased? Hadn't she run away? This was new information. Caroline's heart raced.

"Who chased you? What did you see?"

"I know I should have told you, Madame! I was afraid you'd think I made it up after everything my mother said."

"Oh, I'd have believed you!" Perhaps it had been a soldier. "Did they wear red? Or blue? A uniform?"

During the revolution, the Swiss artillery had worn red, the French blue. But the presence of military hadn't frightened Caroline as much as those who'd rioted in Geneva.

Don't think of that now.

"Red. Maybe purple. Definitely not blue. Not a soldier," Justine admitted in a low voice. "A golem."

A golem? Caroline laughed, unsettled. "I'm uncertain what that is."

"A monster. Something my father spoke of. It's a tale he told me . . ." Justine's voice broke. "The golem chased me into your garden. He was dressed in red, larger than I've ever seen—"

"A Swiss soldier passing through." Caroline's tone suggested she'd have preferred it to be a monster. She recalled the bloodied bodies she'd spied after Alphonse's release, the bitter screams, the bonfires encircling Geneva . . .

"You don't believe me, do you, Madame? I'm not a half-wit! Nor am I a liar. Not like my mother said."

From the wild look in her eyes, Justine was a blink away from tears. Caroline handed her a handkerchief. "I believe you did see something, Justine. I also believe whatever you saw is now gone, yes?"

Justine offered a vehement nod. Snot dribbled from her nose. She really wasn't much more than a child. So different from Elizabeth and Victor. Uneducated. Simple. She probably knew nothing of revolution and soldiers. Well, best not to tell her.

"So, from here on, we'll only think of the future, Justine. If you notice anything, you'll tell me." Caroline slid a cube of sugar toward Justine from her breakfast tray. The girl gave the sugar a cautious lick before popping it in her mouth. "Will you do this for me?"

Justine nodded, wiping her eyes. "Yes, Madame. Anything you need I shall do for you. I promise!"

"Thank you, Justine."

Caroline picked up a pair of gloves off her desk. A walk. That's what she needed. Afterward, she'd prepare for the Christmas soirée, though the anticipation made her lightheaded.

I'm safe. We're all safe.

* * *

Hours later, these ruminations still troubled Caroline as she descended the great staircase to greet their soirée guests, Elizabeth by her side. At the bottom of the stairs, Justine held a platter of wineglasses that appeared to weigh more than she did. The girl offered a wide smile toward Caroline, but the girl's grateful presence did not ease her mood. Already there were too many guests—it appeared as though Alphonse had invited everyone they knew. Their aggressively festive chatter and laughter rose up the staircase, as though they were reassuring themselves all was as it had been before the Geneva revolution, that this Christmas would be like the others. But how could it be? Two Christmases ago there'd been no violence to recall.

Caroline glanced at Elizabeth, whose brow was as serene as ever. The girl looked lovely in her new sack-back gown, sewn from a creamy embroidered brocade. Its back pleats draped along the stairs, whispering with a faint crinkle every time Elizabeth moved. She'd kept her gold curls unpowdered, which also won Caroline's approval. Powder spoke of artifice and cunning, neither of which Elizabeth possessed.

The pleasure Caroline took in her ward's appearance faded with each step toward their guests; there appeared near to a hundred. In addition to this crush, Alphonse had invited a Dr. Galvani visiting from Bologna. "It's the holidays," he'd said. "We can't remain hermits forever. Plus I have a surprise for Victor." What this surprise was, he refused to say; Caroline wondered if it had anything to do with this mysterious doctor.

Caroline murmured to Elizabeth, "Did your uncle say anything to you about a surprise for Victor?"

"Victor?" Elizabeth waved over the balustrade toward their guests, smiling broadly. How loud it was! "There he is! He's downstairs. Uncle too."

"That's not what I asked."

"What, Aunt?"

"Never mind, darling." Change made people skittish, Caroline decided. Everyone, not only aristocrats. Change felt as slippery as the soles of her new shoes against the marble stair—

Caroline stumbled on the polished step. Elizabeth grabbed the soft of her guardian's arm.

"Aunt! Are you alright?"

Caroline clutched the balustrade. "I am now, dearest."

A nervous smile as she pulled herself upright. One step down. Another.

Viewed from above, the Frankensteins' guests resembled a kaleidoscope of color and silks, all glimmering beneath the candle-lit chandelier. Their servants circled about them, even Justine with her platter of glasses. Their gatherings had never appeared so overwhelmingly large in Geneva. Perhaps it was because the doors to the ballroom remained shut, forcing their guests to congregate in their entry hall, which wasn't intended for a soirée. Despite the crush, several couples were dancing a minuet to the string quartet Alphonse had engaged. Joyful, colorful, stately. As life had once been.

To her surprise, Caroline felt her heart lift with pleasure.

Surrounding the dancing couples were clusters of ladies and gentlemen, all of whom had traveled more than a league from Geneva to join the Frankensteins on a cold winter night. All were dressed in their finest, though this varied by class and modernity. Some chose stiff court dresses adorned with wide panniers and ruffles, others simple white chemise dresses flouncing with lace.

There was Madame Tavernier, their lively neighbor from Geneva. She was a gossip who enjoyed making Caroline uneasy. Of course, she stood beside the oil portrait of Caroline, her ostrich feather-adorned head cocked with a knowing air; of course, she wore a blue satin court gown. There was Madame Tavernier's awkward daughter Marianne, whom Elizabeth had befriended, along with the Biron girls, who were near Elizabeth's age. Judging by the flutter of their painted silk fans, they'd already drunk a glass of wine. Behind them, Monsieur Lenard, the kindly lawyer whose opinion Alphonse relied upon, and his charming wife, who appeared with child. They were dressed in unadorned clothes sewn of fine fabrics, suggesting their republican ideals.

As Caroline descended the stairs, many raised their eyes her way and smiled as though she was a queen. Her mood rose. *How lovely this is,* she thought, just as the string quartet finished the minuet and began a lively contredanse.

Amid the swirling skirts and joyful laughter, Caroline's eyes picked out Victor, who awaited by the wall beside Alphonse—Victor who looked so handsome in his satin cutaway and black breeches. Caroline's chest felt near to bursting with love and pride. Alphonse appeared dignified in the waistcoat she'd embroidered with flowers for him.

Beside Victor, a tall young man with fawn-colored longish hair and a sensitive air. Henry Clerval, Victor's closest friend. He was still in that awkward stage of life where he appeared neither boy nor man. He wore a simple brown jacket bearing a white rosebud in a buttonhole, more artistic than noble. He'd brought along his widower father, who fidgeted amid the aristocratic company. Monsieur Clerval was a merchant with a shop off the Place du Bourg-de-Four in Geneva. He appeared dressed as though for a midday stroll.

"Look, there's Henry!" Elizabeth said, releasing Caroline's arm. "I must greet him."

"Go, dearest!"

Finally, Caroline saw the doctor Alphonse invited—he could be no other. The dancers seemed to fade from view as she stared. Her stomach gave an odd flip though she was uncertain why.

Dr. Galvani stood alone in the crowd, hands cupped behind his back as though deep in thought. The doctor's unpowdered greying hair was gathered at his neck with a thick black ribbon. His coat was decidedly shabby, but his linens blindingly white. Caroline sensed an air of self-satisfaction in the doctor's posture. Confidence. For some reason, his hands drew her attention even from a distance. They were stained along the fingertips.

Before she could mull this significance, Victor swept up the remaining stairs to greet his mother. He bowed gallantly.

"How lovely you look, Mother! May I escort you?"

"You may." Caroline rushed with pleasure. Her son guided her toward Alphonse, who offered a shy grin that reminded her of the courtly gentleman who'd sheltered her after her father's untimely death.

"You look happy," Alphonse said, draping his arm about her waist.

"I am—you were right about the soirée." Caroline swept her arms toward their guests, eyes searching for Dr. Galvani and his stained fingers. "Everyone is so happy! And the music—I've forgotten how I've missed it."

Ah, but your happiness is best of all, my dear."

"Your doctor appears lonely," Caroline observed. "I should introduce myself."

"No introduction is necessary. But trust me, you won't forget Dr. Galvani. It's fortunate he was visiting Geneva for Christmas."

"What sort of doctor is he?" Her tone was sharper than intended.

Alphonse offered a knowing smile, the kind he used when they were alone, a rarity these days. "A natural philosopher."

Victor piped up, "Why is he here? Why are the ballroom doors shut?"

"I'd wondered the same, Uncle." Elizabeth and Henry joined their circle. Lanky Henry leaned against petite Elizabeth in a protective manner; Monsieur Clerval had drifted away to God knew where, probably eager to avoid conversation. "How secretive you are about him!"

"Patience, my dears." Alphonse pulled two glasses of champagne from a tray. One for Caroline, the second for him. "All will be revealed soon."

Before Caroline could posit another question, the string quartet silenced. Alphonse approached Dr. Galvani.

"If you please, let us begin."

"As you will, Signore Frankenstein." The doctor spoke with an Italian inflection.

The ballroom doors glided open as though guided by unseen hands. An unexpected icy breeze blew in.

Alphonse raised his voice to address their guests. "Mesdames and messieurs! To the ballroom! The entertainment is about to commence."

CHAPTER IV.

"On this occasion a man of great research in natural philosophy was with us, and . . . he entered on the explanation of a theory which he had formed on the subject of electricity and galvanism."

* * *

INSIDE THE BALLROOM, the air felt as though ice crystals were suspended within it. A quick glance revealed all the windows had been opened. The ballroom was also unlit. Caroline shivered as she accepted her husband's hand in the shadowy room. Her excitement surprised her.

Once the Frankensteins and their guests were inside, a bevy of servants shut the ballroom doors and windows with a snap. The room turned pitch-black; Caroline's excitement shifted. *Oh, for a single candle!* she fretted, her fingers searching for the edge of the door.

Unable to see, every sound grated. Giddy chatter rising and falling. The shuffle of feet as people settled. She struggled to find an anchor in her disorientation, something besides the door frame. There was Elizabeth with her nervous giggle. Henry's mild scent of trade and ink. Victor clutching a purloined glass of claret, judging by the scent of fermented fruit.

"We're all inside, yes?" Alphonse sounded from the other side of the ballroom. "We'll begin. I've invited you here to witness a miracle—"

"A Christmas miracle?" a woman's voice scoffed. Madame Tavernier, who'd been staring at the oil portrait earlier; Caroline's mouth tightened.

"A miracle at any time," Alphonse clarified. "A miracle my guest Dr. Galvani, a natural philosopher from Bologna, will reveal."

Caroline awaited a rush of chatter or applause. Silence. Perhaps their guests were as uneasy as she felt.

"Dr. Galvani?" Alphonse prompted. "You are ready to commence?"

"I am, Signore Frankenstein."

A match hissed. The scent of sulfur. A candle offering scarce illumination to a man's face. Dr. Galvani's face. He emerged from the darkness, as uncanny as a ghost. Caroline's stomach gave another odd flip.

Dr. Galvani called out, "Your guests can all see me, yes?"

A rush of assent. Dr. Galvani's tone was forceful. "I apologize for the cold air, but it is necessary for reasons I will later explain. I beg your patience as I reveal newly discovered wonders, which will bring us closer to the source of all that animates life." He clapped briskly. "If you will, clear the center of the ballroom! Against the walls, if you please."

A rustle of skirts and heels. Laughter. "Ouch, you stepped on my foot!" Apologies. Caroline shivered anew. She sensed Alphonse beside her; yes, that was the camphor liniment he used for his stiff neck.

"Are you frightened, my dear?" he asked.

An unexpected ripple rose along her spine. "Should I be?"

"Watch. Whatever happens, don't shut your eyes."

Dr. Galvani's voice boomed. "*Signore e signori*, are you ready?"

A chorus of impatient, excited applause. Caroline recognized Elizabeth's bell-like giggle in the mix.

"Bravo!" Dr. Galvani called. "Three rules before we start. *Primo*: do not look away from the center of the room. *Secondo*: do not move no matter what you might behold. *Terzo*: remain silent and calm . . ."

He blew out his candle.

"*Ecco!* Let us begin!"

Devoid of that single candle, the ballroom seemed as dark as Hades. Caroline resisted the urge to flee.

After what felt like the longest moment, her ears made out a soft metallic click. The door that led to the garden. Had someone entered? Her throat grew tight.

A shifting, slippery sound. Soft footsteps on the marble floor from the center of the ballroom—this must be why Dr. Galvani had insisted on their vacating it.

And then just as unexpectedly, a pinprick of light.

A spark.

Flurries of sparks. They twinkled like stars in the middle of the ballroom, each about three feet above the floor. No, higher. The stars appeared as Caroline imagined the sky must have shone the night of her Savior's birth. Her mouth spread into an unforced smile. How magical the stars appeared, the sparks rising and falling! They were accompanied by a soft sizzle that snapped and popped.

Amid the sparks of light, she made out the silhouettes of legs, each pressing against the others as they danced. Men—or were they women? —adorned in breeches and stockings, their arms waving with unexpected grace in circle patterns. They must have been wearing slippers, for their steps made nary a sound.

More sparks. The audience gasped. A chorus of *"Oooohs!"*

Caroline's hands relaxed. Yes, it was good. All was good. Whatever Dr. Galvani was presenting, it was a miracle, as Alphonse had promised. Her eyes watered. Was it from squinting into the dark? Or emotion? No matter. Dr. Galvani's display had been beautiful, and beauty was required these troubled days—she understood this now.

The stars dazzled. Circled in a celestial display. And then just as suddenly, they faded from whence they came.

"Ecco la!"

Light returned in a blaze of candles. Caroline blinked, eyes stinging. Once her sight adjusted, she made out the silhouettes of six men, all adorned in stark ebony from their toes to their fingertips. They wore black breeches above black silk tights with matching slippers and gloves, to blend in with the night. Each of them held a lit brass candelabra as though God Himself had declared "Let there be light."

"Electricity!" Dr. Galvani proclaimed with a bow.

"Bravo!" Caroline beat her palms together until they burned, her face aching with joy. Others joined her applause, along with a soft "Brilliant," from Henry.

"Brilliant indeed," she heard Alphonse murmur, his tone lighter than she'd witnessed in months. "Victor? What think you?"

No answer came. Where was Victor? Caroline glanced about the ballroom. There was Elizabeth, Henry . . . At last she found Victor on the other side of the door from her. His arms were folded against his chest, his face long.

"Darling." She nodded toward Victor.

Alphonse waved away her concern. "Look."

He pointed toward Dr. Galvani, who'd returned to the center of the ballroom. What was next? Caroline found herself eager to find out; she forgot about Victor. Such wonders and marvels! She'd never forget them.

"The demonstration of static electricity you've just witnessed," Dr. Galvani explained, "was created by rubbing silk in a dry, cold environment—hence the open windows. The friction creates negative and positive charges. But this is but a fraction of what electricity can accomplish.

"Sir Isaac Newton is said to have avowed that he felt like a child picking up shells beside the great and unexplored ocean of truth—thus is how it is for me. Good people, though I have devoted much of my life in an attempt to unveil the face of Nature, her immortal lineaments remain a wonder and a mystery." A shrug. "Still, one tries. I am encouraged by the writings of other natural philosophers such as Signore Priestley of London with his *History and Present State of Electricity*, Signore Marat's recent *Memoire sur l'electricite medical—*"

"What about Cornelius Agrippa? Paracelsus?" Victor's voice rang out.

Dr. Galvani smiled. "Ah, young Signore Frankenstein! I am honored by your interest. I would prefer not to discuss Agrippa or Paracelsus. Alchemy is not the focus of my display."

Alchemy? Hadn't that to do with transforming lead into gold? Caroline remembered an old tale her father had told her before his death, one he believed as truth. Dr. Galvani continued speaking, but she was distracted.

She glanced over at Victor. His mouth was pursed, arms still crossed.

Why is he so disapproving?

Once Dr. Galvani finished—Caroline recalled him explaining electrostatic generators, a Dr. Nollet as inventor—his assistants rolled out a waist-high cart holding the square-shaped contraption. A hollow glass globe rested in the center of it, an immense hand crank on one side.

The cart's wooden wheels clattered like a peddler's wagon against the marble floor.

At the doctor's command, everyone in the room, even her servants, circled the electrostatic generator to hold hands tightly. On Caroline's left, Alphonse. On her right, Elizabeth; her ward's palms were moist. Caroline looked over her shoulder. There was Victor beside Elizabeth, then Henry with his father, who yawned. Across the circle, Justine, who appeared more blanched of color than usual, Sophie with her bright red hair.

Dr. Galvani ordered, "Whatever you do, do not release your neighbor's hand. Trust in the mystery of Nature as the electrical fluid is passed from source to end and back again!"

As Dr. Galvani turned the crank of the electrostatic generator, the glass globe glowed with a blue light. Mercury. A sharp ting sizzled through Caroline's palms, passing from Alphonse to Elizabeth and around again. Smoke filled the air, a charge thick as cotton.

Caroline was riveted. Nature Herself was among them. Nature who possessed unfathomable wisdom. Nature who'd let Christmas arrive on the longest night of the year.

"Elizabeth," she said, raising her chin, "your hair!"

Elizabeth's golden hair floated in the air, cracking with light. It enveloped her face like a halo, reminding Caroline of an experience she had as a young woman, when she'd viewed a lightning storm atop a mountain. She'd watched in wonder, stunned by its celestial power.

Caroline felt her mouth widen. Joy, that's what she felt. But not all felt such.

A scream rang out. Another.

"It's fine! You're safe!" Caroline reassured Elizabeth.

"It's not me, Aunt." Elizabeth let go of Caroline's hand and pointed across the ballroom. "Look!"

Justine had broken from the circle, releasing Sophie's hand. She stood alone, a pale figure staring at the ballroom windows. Another scream. The sound of shattering glass. The window smashed. Now Sophie shrieked.

The remainder of the circle scattered in a clatter of rushing limbs and shouts. Caroline resisted the urge to scream herself.

"The golem!" Justine shouted. "It's here!"

Someone tall and dark staggered into the ballroom from the garden.

Someone hulking and gasping. Glass crunched beneath his footfall. His arms were full as he approached Caroline. Was he holding a basket?

Justine screamed again. "The golem!"

"Back!" Alphonse ordered. He pulled out what appeared to be a pistol. Where had it come from?

The intruder's silhouette grew close enough that Caroline made out the sallow gleam of his eye. *"My children!"* she wanted to shout, but no words came. Out of the corner of her eye, she saw Henry push Elizabeth from the intruder's path, and Victor reaching for Elizabeth, shouting, shouting.

They're protecting her. But I must protect them.

Caroline set her body before Elizabeth, Victor, and Henry, her knees buckling. She collapsed to the marble floor. Breath knocked from her lungs. Her body arched. A charge flowed into her spine, from her heels to her forehead.

Dr. Galvani. The electrostatic generator.

It still whirled, still glowed. Somehow Caroline had brushed against it in her attempt to protect Elizabeth and Victor. She managed to break away.

"Victor! Elizabeth! Where are you?"

"Behind you, Mother!"

Before Caroline could turn, a flurry of papers assaulted her face, edges sharp against her cheeks. Pamphlets. Dozens of them. A hundred. They scattered across the floor. The pages flipped open, legible despite the scant light. A forest of woodcuts depicting a chorus of unclothed Marie Antoinettes. Men, women, animals. Genitals, breasts, limbs, taunting and depraved.

The intruder stepped forward, blocking Caroline's view of the pamphlets. He was daring her to move. Daring her to leave. Well, he'd have to kill her before she'd let him hurt her children.

He was tall. Foreboding. His mouth cracked open, a corner raised. Lips shifting. *Hate you,* he appeared to be saying. Or was it *Help me?* Was he wearing a red jacket? Yes, he was.

Screams, but not her own. Another surge ringing through her veins. Panic, not electricity.

Caroline looked down.

Blood on the floor. Blood on the intruder's hands. Wet. Sticky.

The intruder's hands stretched toward Caroline, but she couldn't turn away. How sorrowful his eyes appeared! Her compassion rose, surprising her.

"Madame!" Justine shouted, throwing herself between Caroline and the intruder.

A spark of light. A blast. Smoke.

When the smoke cleared, the body of a tall raven-haired man dressed in a red uniform lay on the ballroom floor, a pistol beside him. A Swiss soldier.

"He's dead," Alphonse confirmed. "But not from gunshot."

CHAPTER V.

"When I look back, it seems to me as if this almost miraculous change of inclination and will was the immediate suggestion of the guardian angel of my life—the last effort made by the spirit of preservation to avert the storm that was even then hanging in the stars."

OUTSIDE THE FRANKENSTEINS' *maison de campagne*, a line of coaches departed for Geneva, their lanterns hanging like stars in the night. These coaches transported all of the Frankensteins' guests, including Dr. Galvani with his electrostatic generator. The lifeless body of the intruder had been dragged into the garden shed, where the new gravedigger would collect him come morning. The pamphlets had been gathered and burned, judging by the weight of smoke in the air.

Caroline observed all this with a peculiar detachment. How much time had passed since Alphonse's Christmas soirée staggered to a halt? An hour? More? She couldn't be certain—time seemed twisted, strange. She glanced toward the lake, toward the horizon. The sky remained ink-dark, but she sensed dawn would arrive soon. Victor and Elizabeth stood behind her. They were safe. Beside her, Alphonse clutched her hand. He stroked it with his thumb.

"Are you listening, my dear? He'd been a Swiss soldier," he repeated in a soothing tone. "A mercenary. A revolutionary probably on his way from Geneva to God knows where. He'd collapsed before I discharged the pistol."

Victor remarked, "Just think, he was alive this morning, went through his day, and now he's dead."

Caroline shivered, but not from cold as she had in the ballroom. She watched Elizabeth and Victor drift away. They appeared headed for the garden. "Don't go into the shed!" she wanted to shout. She didn't. They should go to bed. She should go to bed. She couldn't. Not yet.

She inhaled deeply. The air smelled moist. Dangerous. Everything was dangerous. It hadn't mattered they'd left Geneva for this house one league east in Belrive. It hadn't mattered she'd been vigilant. *One, two, three . . .* Yet again, Marie Antoinette's half-clad torso rushed behind Caroline's eyelids. Those pamphlets. Everyone had seen them, though no one said anything. They were frightened, as she'd been.

But she'd protected her children. She'd done what was necessary. Afterward, Victor had embraced her, muttering how afraid he'd been to lose his mother . . .

"Caroline? Did you hear me?"

"I-I'm listening, Alphonse," she replied. "A man died in our ballroom. A soldier. A Swiss revolutionary. The gravedigger will gather him in the morning."

He pulled her close against him, his heart a steady rhythm. "He was already dying when he burst through the window. Someone must have knifed him days earlier. His chest had savage wounds, which were green with pus. Frankly, it's a miracle he didn't expire earlier. He'd taken shelter in our greenhouse—there's bloodstains on the floor, a knapsack. He probably planned to leave once he felt hale."

What had Victor said? *"He was alive that morning, went through his day . . ."*

Alphonse continued, still clutching her hand. "When he didn't improve, he grew desperate for help. That's why he interrupted the soirée. He'd heard people, noticed the candlelight."

Caroline struggled to comprehend. Alphonse's individual words, yes, she understood. But the compilation of these words into thoughts . . . it was too much. Her knees felt wobbly. When she shut her eyes to calm herself, all she saw was the soldier's eyes when they met hers. She'd felt a strange kinship with him she couldn't explain. An affinity.

But that wasn't all Caroline felt. An unexpected joy rose from the core of her body, similar to the one she'd felt during Galvani's celestial display. Was it that she survived what she'd most feared? Or something else?

"She protected me," Caroline said. "As I hoped."

Alphonse's thumb paused on her hand. "Who protected you?"

"Justine. The new maid. She threw herself before the soldier after he broke the window. All to protect us."

Another realization, one that brought a hope into Caroline's heart brighter than Dr. Galvani's display.

"Justine mentioned she'd seen the soldier the night we found her. She spoke of someone chasing her into our garden, a monster. A golem, whatever that is. She said it was a story her father told."

"A golem . . ." Alphonse offered a reluctant smile. "My dear, I have a confession to make. It was due to Justine that this entertainment, if you will, took place."

"Justine invited Dr. Galvani?" How could this be?

"No, but she reminded me of him—I met Dr. Galvani last week in Geneva at the Assembly. I'd forgotten about him until two days ago, when I startled Justine in Victor's room looking at his books. At first she was distressed, for she feared I'd send her back to her mother. I finally teased out the truth: you wanted her to pay mind to anything unusual."

"*Whatever you want of me, I shall do.*" Somehow Justine had sensed Caroline's needs, her worries, even before Caroline asked her to spy.

Caroline replied, "What was in his books?"

Alphonse shrugged. "She can't read, so she couldn't say—she said the pictures alarmed her. But I understood what the books contained. Cornelius Agrippa. Paracelsus. Albertus Magnus." He shook his head. "Alchemy. Fantastical rubbish to rot his mind."

The cold air transformed while he spoke. Sharp breezes, clouds gathering; the shift in weather mirrored the passion of Alphonse's words.

He continued, "I noticed Victor was secretive and behaving strangely. I questioned him. He remained tight-lipped. Caroline, I've been a poor father."

"You? Never."

Across the lake, a slash of lightning over the Juras. Too far away to affect them.

"Listen, and judge, Caroline. Last summer when we visited the baths in Thonon, that day we were rained out at the inn? He'd shown me the Agrippa, which he'd found in the library there. I'd laughed and said, 'Ah, Cornelius Agrippa! Do not waste your time upon this; it is sad trash.'"

"How did Victor respond?"

"He didn't. But to be fair, I didn't say *why* it was trash—I was distracted, for I'd received a letter from Ernest's doctor that morning. Perhaps if I had, Victor wouldn't have read the other books."

Another flash of lightning, this one closer.

"If I'd been a good father, I would have explained the principles of Agrippa have been entirely exploded and that a more modern system of science has been introduced. I would have arranged for him to have a tutor or go to school." Alphonse's tone turned gentle. "But I feared upsetting you after sending Ernest away."

Ernest. Away. The words dangled between them.

"And so when Justine showed you those books in his room," Caroline said at last, "you invited Dr. Galvani here to educate Victor." Now the entire evening made sense.

Alphonse hung his head. "I worried if I said anything critical of the Agrippa, I'd make it worse. Victor is so passionate, so independent of thought—he should really be in school. But I would have never known about his interest in alchemy unless Justine had found those books. She's loyal."

Caroline squeezed her husband's hand, wrinkled beside her smooth one. "I should have confided in you that I asked her to pay attention to anything irregular. I ought to ask your forgiveness."

"There is nothing to forgive." He pressed his lips against her cheek, his grey eyes gleaming in the dark. "You, Caroline Beaufort Frankenstein, are ever perfect in my eyes, ever lovely. Exactly as when I first met you all those years ago at your father's side." His voice broke. "I know I am much older than you. I know I could not have been your first choice for a husband."

"That's not true," she protested, though it was. The truth was she'd had no choice. Not really, unless you considered a life plaiting straw for hats a choice. Anyway, no woman's life was her own—she'd known this for as long as she could recall. Nor was she the first girl to wed for security over affection. All these years later, her prosperity still felt so undeserved, especially once she learned Alphonse had married her out of love, not pity over her father.

"You have been a good husband, Alphonse," she said, eyes stinging. "A good father. A good man. You are *good.*"

With this declaration, Caroline allowed her hands to settle as though she'd been relieved of a burden too heavy to bear. No tapping. No counting. She stroked Alphonse's white beard; it had been grey when they'd first met. Alphonse had been true all these years. He'd loved her when they'd wed even if she hadn't loved him then as she should.

Sensing her softening, Alphonse reached for Caroline as though to breach the years between them. He kissed her gently. Tentatively. But it was a true kiss nonetheless.

He pulled away, awaiting her reaction. His breath warm upon her cheeks, his skin scented with tobacco and wine and, yes, gunpowder.

Despite her turning him away for so long, he still loved her. This felt more of a Christmas miracle than Dr. Galvani's display that evening. All their troubles dissolved—the loss of infants, the illness of their younger son, the difficulties of their eldest, the hopes they held for their ward— until all that remained was her vast white bed, which awaited them upstairs in her tower room.

* * *

One house. Four beds. An hour before dawn.

In Caroline's bed, her husband slept soundly beside her for the first time in six years. She smiled in the dark. How warm Alphonse had been, how gentle! She hadn't protested when he'd blown out the candle she always slept with. Then he'd embraced her, setting her adrift in her bed but not alone. They could be alone together, couldn't they? Wasn't that what marriage was? It was joining forces against an unpredictable world, even when this world included wounded soldiers and revolutionary pamphlets and natural philosophers and troubled sons and alchemy books.

Love is a form of alchemy, she thought.

She smiled in the darkness, hands flat against her counterpane. *There's much more to this world than I am comfortable considering. But I am safe. I am loved.* Nor was she alone. She had Alphonse, Victor, Elizabeth, and now Justine, who'd proven her worth that night.

And what of Justine? Was the girl resting comfortably? With all the turmoil, Caroline had never checked on her. Had she been injured when she'd thrown her body before Caroline's? Was she distressed? Caroline would speak to her in the morning. Perhaps she'd offer the girl an education, now that she knew Justine was illiterate. After all, the Frankenstein household wasn't like those in England or France. They treated their servants as their equals. She'd raise the girl above her station. Win her devotion, which was of greater value than loyalty.

Heart at ease, Caroline watched Alphonse's eyelids tremble as he slept. He was dreaming. Soon she would too. She set a kiss against his bristled jaw and shut her eyes.

A refreshing slumber overtook her, one that led her to pay no mind to the flash of lightning, where cold air met warm; for once, a storm would not disturb her. However, a flash of lightning awakened Sophie upstairs in her bed.

The girl's eyes shot open. Beside her Justine snored softly, arms relaxed across her pillow. How could she sleep after everything that night? As though a man had not died before their eyes—a man who'd appeared so tall and scary?

"You're brave," Sophie whispered. "I hadn't expected that."

With this, she returned to sleep, unaware that both Victor and Elizabeth's beds were empty, for they'd remained in the garden after Caroline and Alphonse had gone inside.

Lightning or no, Victor paced before Elizabeth, his jacket unbuttoned; it had turned strangely warm for December. The shed holding the intruder's corpse was but a few yards away.

"Just think, that soldier was here this morning, went through his day, and now he's dead," he said yet again, pointing toward the shed. "He'd been hiding in our greenhouse for days. More! Ever since Justine's arrival. He could have killed my mother!"

"I know," Elizabeth replied. "It's a shock."

He turned toward the shed. "I want to look at him a last time. To make sure he's really dead. I've never seen a corpse before."

"No, you mustn't! We should go inside. Come!"

Elizabeth took his hand to calm him. It was an old habit, one engrained from their childhood. Instead of Victor tugging her hand in their old way—a quick squeeze of the fingers as though to say *You are my friend and I am here with you*—he released her hand.

"Not yet. I want to speak to you first."

How strangely Victor was behaving! "Not about the corpse, I hope."

A deep rumble of thunder shuddered across the sky.

"Something else . . . I've been a fool, Elizabeth."

"Because you never noticed the soldier?"

When Victor answered, his voice was low. "Something far more humiliating. Dr. Galvani made me realize how useless—no, despicable —my studies have been."

Another lightning flash. Elizabeth waited for him to continue.

Victor's words rushed and tumbled like a broken dam. "I've been studying alchemy. I found some books. Cornelius Agrippa, Albertus Magnus, and Paracelsus, they've been the lords of my imagination for the past two years. I kept my studies a secret from my parents, from you, from Henry. Under the guidance of the alchemists, I searched for the philosopher's stone and the elixir of life. All I considered was the glory I'd gain if I could banish disease and death. But after tonight, I'll quit those pursuits. I'll turn to something else. Mathematics perhaps."

With his confession, Victor smoothed his curls, drew a deep breath. He even yawned. Still, there was an oddness about his affect that troubled Elizabeth.

She stole a glance at the shed, thinking of the corpse within. "We should go inside, Victor. It must be nearly dawn."

"Not yet. Let's watch the storm from beneath the doorway first. Come!"

Elizabeth agreed, letting him lead her toward the *maison de campagne*. They stood hand-in-hand, their backs pressed against the door, as the elements stirred in their direction. Another swish of lightning, this one from the north. In the east, where the sun edged the horizon, rain lashed the sky until it lightened to the hue of a fading bruise. A deep rumbling rose from the core of the earth itself.

"Look, Victor! The storm's nearly upon us!"

Together, they watched the storm's progress with curiosity and delight—well, the curiosity was Elizabeth's, the delight Victor's. Thunder burst with frightful loudness from the heavens, but they were protected beneath the doorway. Safe. A deafening rain soaked the garden. A downpour.

All of a sudden a stream of fire issued from the old oak that stood about twenty yards from the house, the same one they'd found Justine beneath two weeks earlier. As soon as the dazzling light vanished, the oak disappeared from sight. "No, don't go to it, Elizabeth," Victor warned. "We'll look in the morning—it's unsafe." Too late: she'd run toward the oak, not believing her eyes.

A jolt. A shake. Elizabeth slammed against the wet soil, face up toward the heavens, rain splattering her body. Somehow a minuscule fraction of the force hitting the oak traveled through the soaked ground, across the garden. Elizabeth shuddered as energy surged up her spine, through her hands and beyond her fingers. Toward the sky. Then, just as suddenly as the electricity had risen, it was gone, leaving her flat-backed on the earth.

Elizabeth sat up, woozy but untouched save for her rain-soaked body. "Victor . . ."

Victor sank beside her, grasping her hand in his. Now he was drenched too.

"I know, such wonders," was all he said, his eyes gleaming. "Such marvels."

CHAPTER VI.

*"So soon as the dazzling light vanished, the oak had disappeared, and nothing
remained but a blasted stump. When we visited it the next morning, we found
the tree shattered in a singular manner."*

* * *

WHEN CAROLINE VISITED the garden the following morning to pay the
gravedigger, she found the oak tree gone. Instead of being split by lightning, it had been reduced to thin ribbons of wood—she'd never beheld
anything so utterly destroyed. "Nature," Victor explained. "Electricity,
like Dr. Galvani's demonstration."

Beneath where the oak had stood, the Frankensteins found the pale
feathered remains of what had been an owl, and a ruddy fox slinking
away into the underbrush. To her surprise, Caroline watched Elizabeth
kneel to paint the owl's remains in careful watercolor, using the kit
Caroline had given her as a birthday present. Justine accompanied her
ward, holding Elizabeth's brushes and paints for her.

In time, new life would replace the oak tree. Before the arrival of
summer, celadon-hued leaves would sprout from black earth made
fertile with ash. After a complete turn of the sun's wheel, birds and
squirrels returned to where the oak once stood, in search of acorns and
worms. Within four years' time, a thin sapling had set down roots to
grow nearly as tall as Caroline. But none of the Frankensteins would

witness this phenomenon, for they had abandoned their *maison de campagne* in Belrive to return to Geneva.

"It's so Victor can attend school. He's taken an interest in mathematics. Also, Elizabeth wanted to take art lessons," Caroline claimed when asked, though this wasn't the complete truth. Whenever she stepped beyond their *maison de campagne*, she couldn't stop recalling that night with Dr. Galvani and the dead soldier, those pamphlets with the twisting, naked bodies, the shattered oak. No place was safe: instead of Geneva, it was now Paris and the Netherlands that stormed with revolution. And so Caroline reluctantly told Alphonse they should return.

Justine gladly accompanied the Frankensteins back to Geneva—Justine, who'd developed into the perfect servant in every way. Loyal, discreet, hardworking. Educated, thanks to Victor and Henry Clerval. Grateful. Even Sophie had been influenced by Justine's placid temperament and became amiable. The Frankensteins' middle son Ernest remained in the Alps for the sake of his lungs; Caroline visited as often as she could. She prayed he would soon grow healthy enough to return home. He was finally old enough to write them regularly, which brought her comfort.

Once the Frankensteins were settled anew in their three story townhouse on the Rue des Granges, Alphonse increased his attendance at the Geneva Assembly. As a syndic, Alphonse had access to more information than most about the revolutions taking place outside Geneva. In Paris, armies of emaciated beggars were dying on the streets, and prisoners rotted in fetid cells for offenses mild as smuggling salt. Citizens wore red hats signifying liberty for all and tricolored cockades representing revolution. Hangings and starvation. Riots and pamphlets.

In the Netherlands, revolutionaries issued a declaration of independence. Liberty trees were set in town squares. At least in Geneva they had the protection of Swiss and French armies, though that hadn't stopped rebels from taking Alphonse hostage years earlier. All this served to make Caroline deeply anxious.

By the time February of 1788 arrived, Alphonse assured her that since Geneva had already experienced one revolution, another wouldn't occur. Lightning couldn't strike twice in the same place—

* * *

"Don't you agree, Madame Frankenstein? Madame?"

Caroline came to with a start. She'd become lost in her thoughts, thinking of Alphonse and revolutions, all that had occurred in the five years since that Christmas soirée in Belrive when the soldier died.

She recalled where she was. A tea at Madame Manoir's, not far from her home in Geneva. Madame Manoir was the mother of Victor's favorite schoolmate, Louis. But to be fair, Caroline was often daydreaming these days, for she was again heavy with child. She still couldn't believe it—how blessed she felt!

"My apologies. I was distracted by the sun," Caroline replied, cupping her ripe belly. It *was* exceptionally bright for a February morning, but that's not what had happened. The chaise Caroline had taken at Madame Manoir's insistence had proven too comfortable. "You were saying, Madame?"

Madame Manoir repeated, "Surely you don't believe another revolution will happen in Geneva?"

Caroline reached for her tea cup as she considered her response. She shifted against the chaise to ease her back; inside her womb, the baby mirrored her movement. With less than a month until her confinement, Caroline really shouldn't have been out in public, but Madame Manoir insisted on the visit because Elizabeth had painted her daughter's portrait. Justine accompanied them.

Justine sat on the other side of the room, eyes trained on a copy of *Paradise Lost* while she awaited any needs Caroline might have. A good pair of stays helped disguise Justine's twisted spine; a good education helped her gain confidence, though she remained distinctive of appearance with her silvery hair and strange pale eyes. She was devoted to Caroline. The girl had even begun to speak with Caroline's soft lisp, and dressed her hair in a similar looped chignon. It was all very gratifying.

Caroline answered after a sip of tea, "My husband assures me all will be well." It had to be.

"Monsieur Frankenstein is very wise," Madame Manoir concurred.

"Indeed he is." Caroline offered a beatific smile. Backache or not, pregnancy agreed with her. Though she was older than other mothers, she felt reinvigorated at the age of forty-four. She'd never expected to conceive again. Nor had Alphonse. Thus far her pregnancy remained uncomplicated; usually by this stage, the baby had stopped stirring or she'd miscarried.

Caroline offered her womb a gentle pat. *Stay with me. I love you already.*

"I assume you'll remain in Geneva for—"

Madame Manoir's words came to a halt; it wouldn't do to mention Caroline's pregnancy.

Caroline smiled again though her back panged. "We'll remain in Geneva. It has advantages for my family." Alphonse was eager for her to be attended by his favorite doctor, which would be impossible if they returned to Belrive. "Ah, there's Elizabeth at last!"

Elizabeth glided into the drawing room, accompanied by Madame Manoir's son Louis and youngest daughter Genevieve, who was the same age as Elizabeth, now eighteen.

"Behold!" Elizabeth said, propping the tall watercolor of Genevieve on a chair. "Is it not like life?"

Caroline struggled to her feet for a better look. She rushed with pleasure. Elizabeth really was talented. The portrait's composition reflected the changing times. Genevieve's hair was unpowdered and fell in natural curls over her shoulder, without any puffs to raise it off her forehead. Her only ornament was a spray of wheat tucked over her ear, for Elizabeth had portrayed the young woman as the spirit of Nature, like an ideal from Rousseau. Instead of hoop petticoats, Genevieve was depicted in a diaphanous shift-like gown collected beneath her breasts with a sky-blue ribbon.

"Isn't it beautiful?" Genevieve asked, preening. "We must frame it, Mama."

"Indeed we must!" her brother Louis concurred.

"It helped to have such a lovely model," Elizabeth said, her cheeks rising with color.

"Indeed," Caroline said. The baby kicked her bladder—so active! Her back spasmed anew. *How much longer until I can leave?* "I appreciate your hospitality—"

"We must celebrate!" Madame Manoir interrupted before Caroline could complete her farewell.

As if anticipating Caroline's desires, Justine announced, "Forgive the interruption, but I recall Monsieur Frankenstein expects us home soon." A curtsey to Madame Manoir. "We so enjoyed our visit!"

* * *

"That was clever of you, Justine," Elizabeth said, taking Caroline's arm as they picked their way home along the icy pavement from Madame Manoir's. On the Place du Bourg-de-Four, the shop windows were laced with frost. Caroline glanced at her reflection in one: her mouth was a seam of discomfort.

"Yes, thank you, Justine," Caroline said, wincing as she avoided a frozen puddle. "I couldn't think how to leave without being rude."

Justine explained, "I noticed you were rubbing your back, Madame."

"Aunt, you look weary. Take my arm," Elizabeth offered. "I should have insisted you stay home."

Justine clutched Caroline's other arm. "Come, Madame, let's—"

"Justine! Is that you?"

Justine turned in the direction of the voice. Color drained from her already pale face.

Madame Moritz. Could it be?

Caroline watched a skinny grey-haired woman dressed in black loop her way across the square, her arms open wide, fingers spread as though to embrace all the world. Yes, it was Madame Moritz. Even if Justine's mother had never visited in the five years since Justine had joined the Frankensteins, Caroline hadn't forgotten her—especially since she'd continued sending Justine's pay to Madame Moritz. Caroline vaguely recalled the boy and the girl who'd accompanied Madame Moritz that day so long ago. She'd been heavy with child then, as Caroline was now. Today, Madame Moritz was alone.

"Madame." Caroline's tone was brusque.

Madame Moritz ignored Caroline's greeting; her eyes were only for her daughter.

"How different you appear, Justine! So grown! So pretty! I nearly didn't recognize you at first. Your hunchback . . . well, 'tis not as bad. Haven't you anything to say?" A nervous half-smile as Madame Moritz extended her arms anew. "Surely you can speak!"

"I bid you good day, Mother," Justine said, flinching at her mother's touch. "Excuse me."

"How formal you are! I only wanted to say that, if you ever wished to visit . . ."

Justine avoided her mother's gaze. "I am kept quite busy by the Frankensteins."

"Well, surely you're afforded a day—"

Caroline interrupted, "Justine is not at liberty, Madame. You may visit her another time."

"Would you like that, Justine?"

Justine's lips remained tight. Within her tense jaw Caroline sensed the girl's fear, anger, and, surprisingly, longing. After all, how could one not yearn for a mother's love?

"I suppose not . . ." Madame Moritz's mouth twisted in a strange grimace. "I suppose I did treat you unkindly at times."

At times? Caroline's rage rose so bright she forgot about her throbbing back, the weight of the baby across her hips, the icy pavement. Caroline recalled the bruises, the scars, the burns she'd discovered on Justine's body that first morning. The lice crawling from her filthy, tangled hair.

She was about to clutch Justine to protect her, but Elizabeth intervened. She whispered, "Let Justine speak for herself."

Justine turned back slowly. Reluctantly. Her jaw remained firm though her eyes appeared glassy.

"Adieu, Madame."

I did not expect that, Caroline thought.

Justine took Caroline and Elizabeth's hands. "We must return home, Madame Frankenstein. Be careful! The ice is so slippery! Are you feeling any better?"

Caroline nodded; her stomach roiled. Perhaps it was meeting Madame Moritz, the rich tea. The baby adjusted its position. Despite her discomfort a smile tugged at the corner of her lips. How satisfying it had been to see Justine vanquish her mother—perhaps it was petty of Caroline, but there it was. Anyway, Madame Moritz had three children at home. Let her soothe her guilt with them.

"Nearly home!" Elizabeth called out in an aggressively cheerful voice.

Another step. Two more. A long clench overtook Caroline's hips, one that lasted longer than the cry of a blue jay overhead. She heard a strange pop, one scarcely audible.

A rush of water spewed onto the pavement from between Caroline's legs, soaking the hem of her gown.

The puddle appeared tinged with scarlet against the ice.

* * *

"She's having the baby!" Elizabeth shouted when they reached home. "Uncle! Where are you? Come!"

Caroline's arms ached. Justine and Elizabeth nearly carried her the remainder of the way, clutching her beneath her shoulders. They helped her up the stairs to her bed chamber, each step a country to be transversed. More water leaked between her legs. The baby was squirming. Kicking at her portal.

"The doctor! We need him!" This was Justine; Caroline made out her strange pale eyes, the alarm within their depths.

"I'll go." Victor's voice rose from downstairs. "Justine, my father is at the Assembly. Can you fetch him?"

In her room, Caroline was led to her bed. Justine set linens beneath her hips before rushing for Alphonse. Another contraction. Caroline stared up at her embroidered bed curtains, which Elizabeth had closed about her. The tapestries were swaying. How bright they were, their threads shimmering as though they were untangling. Her heart ticked in rhythm with the mantel clock.

A pigeon cooing on the window ledge. Ice cracking on a tree limb.

Another wave of pain. Had labor been so abrupt with Victor? With Ernest? Such violence! One moment her back ached, the next she was asunder in a sea of agony. A sea of water and blood and split flesh.

The sea rose and pulled her down into its depths.

* * *

Hours passed, judging by the shift of light. How long had it been since they'd returned from that tea at the Manoir's? Caroline couldn't recall. "I couldn't find the doctor," Victor said when he returned; she'd never heard him so panicked. "I asked the Clervals for help. Monsieur Clerval recommended one with an excellent reputation—Henry's gone to fetch him." He drew closer to her bed; his brown eyes were wild with fear. "Mother, what else can I do?"

"Nothing, darling . . ." With Victor's return, her room felt more crowded than ever. In one corner of her room, Justine perched on a chair, a bowl of cloths on her lap. Another corner, Sophie and Alphonse. Elizabeth leaned over Caroline, plaiting her hair, which had grown tangled on the pillows.

She let out a long moan.

"How soon can the doctor be here?" Justine asked, fear jangling her voice. Her eyelids were swollen; Caroline hadn't recalled her weeping before.

"I don't know," Victor admitted.

Another wave of pain. Caroline panted.

"A midwife would be better," Sophie said, pacing; Caroline made out her bright red hair. "There's one in Chêne—she attended my sister. She's a miracle worker. She even offers love poppets for those in need. I know a girl who got married after buying one."

Justine shook her head. "Superstition. The church doesn't like that. I can seek another doctor, Monsieur Frankenstein."

"Church doesn't matter," Sophie countered. "If someone could take me in the carriage, I'll show you where she is. Down the road to Chêne. You can't miss her cottage! It's set beside a foot bridge and has a bright green door—"

"No," Alphonse snapped just as the bell jangled downstairs. "You'll remain here, and so will everyone else in this household in case we have need. Hopefully that's Henry with a doctor."

Elizabeth rose for the door. "I'll get it."

Caroline heard footsteps from the hall. An impatient hand turned the doorknob. *Let it be the doctor.*

Suddenly her room emptied of family and servants, leaving her alone with a man she'd never seen before in her life.

The doctor was tall, dark, with hands bearing roughened flesh, sprouted hairs. They appeared stained, spotted. Muscular. Not dissimilar from Dr. Galvani's in a way.

"Madame Frankenstein," he greeted in booming tones. "How long since labor commenced?"

"I'm uncertain," Caroline managed to answer before another contraction arrived.

"If you'll allow me, Madame . . ."

He yanked her legs open. Fished beneath her chemise.

* * *

Some time later, Caroline opened her eyes with a start. How long had she been unaware? Since the doctor's arrival? Her room was unlit save for one candle. Night. The bells chiming from St. Peter's. How late? *One, two, three* . . . She lost count. Her entire body ached. Her throat ached. Had she screamed? She must have.

Someone daubed her face with a soft cloth dipped in water. Someone gentle. The water was scented with lavender.

"Justine?"

"No, it's me, Aunt. I sent Justine to bed. She'd been here with you for the past four hours."

Elizabeth sat beside her bed, her touch gentle as she washed sweat from Caroline's brow. The stench of iron hung on the air. The shutters remained closed, the room dense with shadows.

"The baby?"

"Breech." Elizabeth's brow clouded. "The doctor turned it—you fainted during the worst of it. The baby is quite large though it's early." She drew a shaky breath. "Things should go more easily now."

Breech. Large. Easily. The words made the uncontrollable seem controlled. Caroline knew better.

"Not much longer. Bring me my jewelry box, the one on the dresser."

Elizabeth fetched a square wood box adorned with painted cherubs and bluebirds, a veritable garden of decoration. The jewelry box bore a small gold lock in the center of the lid.

"The key is in a hidden compartment on the side, Elizabeth. Don't forget."

Elizabeth unlocked the jewelry box, hands fumbling, for the tiny gold key was the width of a darning needle. Her eyes widened as she took in the box's contents. A ruby diadem, which Caroline wore on the rare occasions when the syndics gathered at the Hôtel de Ville, which was as close to a court as Geneva offered. Gold rings, strands of pearls, engraved bracelets. The box also contained relics from Caroline's life: lockets inscribed with initials, two fob chains formed from locks of hair. One was dark, the other white. Her mother and her father. She'd held onto the one from her father reluctantly.

"All these are to be yours. The emerald ring was for my engagement," Caroline said, gritting her teeth. An agonizing band tightened about her body. "Tell Victor."

Elizabeth pulled out a letter that bore the seal of the Frankensteins. "What's this?"

"For you when you marry. If I don't survive, open it then—"

"You mustn't say this, Aunt!"

A roll of pain. Caroline let out a long moan, one that shamed her. A scream. ·

Her door opened. The doctor. He'd returned.

"You must leave, Mademoiselle," he said, clutching Elizabeth by her elbow.

Once the door shut behind Elizabeth, Caroline gave way to the tide of pain breaking across her body. Soon after, she heard someone enter her room. Not the doctor, for he stood at her side. Had Elizabeth returned?

A male voice. Victor's. He was speaking to the doctor, their conversation low. Scattered phrases leapt out. "She must survive. There should be a better way to bring forth life. A kinder way—it's unfair the female should suffer so . . ."

Why is Victor here? Caroline tried to say. *He must leave.* She had no desire for her eldest son to witness her giving birth. No words rose from her throat, so he remained in that dank, bloody room as Caroline labored.

She remembered nothing more—or did not want to.

CHAPTER VII.

"When I had attained the age of seventeen, my parents resolved that I should become a student at the university of Ingolstadt . . . but, before the day resolved upon could arrive, the first misfortune of my life occurred."

* * *

CAROLINE NEXT RECALLED light stinging her eyes, the windows open wide. Morning had arrived. She made out the silhouette of a slender girl with a curved spine. Justine. She stood at the foot of her bed. Justine, whom Caroline had forgotten about in the midst of it all. The maid appeared gilded. She was holding a baby.

"Here she is!" Justine's gentle sing-song voice rang out. She approached and angled the swaddled bundle toward Caroline. A soft coo rose from his rosebud mouth. "Do you want to meet your mama, little one? Look, you've a son, Madame! See how handsome he is!"

Caroline stretched toward the baby, her hands empty. Her womb empty.

"Give him to me."

Caroline took the baby, his downy blond head still tinged with blood, into her arms. He opened his eyes. Blue irises, more hue than color. His pupils constricted as he took in light. The baby was a human. A soul. An individual separate from her.

He lives. And he's mine.

How strange it all was. How unexpected. How joyful. She'd grown more accustomed to loss than life. A rush of euphoria overtook her until Victor returned to her room, exclaiming all the while, Elizabeth clutching his hand.

Caroline forced a smile as she introduced her eldest son to her youngest, but she couldn't look Victor in the eye. She remained troubled he'd entered her room while she was giving birth, but there was no point in speaking of it. Clearly he feared her dying. That was all.

Still, how disquieted she felt! Whenever she looked at Victor she sensed the skull beneath his flesh, as though he'd donned a mask of death. It made no sense.

* * *

They named the baby William, though initially there'd been confusion. But later, when Caroline grew alert again—after the birth the doctor needed to pack her womb with ice to stop her bleeding, which was why Victor had appeared so peculiar at first—she corrected them. "His name is William, after my mother's uncle in England," she explained, folding the baby against her breast. "He's adorable!" Elizabeth exclaimed, Justine by her side. Victor held himself back from his mother and new brother with an expression Caroline couldn't quantify. Or, more likely, didn't want to. She told herself she'd imagined him in her room during the birth. After all, she had lost a lot of blood.

But now all was well. Better than well.

How sweet William smelled! How precious! His dimpled thighs were soft as velvet, his yeasty scent delectable. He grew quickly. Caroline spent hours examining his face, searching for signs of herself and of Alphonse. *He's the most like me*, she decided, taking in his pretty curls and straight nose. *He is the last of my womb. He'll grant us comfort in old age.* This felt a gift, especially since Victor and Elizabeth could no longer be considered children. Soon Victor would leave her to take his place in the world.

Alphonse's seventieth birthday arrived exactly six months after William's birth, which coincided with Victor's departure for the University of Ingolstadt. "It's best Victor be exposed to other cultures," Alphonse explained; Caroline was so enthralled with the baby that she didn't protest. *It's time*, she agreed. *Best for him. Best for Elizabeth.* While

Caroline had always entertained a *tendresse* that Victor and Elizabeth should marry, she feared pushing the two into an unwanted alliance. "If they've time apart, they'll know their hearts," she told Alphonse. She'd really had no choice when she wed, though she considered herself the most fortunate of wives.

The day for Alphonse's birthday celebration bloomed bright and hot, for it was the heart of August. Instead of remaining at home, they took a carriage down to the grassy field of Plainpalais, settling where their vantage offered the loveliest view of Mont Blanc. They brought wine, a basket of bread, cheese, and meat. No servants attended them but Justine. Henry accompanied them, for he was as loyal as a brother to Victor.

The chatter among them that day was the sort expected for a summer party: teasing jokes and happy laughter; recountings of memories; moments of solemnity amid revelry as they considered Victor's imminent departure.

Gifts were given. Elizabeth gave Victor a beautiful green journal bound in Florentine paper, which she had custom-made. Victor glowed with pleasure. "I thought you needed one for Ingolstadt, to remember me by," she said shyly. Toasts were made. Victor proclaimed as they refilled their cups, "To my father! The man who has taught me so much, but is also wise enough to let others teach me." Alphonse seemed especially pleased by his speech; he confessed he feared Victor would resist leaving for Ingolstadt, where he knew no one. Elizabeth read aloud the letter Ernest had sent for the occasion:

It is with great joy that I write to wish my Papa the happiest of birthdays. Here, I have grown strong enough that I am now allowed long walks on Alpine paths without my nurse. When you next visit, I promise to show you all I have discovered!

His words brought the Frankensteins much pleasure, for the letter offered completion: they were all together, all in accord. Caroline blinked away a tear. She'd visit Ernest once William was a little bigger— she hadn't seen him since she'd discovered her pregnancy. Maybe he'd improved enough to come home.

"Alphonse," she said, offering a meaningful look. "October?"

"Yes, my dear," he said, understanding. "We'll bring Ernest home."

Her heart swelled. Her three sons. Her ward. They'd live together as one after Victor returned from Ingolstadt. Alphonse embraced her, which encouraged another round of applause that woke William, who'd been napping. He wailed with tears.

Victor offered a mock shudder. "That child is never silent. Even when he sleeps, he's making noise. Cooing. Yelling."

"Victor's acting cranky because he'll be leaving soon. He wants us eager for him to leave," Elizabeth teased. "Don't forget us while you're in Ingolstadt!"

"Forget you? Never!" Victor replied, matching her light tone. "Anyway, Henry's promised he'll visit while I'm away. You won't lack for companionship."

"Indeed I shall," Henry said, leaning in to shake Victor's hand in solidarity.

"I'll watch over her too," Justine said. "I promise."

"Make sure to write us often, my son," Alphonse said. "I know that when you are pleased with yourself you will think of us with affection, and we shall hear regularly from you. You must pardon me if I regard any interruption in your correspondence as a proof your other duties are equally neglected. I'll expect you to keep me apprised of your studies and their progress."

Caroline smiled at her husband's pedantic lecture. So predictable, though she understood why: those alchemy books Justine found way back when. Luckily, Victor had firmly settled on mathematics as his course of studies.

William let out an even longer wail at Alphonse's lecture. Justine set down her mending, her expression as serene as ever. "I'll attend him, Madame. Come, dormouse!"

William lifted his chubby arms toward Justine, cooing. She took off across the grass with the infant, bouncing him against her shoulder.

By then, it was late in the afternoon. Between the wine and the food, Caroline released a soft belch that everyone pretended not to hear. How high the sun had grown! The sky so blue without a cloud in sight! The breeze let up, though it was still pleasant. Caroline fanned herself while she gazed at the vista, bees buzzing lazily as ants led an attack on the blanket where they'd set out their rustic feast. She listened to Victor and Alphonse speak softly, cicadas rising and falling in concert. Alphonse droned on with details regarding Victor's education: the letters of introduction to professors; the rooms near the university, where Victor would live alone for the first time in his life. "Best you have solitude. I don't want you distracted by socializing, though I expect you to make friends." Details, one blurring into the next. Elizabeth chimed in with an occasional comment. She seemed quieter than usual that day.

Caroline took another sip of wine. It was a fine muscat. Her teeth ached from the sweetness. A rush of song. She glanced up. Justine and Elizabeth were dancing in a circle, William in the center, the baby adorned with a crown of milkweed. Every so often they rushed over and tickled his belly. The baby chortled with glee, his legs and arms squirming toward the sky. Victor looked on at the tableau, leaning on his elbow against the soft grass, a soft expression as he stared at Elizabeth.

They'll wed, Caroline thought. *How could I ever have considered myself cursed?*

The sun grew brighter. The air warmer. Caroline's eyelids flagged. She dozed. But instead of dreaming of her father and her blistered fingers and the plaited straw as she sometimes did, she dreamt she was in Ingolstadt in Victor's rooms, which were different than Alphonse's description. A winding wood staircase. A gallery leading to an attic chamber. Dormer windows overlooking the university entrance. The town square. A skylight. In her dream, Caroline took in everything with pride. Her son, a scholar. Away from his family. Grown. Somehow she was pregnant again. How satisfied she felt!

In the attic, Victor had already set up his books on a long table. A long board with sums. Or were they drawings? She couldn't tell.

"You're here," Victor said, approaching her. Yet he wasn't the Victor she knew. It was an older Victor. A Victor who appeared exhausted. Pale. Emaciated. For some reason, he reminded her of her father after his ruin. The curse he'd embodied.

He asked, *"What do you think of my work, Mother?"*

"What work?" She clutched her belly. The baby kicked.

"Over here."

He raised his hand, pointing. Caroline followed the line of his finger toward a corner of the attic, where a long shadow fell across the wood floor. Someone tall. Silent. The scent of rotting leaves. Death. Who could it be?

Whoever he was, he approached Caroline, the yellowish gleam of his teeth shifting in a strange grimace.

Caroline felt her heart rush. The blood within her womb.

The baby kicked again.

"Who's this, Victor?" she asked, cradling her belly. *"Were you expecting a guest?"*

"Not a guest," Victor answered, his dark eyes sorrowful. *"Let me show you. Over here. Down here."*

Caroline looked down. A puddle of scarlet beneath her bared feet. Along her ankles.

Blood splattered the hem of her gown.

* * *

"Caroline. Wake up!"

Someone was shaking her shoulder. Alphonse.

"Wake, my dear! Come, we must leave," he said. "Immediately."

Caroline shuddered awake. How long had she slept? She blinked at the sky. The sun had disappeared behind a bank of clouds. The bottle of wine had spilled onto the blanket where she had been lying, a river of sour; the shoulder of her gown was damp and sticky. Luckily, it had been white wine, not red. But oh that dream! That dream! She tried to shake it off. It hung off her like rot on a vine. For a moment after she'd awakened, she even believed herself pregnant again.

"What's the matter?" she asked, disoriented. "Is all well?"

"Well, obviously not all is well. Otherwise why would we wake you?" Victor retorted.

Caroline's jaw tightened. Victor could be so impatient at times. Yet she welcomed this abrasiveness, a reminder of reality; her son wasn't the wraith she'd encountered in her dream. *The blood. The stranger. Her womb.* Whatever the dream signified, it was her fears. Her desire to protect Victor before he left their home. Nothing more.

He'll be fine. The dream means nothing.

"It's Elizabeth," Victor explained before he dashed off. "I'll arrange for the carriage." As he ran, a rush of crows scattered from the tall grass.

Caroline staggered to her feet. Where was Elizabeth? The last Caroline recalled she'd been dancing with Justine and the baby. She must have slept longer than she realized. Their food basket appeared packed save for the blanket where she'd been sleeping. She picked up the empty wine bottle, brushed ants off it. She'd drunk more than she should, though it didn't seem that way at the time.

"We must return home immediately," Alphonse said. "Elizabeth doesn't feel well—she's lying over there in the shade. It came on her all of a sudden. It's been a wonderful day, but we probably shouldn't have remained in the sun for so long."

"Can we hurry? My head is pounding," Elizabeth called out; her face appeared ruddy. "Uncle, perhaps you should take me back in the carriage?"

"Victor already went for it," Caroline said. Her heart raced. She shouldn't have slept. That last glass of wine. Her dream. It was a sign.

At last Victor returned. "The carriage is down toward the gate. Here, let me help you, Elizabeth." To Caroline: "Tell Justine I'll send the carriage back for you and everyone else."

"No, I'll accompany Elizabeth. So will your father."

"Let's go," Elizabeth cut in, clutching Caroline's hand to stand. "I feel truly horrid."

The trip up the hill to Geneva had never felt so long to Caroline. For some reason there was a delay at the gate, and then the horses were stubborn once the guard gave them clearance. "We'll be home soon, darling," Caroline promised, her lips against Elizabeth's brow. "You'll feel better soon. I promise!" She stroked Elizabeth's head, which lay on her lap inside the carriage, setting cool hands on her cheek. Elizabeth pressed her lips tight, grimacing.

"She's burning," Caroline whispered to Alphonse. "It's a fever."

"Heat stroke," he said. "A cold bath will help. We're almost home."

CHAPTER VIII.

*"Elizabeth had caught the scarlet fever; her illness was severe,
and she was in the greatest danger."*

* * *

"Scarlet fever," the physician told Caroline and Alphonse. "Her condition is grave. Madame Frankenstein, you and your baby must remain apart from her."

"No! This cannot be!" Caroline cried. That dream. It was a warning . . . yet it was Victor she'd dreamt of, not Elizabeth. For some reason this troubled her more, though she couldn't explain why.

There's something else I don't know. Something I should fear.

"Come, my dear," Alphonse said. "You should rest."

"I can't. Not until her fever's broken."

Downstairs in the parlor, Victor, Caroline and Justine sat a floor away from Elizabeth, awaiting any news from the sickroom. Victor postponed his departure to Ingolstadt; Henry Clerval showed up after Victor sent a note. "I cannot bear anything to happen to her," Henry said, more distressed than Caroline had ever witnessed him.

The hours of the night passed slowly. Soon after midnight Alphonse went to bed, unable to stop his eyes from flagging.

"A quick nap," he pledged. "I'll be back in an hour."

"Victor, you should rest too," Caroline said. "I'll remain awake for news."

"I cannot sleep. Not until I know Elizabeth is safe."

Victor's voice was high with panic. By then they'd moved into the drawing room where he, Caroline, and Justine remained with Henry, who'd refused to leave. All were sewing to pass the time save Henry, who was attempting to read a book, though how could anyone read at such a time? Sophie brought them coffee, which went cold in its engraved silver urn.

Caroline glanced across the settee at Victor threading his needle—she hadn't known he could sew until that night, when he'd brought out his sampler. How neat his stitches were, finer than any she'd ever beheld! White thread on white linen, like snow on ice. At the end of each seam he'd sewn a tiny triangle. "My signature, if you will," he'd admitted with a bashful glance. Caroline understood. The holy trinity, sacred to God. Such a good son!

"We'll remain awake together then," Caroline said, curled over the bonnet she was embroidering for William. Roses, lilies, and willows. She glanced over at Justine, whose face was a mask of determination while she mended linens. Every so often, the girl wiped her eyes.

Another low groan drifted downstairs. Caroline could hear the doctor pacing above them in Elizabeth's room. Surely her fever had to break soon. How long could this continue? A long moan. Justine flinched; she sat beside Henry on the low chaise nearest the fireplace. Her mouth tightened.

"I'll read to us," Henry offered, opening *Le Morte d'Arthur*, his favorite book.

"How kind you are to stay with us!" Caroline replied, biting off a thread. "What of your father? Won't he miss you?"

"He'll understand." Henry turned a page, his face rigid. "The story of Lancelot and Guinevere? Or Galahad?"

"We need something more exciting than King Arthur," Victor said, lifting his sampler toward the light. Again, Caroline was astonished at the precision of his stitches; Justine exclaimed as well.

"A fairy tale instead," Caroline suggested. "The story of Blanchette the cat. Or 'La Belle et la Bête.' You remember that one, Justine?"

"Indeed I do, Madame," Justine said in a shaky voice. Caroline had shared her book of Madame d'Aulnoy's fairy tales with Justine when

Henry was teaching her to read. "Shall I get the book? Or tell it from memory?"

A scream from upstairs. The candles flickered. Justine grimaced anew.

How long can this go on? How can she bear this?

"On such a night," Victor said, cutting a new length of snowy thread, "I suggest we tell ghost stories. Something to take us far away. I recently read a German book of them. Shall I get it from my room?"

"No ghost stories," Caroline said, her voice uneven. "Something else. If not fairy tales or King Arthur or—"

"I've a story," Justine said. "It's not a ghost story, but it is magical. The tale of the golem, the one my father told me from his childhood in Prague." Her pale cheeks flushed with color. "What I thought chased me into your garden the night I came to you."

Caroline was surprised Justine had brought this up—she hadn't once mentioned the golem since the night of the Christmas soirée. Such a long time ago! Her stomach gave an odd flip as she recalled the soldier dying in her ballroom.

The wind began to rise. Another candle flickered.

Above their heads, several bangs on the ceiling.

Caroline rose from her perch. "I'll check on Elizabeth."

"Mother . . ." Victor offered a pointed look; she forced herself back into her chair. "Go ahead, Justine. Tell your story."

Justine began: "Once there was a wise man who wanted others to believe him grander than he was—"

"You mean a rabbi?" Henry interrupted. "I read this story in my language studies. The tale comes from the middle ages, from the Hebrews. Was your father's family originally Hebrew?"

Justine colored again. "No, Monsieur Clerval. We've always been Catholic."

Caroline had no idea. All those years Justine had accompanied the Frankensteins to St. Peter's Protestant services without complaint.

"No interrupting, Henry." Victor sounded agitated. "Continue your story, Justine."

Justine complied, her voice growing in confidence. "Hoping to win favor with those above him, the wise man bragged he possessed a servant who was the most obedient in all the land: 'He waits on me as though I am a king.' However, the wise man was poorer than a student; his lie was soon uncovered.

"'But I do have a servant!' he claimed, pride overtaking reason. He'd have his servant, come what may." Justine's voice dropped as her father's must have. "And then he did something that went against God. To create his servant, the wise man gathered clay from a graveyard to mold a man. A creature. A golem. But in creating his golem, he'd created an immortal monster—"

"I don't believe this story is true," Sophie called out from a corner across the room; she'd entered the room so quietly they hadn't noticed. "You're making it up."

"True? All stories are true if they're told." Justine sounded as though she'd cry. "And my father *did* tell me this story many times. It's an old one."

"And your father was a gravedigger, was he not?" Victor asked.

Justine stared down at her mending, pretending not to hear. Caroline flushed, disquieted by his bluntness.

Henry, bless him, piped up, "Monster or no, the story goes that the golem wasn't truly immortal, for he could be brought to death."

Caroline willed herself to ask, "How did the wise man destroy the golem, Henry?"

"Let me think, Madame . . . Now I recall! It had to do with the golem's name. He was called Emet, which means 'truth' in the language of the Hebrews. This was the word the rabbi had written on his forehead to bring him to life."

"But what of his death?" Victor asked, eyes intense.

"Yes, tell us," Justine pressed. "My father never spoke of it."

"It's quite clever," Henry said. "To destroy him, the rabbi removed the letter 'e' from 'emet', which created the word *met*—'death.' And thus the golem dissolved to dust."

"Then the golem became a ghost, didn't he?" Sophie asked. "I thought we weren't supposed to tell ghost stories."

Caroline could no longer bear it. She set down her embroidery. "I'm going to rest my eyes."

Upstairs in her room, Alphonse was snoring softly in her bed. She sat on the edge of the mattress, too tired to ask him to move over.

A soft knock. Justine—she must have followed her. Her eyes were wide.

Caroline's heart sped. "Elizabeth?"

"No, something else, Madame. Something you should know about."

Somehow Caroline found herself inside Victor's room, led by Justine's insistent hands. She handed Caroline a bound journal from a drawer. Victor's old journal, which wasn't nearly as nice as the green Florentine volume Elizabeth had given him at the picnic. This one was bound in cheap brown paper, worn at the corners. Victor's handwriting slashed across the front label. His name. The year.

Mathematics, that's probably all it was.

"How did you come upon this?" Caroline demanded. Her tone was sharper than intended, but she hadn't time for domestic affairs. Not while Elizabeth was so ill.

"I was looking for that book of ghost stories Victor mentioned, and . . . and . . ." Justine blinked, her rabbit-pale eyes glassy. Afraid, that's what she was. "I-I thought you should know of this."

"It's fine, Justine. You can go back to the others."

Caroline leaned against the door frame after glancing over her shoulder to make sure Victor wasn't near. Over the years Justine had found pamphlets in the kitchen, letters from disgruntled employees, and even love letters to Sophie from a boy in the village. Never anything shocking. Never anything where Justine revealed fear.

She's anxious. We all are. I'll look for a moment and then rest.

Caroline opened the journal, stifling a yawn.

What she found inside made her clutch her throat. Pages upon pages of words and sketches. The sketches were lurid, invasive. Her son—her son!—had drawn her with William gaping from her vagina, rivulets of blood easing his way toward life. She hadn't known Victor could draw, though there was a cold imprecision to his depictions as well as a lack of refinement, unlike the elegant skill of Elizabeth's art. His drawings were untrained, crude, but they were made to relay information, not create beauty.

Each journal page revealed similar secrets from Caroline's labor. There she was with her most private flesh torn asunder, her mouth agape in a scream. On another page, Victor had diagrammed the organs in her body, her heart exposed like a wound as it coursed blood toward her extremities and back to her womb, where life awaited birth.

On a last page, he'd drawn a miniature man unlike anything she'd ever seen. Beneath his sketch he wrote a single word: *Homunculus.*

A human grown inside a glass vial. Life created of man, not woman. An unnatural creature.

Too upset to think clearly, Caroline immediately burned the journal. Her hands shook as the flames rose. She should speak to Victor, but what could she say? She felt as though she'd been betrayed, exposed, violated. She even wept.

How could she explain her distress, which she didn't fully understand herself? Should she tell Alphonse, who'd been upset by Victor's interest in alchemy? They'd been so relieved when he'd turned to mathematics.

The fire continued burning. Caroline clutched her skirt, the length of her thigh, fingers tapping. *One, two, three.* She'd thought she'd left these habits behind.

How strange to build such a fire in the midst of summer! To feel such heat when all one craved was cool water and lake breezes! Tendrils flared from the journal, chaffing her face. Would anyone think her peculiar for making the fire? She'd been so startled, so distressed.

Then she remembered. That dream of Ingolstadt she had at the picnic. It was a warning. Something dangerous awaited Victor in Ingolstadt. Something evil. Not the Swiss soldier. Not a homunculus. Something else. Ingolstadt was home to philosophers, wasn't it? Revolutionaries.

He mustn't go to Ingolstadt. But how could she stop him?

CHAPTER IX.

"During her illness, many arguments had been urged to persuade my mother to refrain from attending upon her . . . but when she heard that the life of her favourite was menaced, she could no longer control her anxiety."

* * *

Caroline had no idea how long she'd remained in Victor's room, watching his journal smolder into ash. Her eyes dried as she regained her composure. *He must never know I did this.* Well, Justine would never speak of it—Caroline was certain of that. Suddenly Caroline recalled those pamphlets of Marie Antoinette with their brazen woodcuts. She shuddered. What if someone else had found Victor's journal? Would they recognize Caroline in his foul sketches?

And then Victor appeared by her side—how could she not have heard his approach? His hands were taut. Fisted. His chest puffed like a rooster. Caroline found her mouth dry with fear.

"What have you done, Mother?"

"Done?" she countered, heart pounding.

"My journal. You burned all my research!" He pointed toward the grate; she'd missed part of the binding. "I saw you sneak in here, but can't believe you'd do such a thing. Why?"

"I don't want you to go to Ingolstadt," she said in a low voice. "It's not safe."

He shook his head. "It's all arranged. I must go!"

She couldn't answer him. It was hard to meet his glare. Every time she looked at him, those transgressive illustrations flashed before her eyes, like he was attempting to unearth the secrets of her womb—the womb that had brought him life.

As suddenly as Victor's rage had flared, it faded as though doused by water. "I'm sorry," he whimpered. "I should be thinking of Elizabeth, not this." He embraced his mother, kissed her cheek. "It doesn't matter, Mother. I'll start over with a new one. I shouldn't have yelled. Not now."

The door opened anew. "Caroline?"

Caroline looked up from Victor's arms. Alphonse, accompanied by the doctor. *Elizabeth. Something's happened.*

Caroline doubled over as though she'd a blow. "No! Tell me she's not dead. Tell me!"

Alphonse soothed, "She still lives, but you must be strong."

"Madame Frankenstein," the doctor interjected, "if her fever doesn't break—"

"She can't die. She mustn't!"

Alphonse said, "We must trust in God's will."

My will shall be God's will. Caroline addressed the doctor in a voice calmer than she felt, "I'll nurse her myself. If I'm by her side, she'll live."

Elizabeth must survive to become Victor's wife. If they wed, Elizabeth would influence Victor more than Ingolstadt could. Surely she'd find a way to contain his forbidden interests.

* * *

How many hours had passed? Nights? Caroline couldn't recall. The important thing was Elizabeth's fever had broken—Caroline had saved her. Elizabeth would live to wed Victor. But how weary Caroline felt! Warm. She mustn't take ill. "Madame, you must rest." This was the doctor, wasn't it? Not the one who'd attended her during William's birth, who'd let Victor into her sanctuary while she struggled to give birth.

The door slammed open. Victor entered in a jolt of steps.

"Victor, did you hear the good news? Elizabeth—"

"I still can't believe you burned my journal! What were you thinking?"

The journal again? She forced a smile, more troubled than she cared to reveal. "It's not important, darling, not now! Look at Elizabeth! She's better!"

Victor rushed from the room, cursing. Had she called after him? What had she said next?

I must have said something. He must have answered—he loves Elizabeth, doesn't he?

The physician leaned over Caroline, his hand cool against her forehead. "Madame, are you well?"

"I just need to rest . . ."

She lay on the bed beside Elizabeth, who slept serenely. Caroline listened to the sweet rise and fall of her breath, and nuzzled her face against her cheek. Elizabeth's long gold hair smelled sour from sweat.

Caroline should arrange for a bath for Elizabeth, have Justine wash her hair. But first, she'd sleep.

* * *

Three days passed. Three nights. Hot. All was hot. Well, there was a reason they called it scarlet fever, Caroline decided; her flesh burned like that fire she'd built for Victor's journal. She couldn't swallow. Her throat was too raw. She seemed to recall Victor throwing a fit once he understood how sick she was. "My mother can't die! She mustn't!" This seemed so long ago.

Caroline looked down at the flesh on her arms. Her skin was peeling. She was a monster. Shedding her skin like a snake. A tree losing bark.

"I . . . I need a bath."

These words were ignored as she gave way to the sensation of hands around her neck. Was someone strangling her? No, a girl forcing water down her throat. Was Sophie feeding her? No, Justine. Always Justine, though the doctor had warned her to stay away.

The moisture hurt. Everything hurt.

A male voice said seemingly from a distance, "Swollen glands. Hopefully they'll come down."

Who spoke? Not Victor this time. The doctor. She was glad the doctor attending her wasn't the one from William's birth. She grimaced, remembering the unkindness of his hands as he turned the baby; she'd thought he would tear her asunder until she resembled that lurid sketch in Victor's journal.

At this memory, her throat ached anew.

Why had Victor drawn this? What was wrong with him?

"She's going to vomit," another voice said. Victor, calmer now. He was seated beside her bed, Elizabeth too. He clutched Caroline's hand in his right hand, Elizabeth's in his left.

But Caroline didn't vomit. Instead, her laughter rose though it made her stomach ache.

"Why are you laughing, Aunt?" Elizabeth, alarmed; she'd recovered enough to speak.

"You'd never believe me if I told you," Caroline rasped. It was an odd relief to have all you dread come to pass, like when that soldier invaded their Christmas soirée. A curse fulfilled. Her laughter gave way to tears. She was Victor's mother. She bore responsibility for him. She'd brought him into the world.

Elizabeth sobbed, "I'm so sorry! I don't know where the fever came from. I felt fine during Uncle's birthday!"

"It's not your fault, darling." Caroline searched Elizabeth's face. Her ward's eyes were bright. Glazed. But she lived, that's all that mattered.

"Where's Justine?" Victor asked, rising from the side of the bed.

"I'm here," Justine said. "I'll stay with Madame."

"No, no," Caroline whimpered. "You'll take ill."

Justine refused to leave. She kissed her brow as though Caroline were her own mother.

"You must survive, Madame," she whispered, weeping. "Please."

Suddenly Caroline recalled the change she'd sensed accompanying Justine's arrival in their home, that sense of fate. She understood now.

This change began when Justine unearthed Victor's alchemy books way back when. This discovery spurred Alphonse's Christmas soirée with Dr. Galvani, which in turn, encouraged Caroline's reconciliation with Alphonse. This led to William's conception, and Victor drawing her mid-labor in that foul journal of his. Once Justine discovered Victor's journal, Caroline was left with no choice but to nurse Elizabeth to ensure her survival. Change upon change upon change.

And now . . . well, who knew what would happen?

* * *

"Victor, come here."

Her husband's voice. Alphonse. Had she loved him? She must have, if she'd married him. Yet she could remember little of their marriage save that awful oil portrait he insisted on, the one with her dressed like a beggar. She should have burned the painting during the revolution in 1782, when no one would have noticed.

"Victor," Alphonse said again. "Your mother's awake."

And so Caroline woke. Light flooded her eyes. It stung, as did the hope in Alphonse's voice.

Caroline was in her bedroom. She was surrounded by her family—how glad she was to see them all! Elizabeth's bright gold hair dazzled in the sunlight, though her face was so thin. Victor's eyes were shrouded with emotion. Alphonse appeared to have aged a decade. No William. He'd probably been sent away to protect his health. (Was he with Ernest in the Alps? She couldn't recall.) No Justine. She remembered: Justine had taken ill while nursing her, but would survive.

Dear Justine. Caroline had done well taking her in. She was loyal to the end, even if she'd spurred everything leading up to Caroline finding Victor's journal.

It's not fair to blame Justine for what happened. It's fate, that's all. A curse.

Caroline tried to smile. Tried to grant her family hope. Even while she lay dying, she couldn't forget her responsibilities as a mother. What would William and Ernest contribute to the world? How would they reflect her legacy? She'd done so little to shape them, unlike Elizabeth and Victor, who'd spent years under her influence. She'd raised four humans—five, if you included Justine. She'd never know how they would fare.

Now she wept in earnest, for there was one last thought troubling her: Victor and that foul journal. Of all her children, he had the most power to shape the world. He'd lied about mathematics to put her off the scent.

What have I unleashed on the world?

She'd have to trust Elizabeth to mold him. To teach him what was right—and she'd taught Elizabeth well, hadn't she? Elizabeth would protect him from the temptation of knowledge without compassion. Caroline must make sure they'd marry.

The doctor spoke in a low voice. "I doubt she'll last the night."

Well, if she didn't have long, she'd say what she must.

"I want to speak to Elizabeth and Victor. Alone."

Alphonse backed away. Caroline extended her hands toward Elizabeth and Victor, who took them.

"Mama." Victor pressed his forehead against her hands. *Mama.* He hadn't called her that in years. Caroline's tears fell in response. William was but a baby. She'd never hear his voice, never know him grown. But she must contain her emotions—Victor was her concern now.

Elizabeth and Victor settled on the chaise beside her bed. How would she say all that was on her mind before it was too late? Somehow she would. She'd find a way not to lisp. She must be understood.

She began, her words more air than sound. "Elizabeth, you must supply my place to my younger children. Promise you'll protect William. You'll love him as your own?"

A tearful nod. "I will, Aunt."

Caroline managed to pull off her emerald ring, which she hadn't removed since Alphonse's birthday fête. She set the ring in Victor's palm, or tried; it fell on her white counterpane.

"Victor, my firmest hopes of happiness were placed on the prospect of your union to Elizabeth. This expectation will now be the consolation of your father."

"'Of course, Mother." Victor set the emerald ring on his pinky, sniffing.

But this wasn't enough reassurance—Elizabeth must promise too. Caroline drew Elizabeth close. "You'll marry Victor. Promise?"

"I promise, Aunt."

They'll wed. I can go now.

"My husband," she said. "I want him."

Alphonse returned to the room. Whispers of conversation. Caroline managed to gather what life remained in her—she's parceling it like teaspoons of brandy—to address her family a final time.

"Alas! I regret I am taken from you. But these are not thoughts befitting me; I will indulge a hope of meeting you in another world."

She closed her eyes. But not all was over. Not yet. There was one last thought weighing her. One last consideration. Elizabeth loved Victor, didn't she? Caroline had been so concerned about Victor's future. What of Elizabeth's?

Have I cursed her?

No answer ever came, for her room flared with a light more brilliant than any she'd ever witnessed. Suddenly she sensed the threads of her past and present braid with the future. There she was, a girl trapped by her father's ruin of a life inside that vermin-laden cottage, then later with Alphonse and their babies and her poor sore mouth, and then there was Justine with Victor's books, and the revolution and soldiers and red caps. Ernest as a sickly boy torn from her arms in the Alps. There was Elizabeth with Victor as husband and wife. A shadowy figure followed them, the one she'd dreamt of that day in Plainpalais.

Whoever he was, his face was scarred. Black flowing hair. Flesh the hue of bone. What had he to do with Victor? Or Elizabeth?

He'll be with them on their wedding night.

All of a sudden the shadowy figure was gone and so was the light. Caroline stretched her arms toward the void, as though she could halt fate from colliding with time.

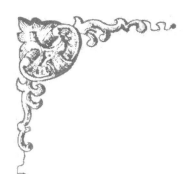
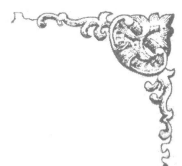

VOLUME TWO

THE BETROTHED

* * *

Three years later

CHAPTER I.

"The saintly soul of Elizabeth shone like a shrine-dedicated lamp
in our peaceful home . . . And Clerval—could aught ill entrench
on the noble spirit of Clerval?"

* * *

ON THE COLDEST day of the year, the Cimetière des Rois would usually be empty save for clatterings of jackdaws perched on gravestones. But when the coldest day also marked the first day of 1792, the cemetery was crowded with families yearning for communion with the dead. Elizabeth Lavenza was distressed. She understood this to be a possibility when she'd insisted on William accompanying her to Caroline's grave, but told herself the snowy weather would act as a deterrent. She was wrong. New Year's Day was New Year's Day no matter how frigid it might be.

"Come, dormouse." Elizabeth reached for William's hand in the carriage. She fought her rising irritation. "We won't stay long."

"No, Lisbeth. Cold." The almost four-year-old boy folded his arms and scowled, reminding her of Victor when she'd first met him as a child. Gold curls. Strong jaw.

"But we're going to visit your mama." She adored William, but how stubborn he could be!

He jutted his lip. "She's not there. She's dead."

Elizabeth's chest caught. *Yes, she's dead. And it's all my fault.*

"There's no reasoning with him when he's like this," Henry Clerval intervened. "Let him wait in the carriage." He had agreed to accompany Elizabeth and William for the New Year's cemetery visit when Alphonse complained of exhaustion after church; Ernest had disappeared to wherever he went these days, now that he'd rejoined the Frankenstein household. He'd returned from the Alps transformed from a sickly boy into a tall fifteen-year-old who appeared older and acted such—or attempted to.

"You'll watch him then?" Elizabeth cast an eye toward the main promenade, where Caroline's tomb awaited. "I won't be long."

"I'd rather accompany you. Antoine can stay with William, Beata." Beata was the childhood nickname Henry had settled on her years earlier.

"I'm happy to, Mademoiselle," Antoine replied.

The groomsman was dressed in a dark frock coat and breeches instead of livery. All that had been done away with during the revolution of 1789, which occurred in Geneva soon after Victor's departure for Ingolstadt. Since then, the republic had settled into an uneasy peace. Not so in France, where turmoil still reigned.

"Very well," Elizabeth muttered, again fighting that conundrum of rage and guilt she'd lived with since Caroline's death. She would do anything to relieve herself of it.

Once William was settled, Henry alighted from the coach holding a small bouquet of lush red roses.

"You forgot these for your aunt."

"Thank you." How kind Henry was! A true friend.

He pointed down a path. "This way, yes?"

Elizabeth nodded. Without thinking, her fingers sought out Caroline's emerald ring, which twisted on her right hand; she'd yet to have it resized since Victor's proposal. They'd marry after his return from Ingolstadt. She prayed soon. At least then she'd make amends for essentially killing Caroline.

It was all her fault. Elizabeth knew it, though she'd never confessed as such to anyone, especially not Victor. That green Florentine journal she'd given him at the farewell picnic—it was a custom binding she'd commissioned. She'd insisted on purchasing it though the shopkeeper was ill. She even warned Elizabeth as much.

"I've a fever, Mademoiselle—you mustn't come near me. Come back next week for your gift."

"Next week will be too late," Elizabeth had pressed. *"I'll be but a moment..."*

A moment too long: the next morning Elizabeth awoke with a headache that worsened during the day. By the end of the picnic, she'd never felt so ill . . . and now. Well, now she was no longer ill. Only cursed, or so she felt.

Once I wed Victor, I'll feel better. I know it. I'll have kept my promise to Caroline.

As she and Henry strolled into the heart of the cemetery, gravel crunched beneath their boots. Denuded of leaves, the snow-covered oak trees lining the promenade looked deflated, like a court gown without panniers. Not that anyone wore these anymore—instead, all was delicate linen tunics and long shawls.

Elizabeth stared above the oaks, the cold air sharp against her cheeks. The sky was a cerulean blue that spoke of sun and heat, lazy days boating, not snow and frost.

Behind them, a family argued. A husband and wife clutching an infant, who was wailing. Why was it that raised voices sounded so much harsher in winter? The feuding couple stomped off, leaving the remaining families crowding the Cimetière des Rois in their separate but equal universes of loss. A young woman hooded in a nut-brown cloak limped before vanishing into a wooded lane.

The sight of her solitary figure tugged at Elizabeth. *No one should be alone and mourning on New Year's Day.* She gazed up at Henry, grateful for his presence. He'd truly kept his vow to Victor to keep her company.

As they walked, the cerulean sky softened to grey. A fresh show of snow, so fine it glistened in the air. It muffled their footfall.

Then they were there. Caroline's tomb. Snow or no, Elizabeth dropped to her knees before it.

Alphonse had spared no expense on the tomb, even arranging for the famed sculptor Jean-Antoine Houdon to carve a life-sized marble representation of Caroline, inspired by that oil portrait from years earlier. The statue was set on a monument base almost as tall as Elizabeth. It was so different from the small watercolor Elizabeth painted of her aunt soon after her death, which she set in a gold locket around her neck. She intended the locket for William in time.

Snow cloaked Caroline's ivory statue, causing it to shimmer like an apparition. White upon white; it would be impossible to paint, Elizabeth decided. The statue lay some steps from the Frankenstein mausoleum, which housed every generation since the family's arrival in Geneva two centuries earlier from Darmstadt. The mausoleum was among the largest in the cemetery, an architectural mirror of the Frankensteins' influence upon the city-republic.

During fretful moments, Elizabeth imagined Caroline lonely away from their ancestors, but she'd come to appreciate Alphonse's decision to set her tomb apart. In this setting, surrounded by elms and oaks, it was easier to sense Caroline's serene presence; the mausoleum always seemed a clatter of individual histories clamoring for attention. Here, there was only Caroline—perfect kind Caroline who'd loved Elizabeth like a mother. Caroline who'd been the perfect wife to Alphonse, as Elizabeth prayed she'd be one day for Victor. Marrying Victor was the least she could do after all that happened. Perhaps she wouldn't feel cursed then.

Henry stepped away, affording Elizabeth privacy. The words she'd said so often and in so many ways since Caroline's death fell from her lips.

"I'm so sorry," Elizabeth whispered, letting the roses fall from her arms. "If only . . ."

If only I hadn't taken ill.

If only you hadn't nursed me.

If only you'd survived. . .

Elizabeth shivered despite her thick wool cloak. The roses appeared a shock of scarlet against the soft white snow. She should finish paying her respects and return to William. Return home. Yet all she could recall was Caroline's face after she'd promised to marry Victor. The ecstatic relief. The peace.

Elizabeth set her palms against the ground to stand. She couldn't seem to. *Guilt is heavier than lead.* This sounded like one of Victor's alchemical formulas.

She had no idea how many seconds passed before Henry helped her to her feet.

"Her death wasn't your fault, Beata." His tone was akin to those used to soothe an invalid.

"Will I ever feel it's not?"

"In time." Henry let out a long breath; snow fluttered about his face. "Time will help."

"But time changed everything," she choked out. "So many I love are now gone. Not only Caroline. Victor in Ingolstadt. Even Justine—I loved her like a friend, and she nearly died because of me."

Justine had also been afflicted with scarlet fever, but not as severely as Caroline and Elizabeth. Soon after her recovery, Justine returned home to her mother. Elizabeth was surprised—hadn't Justine refused Madame Moritz's apology that day? The Frankensteins hadn't heard from Justine since.

Henry said, "Justine's in a happier place now."

Elizabeth offered an unusually harsh laugh. "You make it sound as though she's passed too."

"I meant to say it's good she's reunited with her family. I'm sure it was difficult for her to forgive her mother, but I'm glad she was able."

"You don't have to protect my feelings, Henry. I've no doubt Justine blames me for my aunt's death. I've sent notes, gone to her doorstep. She refuses to see me. Victor blames me too. Since he left for Ingolstadt, I've received a total of six letters in three years. Six!"

"He's barely written anyone." Henry also rarely heard from Victor save for brief, distracted letters he showed to Elizabeth. Victor seemed particularly enamored of a professor named Waldman, who'd advised him to study chemistry instead of mathematics.

The two friends fell into an uneasy silence. The snow continued to fall, broken only by flickers of movement toward the cemetery gate. A line of children holding hands following a stout squat woman. An elderly pair of women shuffling, careful not to slip on ice. That girl in the brown cloak she'd spotted before.

"I'm sorry to be so mournful," Elizabeth said at last.

"It's hard not to. Your aunt was the kindest gentlewoman I've ever met. As close to a mother as I've known."

Just as she was for me. But you didn't cause her death.

Henry looked about the graveyard at the thickening snow. He pushed his unruly fawn-colored hair from his eyes. "We should leave soon."

"I'll hurry. William is probably fidgeting by now."

Elizabeth drew from her muff a slender flask containing water for the flowers. The snow surrounding Caroline's tomb wasn't deep, but it was thick enough to obscure the lip of the glass vase set into the base. Elizabeth cleared the snow, using her hands.

A jag of pain. Her finger. She dropped the flask.

Three drops of red blood fell, blossoming on the snow like poppies.

Blood. *Her* blood. The sight of it made her stomach flip.

"You cut yourself." Henry pressed his handkerchief against her fingertip. The linen bloomed scarlet.

Elizabeth sucked in her lip, finger stinging. Somehow the vase had cracked. She bent over it, spying something small and dark inside. Something shiny. Something curved. An acorn?

To avoid cutting herself again, she scooped it out with Henry's handkerchief.

"A bullet," she said. She shuddered, remembering the soldiers she'd seen three years earlier. Mobs. Thankfully she hadn't seen the worst of the violence. But she'd seen enough.

Henry's face drained of color. "We should go. It's too cold for flowers anyway. We'll place them by your aunt's portrait instead. Let me accompany you home. Perhaps there'll be a letter from Victor."

Good Henry. Kind Henry. What would she have done these past three years without him? Elizabeth stole a glance at him. He really was handsome, though in a different way from Victor.

"Yes, time to leave," she agreed. "William is probably restless."

By then the cemetery was emptied of everyone save that solitary female mourner with the patched brown cloak. The girl crossed the avenue beside Caroline's tomb. Elizabeth nodded out of habitual politeness as she passed.

A dragged leg. A curved spine. Beneath her snow-dappled Thérèse hood, silver-pale hair. Light grey eyes.

Elizabeth turned, heart flooding with emotion. "Justine? Is that you?"

The mourner didn't respond. Her pace evened as she continued down the promenade. Elizabeth hadn't imagined the limp, had she? The hair, the eyes?

"I'll go after her," Elizabeth told Henry. "I don't think Justine heard me." She could apologize again, win her affection back.

Henry circled. "Where? I don't see anyone."

He was right. The cemetery was empty, the mourning girl gone.

Henry took Elizabeth's arm. "It's hard to see anything in this snow.

Come, it's getting heavier. No, don't look behind—you'll only get snow in your face."

And so Elizabeth didn't look behind. If she had, she would have seen Justine emerge from behind an elm to approach Caroline's tomb.

Justine dropped to her knees and kissed the base of Caroline's statue, ignoring the drops of blood dotting the snow. She clutched her hands beneath her chin, knuckles tight.

"I'm so sorry, Madame," she whispered. "If only I could have saved you. If only I hadn't taken ill. If only you'd survived . . ."

A moment later, Justine crossed herself. She staggered to her feet and limped away.

CHAPTER II.

"My father made no reproach in his letters, and only took notice of my silence by enquiring into my occupations more particularly than before. Winter, spring, and summer passed away during my labours; but I did not watch the blossom or the expanding leaves."

* * *

W<small>HEN THEIR CARRIAGE REACHED THE</small> F<small>RANKENSTEINS</small>' home, Henry fled before Elizabeth could offer her customary invitation of a visit and a meal. "The weather. My father," he said, his words limp as wet paper. Elizabeth nodded with disappointment—she'd grown fond of his companionship—and hurried inside, clutching William's sugary hand. Anyway, time for her to hide any desires or needs. To be loving and perfect, as everyone needed her to be.

Once William was settled with Sophie, Elizabeth found Alphonse in his study slumped before the fire. Like Elizabeth, he'd never ceased mourning Caroline; unlike Elizabeth, he didn't blame himself for her passing. A pile of papers rested on the table beside him, where a tea service awaited. Both tea and cakes appeared untouched.

Elizabeth hurried to his side. "Uncle, are you well?"

He waved away her concerns. "A letter from Victor. It just arrived."

Elizabeth's heart gave a stutter as she took the half-sheet from Alphonse.

I bid you all a loving greeting in anticipation of the coming New Year. I will write anew once this round of my labor is complete. —V.F.

Two sentences. That was all. Victor's handwriting looked rushed, as though he'd dashed off the letter without consideration. Small red splatters dotted the letter. *Not blood,* Elizabeth thought; her finger still stung where she'd cut it, but it had ceased bleeding.

She said in a careful tone, "His studies must be heavy."

"Perhaps." Alphonse's spoon clattered against the china as he stirred his tea with a desultory air. "Elizabeth, do you remember what I told him at the picnic that day?"

How could she forget? "You'd said that you'd regard any interruption in your correspondence as proof he was neglecting his other duties."

Alphonse offered a half-smile. "How good your memory is! Well, now you understand my concern. I'm tempted to travel to see him, but Ingolstadt is so far, and with the turmoil in France . . ."

Elizabeth bit her lip. That bullet near Caroline's monument, the shattered vase. She wouldn't tell him. It would only add worry. Nor would she confide that she thought she'd seen Justine. He'd be saddened; he'd been particularly fond of the maid.

"It *is* far, particularly in winter," she finally said, forcing a cheerful smile. "He did promise he'd write again soon. If he isn't home by this summer, we should travel to see him. I'll accompany you. I'm sure Ernest will too."

"A good plan! Thank you, my angel."

She pressed a kiss against his wrinkled cheek. "Shall we write Victor before William interrupts?"

* * *

Once their letter to Victor was complete, Elizabeth crept back to her room to compose a private one.

Beloved friend, she began, *It's been so long since you've written me directly —six months, more. Though I am grateful for your letters to our family, I yearn for us to confide in each other as we used to. How I miss you!*

Her hand stilled; her guilt turned back to that rage she didn't fully understand. Fury at Victor rather than yearning . . . but it was more than this. In Ingolstadt, Victor's life had continued without Elizabeth's involvement as though she didn't matter. In Geneva, Elizabeth was trapped waiting for his return. Waiting to make amends for Caroline.

I have no reason to be so angry. He's busy, that's all.

With this, Elizabeth continued her letter, making her words as bright as the smiles she feigned in her family's presence. She wrote to Victor of people they knew in Geneva, teas to offer philanthropy to the less fortunate, outings to concerts where she hadn't noticed the music. Since Caroline's death, society had welcomed Elizabeth in her aunt's stead. Once she married Victor, her position would be even more secured: she'd be a wife, a Frankenstein by law and before God. She'd no longer be an orphan dependent on their favor. She'd have fulfilled her promise to Caroline. Maybe then she'd be less angry. Less filled with remorse.

"I hope my words have brought you the sense of an afternoon spent with your family at home," Elizabeth concluded. *"If this letter has offered a moment's respite, please write to let me know. I love you and yearn for your return."*

Yet as she reread her words, all she thought of was Henry's face when they'd parted at her door. How lonely he appeared with Victor gone.

Henry. If only he'd stayed for a visit; she'd grown used to having him near. They could have spoken of Victor, reconstructing memories as though to recreate his presence. This would have offered more comfort than that terse letter Victor had sent, which a stranger could have written.

Perhaps Victor had changed while he was in Ingolstadt. Maybe that's why he rarely wrote, not that he blamed her for the loss of his mother.

But what of herself: had she also changed?

Elizabeth couldn't turn from the question. As if pulled by a thread, she rose from her desk. A standing mirror stood across the room where the light was best. She always tried to avoid the sin of vanity . . . but in this case, she couldn't resist.

Elizabeth bolted her door. She unlocked her desk drawer and took out a sketchbook she kept secret. Her pencils and charcoal too. She approached the mirror and unbuttoned her gown, slipping it from her shoulders, her chemise too, until her torso was bared. She narrowed her eyes and imagined Victor viewing her on their wedding night.

Once she'd gotten a good look at herself, she opened her sketchbook. She turned past the drawings she dared not share with anyone—mice caught in traps, birds victimized by cats, butterflies found with abandoned wings, glimpses of her unclad body—until she found a blank page. She sharpened her charcoal.

As Elizabeth drew herself, a peculiar calmness fell across her soul. These sketches felt a compulsion. A hunger. This act of observation and recording was necessary, a ritual to quiet her turmoil. A way to view what was true, rather than the serene surface she felt compelled to present to the world. She never sketched her entire body, only details. This way, should the sketchbook ever be discovered, no one would realize the drawings were of her. Still, she was careful to always lock the sketchbook away.

Her drawing quickly took shape on the page. Her breasts appeared smaller than before she'd taken ill with scarlet fever—two small nipples with softness about them, like a thirteen-year-old girl's. Her ribs protruded beneath her greyed flesh; she'd never gained back the weight she lost then. Decidedly not as pretty as she'd once been. Did she dare to completely undress? Outside of herself, she'd never seen a naked woman, not even when Caroline had given birth to William.

As for the male form . . .

Instead of imagining Victor on their wedding night, Elizabeth recalled the last time she'd seen him. It was the night before his departure for Ingolstadt, several months after Caroline's death. Victor had taken her passing especially hard; his sorrow had been such that he'd been unable to speak to anyone for days. That night, he'd come alone to Elizabeth's room after everyone else had gone to bed.

"I'll be leaving early," he'd said. *"Far earlier than you usually rise."*

"I wouldn't miss seeing you off," she'd replied; she felt her tongue dash against her lips. *"I'll wake early."*

"That's not what I meant, Elizabeth. I wanted to bid you farewell in private."

He took a step toward her, gazing at her in a way he never had before. Then she noticed he was holding the journal she'd given him at that last picnic. It flashed green in the dusky light. Her stomach had flipped. Panic.

Victor offered the journal to her with a yearning smile. *"I want you to inscribe it for me, beloved. Something to remind me of you while I'm away."*

She wrote on the flyleaf: *I will love you until my last breath.* Beneath this, she signed her name with the bravado of the guilty.

Once Victor read her inscription, he embraced her as though something had changed in him. In her. There was an insecurity to his gesture, as though he was exploring what it meant to be a lover instead of a friend.

She suppressed a shiver as he set his dry lips against hers. He laid on the bed beside her. Though nothing happened save some innocent caresses, she told herself Caroline's death hadn't cursed her, for she could tell she pleased him. He murmured how much he loved her, that she was his angel. Perfect. They'd marry upon his return.

Once he'd said this, she wept with relief. She dared to hope their future might be happy. She even thought of their wedding night and—

Bang!

A crash on her window like a gunshot. With this, Elizabeth came back to herself with a start; she was alone in her room, her breasts exposed while she drew. She covered herself and rushed to the window, where a tar-black shadow fluttered.

A bird dangled midair, squawking. A jackdaw—it must have dashed itself against the glass, which miraculously hadn't cracked. Thankfully, it appeared unhurt.

Once she opened the window, the bird took off in a blur of somber iridescence through the snowy garden. She shivered.

The bird means nothing.

She dressed herself and locked her sketchbook inside the drawer. She told herself, "All is well. Victor will write soon."

*   *   *

Victor didn't write.

While Elizabeth and the Frankensteins awaited any news from Ingolstadt, snow melted into spring and tulips gave way to roses. French troops began to arrive in Geneva like they had during the revolution of 1789. More ominously, a new instrument of state appeared in Paris to bring order.

"A guillotine," Ernest explained. It was still strange to have him home. Perhaps it was his time in the mountains, but Ernest considered himself Swiss rather than Genevan, which distressed the patriotic Alphonse.

"What's that?" Elizabeth asked.

"Look." Ernest opened the latest *Gazette de France* to reveal an illustration depicting a tall framed apparatus with an angled blade, a smiling executioner displaying a severed head. "Such is the French devotion to an equal society for all. They've set the guillotine in a field outside Paris to avoid attracting crowds."

Alphonse frowned. "I don't see how the ability to execute criminals more efficiently encourages equality in a country. Better they be banished from their motherland—that, to my mind, is punishment enough."

Elizabeth did her best to make peace between them, as Caroline would want. She smiled, she soothed. She took care of William as though he was her own. She did everything but tell the truth: that she felt as though she was going to jump out of her flesh with each passing day.

By the middle of September, the guillotine had been moved from the Parisian countryside to the Place du Carrousel, which was followed by the massacre of over a thousand people in less than a week. Ernest spent hours in coffee houses debating the situation with other students. That morning, he brought home newspapers proclaiming that French troops had attacked the Duchy of Savoy with the intention of incorporating it into the French Republic; Savoy was south of Geneva. Worse, the French confiscated the Genevan artillery for their use, leaving the city-republic defenseless.

The news transformed Alphonse's unease into a disturbance that Elizabeth couldn't soothe. Even William sensed his father's distress and played quietly for once.

"We should leave Geneva, Uncle," Elizabeth urged. "It's time. Please."

"Not to Belrive," Alphonse replied, glancing up from his pile of correspondence. "Not far enough—look at Chêne." Chêne, a village a league outside Geneva, had been recently captured by the French without a blow.

Ernest challenged, "The French are our allies. We should follow their lead for a more egalitarian society. 'Man is born free but is everywhere in chains.'"

Rousseau again. Elizabeth had read the philosopher at Ernest's insistence, but feared his books encouraged violence.

Before Alphonse could respond, a lanky boy with a mop of sun-dusted curls appeared at the door. A messenger from the Assembly. More letters. More words delivered in an urgent tone. Alphonse ordered Elizabeth and Ernest to leave his study.

"Let your father be," Elizabeth warned Ernest once they were alone.

Ernest's eyes widened, mocking. "Why?"

"You should have more compassion for him."

"You're saying this because you're dependent on his favor until Victor returns," Ernest snapped. "As for my father, he should have more compassion for those who rely on his position to ease their lives."

"And you're the one to enlighten him?"

For a moment, Elizabeth thought Ernest would scowl as he often did; though he resembled Caroline in appearance, his temperament was as stormy as hers was serene.

He only laughed and all seemed set right. In that moment.

"Elizabeth, you forget I didn't spend my childhood here." His tone grew bitter. "My father doesn't really know me. Not yet. As for my mother, I shall never truly know her."

She said quickly, "I understand. I know nothing of my parents myself." She recalled so little of her life before the Frankensteins.

Their conversation silenced as Alphonse emerged from his study, his shoulders taut.

"I was mistaken in my complacency," he said, grave-faced. "French troops are on their way from Savoy to surround Geneva. Elizabeth, you must leave immediately with my sons. I won't accompany you."

"No, you must come!" Elizabeth protested. "Please, Uncle."

"I can't. Nor do I want to," Alphonse said, ignoring Ernest's glare. "Forgive an old man for insisting on remaining in his homeland."

Her uncle handed her a sealed letter. She recognized it from Caroline's jewelry box.

"This is where you shall take sanctuary, children. Elizabeth, your aunt intended this to be your wedding present. I think she will forgive me for giving it to you early."

* * *

Alone in her room, Elizabeth broke the letter's seal:

My dearest Elizabeth,

If you are reading this, you have wed Victor and are now a Franken-stein. As such, it is time for you to learn the truth about the family whose name you came to us bearing: the Lavenzas.

I must warn what I am about to share may bring sorrow as well as joy. However, I trust in time the joy will outweigh the sorrow.

You, of course, know the story of how you came to me so many years ago; how I'd yearned for a daughter of my own, and how I loved you from the moment I first laid eyes on your face. The beggar woman who served as your nursemaid confided of your noble family name, which was of an ancient lineage. She knew little of your parents save they were deceased. I still recall the first time you met Victor. "Here is a pretty gift for my Victor," I told him; but the truth was that even then you were already more than this to me. You were someone I cherished. Someone who, in time, I prayed would become Victor's dearest friend and life companion.

Yet though I'd embraced you as my own, I understood there was a lack in your heart from not knowing your parents. I resolved to fill it. After many letters, I received confirmation that your mother was a German noblewoman who died in the act of giving you life. As for your father, he was an Italian nobleman who plotted to obtain liberty for his native country from Austria. He was arrested soon after your birth, his property confiscated. Alas, a decade later, he was discovered lifeless in his prison cell, leaving you the last of the Lavenzas.

After much petition, your uncle and I were able to restore a property on the shores of Como as your family inheritance. The Villa Lavenza is located near where I first met you as a child. Though the villa has not been inhabited in years, the property has been maintained by loyal servants and is a place of natural beauty. It only awaits you to take possession.

My darling Elizabeth, I pray you and Victor shall find much joy there.

With greatest affection and devotion,
CAROLINE FRANKENSTEIN.

"I'm an heiress," Elizabeth whispered to herself. She truly had no idea.

She folded the letter away, her mind a dark jangle of surprise. Within this confusion, a shocking thought arose, stunning in its disloyalty: would she have agreed to marry Victor had she known she was an heiress?

Of course I would have, she reassured. *I've always loved him.*

And then: *I must. I promised Caroline.*

For a moment, she felt as though she'd retch. She didn't. Instead, she left her room to fetch William, smiling as she always did. "Come, dormouse! We're going on an adventure. Shall we pack?"

CHAPTER III.

"Through my father's exertions, a part of the inheritance of Elizabeth had been restored to her by the Austrian government. A small possession on the shores of Como belonged to her. It was agreed that . . . we should proceed to Villa Lavenza."

* * *

THEY LEFT THE FOLLOWING MORNING.

The journey to the Villa Lavenza would take Elizabeth, William, and Sophie three days—long days that included a ferry to Evian and several coaches to Lake Como; days in which Alphonse did not want Elizabeth to travel without an escort due to the turmoil.

Ernest refused to accompany them, to Alphonse's displeasure. "Can't you see I can't leave Geneva?" Ernest pleaded, his eyes feverish with excitement. "This is a new world. A better world." *A world where many will die,* Elizabeth fretted though she didn't say such; it would have upset William. Anyway, Ernest was only fifteen. What protection could he truly offer?

But someone else volunteered to take Ernest's place: Henry Clerval. Elizabeth had rarely seen him since their New Year's cemetery visit nine months earlier; he claimed to be busy with his father's shop. She'd accepted his excuses with a graceful smile; in private, she felt abandoned. But once Henry learned she'd be leaving Geneva, he immediately appeared at the Frankensteins' door prepared for the journey.

"I will accompany you to Lake Como," he said. "I insist."

Elizabeth's heart leapt at his presence—she'd truly missed him. Alas, he proved to be a somber travel companion. Though he and Elizabeth did not discuss the French invasion of Geneva, it seemed an invisible weight on his spirit. Usually Henry was the placid one, the one who found the good in every situation, the one who enthused over beauty and nature and literature.

Henry's mood did not shift even as they drew closer to Lake Como. Nothing attracted a cursory remark from him, not even the sight of cascading waterfalls or glaciers veined with color. Elizabeth suspected a reason for his preoccupation besides revolution: Victor. Henry was thinking of the promise he'd made to protect Elizabeth. He'd left his father to honor this vow. She could imagine Monsieur Clerval's disapproval, especially during such a tumultuous time. Well, Elizabeth supposed she liked Henry's company more than he liked hers.

"We've missed you these months," she ventured in a careful tone; by then they were onto the next to last leg of their journey and William was napping on her lap. "But we understood you had needs of your own. I hope your silence isn't because of your father's displeasure."

She snuck a glance at him, curious how he'd take her words.

"It's not that, Beata." Henry's voice was so low that Elizabeth had to lean in; his hair bore a faint citrus smell, like sunlight. "My father wants me to become his partner. In time I'm to take over his business."

"Ah. I suspected he may have intended such."

His silence wasn't because of Elizabeth after all. She was surprised by relief, though she knew it was selfish of her. She resisted the urge to take his hand. *I'm sorry,* she wanted to say. *You must be so disappointed.*

She said nothing. Knowing Henry, he'd feel shamed by her pity. She knew he'd hoped his father would allow him at least a year of university before he settled into trade. He wanted to study languages, not business. He once told her and Victor, "The world is so big and wide. Understanding languages is the best way to understand different cultures." Before Caroline's death, the three of them had imagined bright futures where Elizabeth would make art, Victor uncover the mysteries of mathematics, and Henry study other cultures. An enchanted circle of three.

Henry stared out into the vista, letting his hand trail from the open carriage as though to gather sunshine. The September day was warm enough that they had no need for a canopy.

He said at last, "I've another reason for accompanying you besides revolutions and promises. A reason I will tell you by-the-by. I shan't speak of it at this time, for look how lovely the day is! So beautiful! So unaware of the world's troubles . . ."

With this they fell into a new silence, one that felt scarcely less awkward than the first. They remained so for many leagues, even after William woke and they stopped to switch to a hired carriage outside Mont San Giorgio. However, Elizabeth's melancholy faded once they approached the Villa Lavenza and the scenery grew more exquisite. The road twisted and narrowed as it sliced through the mountain. The sun winked through the trees. Vineyards rose beside them, heavy with fruit nearing harvest.

A curl of excitement, anticipation rose from her stomach. With this villa, this *home*, she would at last possess tangible evidence of her parents' lives. A life separate from the Frankensteins. Before Caroline. What would she find when they arrived?

"We're there soon, I hope?" Sophie asked. "Please say yes, Monsieur Clerval!" Suspension coach or no, the unpaved road was bumpy and prone to induce vertigo.

"Now?" William cried.

"Almost," Henry replied examining the map. His spirit also seemed lighter.

"Where's the lake?" Elizabeth asked, sitting up straight.

Henry pointed at the map. "Over here. See? The Villa Lavenza is near the village of Lenno."

"Lenno." The word tripped off Elizabeth's tongue, languorous in its syllables. Alphonse had described these details, but she'd been too stunned by the news of her inheritance as well as panicked by their sudden departure. "How close are we?"

Henry traced a curling shape on the map with his forefinger; Elizabeth had never noticed before that he bit his nails. "See the upside-down Y? That's Lake Como. Over here is Lenno; it's one of those villages along the north perimeter." He looked up from the map. "And here we are, if I'm correct."

There it was, the entire lake revealed like a bride made brazen on her wedding night. Even William gasped.

Lake Como was a blue basin of water, wider than Elizabeth's eyes could contain. Broader than life. Over her right shoulder, a thin island interrupted the pristine span. Where the southern expanse of the lake met the horizon, a distant mountain range rose. A single white cloud floated above their heads, the sole discord marring the sky.

The coach juddered to a stop. William and Sophie spilled out from it, Henry too. Elizabeth's heart raced, reminding her of when she was a child awaiting Christmas.

"Is this real? Am I awake? Am I dreaming?"

"Awake," Henry said, his eyes sparkling, "though it appears a dream. Look, there's your villa!"

And then Elizabeth could no longer deny the truth of what she was experiencing.

"Oh," she breathed. She'd expected to find something humble, something akin to their *maison de campagne* in Belrive. Not this.

The Villa Lavenza was a three story ochre-colored horizontal box crowned by a grey slate roof with matching shutters and balconies. Two shallow gables broke the expanse of the roof, like eyes peering out at the sea. The villa's windows were symmetrical, as were its chimneys, from which a thin drift of smoke emerged.

Before Henry could offer his hand, Elizabeth climbed down from the carriage. She discovered herself inside a long formal garden delineated by two banks of cypresses pruned like pyramids. A long reflecting pond was set between the cypresses, within which a family of nearly grown ducklings and their mother floated placidly. Beyond it, an apple orchard. The villa's gardens were framed by banks of mountains stretching toward the heavens.

All this. Mine. Elizabeth could scarcely breathe.

Henry wrapped his hand around her elbow as though he feared startling her. She leaned into his touch, welcoming his warmth.

"Come, Beata. Your household awaits."

* * *

Inside the villa's foyer, Elizabeth found Sophie already seated on a fine mahogany bench that appeared carved centuries earlier. The maid's grey eyes were as wide as Elizabeth's. William lay in her lap, sucking his thumb from exhaustion. How long had Elizabeth remained in the garden? Long enough for Sophie and William to find their way inside, and for the small household that made up the Villa Lavenza to arrange themselves by height. None were dressed in livery, but that was to be expected, Elizabeth decided. Revolution had affected even these far corners.

First was a grizzled lank of a man who appeared a decade younger than Alphonse. He bowed. "Martin Frizten," he informed Elizabeth in careful German-accented French. A golden-colored hound stood by his side, tail wagging like a whip. "I maintain the grounds. I'm also qualified as a groom, if you've need."

The housekeeper was next, a thick-waisted voluptuous woman with stubborn grey curls escaping her white lawn mob cap. Signora Giulia, Elizabeth was told in Italian. "Your uncle wrote of your arrival. I cook and oversee the staff." As for the housekeeping staff, it was comprised of two skinny girls, one fair-haired and the other dark. Rosa and Ella. They giggled as they bobbed curtseys.

"This is their first placement away from home," Signora Giulia explained. "They are children really, but they will work hard. You must forgive their awkwardness. You have need of a maid to help you dress? I would recommend Ella—she's very clever."

"I've no need, thank you. I've brought a maid with me."

"The red-headed girl?" Signora Giulia gave a dubious shrug in Sophie's direction. Sophie cuddled William and yawned.

"Sophie is very capable," Elizabeth interjected.

Another shrug. "As you wish, Signorina. We are isolated here and it is difficult to find help, so we do as we must. Only I remained here all these years, along with Martin. You must understand it was surprising to learn the villa was to be inhabited again, after so many years with your father gone."

"You were acquainted with my father?" How strange to refer to her father as someone with a history. A life.

Signora Giulia nodded. "And your mother."

This Elizabeth had not expected. Her hands clenched like she'd received a blow. "You knew my mother?"

Signora Giulia replied, "Yes, though I did not wait on your parents— I worked in the kitchen then. Your mother was particularly kind."

What did she look like? Elizabeth yearned to ask. *Did she resemble me?* She didn't trust herself to speak without emotion.

Henry took her hand, gentle as ever. "We can speak with Signora Giulia later, Beata. We should view the rest of the house, don't you think? Soon the sun will be too low to see it properly. I know I am too impatient to wait." He offered a bow. "Milady, may I escort you about your villa?"

Elizabeth's cheeks lifted into a wide grin. "Of course, m'lord."

"Not a lord. Imagine me your knight. I am here as your liege, if you will." Her heart leapt at his words; she could never imagine Victor being so fanciful.

He's inspired by this place, not me.

Henry pointed toward the foyer's widest archway. "I suspect this leads to the rest of the public rooms. I have no idea what they're called in a villa. The reception room? The ballroom? The gallery? To call it a drawing room seems an insult."

Elizabeth laughed, her chest releasing. She dismissed the servants and gave William a kiss before passing him back to Sophie. She reached for Henry's arm. "Shall we, my liege?"

As Henry predicted, the archway led into a room so grand that it must have been a ballroom at one time in its history. A crystal-hung chandelier glittered rainbows from the dying sun. The walls were frescoed in colors faded by years of sunlight, the paintings so skillfully done that they appeared three-dimensional. These frescoes extended toward the ceiling, where they dissolved into a pastel display of sun-drenched clouds and gold-curled cherubs. Paint mimicked faux windows framing views of fantastical landscapes and mythological creatures.

I'm really here. I'm not dreaming.

"You don't remember living here?" Henry asked.

She shook her head. "I was only a baby."

For a moment, she nearly began to tell him again the story of her parents from Caroline's letter, as though to restore them to life in this place where they'd loved each other. She couldn't. Not yet. Instead, Elizabeth's eyes drank in the villa's beauty like water on a parched day. Her fingers itched for her brushes—if only she'd brought her water-color kit! They departed Geneva so quickly that she'd neglected to pack them. She'd have to remember the best she could.

But Henry is here. He won't forget.

Elizabeth turned in a circle. The frescoes surrounding the room were interrupted by a wide marble fireplace. Above the fireplace, the artist had painted two cherubs holding a winged crest.

Henry raised his head and pointed. "This must be the heraldic shield of the Lavenzas."

Elizabeth found she could only nod, for she didn't trust herself to speak.

I may be the last of the Lavenzas, but I can bring a new family here. A new history.

As though conjuring the future, she imagined two children, a boy and a girl, chasing each other through the ballroom, their laughter rising toward the frescoed ceiling, like Victor and herself. *Their* children. A life apart from Geneva, where she wouldn't blame herself for the death of Caroline.

"Are you tired, Beata?" Henry asked. "It's been a long day. Forgive me—I was so eager to see everything that I forgot myself."

"No," she said. "No. I want to see my house."

She giggled. *My house.* How easily the words sprang to her lips. She must see every corner before it grew too dark. Another giggle rose, like water bubbling from the earth.

She broke into a trot, running from room to room much as William would. Henry's boots clattered along the marble floors as he chased her. "Wait for me! You're too swift—I want to take my time taking in everything."

"As do I," she laughed. "We can linger tomorrow. Hurry!"

They approached a set of wide French doors, which opened onto a terrace overlooking Lake Como. To the right of the doors, a staircase led upstairs to more bedrooms than Elizabeth had patience to count. The largest one had walls painted in warm yellows as though from the time of ancient Rome. It held a desk, a gold lacquered screen, and the largest bed, also curtained in yellow.

This must be my room, Elizabeth decided—yes, there was Sophie unpacking in the adjoining antechamber.

Before she could address Sophie, Henry tugged at Elizabeth's arm. They raced down the stairs, out toward the terrace that overlooked the lake, where the sun had sunk low, staining the water a brilliant scarlet. Below the terrace laid an ivy-covered boat house, which was also covered in frescoes. It was here Elizabeth and Henry finally came to a rest, all thoughts of Geneva and revolution and loss far from their minds.

They looked out toward the mountains, the lake, the sky beyond. Henry's mouth shifted as though to conjure words, but he said nothing. She understood. She mirrored his silence, her heart full.

This was worth bearing the loss of a father and a mother. This house. This beauty. Wasn't it?

Again, she tried to imagine the children she might have with Victor. She found she couldn't; she was too aware of the weight of Henry's hand against hers. When had she grasped it?

"Beata," he said, turning toward her. "Elizabeth, I must . . ."

Her stomach pulled with something she refused to identify. Her mouth grew dry. How well his hand fit in hers!

No. Yet she took a step closer.

Behind them, the eager swish of skirts, the rustle of steps. Someone was approaching the boathouse. Elizabeth released Henry's hand as though she'd been caught stealing.

"There you are, Signorina!" Signora Giulia called, puffing for air. Her overgenerous bosom spilled from her black gown; Elizabeth averted her eyes. "I've been looking all over for you!" More huffing. "Dinner is served, but it will be only you and the gentleman, yes?" She bowed to Henry. "Forgive me, Signore—I did not acknowledge you with the respect you deserve. Signore Frankenstein wrote that the Signorina was to marry his son, but I did not expect your arrival too."

"Monsieur Clerval isn't my intended," Elizabeth admitted, her face hot. "He is like family to the Frankensteins."

* * *

By the time the second glass of wine was poured at dinner, Elizabeth forgot her embarrassment before Signora Giulia. She raised her goblet to Henry.

"To family," she said, "and the love that binds."

Love? Where had that come from? A flush crept along her neck.

"To family," Henry repeated, downing the remainder of the wine in a considered gulp. He set down the glass. How delicate the crystal stem appeared against his hands, gnawed nails or no. He ran his forefinger around the rim. "So, what shall you do next with your villa?"

Elizabeth let her wineglass linger against her lips. *Your villa*. She still wasn't accustomed.

"There's not much I need to do. From the looks of it, Signora Giulia and her staff are quite capable. I only wish I'd convinced Uncle Alphonse to accompany us."

"He'll be safe. Your uncle is too good a man to be threatened," Henry assured. Yet Elizabeth sensed there was something bothering Henry, something he'd yet to speak of. *"A reason I will tell you by-the-by,"* he'd said in the carriage. She'd forgotten in the excitement of their arrival.

She shouldn't press him. Not yet. He'd already sacrificed so much to accompany her.

"I hope you're right," she replied. "It's good Ernest remained with him."

"And what of you?"

"Well, I suppose I'll stay here with William until my uncle writes for our return."

"That's not what I meant. Will you live here?"

With Victor after you marry him. Though Henry didn't say it, the implication was impossible to ignore.

She felt another rush of heat on her neck. "I don't know . . . Perhaps a summer house. I can't imagine leaving my uncle alone in Geneva."

"Yet a family needs a home of their own. Children need room."

Perhaps it was the wine, but now she couldn't sense those children with Victor she'd envisioned earlier. This troubled her. Still, she forced herself to answer Henry.

"It's not practical. Lake Como is so far from Geneva."

"True. But this house . . ." Henry swept his arms toward the frescoes, the candelabra, the sea beyond. "How can you abandon all this beauty?"

Elizabeth's fingertips relaxed on the stem of her wineglass. Beauty was a far easier conversation subject. She drained the remainder of her wine. "I have something I must confess."

Henry raised an eyebrow. "Consider me your confessor then."

She giggled, unable to suppress the sound as it rose up her throat. "You would say such a thing. About beauty that is." Another giggle.

Henry refilled his wineglass. "Beauty is no laughing matter."

"I know. This is where you differ from our Victor." Elizabeth spoke quickly without thinking. "You know how Victor talks about the beauty of science? Of logic?"

Henry nodded seriously. "Yes, but I don't follow how that relates to this beautiful villa."

"It's this. He'd never understand this house. The nature surrounding it. The beauty."

"That's not true," Henry said, unusually passionate. "He sees beauty. I've heard him enthuse over flowers, sunsets, nature."

"But he's not seeing the true beauty of it, as you and I would."

True beauty? You and I? She was being too familiar. Still, she plunged on, attempting to make order of her thoughts.

"He's always analyzing his experiences according to the principles of science. For example, tonight's sunset. Wasn't it glorious? Victor would say that it's nothing more than light plus the movement of the heavens and the ability of our brains to perceive what our eyes have witnessed. Not beauty. Do you understand the difference, Henry?"

"Yes. But—"

"It makes me happy that you're here with me, witnessing the beauty of this place. Now I'll never forget my first visit here. I won't recall it as something created by science. I'll recall it as a miracle. A thing of beauty."

Whether it was the wine or the setting, Elizabeth continued vocalizing ideas that made her feel vulnerable: how beauty made her feel, the inspiration that led to her interest in art; the beauty she yearned to remember. As she spoke, she found herself staring at Henry. He really was handsome. Different from Victor, though her betrothed was striking too, with his dark curls and intense eyes. Henry was like a poem. Victor was a storm.

"There's more," she tested. "To beauty, that is." An uneasy giggle. "It's a secret I haven't told anyone. I have this unyielding curiosity to uncover what lies beneath the surface of beauty . . ."

"Such as?"

She drew a deep breath. "I've been drawing animals. Birds. Insects. No one's seen them. I mean, I don't show anyone. I've a secret sketchbook."

Henry leaned in. "For anatomical subjects?"

"Yes. But not like the ones in Victor's books," she answered quickly, the wine tripping her tongue. "I only draw them when I find these subjects . . . unmoving." A breath. "Without life."

"Deceased?"

She flushed. "Well, I also draw myself. Studies in the mirror. The parts I can see, that is." She wouldn't confess these parts were unclothed. "I began the sketchbook after my aunt's passing."

Henry's eyebrows raised. How vulnerable she felt!

"I've shocked you," she said.

After a long moment, he replied. "You're not as people believe, are you, Elizabeth Lavenza? You hide your sorrow behind your smile. You seek comfort by examining the shadows."

"I don't know about that." She'd never thought of her sketchbook that way. But maybe . . .

"It's because of Caroline," she said all of a sudden. "Because of some-thing I did—oh it's so awful! I can't say it."

Henry leaned in. "Whatever it is, it can't be that bad."

"I can't. You'll think less of me."

"That's impossible," Henry said. "I *esteem* you, Elizabeth. Very high-ly." A gulp of wine before he continued. "As for your secret sketches, I'm sure they're not as peculiar as you believe. Artists have drawn such studies for centuries."

Somehow his reassurance loosened her chest. She forgot about Caroline, her guilt. Even her anger.

"Now that I'm here," she said, "I think I know why I became so obsessed with these drawings. Somehow seeing where my parents once lived . . . well, perhaps I can put these strange obsessions behind me. Do you understand, Henry?"

"I do understand. I'm glad. You should be thinking of life, not death."

"And beauty," she added, grasping his hand anew.

"Yes, and beauty." Henry's face clouded. "Elizabeth, I have a secret I must tell you myself."

"I'm glad I'm not the only one!" A bright smile as she reached for more wine. "Was this what you tried to tell me in the carriage? The reason you accompanied us? I've been waiting for you to tell me."

He released her hand to drain the remainder of his wine. Once he set down his glass, Elizabeth detected a tremor in his grasp. Perhaps her confession had shocked him after all.

"It's nothing really. Only that it's been a long day." He abruptly rose from the dining table. "I will see you in the morning."

* * *

When Elizabeth returned to her room (her room! how amazing this remained!), she discovered Sophie had set out her nightrail, her hairbrush, and a bowl of water scented with rosemary and lavender to wash herself. The fire had been stirred, emitting a steady warmth to cut the cool mountain night. The golden-haired hound who'd greeted Elizabeth upon her arrival lay across the bed. He offered a slow wag of his tail before returning to sleep.

However, instead of going to bed, all Elizabeth wanted was to make art. Her conversation with Henry had spurred this desire, though how peculiarly he'd behaved when he'd bid her goodnight. But she'd been peculiar too—it had felt so intimate to dine alone with him. She confided too much, but he wasn't shocked. She felt freed. Instead of death, she'd paint life. Her new life.

I'm drunk, she realized with a start. *That's why I confessed so much.*

A knock on the door.

"Who's there?"

Her door creaked open. A small girl. Ella, the dark-haired one. She appeared the same age Justine had been when she arrived at the Frankensteins. Despite the late hour, the girl's deep brown eyes were wide and awake. Anxious to please. How sweet she was!

"Signorina, I heard your steps," she said in Italian. "I thought I should see if you needed anything else."

Elizabeth fingered the locket of Caroline dangling from her neck. "Perhaps one thing . . ."

"I will get it, whatever it is."

Elizabeth told her.

In lieu of a sketch pad and watercolors, Ella located paper and ink with a quill in the library downstairs. "Will this do, Signorina?"

"Yes." Though paper and ink weren't watercolors, they'd fulfill Elizabeth's needs.

Elizabeth set to work, though her head ached slightly from all the wine. Instead of drawing from observation as she usually did, she'd draw from imagination.

She began by sketching a man's face in the center of the page. Victor's face, as he was before Caroline's death, when they were young and unscathed by loss. Her lips spread into an unconscious smile as she drew the dark beauty of his eyes, their flash when he was laughing or arguing. *I do love him. More than anyone else.* She recalled Victor in the rain. Victor and the tree blasted by lightning. Victor kissing her goodbye after she inscribed that green journal . . .

Don't think of that journal. Let it go.

Her pen lines on the page appeared warm and soft beneath the candlelight. Glowing. But then something took over Elizabeth's hand. Something she couldn't describe.

As she drew, Victor's face transformed into something different. Something base. His hair turned black and luxuriant against his forehead, akin to the wild mane of a beast. An aspect of cruelty in his brow, scarred with age or something else. Something unnatural. His eyes gleamed with madness. His lips black and thin. Vengeful. Demonic.

Elizabeth dropped the quill, splattering ink.

That's not Victor I've drawn.

A peculiar terror tripped along her spine, one she couldn't quantify. Yet as disturbing as the sketch was, she couldn't look away from it. She told herself the sketch didn't signify anything. By the drawing of it, she'd exorcised something from within herself. Something monstrous. Her guilt over Caroline. That sense of being cursed she'd tried so hard to ignore.

She'd burn the sketch in the morning. Whatever was inside her that had led to the sketch . . . well, she wouldn't think of that. *"You seek comfort by examining the shadows."* Henry was right.

She reached for the vial of laudanum she kept by her bedside since Caroline's death. Peace in an elixir, she called it.

Five drops later, she fell into a dreamless slumber as the clock downstairs struck midnight. Her last conscious thought was of Henry. There *had* been a secret he wanted to tell her.

I'll ask him again in the morning, she decided. *He'll tell me then.*

CHAPTER IV.

"Clerval occupied himself, so to speak, with the moral relations of things. The busy stage of life, the virtues of heroes, and the actions of men, were his theme; and his hope and his dream was to become one among those whose names are recorded in story."

* * *

ELIZABETH DIDN'T ASK Henry about his secret in the morning. Nor was his secret mentioned again until the fourth week of their self-imposed exile at the Villa Lavenza. The subject was surprisingly easy to avoid, for their days unfolded so harmoniously: conversation, walks, and books. She'd taken to sketching the landscape around the villa, which was more exquisite than any she'd ever seen.

By the time she learned of Henry's secret, it was nearly November. By coincidence, this was also the morning that the first news arrived from Geneva since their departure.

"The mail packet!" Signora Giulia announced at breakfast. Elizabeth sat across the table from Henry, still in her wrapper as she brushed William's hair, which was long as a cherub's. She'd soon have to trim his gold curls, a bittersweet consideration; he'd appear older without them.

Signora Giulia handed Henry one letter, Elizabeth two. Elizabeth set down the hairbrush. The first letter was from her uncle:

It pains me to admit my worst fears have come to pass, Elizabeth: we've had to summon troops to protect Geneva. Though the French promised to leave Geneva untouched, the view from my window reveals encampments across the lake—invasion is but a matter of time. As for Ernest, I've rarely seen him in recent days. If I am to judge by the pamphlets in his possession, it seems inevitable that Geneva will bend to France in the new year.

Elizabeth folded the letter away, trying her best to remain calm to avoid upsetting William. "Well," she said at last, "I believe we'll remain here through the winter."

Henry looked up from his own letter. His mouth shifted as though to speak before Sophie interrupted.

"What's the other letter, Mademoiselle? Is it Victor?"

"It's from Ernest."

Dear Elizabeth,

I know this will upset you, but you should know the truth. I've begged my father to let me join the military, but he refuses. He still considers me an invalid though the doctors say my lungs are all but healed. However, there's another reason for my need to leave home, which goes beyond anything I shall confide here . . .

"He's involved with the revolution," Elizabeth fretted. "Just as my uncle suspected."

Sophie agreed. "I'm not surprised. I've heard gossip that he goes to coffeehouses to play cards with soldiers."

"I didn't know that." Elizabeth prayed he wasn't gambling. "I'll insist he remain at home. This is not the time to leave my uncle. Not now." She determined to write Ernest as soon as she could, though there was something more bothering her.

Victor. Why was he still so silent?

She'd hoped Alphonse's letter would contain news of him. At this thought a prickle rose along her spine, a surge. She glanced up; Henry's gaze awaited hers. Henry who knew Victor as well as she did. Better even.

His brow was crinkled. Something was troubling him. Something he'd yet to admit; perhaps that secret he'd yet to confide. Then his brow smoothed, and he appeared as he ever was. Calm. Thoughtful.

"Are you well?" he asked.

"The letters are upsetting," was all she said. "I'll answer my uncle immediately."

She tucked both letters away. William pulled at her hand, his grin revealing his milk teeth. "Garden, Lisbeth!" Every morning they went for a constitutional, weather permitting. She excused herself, tightening her shawl over her wrapper. She'd dress upon her return. Anyway, there was no one to see her in her nightclothes. No one who'd care.

Outside in the garden, the weather was peculiar. Though the sun was a bright disk overhead, a bank of dark clouds rolled their way from across the lake. The air was also colder than expected. She needed more than a shawl. "A short walk," she told William. "I must answer your papa." As they strolled past the duck pond toward the orchard, the crisp air chafed her cheeks and stung her eyes.

Just as William ran off to chase a duck, Henry appeared from beneath the apple trees. He offered his handkerchief. "You're weeping."

"It's the cold air." She swiped at her eyes before handing his handkerchief back. "Though those letters—"

To her embarrassment, she found herself sobbing in his arms. Victor. Ernest. The revolution in Geneva. They all seemed one, evidence of her uncertainty and vulnerability.

Henry's coat smelled of coffee and his verdant green scent. She drew another breath to commit it to memory, as though this could banish sorrow. She imagined him lying in his bed an hour earlier, his light brown hair rumpled against his pillow. His hazel eyes opening lazily as he surfaced from his dreams, pupils constricting as they met the first light of day . . .

She pulled away, heart thudding. "You're very patient with me. We should go inside. William?" Where had he gone? She could hear his squeal as he trampled leaves. "Come with me!"

The clouds were now overhead—how swiftly they moved! "Look, Lisbeth!" William ran up, holding a rotting apple invaded by worms. Once she forced him to throw it away, she blew her nose and turned toward the house, wrapping her arms around her chest for warmth. She avoided Henry's gaze.

She chattered as they walked, following William, who ran ahead.

"It's chilly this morning, isn't it? You look cold, Henry. I should ask Signora Giulia to search the attic for warmer clothes. Do you think it's possible? I imagine they're moth-eaten."

Henry blurted, "Beata, I'll be leaving tomorrow morning."

"Tomorrow?" She halted to avoid tripping on a tree root.

He nodded reluctantly, she thought. "I'll be traveling to Ingolstadt to visit Victor. It was planned all along."

She gazed up at him, shocked by how upset she felt. "I don't understand."

"I should have told you earlier, but I could never find the right moment. My father finally agreed to allow me a year of study—it was our bargain in exchange for my becoming his business partner. When he discovered I intended to escort you here, he assumed I wouldn't return to Geneva and made the offer. And then your uncle asked me to check on Victor, and it all seemed of a piece." An unconvincing smile. "I'll be studying languages in Ingolstadt for a year. Persian, Arabic, perhaps Sanskrit."

This felt like a blow, one she hadn't anticipated. Not after the arrival of those letters. How to respond? She lifted her chin, staring beyond the orchard, toward the mountains.

A crisp breeze. A flurry of starlings.

"I do wish you'd told me," she answered in a careful tone. "I could have assured you it was unnecessary. You could have gone directly to Victor, though I appreciate your protection."

"I know. But I also knew accompanying you would bring your uncle peace of mind. Think of it as a consideration to him, if that makes my actions understandable. I meant to tell you about Ingolstadt sooner—I'd intended to leave once you were settled. Instead, I found myself wanting to remain here as long as I could to help."

Elizabeth met his eyes. "You did this for me?"

He flushed. "Well, you and the Frankensteins. But I've delayed for too long." He held up the other letter that had arrived in the mail packet that morning. "Victor."

"He wrote you." *Instead of me.*

"No. His landlady at the university—I'd sent a letter to let her know of my arrival since Victor never answers. She writes he's scarcely left his rooms all summer. She thinks he may be ill."

"So you're leaving me to rescue Victor, like you left your father to rescue me." A nervous giggle; she'd yet to give up this habit from her childhood when uneasy. "So chivalrous. So good."

Softly: "I don't feel very good right now."

"Well, you should." She linked her arm with his in their old way. "I'll miss you, but you already know that. Forgive me for being so ungracious—I had no idea."

"You could never be ungracious." He released her arm and backed away. "I leave in the morning. I know this is sudden. If I am to be honest, I find it painful to leave situations where I have found myself happy." A bow. "I should pack."

It was only after Henry abandoned her in the garden that Elizabeth realized she hadn't expressed any concern over Victor and his potential illness.

What is wrong with me?

* * *

Henry didn't appear at lunch. Nor was he present when Elizabeth came downstairs for dinner. In the meantime, she'd unearthed a cloak for him in the attic. She still couldn't believe she'd barely shown any emotion over the news from Victor's landlady. *Victor can't be ill,* she told herself again. *He's too vigorous of constitution. It must be something else. But what?*

As Elizabeth mulled this over dinner, she stared at her raised hand, silhouetted by candlelight. The skin between her fingers appeared translucent. Blurred, like she felt that night. Her courses had arrived for the first time in months; they were irregular from stress. To ease her cramps, she'd taken a tiny amount of laudanum—enough to dull discomfort, not enough to cause slumber—which emptied the vial. William, bored by the company of adults, had gone to bed early. Sophie had disappeared as well, no doubt eager for a night to herself.

Alone. That's all I am.

Elizabeth looked down at her plate. Risotto and grilled perch. It appeared unappealing though Signora Giulia did what she could to please Elizabeth's palate. No matter.

She stared up at the clock: ten past eight.

He's avoiding me because I'm a burden.

Quarter past eight.

The double doors snapped open and Henry entered in a rush. Elizabeth craned her head over her shoulder, her heart rising in pitch.

"Forgive me," Henry said, approaching the table. "I'm late—I lost track of time."

"Not so late. I was just starting."

"Ah, I'm glad." Henry pulled out a chair, the one furthest from her, and opened the tureen nearest him before turning to the platter of fish. He filled his plate. "No Signora Giulia serving us tonight?"

Elizabeth shrugged. She'd asked Signora Giulia to leave once she brought in the meal. "You're ready for the morning?"

Henry nodded. "Martin will drive me to Lenno, where there's a conveyance leaving for Milan at dawn." He drew a forkful of risotto into his mouth. Once he swallowed, he added, "I doubt I'll sleep much tonight. But I rarely do before travel. I've scant experience with it, to be honest."

"You must write me news of Victor as soon as you arrive. I'm sure he's very busy. Or, I should say, I *hope* he's very busy."

Another fork of food disappeared into Henry's mouth. "Let's trust that's all."

"I'm most grateful. I shall miss your company."

"I . . . I shall miss you too." A sip of wine. "I'm pleased to have been of service. I owe much to the Frankensteins, your aunt especially."

"I know." Elizabeth felt oddly disappointed by his words.

A cool draft rushed through the room, setting the fire to blazing. Elizabeth rose and banked it before returning to her seat. "What a night! On such a night, I swear I can sense my aunt's presence." A giggle, but this one was forced. "I wonder what she'd make of Ernest and Victor."

"I'm sure she'd soothe everyone. That was her way." Henry shifted to the chair next to hers. "You're still sad, aren't you?"

"A little," she admitted, no longer giggling. "I suppose it's Victor. You leaving. Ernest. My uncle. Those letters today. I think there's something else going on with Ernest. Not gambling. Not revolution."

"What could it be? A woman?"

"I've no idea." With the conversation on safer ground, Elizabeth didn't contain her words. "Ernest has been so volatile lately. He's not dissimilar to Victor."

"Because he's passionate of nature?"

Elizabeth nodded, her appetite renewed. She took a taste of the risotto before replying. "I suppose." She tapped the back of Henry's hand lightly after taking a sip of wine. The wine tasted full and sharp, like autumn itself. "In the past he's spoken of the foreign service. Now he wants to be a soldier. A revolutionary really." Another sip. "We should think of another vocation for him. Perhaps he should be a farmer—that's better than a soldier! He'd work the soil to nourish others. It would be good for his health."

"A farmer?" Henry laughed. "No one can truly decide someone's future, though some try."

Elizabeth raised a brow. "Such as your father?"

Henry fumbled with his words. "I hope that my year away at university will shift my father's opinion of what my future might be."

"Ah, then you didn't go into your bargain with him with an open heart?"

"I tried my best." He shook his head. "Can you imagine me a merchant? I've no head for math or accounting."

"No. But I can imagine you doing a fine job if you put your mind to it."

He let out a mock sigh. "Now I understand how Ernest must feel about your opinions. You're not as soft as you appear."

A log shifted in the fire, sending out sparks.

"Very well," she said. "Let us vow not to offer our opinions to Ernest. We shall allow him to find his path in the world, just as you wish to find yours."

"A vow," he agreed. He dropped to his knees on the floor before her.

"Henry, what are you doing? Get up!"

"If one is to vow, one must take it seriously." He gazed up at Elizabeth; she sensed yearning in his hazel eyes. "Elizabeth Lavenza, I hereby vow not to interfere with your cousin's life. Will you do the same?"

"Get up, Henry! What if someone was to walk in on us?"

"Not until you vow too."

"Very well." Elizabeth dropped to her knees across from her friend. Her palm raised to meet his.

"I vow," she said. "Now off the floor! It's cold there."

But he didn't move. Nor did she.

The moment stretched before them, long and elastic. Their fingertips brushed. Henry's lips parted. What would he say? Elizabeth wanted —no, *needed*—to know.

The doors flew open. Donna Giulia.

She cried, "Signorina Elizabeth! Are you well? My cooking hasn't made you ill?"

Henry stumbled to his feet. "No, not at all—we were playing a game. One from our childhood." He offered Signora Giulia a bow. "I depart in the morning. How grateful I am for your kindness!"

"Ah, you were bidding each other farewell. I apologize for the interruption. I'll return to clear the table."

Once Signora Giulia had bustled from the room, the clock chimed the hour. Both found their way back to their chairs. They snuck glances at each other beneath veiled eyes; by then the candles had burned to nubs and the fire in the dining room smoldered into ash. She wondered whether Henry was courting someone in Geneva. If so, he never spoke of such.

I am a fool. We are no longer children as we once were. Then she remembered.

"I have a cloak for you, to keep you warm during your travels," she said. "It's in the foyer."

"I appreciate that."

"Before you leave, I'll write a letter for you to give Victor."

"I'll make certain he reads it," Henry promised, rising from his chair. His hands lingered on the wood top of the chair; again, she noticed his gnawed nails. "I'll write when I arrive in Ingolstadt."

"I'd like that. I'll give you Victor's letter in the morning."

"I leave so early—I hate to disturb your rest. Is there some place you can set it for me?"

"I'll leave it on the dining table."

"A wise plan."

"Then this is farewell, Henry?"

"For now, Beata."

She extended her hand. This time the moments didn't stretch before her. Nor did their eyes or fingertips meet. Instead, Henry offered a quick bow before he fled.

CHAPTER V.

"Clerval continued talking for some time about our mutual friends and his own good fortune in being permitted to come to Ingolstadt."

* * *

UPSTAIRS IN HER ROOM, Elizabeth was unable to sleep. *The letter for Victor,* she remembered. *I'll write it.* How could she have forgotten?

She opened the drawer where she'd set her ink and quill. The drawer also held the sketch of the dark-haired demon she'd created the night of her arrival—she'd found the portrait too compelling to burn. She hid it in the bottom drawer and began to write.

Her words wouldn't come, no matter how she tried.

Dear Victor . . .

Dearest Cousin . . .

Beloved Friend . . .

"Ernest," she decided. *I shall write of him. Like Henry and I discussed. Vow or no, a farmer is a good idea.* But she drew no satisfaction from the laying down of sentences as she once might have. All she recalled was Henry's promise to take the letter. That he'd be leaving in the morning.

She made her words lighter than she felt. She made her words calmer than she felt. Once she blotted and sealed Victor's letter, she opened the door—and there Henry stood, dressed as she'd last seen him.

"You're still awake," she whispered.

"I couldn't sleep. I tried my best. I thought to go downstairs. Get air."

"I see. I meant to bring you . . . Victor . . ."

Her words trailed off, for there she was standing in the corridor clutching a letter. Nothing more need be said.

"I didn't intend to startle you," Henry said. "I cannot abide the idea of leaving you here alone."

"But I'm not alone. Not really." Yet how alone she felt.

"I'm so selfish. Our Victor needs me, but all my thoughts are of you, Beata. You're safe. You're protected."

"Selfish? You're the least selfish person I know."

He took a step closer. He leaned over to finger the gold locket she always wore, the one bearing the small watercolor of Caroline. "I never noticed the portrait of your aunt before—it's so tiny! You painted this?"

She nodded. "I should take it off. It's not meant to be slept in."

"Then you haven't gone to bed yet. I didn't wake you."

"No." She held up the sealed letter.

"Ah, give me it then."

Don't leave, she thought. *Not yet.*

Somehow she took his hand and pulled him into her room; by then the last candle on her desk had guttered out. He didn't resist when she led him onto her bed beside her. They didn't touch save for their hips side-by-side. She closed the yellow bed curtains about them.

"I know I'm being foolish," she said. "Sometimes at night—"

"You feel so alone," he finished, shifting on his side to meet her gaze in the dark. He reached beyond the curtains to set Victor's letter on the nightstand.

"Victor and I, well, we used to sleep like this. As children. Well, we did even before he left for Ingolstadt. Not every night. Sometimes. It was a comfort." She felt vulnerable admitting as much—someone of a less exalted mind would assume the worst. But Henry was pure of heart. Fine of spirit. Of another age. A kinder, more chivalrous age.

"And you want to be comforted?"

She nodded in the shadows. *Comfort.* That's what she wanted from Henry. Nothing more.

"How strange to be here as mistress of this house! Sometimes I try to imagine my father as he might have been. The cloak I found for you—"

"Which was very thoughtful—"

"I doubt it's his—it's too new. Still, I like to imagine him wearing it, how he might have appeared in it."

"What of your mother, Beata?" How warm Henry's voice was in the dark. Soft. Different from Victor's, which was lighter of pitch yet sharper. "Was there anything more in the letter your aunt left you?"

Elizabeth shook her head. "I know nothing except my mother died soon after my birth. I'd hoped Signora Giulia could tell me more—all she said was my mother was kind. Quiet. I know my mother was German. I must look like her, for I have blonde hair. I assume she was also blonde, unless my father was too."

Why was she speaking of her father and her mother while lying in bed beside Henry Clerval, Victor's dearest friend? Yet she couldn't bear to ask him to leave.

"I should go," he said as though reading her thoughts. "Let you sleep in peace."

"No, I like you being here. Who knows when we'll next meet?" Her voice took on a distant tone. "I know it sounds peculiar, but it helps to know you've been here in my family home. That you know of my past."

"I must admit I've wondered about your childhood before the Frankensteins took you in. Your aunt never spoke of it."

"I don't remember much from then."

Somehow this subject made her more disquieted than speaking of her parents—it was difficult to conceive of her life before the Frankensteins. Sometimes in the apple orchard she recollected scraps of memories she'd tucked away like an out-of-fashion gown. The peasant woman who'd taken her in after the death of her parents, what was her name? Marina? Maria? She recalled other children, a man. If she tried hard she could remember the sun streaming through green leaves spotted with red, the faint scent of rotting leaves. The melodic chatter of Italian. Elizabetta, they called her then. Beata, like Henry.

"Do you remember meeting your aunt and uncle for the first time?"

"Not really. But now that I know about my father, I've been trying to imagine what happened after his arrest. Him kissing me goodbye, believing he'd return soon . . ." She let out a long breath. "It's a more comforting story than my father abandoning me, aware he'd die in prison."

"I'm sure your father would never abandon you on purpose. I can't imagine anyone abandoning you."

Like Victor.

An owl hooted outside from the garden.

She replied, "I wish I had more memories from then, something to hold onto."

"I don't recall my mother either," Henry admitted. "My father never recovered from the loss—she passed when I was three. But it helps to remember what I can from his description. It's like bringing her to life, even if it's only for a moment. I close my eyes and list everything he's told me: the timbre of her voice. The shade of her hair. How much she loved us."

"I should try the same, even if I'm imagining it." She'd done this for Caroline after her death, as though she could bring her back to life. Her eyes stung. *That journal. The guilt.* She'd only pushed them away temporarily while at the villa.

Henry must have sensed her thoughts, for he asked, "What troubles you so, Beata?"

She couldn't answer him. Not yet. In that moment, she felt as though she was caught between past and future. In the past was all of her remorse and regret; in the future was her life with Victor, who would never learn that her actions led to the death of his beloved mother. But in the present . . . here she was with Henry. Compassionate Henry. Kind Henry. Henry who was Victor's closest friend, and as close to the Frankensteins as family.

It's unfair to burden him with my guilt, she thought. *And yet . . .*

Before she could reconsider, she began:

"There was a green Florentine paper journal I gave Victor—you probably recall my giving it to him during that last picnic in Plainpalais. I had the journal custom made for Victor because I wanted him to have something special from me to take with him. Because I wanted him to ask me to marry him before he left for Ingolstadt—I thought he'd be moved by my gift."

She felt Henry pull away in her bed. "Did he propose then?"

"Not for several months . . . because I took ill that day. Scarlet fever, as you know."

A long moment of silence. Again Elizabeth sensed the press of the future, the weight of the past.

"But that's not all, Henry," she continued in a quiet, firm voice. "It was because of that journal—" a deep breath "—my aunt died. My fault, if you will—"

"Beata, that's far-fetched. Many had scarlet fever that summer, not just you."

"It's not. Listen."

It all spilled out. The story of the shopkeeper with the fever, how Elizabeth had ignored her warning. That Elizabeth felt unwell the morning of the picnic, but forced herself to go to woo Victor's favor—she didn't want him to leave for Ingolstadt without a promise of marriage. She felt too vulnerable despite Caroline's devotion and Alphonse's protection. After all, she was naught but a penniless orphan.

"And so she died . . . and I can't seem to forgive myself, Henry. Oh, I've tried! How I've tried! But I can't."

"It was fate," Henry said when she finally silenced.

Elizabeth choked out, "I don't believe that."

"But I do. I believe our lives are already marked before our birth—we've no choice but to abide and accept. The consolation of philosophy. It's helped me many a time with my own disappointments."

"Such as your father and his business."

"Along with other losses." A long pause. When Henry spoke again, his voice was ardent. "Elizabeth Lavenza, you are the best woman I know. You're an angel."

Elizabeth's cheeks felt wet. "I don't feel such."

"You are." His hand lightly caressed her arm. "I won't tell anyone what you told me. Nor will I ever mention it to you. Try to forget." A soft kiss on her cheek. "We should get some rest."

"I'll try." Elizabeth's fingers brushed the portrait of Caroline around her neck. *I should take it off.* But she couldn't bear to leave Henry's side.

She settled for turning the portrait against her heart. She wiggled into his arms.

"Sleep, Beata." His voice was tender.

"Sleep, Henry," she answered in turn.

Instead of slumber, she found her head resting against his broad chest, his hand brushing her hair from her brow. His breath on her cheek as he shifted closer. Toward her mouth.

His lips were so soft against hers, barely touching. A press of warmth. Of air. *I'm dreaming this. Nothing more.* Yet she didn't stop herself from reaching for him after he pulled away with a muffled apology. "No, it's fine," she whispered. And then her mouth slanted against his with a hunger she'd never felt before. He tasted of wine from dinner. Warm. Like the present, rather than the past or future.

This isn't happening, she told herself. *As long as we don't speak it's not real.*

Somehow she knew what to do in this ancient dance of men and women. She looped her arms about his neck to draw him closer, feeling no shame, no modesty. He lifted the hem of her nightgown, his palm warm against her bared knee. He let his hand rest there, as though asking permission. Whatever was going to happen between them felt a preordained force, a thread tying them as one, though she couldn't explain what created it. Was it yearning? Or a curiosity similar to the one that led her to sketch her body all those times? Whatever it was, this was a force beyond herself. A force she couldn't contain, though it didn't panic her. Not yet. Instead, a peculiar serenity rose, one she'd never experienced. One she refused to quantify. Not yet.

"I love you," he whispered more softly than she imagined possible. "I always have."

She felt a smile curl along her lips, a surge of joy, but she remained silent. *As long as I don't answer him, I didn't hear this.* But there were other ways she could respond, using hands and lips and limbs, though their caresses remained innocent.

Suddenly her womb ached anew. Her courses. Somehow this broke that force connecting them.

She pushed him away gently. "This didn't happen. A dream. Nothing more."

"Only a dream," he agreed, his voice breaking. He slid his hand from her thigh. "Good night, Beata."

"Goodnight, Henry."

They settled on their backs beside each other, their bodies rigid. Yet it felt too unnatural not to touch. Before she could think otherwise, they'd laced their hands across their stomachs.

Like children, Elizabeth told herself. *Nothing more.*

CHAPTER VI.

"The peasant woman, perceiving that my mother fixed eyes of wonder and admiration on this lovely girl, eagerly communicated her history. She was not her child, but the daughter of a Milanese nobleman . . . His property was confiscated, his child became an orphan and a beggar."

* * *

WHEN ELIZABETH AWOKE in the morning, Henry was no longer next to her in bed. Though she knew she shouldn't have been surprised, she was. Some part of her had hoped he'd remain there, that they'd stay as they were, caught between past and future. Whatever had happened between them was a moment's desire for comfort. As for his confession of love, she'd imagined it. Nothing more.

Then she remembered.

The journal. She'd told Henry. Did she feel lighter? Less cursed? She wasn't sure. Not yet.

She reached for Caroline's portrait locket, to reassure herself the black silk ribbon hadn't broken while she slept. *Still there.* She sat up and opened her bed curtains. The letter to Victor was no longer on her nightstand—Henry had taken it.

He's gone. It's as well.

"Monsieur Clerval has departed," she announced to everyone at breakfast. "He's traveling to Ingolstadt to visit my intended." For some reason not naming Victor made her encounter with Henry feel less of a disloyalty. But what had she and Henry done? They'd held hands while asleep. As for that kiss . . .

A dream. Nothing more.

She shivered, light-headed.

"Signorina, are you well?" Ella asked. "Is the room too cold? I can stoke the fire."

"No, I'm well, thank you." Elizabeth glanced out the window. "It's windy today, isn't it?"

"Rain later, I'd say," Sophie said, who never missed anything; Elizabeth's cheeks flamed beneath her scrutiny. No matter: William approached and begged to run outside.

"The apple orchard," he demanded. "I want to play in the leaves, Lisbeth."

"Later. I need to dress first." It was too chilly to go out with only a wrapper, as she'd discovered yesterday.

"No, *now!*"

William raced from the dining room before any of them could stop him. "Come back!" Elizabeth shouted, chasing the boy. "You can't go alone!"

She rushed into the foyer. No sign of him there. Nor in the ballroom, though the doors to the garden were ajar. She rushed outside, clutching her wrapper, chest tight. An odd panic rose, the sense she was losing control of everyone and everything she cared about: first Victor, then Henry. Ernest, and now William. Even Justine with her mother and Alphonse in Geneva because of the revolution.

In the garden, she caught ear of William's bright laughter. She whirled, stomach cramping, as she panted for breath. The apple orchard. The leaves. He'd gone there as threatened.

His bright blonde head glinted between the trees.

"William! Come back! *Now!*"

"Catch me, Lisbeth!"

He trilled with laughter before he ran off just as Martin the gardener appeared, clutching a basket of manure from the stench of it. This forced the boy to change course into Elizabeth's path, where she grabbed him. He squirmed against her chest like a puppy.

"Let me go!"

"No! Something could have happened—you can't run off alone."

"I'm safe, Lisbeth!"

"But I can't take that for granted. I couldn't see you!"

"I'm fine! Safe!"

She set him down, held his shoulders at arm's length. "What a fright you gave me!"

What a fright you gave me!

The words echoed in Elizabeth's mind. Why?

William whimpered, "Lisbeth? What's the matter?"

"I don't know," she admitted, heart racing.

What a fright you gave me! Where had she heard this before? Who'd said it?

She set the boy down. She stared up at the rain clouds approaching, the apple trees. The wind rustled their gold-hued leaves, most of which had already fallen along the earth. Swallows and finches darted from branch to branch. She inhaled the scent of damp rising from the earth...

And then Elizabeth returned to her past as though she'd stepped through an unlocked door.

Maria—that *had* been her name. The peasant woman who'd sheltered Elizabeth after her father left. She'd seemed more careworn than anyone Elizabeth had known, face creased like an unmade bed, bones poking from all her corners. She had four other half-clad children pulling at her skirts. Elizabeth was around William's age. Younger, actually. Her memories tumbled: Maria throwing away Elizabeth's shoes, forcing her to walk barefoot in the ice. *"We'll gain more sympathy."* Maria yanking her from a bank of flowers. *"What are you doing? You're supposed to be here, not there!"* Elizabeth's tiny hands splayed like starfish as she tried to clutch the colors of the twilight sky.

That was the first day Maria hit Elizabeth, but not the last.

Another memory beckoned, one where Elizabeth's dress was short, her bare feet caked in mud. An autumn day. There had been apples, but not from this orchard. Another one nearby. They were all harvesting fruit for coin; she recalled flies buzzing beside their necks, the stench of horse dung. Maria scolded her for laziness. Elizabeth ran off, much as William had.

"What a fright you gave me!" Maria cried, brushing dirt off Elizabeth's cheek. And then Maria slapped it. "Where did you go?"

"Nowhere," Elizabeth lied; for she'd chased a carriage approaching the road. A lady had emerged from it. A beautiful lady.

And then Maria slapped her a second time.

"Liar! Tell the truth."

"I saw the Madonna," Elizabeth admitted after Maria pressed. "She had long brown hair and a silk dress, a red ribbon on her bonnet."

Maria cocked her head. "The Virgin Mary came to you? And not even on a feast day! Where is she then? Did you ask her for a coin or two?"

"I forgot." Elizabeth cringed. She had good reason, for Maria slapped her a third time.

"What a liar! If only I'd let you starve!"

"Ow! I'm not lying! She's going to return tomorrow with her husband. She's going to take me with her to her palace, where she lives with her son, who's near my age."

"I can hardly wait," Maria snapped. "In the meantime, stop lying!"

"I didn't make this up!" And Elizabeth hadn't—Caroline returned the next day, wearing her finest dress and with her hair dressed and powdered. Compared to Maria, she appeared an angel with her panniers and powdered hair and gold necklaces and ribbons. She smelled of lilies. Beauty.

"My name is Frankenstein. My husband is a syndic from Geneva. I am prepared to adopt your ward," Caroline announced when Maria brought her to their disconsolate cottage. "My husband and I can give Elizabeth every advantage. Most importantly, I already love her."

"I love her too, Signora," Maria simpered with fake sincerity; Elizabeth cringed anew. "Though this child may not share my blood, I've acted as family to her. I've cared for her since she was a babe. She's a Lavenza, you know."

"A Lavenza?"

Maria nodded. "Noble blood. No doubt an heiress, though I haven't been able to find her family. But I will one day, and they will pay me for her care." A hard smile. "I can't let her go."

This was the first time Elizabeth had heard this. She didn't understand what it meant to be an heiress. But she did understand what it meant to have a family, and what it meant to be paid for labor.

Elizabeth wouldn't take the chance. She rushed to Caroline, threw her arms around her knees. She kissed her skirts, grabbed her hand. She'd never let her go.

* * *

Elizabeth returned from her memory with a start. How long had passed? There she stood beneath the denuded apple trees, her villa—her *villa!*—behind her. A villa she would have never possessed if not for Caroline, who'd rescued her. Caroline, who loved her like a mother. Caroline, who was dead after nursing her so she would live. There was William beside her, clutching Elizabeth's hand. There were mountains, a lake. The apple orchard surrounding them. The sky darker than it had been. It would rain soon.

William tugged at Elizabeth's wrist. "I'm sorry, Lisbeth! Believe me?"

"I do believe you," Elizabeth replied, shivering.

"I was bad! What's the matter?"

"It's nothing, William. A sad memory . . ." She squeezed his moist hand. *It was fate.* Wasn't that what Henry said? "Come, let's race to the door!"

And so they did, just as the wind picked up in earnest, though as Elizabeth ran she felt chased by her past. Well, she'd outrace it along with William, though she'd let the boy win at the end. The wind blew her hair against her face, tugged the hem of her wrapper against her ankles. She laughed—"What a morning!"—as she entered the villa with William, the hound loping by their side.

At first, all seemed well. Inside the villa, Sophie offered Elizabeth a shawl to warm herself and yelled at the dog's muddy paws. Life appeared to return to its natural rhythm—but only for a moment. For while she and William raced toward the house, something else entered Elizabeth's mind. Something she'd managed to ignore since she'd brought it into being on the night she arrived at the Villa Lavenza.

The portrait. The one she tried to draw of Victor. It was up in her room, inside her desk. She needed to see it. Now.

She left the table and climbed the stairs toward her room.

"Lisbeth, come back!" William's high-pitched voice trailed after her. "Sophie has tea!"

"I'll be a moment," she called back. "Save me some, please."

"It's my fault you're leaving! I ran away."

She couldn't answer him. Wouldn't answer him—she didn't trust herself to speak without betraying her disturbance.

Hands shaking, Elizabeth opened drawer after drawer, trying to recall where she'd set the sketch of Victor. She found it inside the bottom drawer, where she'd moved it. There it was, that face she'd drawn in ink. It appeared as she remembered: sinister and carnal. The hair dark and luxuriant. The lips thin and black and cruel. The eyes watery and light. Nothing like Victor . . . yet it was, wasn't it?

Suddenly she realized: she'd drawn Victor in this manner because she no longer wanted to marry him. And it wasn't only this—there was more. And at last, she had no choice but to acknowledge the truth she'd resisted until it festered like a blister.

God help me, I love Henry. And he loves me too.

Sketch in hand, Elizabeth sank onto the bed, sobbing until she gasped for air. She pressed her nose against her pillow, yearning for Henry's scent, that subtle tang of verbena and sun. She recalled Henry beside her in her bed. Henry lifting the hem of her nightgown, caressing her knee. The warmth of his breath against her flesh. His lips as they'd kissed. She'd felt no modesty, only desire. *"I love you. I always have . . ."*

She would have made love with him. Given herself to him. She would have betrayed Victor. Betrayed her vow to Caroline on her death bed. Betrayed her promise to the Frankensteins, who'd saved her from a life of abuse and poverty.

Disloyalty and opportunity, that's what I'm made of.

Ella pulled the curtains from her bed. "Tea's ready. Signorina, why are you crying?"

Sophie joined Ella. Their startled faces hung over Elizabeth like apples from a tree. "What's wrong?"

Ella flailed her arms. "I don't know, Sophie! I didn't do anything to her!"

Sophie said in her most soothing voice, "Tea will calm you, Mademoiselle. You're upsetting William. Come, take my hand! Now!"

As Elizabeth stared at Sophie's outstretched hand, she recalled Henry's with his bitten nails, the way he ran his finger around the rim of that wineglass that first night. His palm on her knee. That kiss.

He's gone.

And then somehow Elizabeth *did* take Sophie's hand, for Elizabeth had no desire to upset William, or anyone else for that matter. Sophie's words had somehow returned decorum to her.

"I'm sorry," Elizabeth muttered as Sophie and Ella led her downstairs to the kitchen. "I don't know what upset me." But she *did* know. She glanced out the windows toward the mountains, the lake, the gardens. The villa roofs with its perfectly symmetrical chimneys and windows. The autumnal landscape with the rapidly moving clouds.

Mine. All because of Caroline.

"It's the isolation here," Ella said with a shrug. "And now Monsieur Clerval is gone."

Elizabeth bit back a sob. "Yes, Monsieur Clerval is gone . . ."

And we must never be. If I'm to love him, it must be as a friend.

Where was Henry now? She tried to imagine him in the carriage to Ingolstadt. What would he find when he arrived there? Would Victor sense their intimacies? What if Victor really was unwell?

And then she knew: she had to go to Ingolstadt.

CHAPTER VII.

"I thought I saw Elizabeth, in the bloom of health, walking in the streets of Ingolstadt. Delighted and surprised, I embraced her; but as I imprinted the first kiss on her lips, they became livid with the hue of death; her features appeared to change, and I thought that I held the corpse of my dead mother in my arms."

* * *

ELIZABETH DEPARTED Lake Como as soon as transport could be arranged, bringing Sophie and William with her. In hopes of overtaking Henry, she even hired a carriage in Lenno to speed their way. Alas, their journey to Ingolstadt was affected by the stormiest weather she'd ever witnessed: thunderstorms, hail, and floods. But Elizabeth refused to be deterred. Though it was already night by the time they arrived in Ingolstadt, she resolved to go to Victor after settling Sophie and William at the coaching inn.

"Mademoiselle, shouldn't you wait until morning?" Sophie pressed, clutching a sleeping William in her lap. "It's still raining. You need rest. Food. It's dark out!"

"I must find Victor."

With luck, she'd arrive before Henry—he'd probably been delayed as much as she'd been by the weather. Oh, she'd be welcoming to him, profuse in her gratitude, but she'd make it clear Henry's help was not required, that she still loved Victor and that he was her responsibility, not Henry's. Henry might love her, but his love would have to be that of a brother, not a lover. She'd will herself to no longer desire him.

And so Elizabeth wrapped her still-damp cloak about her travel-fatigued body and rushed into the streets of Ingolstadt, where the night air hung as though clouds had descended over the city like a bell jar. She clutched a small map in one hand and Victor's address in her other, though there was scant light to examine either.

The streets were narrow, medieval, winding, not unlike those in the oldest part of Geneva. She passed the university walls, recognizing a pale steeple and clock tower. It began to chime eleven. She must be close. Victor's rooms were just outside the university walls. Wasn't that what her uncle had said?

By then the rain had slowed enough that Elizabeth could make out the hush of wind brushing against tree branches, the drip of water from eaves. The bang of a loose shutter. She hurried on.

Beneath her feet, cobblestones glittered with moisture. She avoided the occasional puddle. Her breath sounded heavy with fear, though she didn't feel such. It was more of a disquietude rising through her blood. A disturbance she needed to rectify.

How dark Ingolstadt was! How quiet! It seemed as though all the world was slumbering, including Victor. She'd never been out alone so late. Did this make her brave? Or a fool? Perhaps Sophie was right; she should have waited until morning. Yet her need to see him, to make amends, wouldn't allow her to turn back.

Several steps later, she sensed someone behind her.

A shuffling footfall. A low moan.

Though she was seized with the urge to run, Elizabeth glanced over her shoulder. Again, her breath sounded rough.

"Hello?" she called.

No answer but the hiss of wind. The weight of moisture.

She squinted. She made out in the fog what appeared to be the silhouette of a lurching form about eight feet tall standing beside a wall built of stone. Dark hair. Long arms. Whoever—or whatever—it was, the figure was still. Solitary. Thick of form, too massive to be human.

She pulled down her hood to see better; luckily the rain had slowed enough that the sky had cleared. *A tree.* She'd imagined someone. What she thought to be arms were limbs. Fingers, the gnarl of branches. Still, her flesh prickled beneath her stays, like a cold hand on her spine.

She stepped away, feet plunging into icy water. She'd been too distracted to avoid a puddle.

She looked down. In the puddle lay a small dun-hued rabbit, its glassy eyes unnaturally wide. How fragile it appeared, so precious; Elizabeth had the sense its heart had ceased mid-beat, as though it had been startled from life. Her emotions clotted with protectiveness as she thought of William, whom she'd left alone with Sophie at that inn.

Above her, the slap of shutters, a window opening.

"Elizabeth? Is that you?" a familiar male voice called.

She forgot about the rabbit, her morbid fancies, for all she saw was Victor. Her heart gave a lurch. Even in the dark on a rainy night, five years since she'd last seen him, she easily recognized him.

Victor leaned out the top window of a four-storied building, one that bore dormers and a roof steeply pitched in the German manner. "Come inside!" he hissed. "Hurry!"

She rushed toward the door, which swung open at her touch. She rushed up the winding wood staircase toward the attic, taking the steps two by two. An unpleasant odor seemed imbued in the building's very timbers, something sour and foul. *It must be the rain. It's probably been storming here for days.* The higher she climbed, the stronger the stench; she cupped her hands over her nose to avoid gagging.

"There you are!" Victor cried once she'd reached a long wood paneled gallery she assumed led to his rooms. "My dearest Elizabeth! I can't believe you're here! How happy I am!"

His face was illuminated by a solitary candle set on a small table in the gallery. His countenance reminded her of Dr. Galvani's from that winter soirée years ago.

Before Elizabeth could offer a word of greeting, Victor wrapped her in an embrace so tight that she struggled to inhale. *It's a sign of his affection, nothing more.* She took in Victor's features, marking how he'd changed. His hair was the same mass of dark curls, his eyes just as soulful, though he did look shockingly thin.

He's the same, she reassured herself. *We'll be as we were.*

"Closer, beloved," he murmured in a voice rough with desire. "It's been too long."

Elizabeth didn't resist when he tilted her chin up toward him.

He kissed her as he had the night before his departure for Ingolstadt. Mouth against mouth. Flesh against flesh. She recoiled. His tongue felt clammy against her lips.

He tasted cold. Foul, like he'd been ill.

She recalled how Henry had tasted of wine. Warmth. Love.

Traitor.

A blind panic wrapped around her throat. Her chest. She forced herself not to push Victor away. He must have sensed her disgust, for he clutched her at arms' length.

His eyes searched her face. "What have you done?"

Somehow he knows about Henry.

Her anxiety rose. "Done? I don't understand."

His hands tightened like claws about her shoulders. "Then where's Elizabeth? Did you force her to leave?"

"I'm here, Victor. It's me! I'm Elizabeth."

"Don't lie! You're not Elizabeth! You're my mother—well, *had* been my mother." He flicked at the folds of Elizabeth's cloak, brushing something away she couldn't see. "Go! Back to the grave! Now!"

"Victor—"

The gallery suddenly filled with light as a door opened. Someone behind Victor clutching an oil lamp. Elizabeth made out Henry. He set down the oil lamp beside the candle in a fluid motion—he'd arrived before her despite the weather. Her heart leapt at the sight of his dear face. Before anything could be said, Victor collapsed into Henry's arms, still muttering about graves and his mother.

Henry's eyes widened with an aspect of shock. "You should leave, Beata."

"I can't." Not yet.

Elizabeth grabbed the oil lamp and followed them into Victor's rooms, which turned out to be a solitary chamber; it bore an even stronger stench than the hall. Inside, she made out a long table covered in some sort of refuse, an array of what appeared to be scientific implements, piles of notebooks. She had scant chance to look before the oil lamp guttered. All that remained was the dim blue of moonlight from the skylight.

Once her eyes adjusted, Elizabeth watched Henry drag Victor to a long cot draped with blankets and pillows. He forced a glass of fluid into Victor's mouth, some of which dribbled down his unshaven chin.

"What's wrong with him? Henry, tell me!"

"Please go!" Henry said again, his voice pitched strangely high. "Victor wouldn't want you to see him this way."

"But I'm to be his wife!"

"All the more reason for you not to be here. Please!"

"What's happened?"

Victor roiled against the cot like a storm, the whites of his eyes flashing. *He's gone mad.* Henry wrestled with him, tying Victor to the cot with lashes of fabric. Victor struggled at first, but abruptly collapsed into what appeared to be a drugged sleep.

Henry let out a long breath and looked up from the cot. Elizabeth couldn't make out his expression. Was it sorrow? Desire? Fear?

"I didn't expect you to come here," he said after a long moment.

"Nor did I. I was worried about him."

"And for good reason," Henry finished. "I haven't time now to explain his illness. It's best you leave in case he becomes agitated again —sometimes the chloral isn't enough."

"I want to nurse him!"

"It's better you not. Go, Elizabeth!"

"Tell me what's going on, Henry. Please!"

"In the morning. I'll come to you, I promise. I assume you're at the coaching inn?"

"Yes."

All of a sudden Victor let out a yelp and began to thrash again.

Elizabeth fled. As she rushed through the streets of Ingolstadt, she again sensed someone—or some*thing*—following her.

* * *

Henry didn't go to Elizabeth the following morning. Instead, he wrote a letter as soon as the sun rose. He'd barely slept, thinking of her distress at Victor's condition.

Dear Elizabeth,

I cannot imagine the shock you must have felt after encountering

Victor last night. I apologize that I won't be coming to you this morning as promised, but once you read this letter you will understand why I'm loathe to leave him. I must reiterate my belief that it's best you do not see him. Yes, Victor is ill—far more ill than either of us imagined. But let me assure he will improve though it may take months—far too long for you to remain in Ingolstadt.

Perhaps it is best I start by describing Victor's situation exactly, so you may understand his circumstances.

When I arrived in Ingolstadt two days ago, I found Victor waiting outside the coaching inn despite the downpour. At first all seemed well. Once we took shelter, he gave me a warm embrace that soothed my fears. When he pressed as to the reason for my arrival, I did not confess of our concern for him. I only said in a teasing manner, "My father's affection for me has overcome his dislike of learning. At last he has permitted me to undertake a voyage to the land of knowledge." But Victor did not understand my jest until I explained I'd traveled to Ingolstadt to study with him. It was then I noticed his eyes were glazed with a feverish glint; he'd grown thin and pale.

I found myself unable to remain silent on his demeanor: "How very ill you appear. You look as if you've been awake for several nights."

At this statement, any appearance of normalcy dropped from Victor; he trembled like an aged man with palsy; his flesh grew even more blanched of color. He said at great length, "As you can see, I have been busy and haven't allowed myself sufficient rest. I sincerely hope that all these employments are now at an end."

I did not inquire as to those employments, for I was too disturbed to find him thus. I suggested we return to his abode; by then, the rain had slowed to a drizzle. He agreed, though he was hesitant.

When we arrived at his rooms he rushed upstairs, leaving me tarrying at his threshold. Some moments later he reappeared. He clapped his hands like a child. "Now you can enter! Ah, Clerval, dearest of friends, how happy I am!"

As we ascended the stairs to his chambers, the odor was such that I suspected they were set above a butcher shop. The stench lessened once Victor opened the windows in his rooms. He brought out a simple repast for us of bread, cheese, and coffee. I hoped the food would calm him. Alas, his agitation grew. He jumped over chairs, clapped his hands; his laughter became wilder, louder.

I begged, "Victor, what for God's sake is the matter?"

"Do not ask me!" He set his hands over my eyes. "He can tell. Oh, save me! Save me!"

I pushed his hands away, but as I did so, he struggled and fell in a fit. He did not recover his senses for hours. Fortunately his landlady was able to recommend a physician, who diagnosed him with a brain fever as a result of overwork, malnourishment, and insomnia. The physician stated this affliction was more common than one would wish among students of Victor's ambition.

It's unclear what precipitated his collapse. I investigated whether an event had distressed him, perhaps a professor he'd displeased, or a student bearing a grudge. Both of his professors, Monsieurs Waldman and Krempe, assured they held Victor in the greatest esteem: "I assure you he has outstripped us all. A youngster who, but a few years ago, believed in alchemy and Cornelius Agrippa as gospel, has now set himself at the head of the university!" As for his fellow students, though few have witnessed him in class of late, they bear only goodwill.

To facilitate his recovery, Victor is to rest and avoid any stimulation —another reason it is best you do not visit him. A physician will attend him regularly. When he stirs, I've been advised to feed him bone broth and milk bread. As alarming as all this may be, I've been assured he will recover to return to your side in time.

Though this is all I need to relate of Victor, I must address another troubling subject—something I bear all responsibility for. Indeed, it would be remiss of me to send you this letter without mention of our final night together in Lake Como.

Elizabeth, I won't write of what happened, for you know. If it offers any consolation, the fault was all mine. My behavior was predicated by something I've been loathe to confess lest it cause you pain. But now you know the truth: I love you—

Henry jerked his pen away. He reread the last paragraph, those three traitorous words.

I love you.

Overcome, he set down his pen. Anyway, he'd already told Elizabeth he loved her that night in Lake Como. She hadn't responded then. Why did he think she'd respond now? She was fated to be with Victor.

I love you, he read again.

It was clear she loved Victor, not him. That's why she came all the way to Ingolstadt, rushing to Victor in the middle of the night. Still, Henry's heart was stubborn. When he'd first seen her at Victor's door, he'd yearned to press his suit again like a desperate fool.

Disloyalty and opportunity. That's what I'm made of.

Henry glanced at the cot in the corner of the attic, where Victor slept, too drugged to recall Elizabeth's visit. How would Elizabeth react when she read this? Worse, what if Victor were to somehow happen upon his letter at a later date? Or someone else? It made little sense, but Henry sensed someone spying on him.

The night of his arrival, Henry had awakened to find the shadowy silhouette of the tallest man he'd ever witnessed standing at the foot of his bed. By the time he grabbed a fire poker for protection, the creature was gone; Henry told himself he'd imagined him. His foreboding only increased when he discovered two leather trunks in Victor's possession containing what appeared to be surgical instruments and anatomical samples. Bones, rotting flesh, and organs. He disposed of the body parts as respectfully as possible, and aired out the rooms until they were tolerable.

"You're a fool, Henry Clerval," he muttered.

He should rewrite the letter, destroy the first one. But before he began anew, he needed to mourn for a moment. He and Elizabeth would never be. Could never be.

Outside Victor's attic, the clock tower beyond the university walls clanged six of the morning. A cart rumbled by. A street vendor shouted. Victor stirred at the sounds, his lips parting like a child's.

Henry remembered the bone broth, the doctor's orders. He should hurry.

He began a new letter, copying what he'd written until he reached the paragraph where he'd penned those three disloyal words. He composed a new ending innocent of any betrayal:

Now that I have completed my account, I hope you understand why you must leave Ingolstadt immediately—it truly is for the best for Victor as well as yourself. Let me assure he bears no memory of your visit save as a dream; he ranted such to me. I believe it best to allow him to believe this—he'd be humiliated to learn you'd witnessed him in such a weakened state. However, if you or any of your family were to mail a simple correspondence, I will read it to him when he is less volatile. In the meantime, I promise to remain by his side.

Your most loyal servant—
HENRY CLERVAL.

CHAPTER VIII.

"Justine has returned to us; and I assure you I love her tenderly. She is very clever and gentle, and extremely pretty; as I mentioned before, her mien and her expressions continually remind me of my dear aunt."

* * *

ONCE ELIZABETH RECEIVED Henry's letter that morning, she departed Ingolstadt with Sophie and William though their cloaks still bore dust from their travels. However, instead of returning to Lake Como, she insisted they head home for Geneva.

Though Elizabeth had no idea what troubles they'd find in Geneva, she couldn't bear to return to the Villa Lavenza after learning of Victor's illness. Every corner offered evidence of her disloyalty to him and the Frankensteins. The dining room, where she and Henry had spent so many evenings conversing over meals. Her bedroom, where they'd lain together and he'd confessed his love. The desk, where she'd drawn that disturbing picture of Victor, which she later burned. Most of all, the apple orchard, where she'd recalled how Caroline had saved her from a life of abuse.

Their journey back to Geneva was hindered by interruptions, which did little to relieve Elizabeth's anxiety. Though the weather wasn't as extreme as when they'd traveled to Ingolstadt, snow had arrived early in the Alps, making several mountain passings insurmountable.

They ended up dallying extra weeks in small inns tucked in tiny villages. The first delay occurred in the town of Lugano, where she purchased a watercolor kit and brushes. Somehow the act of making art reoriented Elizabeth to who she'd been before Caroline's death; not the Elizabeth who sketched dead animals, body parts, and monsters, but the Elizabeth who loved beauty and the act of preserving it on paper. An Elizabeth less filled with guilt and sorrow.

Save for a portrait she created of William to send Victor, she spent hours painting botanical studies, sometimes without pausing for meals. Sophie expressed concern at Elizabeth's preoccupation, but did not press; perhaps the maid was still alarmed by Elizabeth's strange behavior after Henry's departure.

By the time Elizabeth, Sophie, and William returned to Geneva, it was just after Christmas. The city-republic resembled a ruined woman staggering beneath the weight of her fate, which contributed to Elizabeth's apprehension. She was especially disturbed to find the formerly bustling Place du Bourg-de-Four inhabited by boarded-up shops and broken windows. Monsieur Clerval's shop appeared abandoned; Elizabeth hadn't been able to resist asking their carriage to take that route.

Each street corner hosted hawkers offering pamphlets, some salacious and others thirsting for the blood of the French king and queen, who remained in captivity in Paris. Abandoned pamphlets were found frozen in puddles of ice. South of the city gates, someone had set up a tree of liberty in Plainpalais, where bonfires burned at odd hours. Ash hung on the wind, coating ironwork about the city-republic in a fine grey powder impossible to avoid.

Elizabeth, William, and Sophie arrived home to discover Alphonse in a state of distress. He explained, "Three thousand auxiliary troops were withdrawn from Geneva. Therefore we had no protection when the French invaded us. Can you believe it?" The French had encouraged rebellion in Geneva. As a result, the Geneva Council staged their own revolution to avoid being forced into the French Republic. Many aristocrats fled for sanctuary in Switzerland and beyond—but not Alphonse, who remained in their cream-bricked manor house on the Rue des Granges. Alphonse warned Elizabeth that he feared a bloodbath resembling the September massacres in Paris, though Geneva did not have a guillotine. Ernest appeared agitated by the news; Elizabeth could not tell where his sympathies lay.

Strangely, neither Alphonse nor Ernest spoke of Victor's illness once she confided all she'd seen in Ingolstadt. Or, if they did, it wasn't in Elizabeth's presence. She told herself they feared upsetting her; she was relieved they said nothing. She still couldn't reconcile the madman she'd encountered in Ingolstadt with the beloved friend she'd grown up with.

However, a surprise awaited Elizabeth at home. When she arrived upstairs with her luggage, she discovered Justine making William's bed. Elizabeth questioned her senses before a wild joy bloomed.

"Justine! It really *is* you!"

Elizabeth enveloped the girl in an embrace before holding her out to examine her. How different Justine appeared! But then, it had been five years since they'd last met.

When they'd parted after Caroline's death, Justine was still full-cheeked, awkward of aspect with spotted skin. Now she was a woman though still petite. She was more lithe than Elizabeth recalled, her face incandescent with a peculiar beauty now that her complexion had cleared. Despite her hunchback, her pale eyes and hair made her resemble a princess from those French fairy tales Caroline loved, rather than a fey creature of the woods. Yet there was something sorrowful about Justine, as though she was haunted by loss. Elizabeth understood this too well.

"I did not expect you back so soon," Justine answered, lisping like Caroline in her old way. "Monsieur Frankenstein said you'd return in the spring. He intended me to mind William. In the meantime, I've been aiding Cook in the kitchen."

Elizabeth asked, "What of your mother? She is well?"

Two rosy spots appeared in the center of Justine's cheeks. "My mother has passed. My brothers and sister also gone."

"They abandoned Geneva?"

Justine's brow puckered. "Dead. Cholera—I did not know until after I returned home. Forgive me for not writing you, Mademoiselle, but my responsibilities were heavy."

All the Moritzes dead. Ah, that explained the haunted quality Elizabeth noticed in Justine! She offered the maid another full embrace. "We shall be your family now."

William burst in, and Elizabeth gathered the boy into her arms.

"This is Justine," she said, her tone bright. "She's going to be a good friend to you, dormouse. You don't remember her, but she attended you when you were a baby."

By the time Elizabeth left them, Justine was clapping hands with William in a game, the two laughing as though they'd known one another for years.

* * *

Despite the joy of Justine's return, Elizabeth found dinner that night to be a solemn affair. How could it not be, with fires burning in the squares, raised voices in the street? The lack of flour, the spoiled fruit, the turned meats? However, she chattered to her uncle as though nothing had changed the weeks they'd been away in an attempt to distract him as well as herself, to push away the disturbances of Ingolstadt and Lake Como. And in some ways, nothing *had* changed—the Frankensteins still ate off gilded plates and drank from Venetian glass. Ernest was nowhere to be seen; Elizabeth didn't dare ask where he'd gone.

"Uncle, you are too good!" Elizabeth exclaimed as soon as dinner began.

"I don't feel very good now," Alphonse replied, his brow furrowed. "You should have stayed in Italy. You look thin, my angel. Frail."

"I'm fine," Elizabeth evaded. "And I'm even better now that I've seen Justine. I'm so glad you offered her a home!"

Her return was a sign from Caroline, Elizabeth decided. Hadn't Justine left their household soon after her aunt's death? Hadn't she taken a special interest in Justine, educating her above her station? And now here Justine was, attending to William in Caroline's stead.

Alphonse's weary face finally bore a hint of a smile. "How could I not? It took some persuasion to convince her to return. She was fearful I'd asked out of charity. Poor girl, how she's suffered! Shortly after you left for Lake Como, I found her wandering alone in the cemetery by your aunt's tomb. She confided that her mother had died after a long illness, during which she nursed her."

"Just as she nursed my aunt." Elizabeth's eyes filled.

Alphonse nodded. "Alas, Justine never received gratitude for her devotion. Madame Moritz blamed her for the death of her siblings, though this made no sense. She took every opportunity to flail the girl."

Flail the girl.

With this, color drained from Elizabeth's face.

Maria. The apple orchard. Caroline . . .

Alphonse set down his wine glass. "Elizabeth, are you well?"

"Perfectly." She forced a smile; no need to upset her uncle. "I'm weary, that's all."

She excused herself, unable to remain any longer.

That night she dreamt of a monster playing hide and seek with her and William in the apple orchard. Within this dream, she felt that same foreboding she'd struggled against since Caroline's death. A curse.

She shuddered awake with a start, her heart pounding like a drum. It seemed hours before she could sleep again.

I'm safe. We're all safe.

* * *

By the time Elizabeth rose the next morning, the winter sun was high and the lark had given way to the sparrow. She felt disoriented from that dream. A headache loomed. Outside her room, she heard Justine playing with William, their laughter rising like a melody.

Once Elizabeth dressed, she approached the window. She saw sunlight dancing across William's golden curls as he romped with Justine like puppies in a pile of leaves. A moment later, Ernest joined the game; he appeared cheerful for a change. Elizabeth's heart lightened. Justine had already won over Ernest as well as William. Soon a little girl arrived. Louisa Biron—William liked to call her his favorite wife. William smiled at Louisa's approach, revealing twin dimples on his cheeks.

Elizabeth watched the four of them chase each other about the garden. Their jests and giggles drowned out the cries of street hawkers selling pamphlets, the clatter of carriages, the angry shouts beyond their home. But it didn't stop her ruminations. That sense of being cursed—she'd thought her confession to Henry had banished it. She should write Henry regarding Victor. But not yet.

I'll paint. That will soothe my mind.

She resolved to let her secret sketchbook languish in its locked drawer. Instead, she would continue with those scientific studies of plants she'd begun during their travels from Ingolstadt. She yearned for them to be more than pretty pictures. Sometimes she'd slice the flowers open to reveal the tender organs within: the pistols, stamens and ovules. The secrets hidden in Nature.

Victor will improve, she told herself as she mixed lush purples and greens to paint an iris. *All will be well.* By the time he returned home, she'd love him again like she had as a child. They'd wed.

"We're fated," she whispered aloud.

Elizabeth heard a knock on her door. Justine. She was still wearing her cloak, her cheeks rosy from the cold. How like Caroline she remained, with her hair adorned as Elizabeth's aunt had worn it, her head tilted in tender concern! It really was a comfort.

Elizabeth looked up from her watercolor. "I thought you were in the garden with William."

"I was. But Monsieur Ernest informed me of the news from Ingolstadt."

Justine opened her arms. Again, Elizabeth sensed that haunted quality in Justine, the otherworldly sense of loss. Justine understood, for she'd suffered too.

As they embraced, Elizabeth mourned the shell of a man Victor had become in Ingolstadt. She mourned Henry and the loyalties they must honor. She mourned Caroline, who'd saved her from a life of misfortune. She could never tell anyone what had happened with Maria. But she'd never forget.

"Anything you need of me, I will do," Justine said. "This I promise."

CHAPTER IX.

*"My uncle is not pleased with the idea of a military career in
a distant country; but Ernest never had your powers of application . . .
I fear that he will become an idler, unless we yield the point, and permit
him to enter on the profession which he has selected."*

* * *

VICTOR REMAINED in Ingolstadt with Henry for over a year while the
world tipped further into chaos. By the spring of 1794, a new constitution of Geneva had been formed and the French king and queen
relieved of their heads by guillotine. To avoid reprisal, no one wore
black. Elizabeth feared yet another revolution in Geneva, and suggested
they return to Belrive. Alphonse assured her otherwise, though he
sometimes appeared unwell from stress.

Elizabeth tried to reconcile herself to her upcoming marriage; it was
difficult to forget the Victor she'd encountered in Ingolstadt. *"My
dearest Victor, you have been very ill,* she wrote, *"and even the constant
letters of dear kind Henry are not sufficient to reassure me on your account.
Get well and return to us."* She wrote him of Ernest and of local gossip, of
his father and William as though all was as it had been. There were the
Mansfield sisters, who were desperate for matrimony; the awkward
one had become engaged to a rich banker. Louis Manoir, Victor's friend

from school, had been engaged and jilted twice because he was discovered gambling in a café.

Henry kept the Frankensteins apprised of Victor's condition. He wrote, "*I vow to do all I can to return Victor to you, and am pleased to report it's a matter of weeks before he's hale enough to return to Geneva.*"

This good news did not alleviate the Frankensteins' dread over the troubles in Geneva and France. The servants also sensed this tension, even Justine, whose temperament was usually placid. Elizabeth noticed the maid appeared distracted and slack-cheeked, as though she'd given up sleep to fret.

And then one May afternoon Elizabeth heard a yelp rise from William's room. She rushed to find Justine kneeling before the child, holding a sweet.

William wailed, "Justine slapped me! All because I wouldn't eat my lunch."

"I'm so sorry, Mademoiselle," Justine cried, hiding her face in her hands. "Truly sorry!"

"Is all well?" Elizabeth forced a concerned gaze to cover her confusion. She couldn't imagine Justine hitting a child. Nor could she imagine William lying—he was mischievous but not dishonest. "You do look tired, Justine."

"Forgive me!" Justine reached to comfort William. She began to weep herself. "I'm so sorry! I don't know what's wrong with me today."

She feels the tension too. We all do.

Elizabeth soothed William, "There, dormouse! What did you do to try our good Justine so? You heard her; she's sorry. No need to cry! Look—" Elizabeth pulled from around her neck the locket bearing Caroline's portrait. "Your mama wouldn't want you to cry so, darling. Here, do you want to hold this?"

He *did* want to hold the locket—but not before he also took the sweet from Justine.

"I'm sorry," Justine said again, wiping her eyes. "I don't understand what possessed me."

Elizabeth couldn't think how to respond. For a moment, she thought anew of Maria. *Justine is nothing like her.*

"I've been working you too hard," Elizabeth said at last, her voice catching. "It is I who should apologize."

She couldn't have slapped him before; I'd have noticed. Justine had always been so tender with the boy. Elizabeth pushed her concerns away when Ernest appeared drunk at dinner, earning a scolding from his father. Honestly, in some ways Ernest was more juvenile than William; at least William had the excuse of being a child.

"Why won't you let me go to Switzerland or France?" Ernest whined over his untouched plate of food. "I'm old enough, Father."

Alphonse replied sharply, "You're only seventeen. Your lungs are not as strong as you think—the doctors warned against exerting yourself. We'd hoped to have you home for another three years before university, not join the military. Anyway, this isn't the time to be in France . . ."

Alphonse's voice trailed off in pointed omission. Elizabeth understood. Ever since the French had beheaded Marie Antoinette and King Louis, everyone was fair play. Months later, Elizabeth could still envision the descriptions she'd read of women passing their nursing babies to strangers as they marched to the guillotine, men with their collars folded to reveal the tender flesh of their necks.

"I'll be safe," Ernest retorted. "Please, Father!"

Alphonse offered a stern gaze. "I want all my family to remain together."

Their argument was interrupted by William, who ran into the dining room. He settled below the table, arms and legs flailing. Ernest used the disruption to storm out of the room, slamming the door behind him.

William demanded, "Play with me, Lisbeth!"

Elizabeth soothed, "Not now, dormouse. We're still dining."

"No!" William beat his feet against her chair legs.

"Where's Justine?" Alphonse said, frowning. "Shouldn't she be with him?"

"No, Papa! I want Lisbeth! Not her!"

William began to wail, causing Alphonse to throw down his napkin. "Calm him," he ordered. Just as Elizabeth again offered William her locket to distract him from a tantrum, Justine swept into the dining room.

"I'll take him, Mademoiselle."

"Leave me alone, Justine!" William sobbed, reaching for Elizabeth anew. "I don't like you anymore."

"My apologies," Justine said, curtseying to Alphonse. "He didn't sleep well last night, Monsieur. He's overtired."

Elizabeth laughed nervously as William hugged her knees. Justine looked away, biting her lip.

How strangely everyone is behaving today.

Elizabeth said: "I'll take him, Justine. You may go."

But Justine lingered even after Alphonse left the room.

"If I may ask a favor . . ." Her tone was uneasy, Elizabeth thought. "I received a letter. My aunt in Chêne. She's poorly. May I visit her tonight?"

Well, that explained Justine's peculiar behavior. Still, she shouldn't have lost her temper with William.

"But it's so late to be walking that way," Elizabeth responded, rubbing her temples. Chêne was nearly a league south of Geneva and French territory. "I didn't know you had other family."

"I haven't seen my aunt in years, but . . ."

"What about soldiers along the road?"

"I doubt they'll bother me. Please. I'll be back by nightfall!"

"Go ahead," Elizabeth said just as Ernest returned, ignoring Justine as she rushed from the room.

"Elizabeth, Father wants to stroll to Plainpalais to take the air," Ernest said. "Will you and William accompany us? Please? I need to talk to you."

Elizabeth had planned to return to her room to paint. But there was something odd about Ernest's request. Something that bothered her beyond his argument with his father.

"Very well," she said, seeking her gloves. "Come, dormouse! We're going for a walk. It's a fine evening."

* * *

Plainpalais that evening was luscious and green with spring warmth, soft breezes, and the lazy buzzing of insects. A perfect May evening. Ernest or no, Elizabeth was glad they'd come—perhaps she'd been spending too much time alone painting. William immediately jumped up and down with a shout of pleasure.

"What is it you wanted to tell me?" Elizabeth asked Ernest once they'd settled on a wood bench beneath an ancient chestnut tree. "You're acting very odd."

"I'll tell you once we're alone," he answered, avoiding her gaze. "William, where's Papa?"

The boy pointed toward an oak some yards away. "Over there. With Monsieur Lenard." Monsieur Lenard was a lawyer as well as an old friend of the Frankensteins; Alphonse appreciated his sanguine intelligence.

"Go visit him. I'm sure he misses you."

"I want to stay here with you and Lisbeth."

"But Papa needs you, dormouse."

"But I *need* you."

The boy stuck out his lower lip, looking so akin to Caroline when she was in a contemplative mood that Elizabeth couldn't resist a smile. She noticed the locket dangling from his pocket.

"Let me have it, dormouse." She should have taken it back earlier.

William darted away, laughing. "Come get me!"

"Well, at least set it around your neck so you don't lose it," she said.

"Ah, what a demon you are!" Ernest rose from the bench to tickle his younger brother. "I'll catch you! You'll see!"

"No, you won't!" William dashed across the expanse of lush grass. "I'm faster than you! You're old, Ernest. Stupid too."

Elizabeth laughed as the two ran about the oak, Ernest one way, then William the other. Her disturbances of the day faded. Justine's loss of temper was of the moment. She hadn't meant to slap William. She was fretful. They all were. The times were challenging.

Once William rushed away, Ernest returned to the bench. "I'll give him a minute to hide himself," he explained to Elizabeth. "We have our routine—don't look so worried! He knows the park well. He's a good boy."

Elizabeth glanced over her shoulder. William dashed toward the river, which was a thin stream snaking along the edge of Plainpalais. "I don't want to leave him unattended for long. Is there enough time to speak?"

"I'll be quick." He leaned in, his tone desperate. "I need funds to go to France. My father refuses."

Elizabeth drew back, forgetting William. "France? I thought that was settled at dinner."

"Elizabeth, I can't stay here."

"I can't give you funds—your father would be furious," she said, rising to her feet. "Where's William? I don't want him playing near water."

"He's over there, behind the oak. He's fine. Calm down—"

"How can I be calm about you leaving home?"

"You're more reasonable than Father, so I'd hoped you'd take my part."

"You're in trouble, aren't you?" She'd heard rumors of Ernest partaking in cards at taverns. He looked old for his age; it would be easy for him to persuade someone to allow him entry. "Gambling?"

"No." Ernest flushed. "Well, not that sort of gambling . . ."

Across the field, she heard William laugh. "Come on, Ernest! I'm waiting for you!"

"A woman?" Elizabeth had never noticed Ernest pay anyone mind, but he was barely seventeen. Too young to be courting.

He nodded after a moment. "But don't tell my father!"

"Ernest, you're going to lose the game!" William sounded further away. The burble of the stream chattered alongside his high voice, bird song rising as twilight approached. How idyllic it all was, save for Ernest and his troubles. Elizabeth's impatience rose. Ernest was being so evasive. Why wouldn't he just tell her already?

"I'll be there soon, dormouse," Ernest called out. "Another minute!"

"What happened?" Elizabeth asked. "I won't tell Uncle." She glanced William's way. Where had he gone? She recalled him near the trees. *Not the river.* Well, as long as she could hear him . . .

"I'd rather not say, Elizabeth." An embarrassed smile. "Frankly, it's more irritating than anything. You must trust it's for the best I go away. Not for long. Only a year or two—"

"A year or two!" Elizabeth turned cold. "This is about the revolution, isn't it?"

Ernest scowled. "You have such little faith in me. Oh, I always ruin things—isn't that what Father would say?"

"He does his best. Be kind. He hasn't been himself since your mother passed." Elizabeth choked back a pang of yearning. Caroline would have known how to handle Ernest, just as she'd known how to handle Victor and Alphonse.

Ernest's face crumbled. "I wish I'd never come home. Wish I'd stayed in the Alps. I had more liberty as an invalid than I do here." He rose abruptly, smoothing his trousers. "We should go."

"Ernest, listen to reason!"

"I am being reasonable. And now I understand I was unreasonable to reason with you." He glared into the distance. "I'll get William—he's probably ready to leave. Anyway, the sky is clouding over. It'll be dark soon. I'll meet you back here."

Ernest strode off toward the river. Elizabeth sat on the bench, her chin tucked in her palms. The sky dimmed into twilight. Once she heard the sparrows quiet, she rose to her feet, exhausted and hungry. Had she eaten lunch? She recalled Justine bringing her morning tea, but dinner hadn't appealed; she'd barely eaten.

In the distance, a growl of thunder. A shard of lightning.

Alphonse approached, his hat in his hand. He was smiling for once.

"Ah, there you are, my angel," he said. "Sorry I took so long. I had an interesting conversation with Lenard." His brow knit. "Where's Ernest and William?"

"Ernest went to fetch William. They'll be back presently." Elizabeth set her hand on her uncle's arm, determined not to reveal her distress over Ernest's confession. "Tell me about your conversation. I could use some gossip."

"No gossip, alas. News that I wish was gossip." Alphonse launched into a detailed description of the new revolutionary tribunal, which Monsieur Lenard believed had been instigated by the French government. "I told Lenard this cannot be, but perhaps he knows something I don't."

Elizabeth grew dizzy. Lightheaded. She'd eat when she returned home. She sank onto the bench beside her uncle. The rush of the river had never sounded so loud.

"Sorry, Uncle. You were saying?"

He patted Elizabeth's hand. "Never mind. We should leave."

Another lash of lightning. It appeared a league to the south, in the direction of Chêne. She recalled Justine's mysterious errand.

She must be back by now. No need to worry.

"Ah, there's Ernest," Alphonse announced. "Without William."

"He's probably run off again. I should have insisted he stay near." Hopefully he hadn't lost the locket of Caroline.

Ernest approached, his face moist with sweat, clutching William's spencer jacket. "Did you see William? I can't find him anywhere. I swear I've run the length of the field four times."

Elizabeth asked, "Are you sure he didn't go toward the stream?"

"He's a good boy," Ernest assured.

Alphonse rose as well from the bench, clutching his walking stick. "We'll find him. He couldn't have gone far." He narrowed his gaze toward the sky, where the sun had dropped behind the mountains. "We should hurry before it's dark."

Elizabeth's skin prickled, cheeks flushed. Fear, that's what she felt. Her eyes strained in the gloom. In a field beyond, she made out the lurching silhouette of a tall man. A giant. Her heart gave a stutter of panic.

She squinted. *Nothing there.* She'd imagined him, just as she had that rainy night in Ingolstadt. As for William, surely he must be near.

She turned around Plainpalais, heart pounding.

Where can my boy be?

CHAPTER X.

"I must say also a few words to you, my dear cousin, of little darling William. I wish you could see him; he is very tall of his age, with sweet laughing blue eyes, dark eyelashes, and curling hair. When he smiles, two little dimples appear on each cheek, which are rosy with health."

* * *

WILLIAM HADN'T INTENDED to end up so far afield from Plainpalais. Initially his wandering had been a way to garner attention, for he was riled by Justine slapping him earlier. He was shocked Elizabeth hadn't scolded Justine. She really should have—after all, he was a Frankenstein. As much as he loved Justine, she was only a servant, like Sophie.

"Come find me!" he'd shouted in the direction where the oak with the bench lay, though he could no longer see it. "I'm here!"

But where was here? He couldn't recall.

"Come get me then!"

Silence.

The boy circled about. To his right was the stream, the one where Ernest had taken him fishing earlier that spring. It burbled over rocks and reeds, high for the season, for it had been a rainy spring. Behind him was the woods, which led back into the heart of Plainpalais.

William pulled his spencer coat off; he'd grown hot from running.

Elizabeth and Ernest were still beneath the oak, no doubt still fighting. And it was a fight he heard—though William would soon be six, he'd spent enough time with adults to recognize when conversations turned nasty. This granted him an advantage among his friends, the few he had. Girls he liked. Wives, he called them, mainly because it pleased Elizabeth. Elizabeth always seemed so sad even when she was smiling. Though he was only five, William understood smiles often hid any number of sorrows. How could she not be sorrowful, with Victor ill and far away? He held no memories of his eldest brother, but knew him from Elizabeth's stories; she'd marry him one day. But William's adoration of Victor bore no comparison to his worship of Mama. She watched over him from heaven—the stories Justine told left him with no doubt.

Thinking of this, William's short fingers closed around the locket with the picture of Mama. When he'd removed his coat, he was careful to hang the necklace around his neck to avoid losing it.

By then dusk had fallen, hushing the birds into a stupor. The setting sun glimmered purple and blue over the mountain rim.

Alone. William was alone in the night—this had never happened before. He would be brave, like the soldiers Ernest spoke of. Where was he? "Walk toward the river," he whimpered. That would take him home, wouldn't it? Sooner or later, a river led to Geneva. Geneva was founded on two rivers, the Rhone and the Arne. William was nothing if not smart. Wasn't that what Justine always said?

William walked for some moments in sturdy determination, his short legs tiring as he scrambled over rocks and roots. At last he came to a clearing. The field he found himself in was boring. Flat. Tall grass. Flies. Gnats. Surely the river was beyond this. Surely Geneva was near.

His fist tightened again around the precious locket of Mama. He'd be scolded for running off, but at least he hadn't lost it. His stomach was growling and he was thirsty. When he got home, Justine would make him warm milk, as she always did before bed. He'd wrap his arms around her. Forgive her. After all, she was a servant and he was a Frankenstein. His papa was a syndic. He could grant her mercy.

Some feet away, he saw a cluster of ravens rush into the sky. Below their rising wings stood a man with hair the color of coal, his lurching form silhouetted by the dying rays of the day. The man was taller than

William imagined possible, with a sallow face seamed by scars, long arms bound by muscles and torn clothes. He appeared a giant from one of his storybooks. A creature. A demon. A monster.

The monster turned to meet William's gaze. His thin dark lips spread into a grin.

CHAPTER XI.

"Last Thursday (May 7th), I, my niece, and your two brothers, went to walk in Plainpalais . . . Presently Ernest came, and enquired if we had seen his brother: he said, that he had been playing with him, that William had run away to hide himself, and that he vainly sought for him."

* * *

"William!" Elizabeth shouted into the night. "Where are you?" By then an hour had passed since Ernest had appeared bearing William's abandoned spencer in his arms. They'd searched the riverbanks, checked the woods, and walked the width of Plainpalais more times than she could recall. It had grown dark enough that both the Juras and Mont Blanc were indistinguishable save for stars winking above them. Thankfully the storm Elizabeth witnessed to the south never passed their way.

"He couldn't have gone far," Alphonse said. "He always did like to run off, didn't he?"

Ernest set his arm around his father's frail shoulders. "We'll find him soon, Father."

"He probably went home," Elizabeth suggested, ignoring the panic roiling in her head. "It must be that. We'll find him there."

"A child of five? Alone?" Ernest said, incredulous.

Elizabeth cradled her face in her hands. She imagined William's face submerged beneath the river. William gasping for breath.

"Hush, you're alarming Elizabeth!" Alphonse warned. "He knows his way."

"You're right," Ernest said, his tone gentler. "Elizabeth, go home with Father. Send a servant if you find William there—I'll remain in case he's still here."

But William wasn't home when Elizabeth and Alphonse arrived. Sophie asked, "Shall I send servants to search Plainpalais? They're all in bed—I'll wake them."

"Only the footmen. No need to disturb everyone." Alphonse's face appeared leeched of color. "Bring torches from the carriage house. It's too dark to see otherwise."

Elizabeth insisted, "I want to accompany you. My poor boy! No doubt he's lost and frightened. He's probably sleeping beside the river, cold and covered in dew."

"I'll wake Justine," Sophie offered. "She'd know where he hides. She goes with him to Plainpalais every night."

"Let her rest," Elizabeth replied, gathering her cloak; it had grown chilly now that it was night. "I'll need her tomorrow to take care of him, after being up so late. Anyway, we've six people to search."

Despite it nearing ten of the clock, the gatekeeper let them out with a warning they'd be locked out of the city gates. "We've a boy missing," Alphonse explained. "It can't wait until morning!" By then a small gathering of people had joined the Frankensteins at the entry to Plainpalais: soldiers, servants, and townspeople. Ernest ran ahead, showing where he'd already searched. How dark Plainpalais appeared to Elizabeth! How sinister! She'd never been there before at night. She sensed Ernest by her side; she could smell his scent, which was warm and soapy with an overlay of wine. His breath was heavy from running.

"Stay close to me, Elizabeth—it won't do to have you go missing too. Come!"

From their vantage point, Elizabeth watched the torches spread out across the entirety of Plainpalais in all directions. The lights dashed in and out between trees and fields, swirling and moving like stars dancing in the heavens. If they hadn't been searching for a missing child, the torches would have been a sight to inspire wonder, not fear. Elizabeth understood the more those torches moved, the more unlikely it was they'd located William; once they found him, all the torches would rush to one spot.

Ernest said, "I pray he didn't fall into the river. I didn't dare suggest this to my father."

"You told me this was unlikely."

"Well, I've taken him fishing there, in the stream yonder." Ernest pointed with his torch.

"We already looked there twice," Elizabeth assured, though her words didn't silence the rush of blood in her head. Something bad had happened. Something evil. She felt it. She tasted it. Something to do with what she'd heard murmured in the marketplace and beyond. Someone had kidnapped William. Someone who hated syndics and nobles. Perhaps someone from the revolutionary tribunal her uncle mentioned. There'd even been chatter about the arrival of a strange man scarred from war, who appeared as threatening as a monster. No one knew where he'd come from. She should have told Alphonse. She hadn't, for she hoped it was naught but a rumor. But Ernest knew of the chatter, didn't he?

The thought wouldn't let Elizabeth go. It dug its claws into her like a bird of prey.

"Ernest, you don't think—"

"This has nothing to do with the revolutionary tribunal." Ernest's jaw was set. "They'd never hurt William. Their anger is toward adults, not innocent children." A sharp inhale of breath. "Look!"

In a field just beyond Plainpalais, the array of torches rearranged themselves into a brilliant constellation. The constellation tightened until it blazed like a sun.

"They've found him," Elizabeth breathed. All would be well.

Ernest raced toward the constellation, abandoning Elizabeth to darkness. It took her some moments to catch up—her stays were too tight for running easily. By the time she caught up with Ernest, her face had widened into a grin.

"Ah," she sighed. "Praise God."

There was William lying in the grass. He was sleeping, the poor child. How innocent he appeared, how sweet! His hair was ruffled, his hands clasped before his chest. He must have fallen asleep while saying prayers.

He's safe. Yet everyone was weeping, even Alphonse.

Elizabeth's heart pitched. Why weren't they smiling? They should be happy, shouldn't they? They'd found William. He'd come home with them, they'd give him a hot bath, some warm milk, and all would be well. Tomorrow they'd laugh over the fright he'd given them.

"He's sleeping. That's all!"

"Elizabeth . . ." Ernest shook his head.

"Wake him," Elizabeth said, her eyes filling, her voice shrill. "Wake him! Why isn't anyone waking him?"

* * *

Elizabeth barely recalled accompanying William's body back to the Frankensteins' home—somehow they were in Plainpalais and then they were home. Though Ernest laid William in the morning room away from her line of sight, some part of her did not believe William to be truly dead; he'd live again once they set him before a blazing fire after a warm bath. She'd chafe his limbs, restore breath into him. But all her hope fled once she beheld Alphonse's stricken countenance. He reached for Elizabeth. The tears on his unshaven cheek offered the confirmation she'd denied.

Elizabeth struggled from Alphonse's arms. "Let me go to him!" She next recalled Ernest trying to hold her back from the child she'd loved and nurtured since infancy, her dear Caroline's baby. Alphonse ordering, "Calm her." Sophie crying out, "Get Justine—she'll be able to help!" But Justine was nowhere to be found.

Elizabeth staggered into the morning room where William had been set. All was dark, for the candles remained unlit, shutters still closed. Silent like a tomb. All she could hear was the rush of her breath, the beat of her heart.

Once her eyes adjusted to the shadows, she made out a slight bundle on the settee. The bundle was wrapped in a yellow blanket—a blanket she recognized from William's bed.

"Sweet dormouse," she whispered, her throat clotted with tears.

Outside, a bough of a tree snapped, shattering the silence. Or was it her heart cracking? Though Elizabeth understood the latter to be an impossibility—hadn't Victor, with his books and diagrams revealing the hidden workings of organs and veins and muscles, taught her otherwise?—in that moment, it felt possible. She'd never be the same. Couldn't be the same. As awful as Caroline's death had been, she'd lived a full life. William was but a child. An innocent, lovely child who should still be alive with years before him.

Elizabeth approached the settee, where that small bundle awaited. She pulled at the blanket, revealing William's sweet face. Surely God had taken his soul. He must be at peace . . .

The blanket fell from his shoulders.

His neck. Even in the shuttered light, she made out a chain of bruises around his tender throat, something she'd been unable to see when they'd found him in Plainpalais.

Her eyes swam, knees swayed. Who could have done this to him? Why would they harm a child? The evil was incomprehensible.

Unless . . .

The locket, the one she'd given him. Hadn't she last seen it about his neck? The ribbon holding it couldn't have snapped, could it? Perhaps he'd taken it off. Elizabeth tugged at his clothes, his pockets. Where was it?

Gone. Someone had stolen it.

She cried out, "Oh God! I have murdered my darling child!"

The room buzzed with shadows and regret and sorrow and loss. The flesh of William's neck; the bruises livid and yellow and blue. And then it was Caroline she saw before her. Caroline before her death—a death that Elizabeth had only recently learned to accept as fate. Caroline cradling William as a baby, offering him to Elizabeth. *"Promise you'll protect William. You'll love him as your own?"*

She'd failed William just as she'd failed Caroline.

Cursed, that's what I am.

* * *

Elizabeth did not remember anything more until she awakened in her bed. The scent of *sal volatile* wafted in the air. Alphonse and Ernest were seated across the room, their heads bent toward one another. The windows were open. The sun appeared high, shimmering with brilliance. An afternoon sun—she must have been insensate for hours. The birds were singing as though life was as it had been before she'd accompanied William to Plainpalais the previous evening. A lush perfume mingled with the smelling salts: the lilac beneath her window had started to bloom. Church bells from St. Peter's rang in the distance.

"We'll need to write Victor," Alphonse murmured to Ernest. "Surely he's strong enough to come home."

Ernest agreed. "We should prepare him first."

Alphonse cradled his head in his palms. "Ah my poor Victor! What a homecoming he shall arrive to!"

"What of the police? Have they any suspects yet?"

Their conversation dropped to a halt as Elizabeth pulled herself up, head swimming.

"Justine," she said, weeping. "I want Justine. Has anyone told her? She loved him too."

"Justine is sick in bed," Alphonse said, his tone hollow. "She'd been out all night. She claims you'd granted her permission to visit her aunt in Chêne yesterday. Is this true?"

"Yes. What of it?"

Alphonse refused to answer. Elizabeth discovered why two mornings later, when the locket bearing Elizabeth's watercolor of Caroline was discovered inside the gown Justine had worn the day of the murder.

"I suspected something peculiar about her absence that night," Alphonse said, his face grey. "To think I invited her into our home. Let her eat at our table. Sleep under our roof."

"Uncle, this cannot be! Justine loved William. I would have given the locket to her had she asked. There was no need for her to steal it! None at all."

A sharp scream rang from downstairs. Justine—Elizabeth knew it.

Elizabeth rushed from her room toward the stair landing. Downstairs by the portrait of Caroline, Justine stood in the center of the entryway surrounded by police. How small she appeared, so slight! She was still dressed in her white nightrail, her silvery hair unbound; the tresses dangled below her hips. One officer tried to grab her by her hair, another, the hem of her nightrail. She appeared a will of the wisp, a pale specter, as she slipped and flitted from their grasp.

Elizabeth yelled over the balustrade, "Let her go! She's not a murderess!" She rushed downstairs, shouting all the while. But before she could reach Justine, Ernest pulled her back. As Elizabeth struggled to free herself, the two slipped as one to the floor.

"No, no!" Justine circled from officer to officer until she dropped to her knees. The tallest officer used the opportunity to capture her wrists, which he yanked behind her. "I'm praying for the boy! Can't you see? Let me pray!"

Elizabeth banged her fists against the marble floor. "Justine!"

Justine's head craned toward Elizabeth, her eyes white with terror as the officers dragged her toward the door.

CHAPTER XII.

"It was about five in the morning when I entered my father's house. I told the servants not to disturb the family, and went into the library to attend their usual hour of rising. Six years had elapsed, passed as a dream but for one indelible trace, and I stood in the same place where I had last embraced my father before my departure for Ingolstadt."

VICTOR RETURNED from Ingolstadt within three weeks of Justine's arrest. Elizabeth was leaving the morning room after breakfast when she heard him emerge from the library. At first she didn't recognize Victor—he was so altered from when she'd encountered him in Ingolstadt.

Instead of rushing to him as she should have, Elizabeth hung back. Victor's physical presence shocked her. He was thinner than she'd ever seen, his bones jutting where his flesh was exposed: his wrists, his jaw, his temples. His generous dark curls had been shorn close to his head, revealing the curve of his skull to her eyes for the first time. He'd been far more ill than Henry's letters had said. She recalled how, when she'd last encountered Victor, he'd been so agitated that he'd clutched her shoulders painfully tight; she later found bruises the hue of dying violets on her flesh.

"Don't lie! You're not Elizabeth! You're my mother—well, had been my mother . . . Go! Back to the grave . . ."

"That's in the past," she whispered to herself. "He's better now." Still, she couldn't find it in herself to greet him. Not yet.

She watched Ernest embrace Victor, watched the reunited brothers approach the life-sized portrait of Caroline in the entry hall. A small framed watercolor of William, the one Elizabeth had painted during their journey, lay on the mantel below the oil portrait.

Victor cradled the watercolor of William in his palm. "How he'd grown! He was a baby when I left. Would that I could behold him again!"

"You come to us to share a misery that nothing can alleviate." Ernest's voice was shaky. "Poor William! He was our darling and our pride! Even worse, the murderer has been discovered—"

"The murderer discovered!" Victor cried, color draining from his face. "Good God! How can that be? Who could attempt to pursue him? It is impossible! One might as well try to overtake the winds, or confine a mountain stream. I saw him too; he was free last night!"

"I do not know what you mean," Ernest replied, "but the discovery of the murderer completes our misery. It was Justine, his nursemaid. We've proof."

The locket. Elizabeth's eyes filled; she still couldn't believe it. She'd had to hide her distress before her family, to be the strong one, the stalwart one. Perfect. When alone, her panicked thoughts circled between *How can William be dead?* and *Justine couldn't have murdered him. I must save her.* Alphonse had forbidden Elizabeth to advocate on Justine's behalf, warning the revolutionary tribunal would view this as undermining the scales of justice. "We must trust in our courts," he urged. "If she is innocent, she will be freed."

Elizabeth must not have been as silent as she'd hoped, for Ernest called out in an aspect of alarm, "Who's there?"

"Only me."

Elizabeth's stomach fluttered as she approached Victor—Victor who appeared a stranger from the hale man who'd departed Geneva six years earlier.

She drew a breath to steady the rise of her pulse. There was Victor. There was Ernest. Henry wasn't present—he must have gone home to his father. *For the best,* she told herself. Still, her treacherous heart sped at the thought of his proximity.

I can't love Henry. I won't.

She greeted Ernest, embraced Victor. "Welcome home." How odd such words sounded after such a loss.

"Dearest Elizabeth. Beloved friend."

Victor grasped her hand bearing Caroline's emerald ring and pressed it against his lips. A warmth, a sorrow flickered within the depths of his gaze. His eyes were as welcoming as ever, the same deep brown pools with flecks of gold. "I know Justine is innocent," he whispered as he bent to kiss her cheek.

For a moment, she felt a flare of hope. But at dinner any consolation Elizabeth had found in Victor's return fled. He ignored Alphonse's attempts at conversation, snapped at Ernest. Nor would he answer her when she addressed him. Alphonse mouthed, "He's tired. That's all."

Victor's behavior disturbed Elizabeth enough that she sought him in his room afterward. He was already in bed, the counterpane high over his chest. A candle on the mantel revealed his eyes were wide open.

She knocked softly against the door frame. "May I come in?"

Victor blinked and sniffed. He'd been weeping.

"If you must," he said at last.

She settled herself on the edge of his bed, like in old times when they were children. Just as she'd tried to replicate that night in Lake Como with Henry.

She lay next to Victor and grasped his hand. How cold his skin felt! She was tempted to stroke what remained of his hair, to feel it bristle beneath her palms, to orient herself to the Victor who'd returned to her. She didn't. She was too disquieted.

After a moment he said, "I know who the murderer is."

"You do? We must tell the authorities!"

Victor broke her gaze. "I—I meant to say that the murderer cannot be poor, good Justine—it's impossible." A pause. "Why are you here?"

"I thought we could comfort each other." She tried to push away her memories of Henry, how he'd felt beside her.

Victor let out a huff. "Comfort . . . How can any comfort be found? My brother is dead, Justine in prison."

He turned his back against her stomach. She embraced him. His spine felt a series of protrusions, a long snakelike cord.

"You've grown so thin." Her voice dropped. "What made you so ill? Was it only overwork?"

"I don't want to talk about it. I'd give anything to forget Ingolstadt. Elizabeth, I'm not the man I'd once been. I never will be. You should know that before we wed."

"Nor am I the woman I was," she said, choking back emotion as she thought of William in his grave, Justine in her cell. "Loss will do that. We'll need to know each other anew."

She closed her eyes, trying to invoke the Victor she remembered. The Victor who sat with her in summer gardens and brought her flowers, and spoke of the wonders of Nature. The Victor she'd loved from the moment she'd met him as a child.

She kissed his shoulder, yearning for some show of warmth. Something to reassure they were meant to marry as she'd promised Caroline. That they were fated, as Henry would say. She awaited his response, but all she sensed was agitation; his limbs shuddered before they turned rigid. His candle sputtered and blew out. He gestured wildly, moaning "I can't bear the darkness!" until she rose and lit another. When she returned to bed, he gave no thanks, only a sigh.

The silence grew between them, somber and heavy. She laid a cautious hand against his forearm. She stroked the corded muscles, the long bones. *He's like a cadaver.* He even smelled strange, like rot.

She pulled her hand away, settling it under his pillow. Something cold and metallic met her fingers. Her eyes widened as she drew out a pistol. Alphonse's from the library—Elizabeth recognized it.

"Why are you sleeping with this? You're not going to harm yourself?" Her voice shook.

"God no. I haven't the courage for that." He grabbed the pistol back. "If you must know, after William . . ."

He wanted to protect them. At last her affection ignited; she nearly wept with relief. He feared losing her. All of them. He truly didn't believe Justine murdered William—his strange outburst about knowing who murdered William wasn't only to appease her belief in Justine's innocence. However, the implications of Victor's claims were nearly as troubling: who could have strangled her darling boy? Where could the murderer be? Did Victor really believe he'd strike again?

He tucked the pistol back under his pillow. "You should go, Elizabeth. You deserve some sleep."

He said nothing more, not even when she bid him goodnight. Yet she found she couldn't return to her room. Not yet. She was too unsettled.

She made her way downstairs toward the library, past the entry where the portraits of Caroline and William remained on display. She nodded to Caroline in silent promise. A rise of voices from the kitchen caught her attention. The door was ajar, a lamp burning.

She peeked through the door crack like a mouse. Ernest was seated at the long kitchen table with Sophie, Henry too. Her eyes prickled at the sight of Henry—loyal, kind Henry who nursed Victor. Unlike Victor, Henry appeared much the same as when she'd last seen him, though his hair had grown long enough to dangle over his eyes; every so often he brushed it back. The hour was so late! Had he come to the Frankensteins with the intent of avoiding her?

"How is she?" Henry asked in a low voice. "I know it's forward of me to speak to you in confidence, but I believe you know Mademoiselle Elizabeth best."

Elizabeth pressed her eye against the door crack, unable to turn away.

Sophie set her chin against her hands. "It's as you think, Monsieur Clerval. She blames herself for the boy's death."

"I feared as much."

"On top of that—well, I don't suppose you know what's occurred, Monsieur Clerval . . ."

Sophie described the new revolutionary tribunal, the threats against the syndics, the fears they held for Alphonse. "They want to take power from the syndics, even if it means killing them. It's like what happened in France!" As she spoke, Ernest grew agitated; he chewed his lip, shook his head. "It's not that simple," he cut in, voice rising. "The tribunal will insist on a new constitution for Geneva, one that is fair to all citizens. My father should help them."

Henry raised a hand to silence Ernest. "Your father can sort his own troubles. It's Mademoiselle Elizabeth I'm concerned about. I can't bear to think of anything more befalling her—Madame Frankenstein's death affected her so. You both must protect her. Care for her. Victor cannot. Victor is not as he was."

I know, Elizabeth thought, easing her way from the door. Yet, as she returned to her bed, it was only Henry she thought of. Henry who'd cared and protected her yet again.

Suddenly she imagined Caroline's hand caressing her cheek. The weight of her guardian's emerald ring on her hand.

* * *

It took another month before Justine's trial was brought to court—weeks during which fourteen syndics were imprisoned for crimes against the state by the revolutionary tribunal; thankfully, Alphonse was spared. Though he forbade Elizabeth from visiting Justine in prison, she secretly sent care packages of food and clothes accompanied by messages of support.

During this period, Henry did not visit Elizabeth save for an awkward call to offer condolences for William's death. *It's for the best*, she told herself again. *I should be thinking of Victor, not him.* As for Victor, he remained peculiar. He'd taken to staying awake at all hours, staring out windows like a cat awaiting prey. Other days he refused to leave his room; Ernest brought Victor trays of food after promising he'd tasted everything first. Then there were days when Victor headed toward the lake, sailing for hours even at night. The only one able to calm him was Alphonse, who was preternaturally patient with his eldest son.

"He's had a shock," he explained. "He's been ill."

The morning of Justine's trial, Elizabeth was dressed for court well before its scheduled start at eleven o'clock. "We should arrive early to express our belief in her innocence," she told Victor. "The jury will take note." Not that it mattered—by the time the Frankensteins had shown, the courtroom was already packed with more humanity than it was intended to hold.

By then the wheel of the year had shifted from June to July. It was a fetid July too—the air lay especially heavy in the courtroom. Every so often a matron snapped open a fan. From the chatter Elizabeth made out, everyone wanted to see the trial of the girl accused of murdering a child—far more scandalous than the imprisonment of a handful of syndics for resisting the march of liberty. The voices in the courtroom swelled into a nearly indistinguishable rise of syllables and sentences.

"Can you believe the Frankensteins defend her?"

"The girl is guilty as sin. Anyone can tell."

"The boy was an angel. She strangled him because of the revolution."

"No, because of the syndics—Monsieur Frankenstein is a syndic too, you know."

"She's the daughter of a gravedigger. An unnatural creature. What did they expect?"

"They're wrong," Elizabeth whispered, clutching Victor's hand. "Wrong!"

"Do you see anyone outside?" Victor whispered in turn, glancing around the courtroom toward the windows. "Someone tall? Dark?"

"I don't know who you mean," Elizabeth replied, perspiration beading her brow. How warm the courtroom was! Was he going to start ranting again? From the sharp glint in his eye, she could tell the anxious Victor sat beside her—the Victor who paraded around the house at night checking for hidden enemies—rather than the melancholic Victor who went out in boats at all hours and only slept when drugged by laudanum and brandy. Alphonse and Ernest ignored him, lost in their whispered conversation.

"The judge is about to begin," a clerk announced. "Silence!"

The chatter hushed as the judge called the court to order. A slender door opened to the left of the magistrate's bench, revealing the flash of a black bombazine skirt as its wearer limped into the courtroom.

Elizabeth's hand tightened on Victor's. "She must be found innocent."

Alphonse said, "If she is, God forbid she should suffer as guilty."

Justine's demeanor was serene despite spending two months locked in a cell. She appeared prettier than usual, though this made little sense; Elizabeth prayed this would sway the jury's sentiments. Justine's color-less hair was plaited in swirls around her neatly shaped head. Her mourning gown, the cause for the black bombazine skirts, minimized the appearance of her hunchback. Elizabeth had brought her the outfit —Elizabeth, who wished there was more she could do to save her.

Elizabeth lifted her hand in a tentative wave. A tear seemed to dim Justine's eye as she acknowledged the greeting with a small nod. Her chin jutted and quivered.

"She didn't do it," Victor muttered. "A monster did—"

"I know, Victor. I know."

A long shiver overtook Elizabeth as sweat dripped between her breasts. Who could have hurt William? *Evil exists no matter how we avoid it.* She felt as though she'd vomit. That conundrum of anger and guilt and sorrow she'd felt since Caroline's death flared anew. That sense of being cursed.

She couldn't have murdered my boy.

The trial droned on for hours. Elizabeth remained alert despite the stifling temperatures. Others dozed. Testimony revealed nothing Elizabeth had not known before: Justine had gone to visit her aunt in Chêne, who'd been unwell. However, the aunt was unavailable for testimony; Justine claimed she'd abandoned Chêne once she'd recovered. Justine did not know where her aunt had gone. Nor did any neighbors recall the aunt. Shortly before dawn, a market woman had spoken to Justine near Plainpalais, not far from where William's body was found. When the woman asked Justine why she was out so early, Justine had offered a peculiar reply: "Is it early? I hadn't noticed." Then she'd wandered away.

It was at this stage Alphonse and Ernest were required to testify regarding the locket, which the Frankensteins had discovered in Justine's pocket. Elizabeth followed them. Again, no new evidence was revealed: Justine had gone to visit her aunt in Chêne, who'd been unwell; Elizabeth had granted her leave. Elizabeth tried her best to restrain her emotion, to reveal the facts, but her voice quavered. She had expected Justine's aunt to testify on her behalf; she refused to consider what this might signify.

I cannot bear to lose Justine as well as William.

Once the judge excused Elizabeth, Justine was called. Any serenity she'd exhibited at the start of her trial was gone. As she approached the bench, Victor hid his face in his hands.

"I sincerely trust all shall be cleared by my honest description of the evening in question," Justine began in a faltering voice. "God knows how utterly innocent I am, and how much I esteemed William Frankenstein and his family, who have been my benefactors since I was a child."

She explained she had passed the evening of the murder at her aunt's house in Chêne. On her return to Geneva at about nine o'clock, she met a man who asked if she had seen the child who was lost. "I had no idea the child was William Frankenstein." She spent several hours helping look for him when the gates of Geneva were shut. As a result, she was forced to take shelter in a barn. She spent much of the night awake; toward morning she slept for a few minutes when someone's steps woke her from a nightmare. She found no one there. It was dawn when she quit the hayloft. That she had been bewildered when questioned by the market woman was not surprising, since she had passed a restless night. Concerning the locket found in her pocket, she could give no account.

"I know," Justine said, "how fatally my possession of the locket weighs against me, but I have no power of explaining it. Did the murderer place it there while I slept? If so, why should he have stolen the locket to part with it so soon? If I was a dishonest person, I'd think of a story to tell you to assert my innocence. But I am not." Her voice broke. "I must commit my cause to the justice of my judges . . . yet I see no room for hope. I suppose nothing remains but to trust in God's mercy and the truth of my innocence. If the court will allow, I beg permission to have a few witnesses examined concerning my character."

Several witnesses were called, but they were unwilling to testify due to the foul nature of the crime. Justine's limp appeared especially robust as she returned to her seat. She blinked repeatedly and sighed, hiding her face in her hands. Elizabeth yearned to rush to her, to protect her.

I must save Justine. But how?

The judge said, "If there are no further witnesses—"

Elizabeth raised her hand. "I will speak!"

"But you have already testified, Mademoiselle Lavenza. The jury is prepared to deliberate."

Elizabeth stood before the jury. How her heart pounded!

"But I have not spoken to her character, sir. When I see an innocent creature about to perish, I must do what I can."

A hush fell upon the court as Elizabeth returned to the magistrate's bench. Initially her voice quavered with nerves. It grew in strength as she swore to Justine's loyalty, kindness, and goodness. She spoke of how Justine nursed Madame Moritz and Caroline during their final illnesses, that she'd offered only affection to William and friendship to Elizabeth.

"For my own part, I do not hesitate to say that, notwithstanding all the evidence, I unequivocally believe in Mademoiselle Moritz's innocence," Elizabeth said. "She had no temptation for such an action. As to the locket on which the proof rests, I would have willingly given it to her if she'd asked for it, so much do I esteem her. She is like family."

At last Elizabeth fell into silence, her heart still pounding. She searched the crowded court, seeking any sign of mercy toward Justine. To Elizabeth's horror, a low murmur of indignation grew until it took over the courtroom.

"Mademoiselle Lavenza is too good!"

"What ingratitude! To murder a child after caring for him!"

"What did they expect? Look at her! She's a hunchback."

"A gravedigger's daughter!"

"She must hang after this!"

As their voices swelled and rose, Victor pressed his hands over his ears, rocking in his seat like a madman.

* * *

Elizabeth barely slept that night. At dawn the following morning, she discovered Alphonse wandering in the courtyard still dressed in his nightcap and gown. For a moment, she wondered if he'd been distressed by her testimony. But he kissed Elizabeth's cheek, calling her his angel, as he usually did.

"Come inside, Uncle," she said, taking his arm. "You'll take ill." She recalled how regal he'd seemed when she first joined the Frankenstein family, like a king with Caroline his queen. Now if she didn't know better, she'd think him befuddled.

"But it's warm, Elizabeth." He offered a hand, revealing a bony wrist. "Look, no gooseflesh."

"Someone might see you and think you unwell. Besides, it's going to rain."

He frowned, looking down at his bare legs and feet. "You must think me mad."

Elizabeth avoided his gaze. "I think no such thing."

"Ah, you're a good liar as well as kind!" He pursed his lips. "Unlike *her*—I cannot bear to say her name. No matter. It's been settled." He raised his arms toward the sky, toward the clouds. "At last there is some justice!"

Elizabeth's heart tripped. "Has there been word from the jury?"

"Which one?" Alphonse asked. "The jury for the syndics? Or for *her*?"

It took Elizabeth several more minutes to tease more words from Alphonse—he was too agitated—and a few more to force him inside the house. Then he collapsed onto a chair, shaking his head as the servants pretended not to notice his undressed state.

"Tell me, Uncle! What of the jury?" She prayed her testimony hadn't turned them against Justine.

"Very well, Elizabeth. Tomorrow eleven of the imprisoned syndics are to be executed. Treason, or so they say. They'll shoot them in Plainpalais. Kinder than hanging, they claim." He shook his head. "There but for the grace of God . . . though I'm uncertain if there is any grace to be found these days."

Elizabeth sank into the chair beside his. "What if they arrest you?" This was a possibility she'd refused to consider.

"They won't. I resigned as syndic—this should satisfy the revolutionary tribunal. But Ernest would say that if I need to sacrifice my life for the sake of a new world, so be it . . ." Alphonse began to sob like a child. "And if I am to be honest, I wouldn't mind. Perhaps I'd finally forget what *she* did to my boy. I'll never forgive myself for bringing *her* back here."

Elizabeth wrapped her arms around his frail shoulders. "The jury hasn't decided, have they? She may yet be found innocent."

"Not anymore." He dabbed at his eyes. "The ballots have been thrown; they were all black. She's confessed. They'll hang her tomorrow at dawn."

CHAPTER XIII.

"Soon after we heard that the poor victim had expressed a desire to see my cousin. My father wished her not to go; but said, that he left it to her own judgment and feelings to decide. 'Yes,' said Elizabeth, 'I will go, although she is guilty; and you, Victor, shall accompany me.'"

* * *

"SHE'S CONFESSED." It was this sentence Elizabeth recalled most as she fled Alphonse's side to confront Justine in prison. If she hadn't murdered William, why would she confess? It made no sense. Tiny doubts Elizabeth had ignored during the trial flared in her mind until she could think of nothing else. There'd been that slap Justine had given William that day, the locket found in her gown, her strange inability to produce her aunt as alibi.

Soon Elizabeth was nearly to the city gate, which would lead down toward the prison. It lay not far from Plainpalais, where William's body had been found and where Justine would hang once the sun rose. As Elizabeth ran, despair and anger mingled with shock, as though the cobblestones beneath her step had been turned to sand.

"Elizabeth! Wait!"

Elizabeth turned. Victor. He'd followed.

He pulled her against him. "Listen to me!"

"Let me go, Victor! I need to see Justine, find out the truth. You can't understand how I feel, how I hold myself responsible!"

"Elizabeth, I'm the one responsible! I know who the murderer is. The monster walks among us!"

Victor again, with his talk of monsters and responsibility. "Then produce him! If not now, when?" She struggled from his arms. "Didn't you hear your father? She's confessed! She murdered William! How shall I ever believe in human goodness again?"

"I know she confessed a lie."

Elizabeth snapped, "Then tell me who the murderer is!"

Victor's eyes grew large and dark in his ashen face. "I wish I could! I can't explain how or why I know this. But I do. I share your sorrow, but you can't understand my guilt. I know she's innocent. I know you don't believe her guilty."

"I didn't. But now that she's confessed—"

"I know you want to save her," he said, stroking her cheek. "Dear Elizabeth. Beloved Elizabeth. Elizabeth, my wife to be. Believe my assurances—Justine is innocent."

And now the old Victor was back, the one she'd adored as a child. The good Victor. The kind Victor. The Victor who wanted to save the world with science and chemistry and books. Not the Victor who slept with a pistol beneath his pillow or rocked like a madman in courtrooms. Sorrow and confusion churned within Elizabeth.

"I don't know what to believe!" she cried at last.

"But I do," he said, his tone ardent. "Let me accompany you. We'll visit Justine together." He caressed her cheek. "Beloved, you're trembling. Here, take my hand."

* * *

With Victor by her side, Elizabeth entered the desolate grey-stoned prison, avoiding the rows of family members awaiting the condemned syndics. A long stone hallway, lit by only a handful of candles, led to where Justine awaited. Her cell was dank, scented with urine and sweat, and scant of light; it could have been any season instead of summer. A relentless trickle of water pinged against the stones.

Once Elizabeth's eyes adjusted to the gloom, she beheld Justine sitting on some straw beneath a small barred window, which revealed a narrow patch of leaden sky. Her hands were manacled and her head rested on her knees. Justine slowly rose at Elizabeth's entry; it was then Elizabeth noticed her face was bruised, her lustrous silvery hair shorn beneath her stained linen cap. There was a hollow quality to her eyes. Haunted.

"They've beaten her," Elizabeth whispered to Victor. She'd never heard of such punishment in Geneva, which prided itself on its civility. But she'd also never heard of a woman condemned to die for the murder of a child.

Justine's manacles trailed as she staggered in their direction. When she could go no further, she threw herself at Elizabeth's feet.

"You confessed!" Elizabeth cried. "Why did you rob me of my last consolation? I relied on your innocence, and although I was wretched, I was not so miserable as I am now."

Justine looked up from the floor, steadily meeting Elizabeth's gaze. "Do you also believe me so very wicked?"

"I believed you guiltless until I heard you'd confessed."

"I did confess," Justine admitted, "but I confessed a lie. I confessed that I might obtain absolution from my church. I confessed so they'd leave me alone. May God forgive me!"

"But how could you lie so?" Elizabeth accused, now weeping herself. "You guaranteed your death!"

"I had no choice. Ever since the trial ended, I was besieged by guards and my confessor until I almost believed myself to be the monster they claimed. I confessed to a lie . . . and now I am truly miserable. But what else could I do?"

With this, Justine was overtaken by sobs of the most violent variety. As she wept, Elizabeth recalled Justine's devotion to her aunt, the many kindnesses she'd offered the Frankensteins over the years, her love of William. Any lingering doubts fled.

She couldn't have murdered him.

She offered Justine her hand. "Forgive me for having distrusted you, my friend. There must be something I can do. You perish on the scaffold? This cannot be!" She thought of impossible schemes that could never be. She imagined forging a letter to gain Justine's freedom. She imagined spiriting Justine to freedom. She imagined a miracle. "I would do anything to free you!"

Justine wiped her eyes, calmer now. "No one can free me. I do not fear to die, for that pang is past. God gives me courage to endure."

And, to Elizabeth's surprise, she believed Justine truly meant this. She understood she couldn't escape death, and now only yearned for closure in this world.

Victor must have made some sound from his corner, for Justine acknowledged him. "You are very kind to visit. I hope you do not believe me guilty?"

Victor hung his shoulders, twisting his hands. Elizabeth responded for him. "Victor is more convinced of your innocence than I was. Even when he heard you had confessed, he did not credit it."

Justine offered a wan smile. "I truly thank him. In these last moments, I feel the sincerest gratitude towards those who think of me with kindness."

A bald, stout guard approached. "It's time."

Elizabeth cried to Justine, "I cannot bear to leave you!"

"You must." Justine embraced Elizabeth. "Farewell, Elizabeth, my only friend. May heaven bless and preserve you; may this be the last misfortune you ever suffer! Live, and be happy, and make others so."

Elizabeth's last sight of Justine was her face: stricken, pale, resolved.

* * *

The guard led Elizabeth and Victor outside the prison, where they were confronted by a sky that appeared more ominous than it had been upon their arrival. Elizabeth made out a faint hammering from the direction of Plainpalais. Justine's scaffold—they were building it.

Victor appeared not to notice. "It's going to rain any minute. I'll get a carriage. Stay here beneath the eaves where it's dry."

But Elizabeth couldn't let him leave her. Not yet.

"How can we go on, knowing such evil exists? Knowing she'll die tomorrow?"

Victor kissed her brow, his lips cold. He murmured soft sounds, promises of better days. They offered scant comfort. Her tears released like a cloudburst. Yet as she wept, she recalled the families of the eleven syndics also to be murdered. How small her sorrows must be in their wake! "I know this is selfish of me, but I want my Justine."

Victor stroked her hair. "There's one thing we can do for Justine. One thing to bring her peace."

Elizabeth looked up from his sleeve, which had grown wet with her tears. "What would that be?"

He said with a disaffected air, "We can offer her the honor of burial beside my mother and William."

She drew away. "Your father will never allow this."

Victor's eyes burned bright. "Elizabeth, she *must* be buried there. Otherwise, her body will be abandoned in a pauper's grave. Someone will steal it."

Elizabeth's heart stuttered. "How would you know of this?"

He waved his arms. "Because . . . because I've heard talk of this. They'll desecrate her body. Crack open her ribs to remove her organs, harvest her bones. Peel her flesh, study her hunchback—"

She felt sick to her stomach. "Who could commit such horrors?"

"Medical students, chemists, natural philosophers. They call themselves resurrectionists—"

Elizabeth could listen no more. She fled, abandoning Victor outside the prison. But she didn't return home.

* * *

"Elizabeth? What are you doing here?" Henry exclaimed when she arrived at the door of the Clervals' shop; he was in the process of unlocking the gate for the afternoon. A soft plunk of rain hit her forehead. Another.

She didn't answer. Couldn't answer. She only knew she needed him. No matter: Henry didn't press, only led her inside once he'd opened the shop door.

"This is unexpected," he said, running his fingers through his unruly light brown hair. "Tea?"

"No, thank you."

She stood in the middle of the black and white tiled floor, her hands dangling with uselessness, as she took in the overstuffed shop: the books, the taxidermy owl, the printing press in the back of the long room, the displays of sextants and loupes and telescopes in their low glass cases, the bookshelves. How long had it been since she'd last visited the Clervals' shop? A year. More. Before they'd left for Lake

Como, before Ingolstadt. *"I love you. I always have . . ."* Suddenly she recalled Henry lying beside her in that shadowed, curtained bed in Lake Como; how empty her soul felt when she'd awakened to find him gone.

I must not think of this.

"I suspect you're here because of Justine," Henry said after an awkward moment. "I heard what happened."

"They're going to hang her! Murder her, really. I cannot bear it! On top of that Victor wants to bury her in the family tomb. He ranted that if he didn't, her body would be buried in a mass grave where it would be desecrated by . . . by . . . oh I can't say!"

Henry didn't rush to comfort her as he once might have. He avoided her stare as he set a stack of books inside a locked cabinet.

Elizabeth pressed, "You can't believe she's guilty? You saw how kind she was to William, how devoted to my aunt."

He finally met her eyes. "Elizabeth, I don't know what to think. She's been convicted."

"She confessed a lie to win absolution from a papist priest. Nothing more."

He gathered another pile of books. Rousseau, Milton, Wollstonecraft. He was dismissing her.

"Henry, how can you be so unfeeling? Of everyone I know, I'd thought you'd be sympathetic to her cause."

Unlike Victor who's mad. Victor who rants about monsters. But she couldn't think of Victor. Not now. Her anger toward Henry felt a gift. A distraction. She welcomed it.

He set the books down, his mouth tight. "I *am* sympathetic. But, in retrospect, I will admit there was something about Justine I found disturbing. A watchfulness. An eagerness."

"She was a good servant. A true friend to me."

"But there was also the way she worshipped your aunt. The hair, the accent. It seemed . . . unnatural."

"That's because my aunt was kind to her. She admired her."

"It wasn't only that. Justine's mother. It was peculiar she never visited Justine, that she'd hated her so much. Oh, I know Madame Moritz later tried to make amends. Still, what sort of mother does this without good cause? Perhaps there was something she knew that we didn't."

Elizabeth's mouth tightened, recalling Maria. "There are truths you don't know about the world. Truths you are fortunate to never experienced." An unfair accusation since he had no mother, but he'd forced her.

Henry didn't flinch. Nor did he back down. "I question, that's all. But now, with William gone . . ."

Elizabeth turned toward the door. "I should go home. Forgive me for disturbing you."

He flinched at her sarcasm. "No, don't leave, Beata. Not like this. I'm sorry!" He reached for her wrist. "Please don't leave—I'm begging you. I'm sorry to have been combative. Anyway, it's starting to rain—"

"I was mistaken to come here."

In all the years they'd known each other, they'd never argued, not like this. It was awful. Troubling. She felt worse than ever. Henry was usually the calm one, the considered one. If he didn't believe in Justine's innocence, what hope was there?

"No, I'm glad you came. I missed you, Beata. More than I can say. Again, I'm sorry! I lacked compassion."

And then he fell to his knees before her like a knight of old, as he had during that last dinner in Lake Como.

"Tell me the truth, I'm begging you, Beata. Tell me now, and I'll never ask you again. Are we arguing over Justine? Or because of what happened that night when I confessed I loved you? To punish me for esteeming you above all other women?"

Her head grew light, her heart full. *He loved her.* A year had passed since that night in Lake Como. Not once had he mentioned it, not even when she'd come to Ingolstadt and he'd sent her away. She'd done her best to convince herself she'd imagined his confession of love. She hadn't. A mixture of joy and sorrow churned within her. It felt a physical pain, a twisting. He loved her . . . but they could never be.

She choked out, "Henry, I don't know how to respond."

"Well, I do! I do love you beyond all others. I love you more than I ever thought I could love anything, even Heaven itself, God forgive me. I love you enough to betray my best friend in the entire world and his family. And even though you don't love me in return, I'll love you until my last breath."

There, he'd said it. There felt a finality to his words, an inevitability.

Once he'd finished speaking, he remained on his knees before her, eyes wide as though he'd shocked himself as much as he'd shocked her.

She took him in, this man she'd known for so many years, as though he was new and she was old, that all of her life had passed and she was examining her regrets, her joys. That night in Lake Como, when they'd lain together as though they were the only man and woman in the world. Her confession of her darkest secrets, to which he'd responded with more compassion than she'd shown herself. Those hours they'd shared stories and art, while Victor expounded about science and philosophy. King Arthur, *Paradise Lost*. Agrippa, Paracelsus. Looking back, she realized they weren't an enchanted circle of three. Even in Ingolstadt, they'd been two against one. Elizabeth and Henry. Not Elizabeth and Victor.

And then she realized: vow to Caroline or no, she couldn't be Victor's wife. She wanted Henry—she'd been a fool to deny the truth. Even if she did marry Victor, that night she'd shared with Henry doomed any happiness she might have found with Victor. She'd always wonder what might have been. Most of all, she couldn't marry Victor because she loved Henry. This hadn't changed since Lake Como; she'd only yearned to forget in the same way one would yearn to forget a sorrow too great to bear. For all of Henry's talk of fate, it hadn't mattered.

"I'm sorry," Henry said, struggling to his feet. "I can tell I've upset you. I apologize! I shouldn't have said what I did. I was wrong. Please forgive me. Don't tell Victor—I know your heart has been joined to his since you were a child. I've been so disloyal—"

Before she could reconsider, she raised herself on her toes and angled her mouth toward his. And then she was in his arms, and he in hers. Her throat released a low moan, a softening. His arms tightened about her. He bent to kiss the tears from her eyes, and then his lips were on hers, and their mouths opened as though they'd merge souls if they could.

This time when they kissed he tasted of coffee and regret, of past choices not taken. But things could be different, couldn't they? *Too late,* her mind answered.

Well, if it's too late, then let us have this day. This one time. And never again.

Once they'd broken away, she said, "I love you too."

Caroline, forgive me.

He reached for her with a long sigh. He kissed her again. A pause in their kiss to break away and lock the shop door. When he returned, he pulled her against him anew. She felt her bones grow soft, her body fluid. Electric.

Victor, forgive me.

Another kiss, this one more demanding as he led her toward the back of the shop. Toward the stairs that led up to the rooms he shared with his father.

"Is your father at home?" she murmured, leaning her head against his shoulder.

"Away. Montreux. Business. He'll be home later in the week."

"Servants?"

"Off today."

"We're alone."

"Yes, alone."

And then they were upstairs in his sitting room. Side-by-side on his soft blue chaise, with its piles of books and papers surrounding it like a pathway to wisdom. She'd rarely been inside his residence; usually Henry came to the Frankensteins, not the Frankensteins to Henry. She snuck a glance about the room: a tall fireplace bound in creamy marble flanked by even taller bookshelves; wide windows looking out onto the cobblestones of the Place du Bourg-de-Four; a half-closed pair of green-painted double doors she suspected led to his bedroom; a cup of half-drunk tea beside a chipped plate filled with abandoned toast crusts.

Her gaze returned to her hands, which Henry still held. He stroked her palm with his fingertips, as though awaiting her permission.

She reached for him, her mind silencing at last.

They did nothing that would leave Elizabeth changed from when she'd arrived at his door; she'd go to her wedding night innocent of the act that joined men and women as one. But Henry demonstrated his devotion in ways she'd never anticipated. She soon found herself lying against the chaise in her chemise, flesh bared, arms wrapped about his lean torso. His hands stroking the inside of her thighs until she thought she'd faint with longing. She pulled his body against hers, nudging him toward places she'd been told should remain untouched before wedlock.

"I love you more than you can imagine," he whispered, his breath warm against the length of her neck before he captured her mouth in a kiss. "I desire you more than I thought possible. But we shouldn't."

Another kiss, one that lasted longer than she believed possible.

"I know, Henry. But what if we . . . ?"

"Yes."

Yes. She shut her eyes. Lips upon breasts. Tongue against teeth. Desire and acceptance. Pleasure that made her gasp with surprise. Delight. And then, when it was over, she returned to her body with a shudder.

I'm alive, she thought, filled with wonder. *I live.*

But that wasn't the end of it. Once Henry stirred from her arms, he reached for a journal that laid on a side table, the one with the forgotten tea and toast. He offered a stub of a pencil just as the rain began in earnest. She inhaled the clean scent of wet leaves and clean air. The ping of water in a pot set under a roof leak.

"Draw me?" he asked, turning to a blank page. "I want to see the sort of art you make for yourself when you're alone. Please?"

And so she did, taking care to avoid any details that would reveal his identity to any who might discover the sketch. The curve of his buttocks. The dimple at the base of his spine. The soft forest of hair along his chest. His cupped hand against her breast.

Once she finished, she offered Henry her sketch. As he examined it, his face shifted into an expression she could not decipher. Was he disturbed? Would he tell her to destroy it? Find it vulgar?

A smile returned to his face; she let out a breath.

"It's beautiful, Beata. Like you. I'll treasure it forever, for it'll always remind me of this day."

He reached for her; the journal fell from his hands. She'd always lived in her emotions. Her obedience. But her body, how powerful it was! To know such pleasure! To understand that her body was capable of feeling this, of even creating life from it!

And then it all came back. Justine's body. Soon she would be dead. Hanged in Plainpalais. How could she have given way to love when Justine was suffering? When Henry believed her possibly guilty?

Ah, Justine, forgive me! How I wish I could save you!

Henry must have sensed her melancholy, for he asked, "What can I do to soothe your spirit?"

"Do you still believe in fate?" she asked.

He stroked her hair. She turned away. He did not press.

* * *

Hours later, Elizabeth woke to a sunrise so bright that the sky appeared drenched in scarlet. She was alone in a bed. Henry's bed. When had they ended up there? She vaguely recalled him leading her there in the middle of the night. (Or had she led him?) She should have gone home hours earlier. She hadn't—she couldn't bear to. Yet nothing had happened between her and Henry. Well, not really. On her wedding night, Victor would never suspect.

But I can't marry Victor. Not after this.

Her heart gave a skip. Victor. She'd run off from him. Was he worrying? What of Alphonse? She should have at least sent a note.

She pulled herself up against Henry's pillow. The lime-washed bedroom was small, dark, with only a small window looking out onto an alley. Velvet bed curtains the color of sun-lit amber, fringed in silk.

She drew the curtains open. No sign of Henry. Perhaps he was asleep on the chaise in the sitting room. Perhaps he'd gone down to his shop.

Instead of missing him, she was grateful for the solitude. She needed time to think. To decide what to do. A young woman was to be hanged —a young woman who'd confessed to a lie. A child had been murdered —a child who should be alive and sleeping in his bed. The Frankenstein family would never be the same. Nor would she and Victor. Victor was mad; she loved Henry; Henry loved her. Elizabeth knew this as much as she knew the sway of Henry's spine while she'd drawn him.

Then reason returned. What about her deathbed promise to Caroline? How could she humiliate the Frankensteins, who loved her as their own? She'd break Alphonse's heart, leave him without hope. (Strange she didn't consider Victor's.) Yet the peace she felt being with Henry . . . had she ever felt such before?

The bedroom door opened. Henry. He appeared freshly shaved and dressed, though his eyes were rimmed with shadows. Had he even slept?

"I've just returned from the Frankensteins," he said, offering her a cup of tea. He settled on the edge of the bed beside her. "I received a note from Victor in the middle of the night. No one knew where you'd gone, so I went and made some excuse you'd taken ill while visiting me, which your uncle accepted without a peep. To be honest, he appears more upset about the syndics."

It wasn't Alphonse Elizabeth was thinking of. "Victor?"

"He was also awake—I suspect no one there got any rest last night. And yes, he mentioned Justine's burial when your uncle was distracted." He stroked her cheek, gazing into her eyes. "I don't believe Victor's ill again, only distressed, as we all are. However, I do think there's wisdom to his proposal about Justine's grave." His brow knit. "When I was in Ingolstadt, I noticed practices that were . . . disturbing. I shan't speak of them, but Victor is right: we should intervene to protect Justine."

She shivered despite the warmth of the tea in her hand. What had Victor called these grave robbers? Resurrectionists. *"They'll desecrate her body. Crack open her ribs to remove her organs, harvest her bones. Peel her flesh . . ."* Elizabeth's stomach churned as she thought of poor Justine violated. Disassembled.

"My uncle will never allow her to be interred beside William."

"I know. But I've a plan."

The plan Henry laid out was simple: he'd accompany Justine's corpse to the Villa Lavenza and bury it in the small cemetery that hosted the graves of Elizabeth's mother and father. He'd arrange for a service in her faith to bring her soul peace. His father would need to understand his absence.

He rose from the bed, taking her emptied tea-cup. "It's nearly dawn. I'll arrange the carriage for Justine's transport. I'll write you when all is settled. Until then, adieu, Beata."

Her heart skipped a beat. Was this really farewell? Was he really leaving thus? Without any word of the future? None of the past?

She grabbed his forearm. "Take me with you, Henry."

He met her eyes. "You don't mean that."

"I do."

"You understand people will gossip. Worse."

"I don't care. I love you."

"I love you too, but what of Victor? Your uncle?"

She pressed her lips against his, which provided all the answer he required.

Once they'd parted, breathless and dizzy, he beamed a broad smile.

"We'll go to Italy together. We'll protect Justine. And then, if you'll have me, we'll wed."

He sank to the bed beside her. He kissed her more times than she could count, some of these light and feathery, others deep and soulful. In between these kisses, she'd tell him the truth about her sorrowful past, or as much as one could in such scant time. She'd confess the deathbed promise she'd made to Caroline to wed Victor, and that while she'd loved Victor then, she didn't love him now. Not like that. She'd tell Henry everything, even about Maria—he'd understand, help her find forgiveness. In time, they'd find a way to make amends to the Frankensteins, to Victor. To show gratitude while honoring their hearts. After all, Elizabeth couldn't imagine Caroline wanting her to wed Victor if she loved someone else, vow or no. She'd no longer allow herself to feel cursed.

But now there was only Henry's beloved face before hers and his unanswered proposal.

"Yes, we'll wed," she said, embracing him with the full of her body. *Yes.*

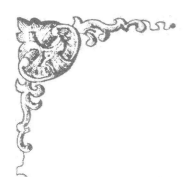

VOLUME THREE

THE MURDERESS

* * *

Twelve hours earlier

CHAPTER I.

"Justine also was a girl of merit, and possessed qualities which promised to render her life happy: now all was to be obliterated in an ignominious grave; and I the cause!"

* * *

ON THE MORNING of Justine Moritz's birth, the doctor had taken one look at the infant's twisted spine and announced her life would be cursed—this was a tale Madame Moritz related when dissatisfied, which was often. Now, as Justine watched Elizabeth and Victor depart her cell, she considered how correct the doctor had been. She'd told them, "I do not fear to die, for that pang is past. God gives me courage to endure the worst." How could she have said such tripe?

She'd lied to Elizabeth. Lied to Victor. Lied because she wanted it so badly to be true. The truth was she was terrified to die; so terrified that her bladder felt as though it would release at any moment; so terrified that she could hear her blood in her ears as it roared from her heart through her veins. Nor did she take any solace in her last confession, for this, too, was a lie. That absolution the priest offered was false— now she was more miserable than ever. She'd never harm William. She'd loved him. No, more than that: she'd adored him. That slap was the only time she ever harmed him. She'd regretted it immediately and apologized profusely. "I'm your friend," she said. "Forgive me? I'll never do that again. I promise."

But oh, that confession! It was false, along with the absolution she gained. This tormented her: where would her soul reside for eternity?

Alone in her barred and locked cell, Justine staggered toward the rancid pile of hay that served as her bed, dragging her manacles behind her. She curled against the hay and tucked her thumb inside her mouth. Her thumb smelled like stale bread. Her ribs ached from where they'd beaten her. Her eyes stung with tears. Scalp itched where they'd shaved her. Despite the bravado of her last speech to Elizabeth, Justine felt very alone and very scared. Absolution or no, God's grace felt very far away.

She squeezed her eyes shut. Before her, she saw Elizabeth and Victor when they'd arrived in her cell, their concerned faces—no, their terrified faces—as they approached. Victor had appeared so different from when she'd last seen him, like a skeletal wraith; Elizabeth was thinner than ever, her sea-blue eyes enormous in her face. They'd been truly shocked at her condition. And then there was the stench of her cell, the water dripping. They'd probably never been inside a prison before. Neither had Justine until two months earlier.

Now she was a murderess by name, if not by deed. Hated by all. Alone. Unloved. Friendless save for Elizabeth.

Outside her cell, Justine heard the rain begin, its soft percussion mingling with moans. The syndics—their cells were next to hers. They, at least, had the coin to guarantee soft beds and clean food; Elizabeth had only been able to send so much to Justine. The syndics would die before her on the morrow in a hail of bullets. Then they'd hang her, a mark of her crime. She could hear distant banging from Plainpalais, where they were building the scaffold. *Her* scaffold. Her heart raced.

Forgive me Lord. I know not what to do. I confessed a lie.

For all of her mother's faults, Madame Moritz had been devout, and this had affected Justine deeply; the prospect of death without divine solace terrified her. She must find another way to prepare for death. And then she knew: she'd make her own confession, even if this wasn't the way of her church.

Justine crawled onto her knees. She clenched her hands. She began, lips dry against her fingers.

"Dear God, this I confess with the hope of winning Your favor and forgiveness. I was born twenty-two years ago in the village of Belrive to a gravedigger and his wife, both whom have passed onto Your light and glory . . ."

As Justine whispered, all of her life rushed before her, brash and bitter. Her first breath to her father's death; her mother's hatred to the loss of her three siblings; and finally, the most significant day of her life: New Year's Day two years earlier. That was the day she'd spied Elizabeth and Henry in the Cimetière des Rois near Caroline's tomb.

"Lord, that day led to the greatest joy I'd ever known," she continued, "as well as my greatest regret—"

The lock to her cell clanked; she looked up. A guard, the kind one. The only one who pitied and believed her, though she never learned his name. He was bald, greying, squat. He held a tin plate, from which an unappetizing stench drifted.

"Praying?" he asked as he opened her cell door.

She nodded, her throat tight. "I hang in the morning."

(How strange to say such a thing! Like she was speaking of a carriage ride or a walk.)

"I heard, Mademoiselle. You confessed." A long pause; Justine awaited a censure that never arrived. "If the rain remains heavy, perhaps you'll gain another day."

(Another day? For what? To fear?)

He offered the plate. The food on it appeared rancid: a slice of fatty meat, boiled potatoes. "Dinner, though I imagine you have no appetite."

"Leave it on the stool, thank you."

Once he left, she ignored the plate. She continued.

"Back to that New Year's Day of 1792, when I saw Elizabeth in the cemetery," she said, her whispers inaudible over the rush of rain, the syndic's cries, the banging from Plainpalais. "I have so much to say that no one knows, Lord. I pray you forgive me . . ."

* * *

That New Year's Day had initially promised to be inauspicious. After avoiding Henry and Elizabeth in the cemetery, Justine had visited Caroline's grave as she often did. She'd been a fool to go on New Year's day, when so many others would come. A deserted cemetery was a welcoming cemetery. Luckily Elizabeth hadn't spied her.

Once she was certain no one watched, Justine embraced Caroline's statue. She noticed several small drops of red on the snow beside the vase. Blood.

If it hadn't been snowing, Justine would have contemplated this peculiarity, but the snow didn't encourage contemplation. In addition, her spine ached from the cold along with her feet; she was wearing a pair of boots Caroline had given her four years earlier, though with twice-mended soles. Therefore, instead of continuing through the cemetery toward Plainpalais, as she often did to prolong her time away from her mother, Justine departed the cemetery. This was a choice that would prove fateful.

Up the steep hill she'd walked, all the way toward the Geneva city gate. Her chest grew tight from exertion, the icy air slicing her lungs. She needed to get before a fire before her chilblains worsened. Luckily, the guard at the gate didn't question her as he usually did.

"1792!" he greeted. He waved her through after belching without apology. "New year, Mademoiselle!"

"New year indeed, Monsieur." What was a new year to her? Only one day leading into yet another. Now that she'd reached the grand age of nineteen, Justine understood how days piled into weeks and weeks into years, each stacked upon another without remorse. Nothing would ever change in her life—or so she believed.

Once past the Geneva gate, Justine continued toward the arsenal and city hall, which were decked in the flags of France, Switzerland, and the Republic of Geneva. Wet boots or no, her steps lingered near the Rue des Granges, where the Frankensteins resided; they didn't live far from the Catholic church her mother favored.

Suddenly it all came back: she'd seen Henry Clerval accompanying Elizabeth Lavenza, who appeared more radiant than ever. Despite the space of three years, Justine had immediately recognized the Frankensteins' ward. How could Justine not take note of Elizabeth's exquisite golden hair and luminous blue eyes that always appeared too angelic for the world? The tremulous smile that accompanied her bell-like laughter? She hadn't responded to Elizabeth's greeting. She couldn't bear to, for she felt so reduced in station. Anyway, it wasn't Elizabeth Justine yearned to behold. While she was fond of Elizabeth and Victor —how could she not be?—it was Caroline she adored.

Justine's eyes clouded. If only Caroline still lived! She'd give anything to view that soft smile of welcome the Frankenstein matriarch offered everyone, whether they were well-to-do or a beggar. Or a fatherless hunchback girl, such as herself. But Elizabeth had survived— beautiful Elizabeth, kind Elizabeth. Perfect Elizabeth. Elizabeth whom everyone loved.

It was your fault Caroline died, a voice inside her whispered. *You could have saved her.*

"Stop thinking of this," Justine muttered. "You're a fool."

Better to accept what was lost. Hadn't the revolution of 1789 taught her as much? Neither God nor man could stop death from arriving any more than they could hold back the tide. Best to accept things as they were, not to yearn for better. This had been her rationale for ignoring the letters Elizabeth sent after Justine's departure from the Frankensteins. Madame Moritz initially seemed so eager for Justine's company, so filled with remorse, that Justine had reluctantly believed her. At last, her mother loved her! At last her mother saw her as more than the sum of a deformed spine and rabbit-pale eyes!

Justine was wrong.

Soon after her return home, she discovered her mother believed God had punished her three siblings with cholera. "It's because I treated you poorly, Justine. I beg your forgiveness." As the sole surviving child, Justine had no choice but to work like a dog for her mother, especially after they left Belrive for cheaper lodgings in Geneva. Soon Madame Moritz's apologies turned to fists: "I am tested like Job. I wish God had taken you instead of the others!" Yes, Justine could have returned to the Frankensteins, but to return felt a humiliation. Yet again, she'd failed to win her mother's love.

Justine's memories ached. They teased. Had she really lived with a great family in a great house for five years? Been taught to read and educated in other ways? Gained friends of a sort? Worst of all, she hadn't learned all she could there, or become polished in a manner that would have afforded her entry into a finer world. Caroline's premature death had left Justine an unfinished creation, forgotten and uncared for.

No matter. Now Justine had a real mother, not an imaginary one.

A mother who still despised her.

And then, on that snowy first day of 1792, Justine knew she'd never return to her mother. She couldn't. Better to find her way alone in the world.

"I'll run away," she decided. But how did one run away from home? This wasn't something she'd considered.

To gain time to think, Justine headed toward an inn on the Grand-Rue. She had a few coins—enough to buy a coffee with change to spare. Justine sipped the steaming beverage slowly, ignoring drunken French soldiers laughing over a round of *bouillotte*, a card game popular from the revolution. Once her stomach was fortified and mind cleared, she left the inn resolved. She'd find a coach, no matter its destination. Anything to leave her mother.

By then, the afternoon was gone, the sky the color of tarnished pewter. The coach stand on the Place du Bourg-de-Four was deserted save for a woman wearing an oversized silk toque despite the inclement weather. She clutched a small spaniel in her arms, who yipped at Justine's approach.

"The coach isn't coming." The woman's tones were clipped with impatience.

"Are you certain, Madame?"

A dismissive tut. "I've been waiting since the snow started, Mademoiselle."

"Why not go someplace dry?"

"Because I couldn't bear to go inside the inn. Those soldiers! Nor could I bear to go home. It felt so . . . hopeless."

This Justine understood too well. *What shall I do?* Then she realized: it didn't matter where she went as long as she didn't return home—and quickly before her mother marked her absence.

Heart pounding, Justine's boots slid in the snow as she rushed away. The gates were still open, the road from Geneva clear. Down she went, skidding on the hill, clutching the stone wall to keep from falling. She'd take shelter in Plainpalais, hide beneath trees until the storm stopped. Then she'd head toward the lake, where someone would row her to the other side in her quest for freedom. Yet, instead of heading directly to Plainpalais, she found herself back inside the cemetery again, as though Caroline herself had beckoned.

By then, the bells were chiming six from St. Peter's. How eerie they sounded, like they'd grown weary of tolling for humanity's follies! As Justine approached Caroline's tomb, she saw a solitary man on the promenade holding a book. As he passed by, she saw he was tall and lanky. He wore a loose great coat that dropped past his thighs. Dark brown hair on the longish side. Delicate nose. He was reading as he walked despite the snow and lack of light.

After a furtive glance in his direction, Justine sank to her knees before the monument. She pressed her fingers along the slim letters carved into the tomb, recalling Caroline's kindness, Caroline's generosity. The blood she'd seen earlier was gone; it must have melted into the earth. She'd sit a moment, then decide what to do.

"It cannot be! Is that you?"

The reading man. He'd returned. His tenor voice was wonder-filled, ecstatic. Justine sidled from the monument, cold air catching in her lungs. He was striding toward her. From the vigor of his step, he was a young man, probably around Victor or Henry's age.

Without understanding why, she broke into a run, her skirts tangling about her ankles. She slammed into the gravel.

Before she could rise to her feet, a pair of legs clad in simple leather shoes and brown trousers arrived before her eyes. His book dangled from his hand.

"You're not who I expected," he said in a flat voice. "For a moment, I thought you were a ghost, though I knew it was ridiculous. Are you injured, citizen?"

Citizen. Was he a revolutionary?

"No."

"The palms of your hands. They're bloody."

"Just scraped. They're fine." Despite his lack of uniform, she was about to ask "Are you a soldier?" She didn't. Better to ignore, to pretend otherwise.

"Are you sure?"

"Quite sure. I must hurry."

Yet she couldn't seem to move. The gentleman knelt by her side.

"Let me help you. The city gate is already locked for the night."

"The gates don't lock until ten."

"Not today," he answered.

"Because it's New Year's?"

The young man chuckled softly. "You're clever." Was his tone sarcastic? Justine couldn't tell. Then he smiled, causing her to suppress a gasp. She'd never seen someone so handsome. He resembled a poet, a hero from a book of French fairy tales. His dark eyes were warm yet sensitive. When they met Justine's, she felt like she'd faint.

His smile dropped. "Your spine! You're injured. We must find you a doctor, citizen. Someplace to sleep. Come, I'll help you."

Justine flushed. "I'm not injured. I bid you good night." She rolled onto her back, brushed off her shoulders. She'd find someplace to take shelter for the night. Perhaps a hayloft, a barn. She'd decide where to go in the morning.

She managed to rise. One step, two . . .

"Wait!" He reached for her wrist. "I beg your forgiveness, citizen."

Justine turned back. "For what?"

"I've caused you embarrassment." He pointed to her spine, his other hand still lingering on hers. "You were born that way. A hunchback. You bear no responsibility for your malformation any more than I do for mine."

Malformation? Justine brushed off his hand. "Again, I bid you good night, citizen."

She emphasized the final word, setting a sarcastic bent to the syllables. She strode away.

"Come back!" He ran to keep up with her. "I insulted you, didn't I?"

She glanced over her good shoulder, thrust out her chin. "You only stated the truth. Yes, I am a hunchback."

Again, his hand on her wrist. "Stop, please!"

His tone bore a familiarity that tore Justine in a place she couldn't name. It brought up memories of Sophie and her talk of love poppets, Caroline and Alphonse in tender moments, Elizabeth with Victor, Henry when he addressed Elizabeth. No one had ever spoken to her in such a manner, not even her father, the best and kindest man she'd ever known.

Her eyes stung. "Leave me alone!"

"You're not the only one with bodily concerns. Look at me! I am also an invalid—well, *was* one."

"You want my sympathy?"

"I do." He offered his book to her. Milton. *Paradise Lost*—Henry had taught it during their lessons.

"You're a student. Not a soldier."

He nodded. "Let me offer it to you as a gift, citizen."

"No, thank you." Books were expensive. What would he want in exchange?

"Then I shall read for you instead." He recited:

"Should God create another Eve, and I
Another Rib afford, yet loss of thee
Would never from my heart; no no, I feel
The Link of Nature draw me: Flesh of Flesh,
Bone of my Bone thou art, and from thy State
Mine never shall be parted, bliss or woe."

As she listened, her heart sped like a rabbit she once held.

"What is your name?" he asked once he finished reading.

She lied though she was uncertain why. "Julie. What's yours?"

He smiled darkly. "My name is Nobody, if I'm to believe my family."

She laughed. She recalled Henry reading the Odyssey to her. It was a sign. "Like in Homer?"

"Ah, you're well read! I'll try again. My name is Adam, like the first man."

"More likely Lucifer from your book. 'Better to reign in hell than to serve in Heaven' and all that." How bold she felt! Clever, like when she was trying to earn Caroline's approval.

He met her eyes. "If I'm Lucifer, you're an angel."

"I'm not as simple as you believe." She laughed again until he set his hand on her cheek. Instead of slapping him away, she pressed against him like a cat—she couldn't resist. How soft his gloves were! They must have been sewn of the finest kid.

"No more jokes," he said, cupping her chin. "My name is Jean."

"Jean," she repeated, unable to pull from his gaze. Her father's name had been Jean. Surely this was another sign.

"We should find a place to sleep, Julie—the gates won't open for hours. Come with me. I'll protect you."

"I shouldn't."

Jean set a hand over his heart. "I promise not to harm your body or your soul, if you believe in such claptrap." A rakish grin. "I also promise if you remain here, you'll freeze by morning."

"I was going to take a boat."

"No one is sailing tonight. Not in this cold. Come."

She couldn't argue with Jean's logic. Nor did she want to. He reminded her of someone she knew. His straight nose. The way his chestnut hair dipped over his brow. She couldn't remember, though. So she followed him, and he kept his promise: he paid for a room at an inn.

Nor did he touch her. Still, when she woke beside him in the morning, hair tangled and breath foul, her fears returned.

"You won't harm me?" she asked as they pressed forehead to forehead.

"Never." He ran a finger along the twist of her spine. "Perhaps this is where God meant to give you wings," he said, his voice husky.

She pulled away. "I should go. My mother will be worried." She wouldn't run away. Not after meeting Jean. Not yet.

"Stay another moment, Julie. Please. There's something about the way you speak, the way you dress your hair that reminds me of someone I lost. Your mother will understand once you explain the gates closed early because it was New Year's."

"She'll wonder where I spent the night."

"Tell her you took shelter in a hayloft." Another stroke of his finger, this time along the rise of her humped shoulder. "You don't have to tell her about me. It'll be our secret."

She drew a shaky breath, overwhelmed by desire and something else. Hope. She hadn't felt hope since Caroline's death.

As they'd parted, Jean said, "I'll be at the cemetery again at four, if you can meet. I'll have time after class." And he *was* there—somehow Justine found a way to escape her mother, to find freedom without running away. It helped that Justine had purchased a fresh bottle of laudanum; her mother was too drugged to slap her anew.

Liberty! It was within her heart. Her mind. Revolution! Now she understood—*this* was what the soldiers meant when they sought it for their country. But first you had to begin with the individual. The citizen. Or a man named Jean.

From there on, Justine met Jean every afternoon by Caroline's memorial. They'd walk together, his hand resting lightly on her elbow. (Who knew an arm could hold so much sensitivity?) He spoke of books he was reading, of events taking place in the world, of the impact he yearned to make once he finished university. She was elusive when she described her life, careful to avoid mention of her mother's hatred and her siblings' deaths. Nor did she speak of the terrible loss she'd suffered when Caroline died, or of the Frankensteins. Each day, their hands crept closer, and so by the time they finally pressed their lips together for the first time, it was spring and the air smelled balmy with hope. When Jean had lain with her in a flower-dappled field one evening, he'd been so gentle she'd wept. He didn't take her innocence though she offered it. Instead, they spent the entire night kissing and caressing.

As they lay together, he vowed:

> *"Flesh of Flesh,*
> *Bone of my Bone thou art, and from thy State*
> *Mine never shall be parted, bliss or woe."*

Only good could come from this, she decided. For once, her body could bring her joy, not shame. Even if they never wed, he'd mold her as Caroline had intended. He'd leave her a finer Justine. A wiser Justine. He'd give her books and kisses and caresses. She'd offer him a gift she'd shared with no one in her life save her father and Caroline: love.

Alas, it was this love that would curse Justine to a dank jail cell outside Plainpalais. Her fate was set by the time Alphonse Frankenstein brought her to live anew in his home after Madame Moritz's death.

"You," she said when she'd seen Jean emerge in the Frankensteins' hall the morning after her return. "It can't be." But it was.

"What are you doing here?" her suitor demanded, his face covered in soap; he'd been yelling for hot water.

"I'm in service to the family," she mumbled. How different Jean appeared! A stranger. An aristocrat. "The Frankensteins."

"You work for my father." His neck reddened and chest collapsed. Suddenly she realized why Jean appeared so familiar. He resembled Caroline, that's who. "You mustn't say anything," he whispered, panicked. "Not to my father or brothers. Nor to the rest of my family when they return from Lake Como, Julie."

"Justine," she corrected, shamefaced. "My name is Justine. I'm here to help the mademoiselle with William when they return."

"My brother William." He bit the soft of his lip. "I suppose I should confess the truth too. My name is Ernest."

Ernest the middle brother? The one who lived in the Alps because of his lungs? Justine had never met him. She recalled Caroline fretting over Ernest before her death, upset Alphonse refused to send for him; by then Caroline was raving with fever, unable to understand they were protecting Ernest from a similar fate.

"It won't do for you to address me by my Christian name here,"

Ernest continued. "My father is impatient with me these days." A rueful smile. "I haven't exactly won his favor."

Justine's cheeks burned. "It seems we've both had secrets."

She recalled how he'd felt lying beside her in the field outside Geneva, like they were the only two people in the world. Now the world rushed in.

"I must go, citizen." He gave her a quick peck on her forehead after looking up and down the hall.

"Likewise, citizen."

"Oh, and when you have a moment, tell Sophie to bring me hot water." Then he'd left her alone in the hallway bearing a pile of linens and a huge secret.

Days later when Elizabeth returned from Lake Como, she said, "I heard you met Ernest while I was away. I do hope he wasn't unpleasant! He's still not accustomed to us after being gone for so long. Fortunately his health has quite recovered. It's best you avoid him unless you relish discussing politics for hours." But Justine wouldn't be deterred. Instead, something hot and strong rose inside her. Something sly. Something she'd never experienced despite all of her mother's accusations.

I'll force him to marry me. God will forgive me.

With this, Justine sensed a shadow fall across her—a shadow that would bring only death.

CHAPTER II.

"She then related that, by the permission of Elizabeth, she had passed the evening of the night on which the murder had been committed at the house of an aunt at Chêne, a village situated at about a league from Geneva."

* * *

WHEN JUSTINE REACHED this part of her confession, heat rose along her breasts, her cheeks. Shame. How could God forgive her if she couldn't forgive herself? Was this even possible?

She gazed up toward the slant of a window as though it might hold the answer she required. The sky was lightening; the rain had stopped; the hammering had ceased. *Not much longer.* She glanced down at the rough black tunic she wore, which they gave her after she'd been condemned. Her hands, still folded in prayer.

I must trust in God's mercy. There's no time for anything else.

"Heavenly Father," she continued, speaking more quickly. "What next happened is the most painful to confess, for it is here I turned my sinful desires into deed . . ."

* * *

Once she learned her beloved was Ernest Frankenstein, Justine spent the remainder of the day plotting how to marry him. After all, Elizabeth was to wed Victor. Like Elizabeth, Justine was an orphan favored by the Frankensteins. But, unlike Elizabeth, she did not have noble blood. Nor had she been raised by Caroline as her ward.

After much turmoil, Justine decided on a path she knew to be immoral. That night, she found her way into Ernest's bed while the entire house slept.

"I love you," she murmured.

While Ernest didn't respond in kind with his words, he did respond with his body—he hadn't the will to turn her away.

For the first time in her life Justine was happy, for she was loved. Even if Ernest never declared as much, didn't his lips confess this? His hands? His fingers? They swam through her long silvery hair, pulling her face toward his, her hips against his thighs until she lost herself in a pleasure she'd never known existed. "You're like moonlight," he murmured against her flesh. "An enchantress." His love was an untainted love, unlike the love of her father, which had been hindered by her mother's disapproval, or the love of Caroline, which Justine had never fully gained.

Only good can come from this, she told herself. *He loves me. He must.*

Yet some things could not be escaped. Some nights after they'd lain together panting and sweaty and whispering each others' names in the dark, she'd return to her room and hear William squirming in the bed beside hers. She'd recall Caroline's screams when she labored to bring him into this world, the blood seeping from her nether regions, the afterbirth. All that to create life—God should have thought of a better way. A kinder way, for it was unfair the female should suffer so; she'd overheard Victor say as much.

And so Justine and Ernest's affair continued. Months passed, comprised of nights that felt endless, days that left Justine giddy with hope. By the time spring arrived, Ernest admitted he loved her too. He gave her gifts of ribbons and marzipan, a lace fichu. Justine hummed as she went about her chores, sleep-deprived but blissful. Elizabeth noticed Justine had grown shadows beneath her eyes and said as much. "I hope William isn't keeping you awake all night." Justine only smiled in answer, for she was holding a secret too precious to share.

Then one day the secret took shape in a manner she hadn't expected. Hadn't Ernest been careful not to spend inside her during their intimacies?

"I think I'm with child," she announced when she next came to his bed; by then it was May 1794 and Victor was still ill in Ingolstadt with brain fever.

Ernest blanched in the dark. "How far?"

She counted on her fingers. "Four months?" Indeed, her stomach was slightly rounded where it had been concave; she could no longer deny this. She again thought of Caroline as she labored. Her screams. The blood.

It will be different for me. It must.

"*Merde.* This cannot be. We were careful."

He turned and ignored her until she'd had no choice but to creep back to her bed where William slumbered, sweet-breathed and innocent. She kissed the boy's forehead, wondering what it would be like to have a child of her own. Trying not to think of her mother. The slaps. The bruises. The insults. *Ernest will marry me*, she told herself. *He just needs time to get over the shock.* This was what was meant to happen, even if it wasn't the same as Elizabeth's engagement to Victor. This was what Ernest needed to be taken seriously by his father. Surely Caroline would approve.

The following morning, Ernest was nowhere to be found in the mansion. Justine located him in a tavern on the Grand-Rue; she heard his voice ring out when she was strolling with William across the square. When she returned to the tavern later, he was still there, smelling strongly of ale and sweat. He and several soldiers were arguing over politics.

Justine sidled up to him, praying no one would consider her a prostitute. Ernest reluctantly acknowledged her after she hung on his sleeve long enough. While she waited, she felt the first stirrings of life inside her womb; they fluttered like butterfly wings. "It lives," she breathed to herself in wonder; she couldn't yet think of the baby as a boy or girl.

"I'd thought we'd speak later," he grunted. "Can't you see I'm busy?"

She shyly took his hand. "I missed you. Did you miss me?"

He grimaced as he took another gulp of ale. "How do you know it's mine?"

Justine blinked away tears. "Of course the baby's yours. I was a maiden until we lay together."

"What of afterward? You could have been with others."

Justine's hand ached with the urge to slap the words from his lips.

The next day, when William was too demanding during lunch, she slapped him instead.

"I'm sorry. So sorry," she wept after her hand lashed out and the child wailed. "Please don't tell anyone. Here, have a sweet. I'll never do that again. Truly." But the damage was done. Worse, Elizabeth had witnessed her loss of temper.

"Is all well? You look tired, Justine."

"Forgive me," she said, bending down to comfort William. "I'm so sorry! I don't know what's wrong with me today."

But she *did* know—she'd never be able to tell the truth to Elizabeth, who was so pure of heart.

"I'm sorry," Justine vowed to both William and Elizabeth, wiping her eyes. Then she saw Ernest in the hall and rushed off, claiming she needed to bring him clean linens.

"What do you want from me?" he demanded once they were alone in his room. "Money? Trinkets? Is that what this is about? I can't marry you, if that's what you're thinking. I'm only seventeen. My father will never allow it."

Seventeen? He was five years younger than she was. She'd thought him nearly Victor's age.

"I thought you loved me," she said once she recovered.

"Perhaps I do—well, if one believes in the love that joins bodies as well as spirits. But I don't believe in the bourgeois institution of marriage," he said, refusing to meet her eyes. "Love is a universal force. It shouldn't be set into shackles with institutions such as matrimony. It should be allowed to grow and shift as required." He pulled a book from his desk, pointing to a dog-eared page. "Rousseau writes, 'Man is born free, and everywhere he is in chains.' I won't live in chains, Justine!"

She slumped onto his bed. "What am I to do?"

"I don't know." He flipped idly through his book. "We could leave it at an orphanage when the time comes. No one need ever know, if we're careful."

"I'm not abandoning our baby!"

"Well, it's *your* baby really—you can't prove it's mine, though I suppose I can give you money. Tell me how much is required. I'll find a way. I also have some gambling debts I need to retire; I'll use those as an excuse."

"I don't want money!"

"What do you want then?"

"Love," she sobbed. "A husband. A child."

"Well, I can't help you with those." His temper rose in a way that shocked her; she understood why Alphonse found him so difficult. Ernest threw his book at the wall, then grimaced as though her physical form repulsed him. "If you don't mind, I'd like to get dressed. Leave!"

As Justine stumbled through the remainder of her day she thought, *Who is this monster I loved?* She'd believed Ernest a man, not barely out of childhood. Someone must be able to help. But who? She ran down the possibilities. Cook, Sophie, Elizabeth. *No, no, definitely no.*

As soon as she'd finished her dinner, which tasted like sawdust, she remembered. That midwife in Chêne, whom Sophie had mentioned during Caroline's pregnancy. "You can't miss her cottage," she'd said. "It's set beside a foot bridge and has a bright green door."

Before she could change her mind, Justine asked Elizabeth if she could have the evening off. "I received a letter, Mademoiselle. My aunt in Chêne. She's poorly."

Before Justine departed, she offered William a kiss. "I'll tuck you in bed later, dormouse," she said, truly remorseful. He turned his face away. "I don't like you anymore, Justine."

* * *

By the time Justine approached the midwife's cottage in Chêne, the afternoon sky had shifted into that absurdly bright cobalt preceding twilight. Her heart pounded until she thought it would fly from her chest; beneath it, she imagined the baby squirming in her womb.

The midwife's cottage was exactly as Sophie had described years earlier yet somehow more, but wasn't life always like that? Someone could tell you what to expect, but nothing could prepare you for the experience. The green-doored cottage appeared to be from a fairy tale, like the ones Caroline read. The bloom of a dark red rose pressed against the window glass, as though lured by the warmth within. To the side of the door, two tall wooden planters spilling fragrant herbs. The center of the door was marked by a brass knocker shaped like a lion's head. It glinted with the last gold rays of the day.

Justine crossed the bridge and sank beneath the arbor, too distressed to pull the knocker.

"Do I know you?" the midwife greeted after she overheard Justine sobbing on her doorstep. She wasn't what Justine expected. The midwife's face appeared ageless, with dark hair immaculately curled down to her waist, like an old engraving from one of Victor's books. Her attire was no less remarkable. She was adorned in an ecru muslin gown suitable for summer. The bodice was gathered with a pale gold ribbon beneath her high, firm breasts. When she moved, the subtle scent of lavender wafted from the folds of her gown.

"No, you don't know me," Justine replied once she'd found her tongue. "But I've been told of you."

Once the green door shut behind them, Justine stood awkwardly in the center of a neatly attired sitting room, uncertain whether she'd happened into Paradise or the devil's den. A tall mirror, framed in gold, hung on one side of the fireplace. It was dwarfed by a glass cabinet filled with bottles and jars, each labeled in a neat hand. Pennyroyal, mercury, cohosh, belladonna. A thick-furred grey cat wound about Justine's ankles, persistent in its affections.

"Ignore the cat. He's a nuisance, but I can't turn him out. As for you . . ." The midwife granted Justine an appraising look. "You're in trouble."

Justine broke down. "Forgive me, Madame! I didn't know where to go!"

"I've heard this before."

"I've been told you sell love poppets?"

The midwife gave a little smile. "Let me guess. Your gentleman no longer loves you, and you want to win him back now that he's left you with a belly-full of child."

Justine nodded, her nose dripping like William's when he was in a temper.

The midwife laughed softly, which only set Justine to sobbing harder. "You're not the first to come to me with such concerns."

"I suppose I've been a fool."

The midwife caressed Justine's cheek; again, that scent of lavender. "Not a fool. A sweet, innocent child. And on top of that, a hunchback." Her tone gentled. "Life has not been easy for you, has it?"

"I don't want to have a baby." And this was the truth; she recalled slapping William earlier that day, her mother slapping her, Caroline shrieking in labor. "But if I am to be a mother, I want my baby's father to love me. Not to abandon me. To cherish me again . . . as he . . . as he once did. Ah, how sorrowful I am!"

"Shush, child. Listen to me. Those poppets don't bring love; they only offer confidence to those who yearn for it. But I can offer you something better. Freedom." A knowing pause. "You'll need to keep it a secret."

Justine immediately understood what the midwife meant. *I shouldn't.* Then she recalled a girl she knew who'd had a child out of wedlock. She'd ended up living on the street, where her baby was found frozen beside her one winter morning. Later, the girl expired from the French pox.

After a long moment, Justine asked, "Will it hurt?'

"No more than your monthly issue. Though it depends . . ." She raised Justine's apron to pat her belly. "How far along are you? If it's too late, I can't help you."

"Three months? Four?" Now Justine couldn't be sure—or didn't want to be.

The midwife nodded approvingly. "That's good. Easier."

"Will it cost much?"

"How much do you have on you?"

Do it. It's for the best.

Before she could change her mind, Justine offered what money she'd brought. The midwife warned, "You must never speak of this to anyone. If you do, I'll curse you and make your life a misery. Understood?"

Oh, Justine understood. Too well.

By the time Justine departed, she was in possession of two small bottles whose ingredients the midwife refused to divulge—"What if you're a French spy?"—along with instructions to drink the first bottle when she reached home and the second if she hadn't begun to bleed by morning. Justine couldn't wait. She drank the first one as soon as she crossed the bridge from Chêne. A mile later, she felt nothing, so she drank the second. This one tasted fouler than the first; she clenched her jaw to avoid retching.

By then it was night, and she approached the final bridge before Geneva, where a host of soldiers awaited. She slowed her step, trying to make herself appear as small as possible. *Don't stop me,* she prayed. *I must get home.* Her womb had begun to clench in a manner that felt more like a vise than the result of menstruation.

"Citizen, halt! Where are you bound?" the tallest of the soldiers demanded.

"Geneva," she explained, gritting her teeth. "I live there."

"Have you papers?"

"I hadn't known I needed such."

"New law."

"I'll know better next time. Forgive me, I must pass. My mistress awaits." The first trickle of blood oozed between her legs. Or was it urine? She hadn't released water since she'd approached Elizabeth with her half-cocked excuse to walk to Chêne. "I must assist my mistress to bed. I'm her maid."

"Perhaps she should be helping you to bed. You're her equal, citizen."

Justine offered her most flirty smile. "I may be her equal in the sight of God, but I am not her equal in worldly coin. So labor I must."

The soldier didn't laugh as she expected. Something else had happened. Something bad. Again, her womb clenched.

"May I pass?" she asked again. "The truth is I'm feeling poorly. My mistress has been ill. Perhaps I've caught it."

"I've orders. A child has gone missing. A boy. We've been instructed to question everyone who passes in and out of Geneva."

"Surely you don't think I have anything to do with this." Yet Justine felt compelled to help them search, unaware who the boy could be. By the time she slipped away from the soldiers, she didn't head toward the city gates—anyway, they were probably locked by then. Instead, she found a hayloft in a farm belonging to no one she knew. She struggled to climb into it before she collapsed.

By then Justine could barely walk, but somehow she tied her apron around her nether regions to keep blood from staining her petticoats. And the pain! The pain! This was no monthly course like the midwife claimed. Her womb constricted and expanded. Her back twisted as though it would break.

As she labored in the hayloft, she heard cows low below her, the horses neigh as she grunted, her teeth and lips clenched. *It's alive*, she thought. *And it will kill me. It hates me, for I have abandoned it.* But whatever was inside her womb didn't kill her. Instead, she felt a slither of something—no, some*one*—snake into her hands.

She glanced down. A clot of thickened blood. A circle of tissue. Whatever it was, it had been something. Now it was nothing.

She wrapped the remains in her apron after saying a prayer for its soul. She fell into a fevered sleep.

As she slept, she dreamt of William, of slapping him that one time. "I'm sorry," she begged. "Forgive me." Next, her mother appeared and hit her. *"I wish you had died instead of my other children!"* Then Ernest was before her, his expression loving like when they'd first met. His features transformed into something akin to the golem from her father's tale. The golem bore a scarred face, black flowing hair, and eyes yellowed with jaundice. He resembled a demon, a monster. He hissed, "Awake, fairest, thy lover is near—he who would give his life but to obtain one look of affection from thine eyes; my beloved, awake!"

Justine awoke with a start, chest thudding. She drew a deep breath and looked around the hayloft.

No one was there.

Larks were singing.

The wind was soft.

Dawn had arrived.

I'm free.

She brushed the hay from her skirts. She buried her apron with the remains from her womb. Whatever discomfort she experienced now was nothing compared to what had been. As for the baby, her mourning would lessen in time. It was for the best. Her life would improve. God would understand. She'd be a better Justine. A finer Justine, as Caroline had intended.

Justine's spirit was already lighter as she headed back to the Frankensteins, though she barely recalled how she walked there—she was so sore and exhausted. She found Ernest pacing in the hall beneath the tall oil portrait of Caroline. His eyes were red, his face blotched.

"I'm not pregnant," she whispered; a smile crept across her lips. "I was mistaken. All is well."

Ernest grimaced. "I suppose you think we can go on as we did."

She didn't say yes or no. She hadn't thought that far ahead. The only thing she thought of was her bed, for she felt so weak.

She answered, "I don't know—I hardly slept last night because I was caught by the city gates. I had to take shelter in a hayloft."

Ernest grabbed her by her shoulders and shook her. "You think that's why I'm here? That I was waiting for you? William is dead, you whore. That's why I'm here, still awake. There were search parties all night after he went missing in Plainpalais."

The boy she'd been searching for, of whom the soldiers had spoken. Now Justine understood.

Ernest continued in a rush, "We found his body in a field—some evil fiend strangled him for reasons I cannot conjecture. Wherever you were last night, you weren't here. If you had been, he might not have been murdered." He shoved her away. "You should have been here to watch him! To protect him!"

William dead? It could not be. She glanced up at the oil portrait of Caroline, whose painted gaze accused. *I'm so sorry.* Another wave of pain. She clutched her stomach. Another clot of blood slid between her legs. She convulsed, unable to stand.

Two days later, the locket bearing the watercolor of Caroline fell from her pocket in front of Alphonse and others. Ernest assumed the worst, though of course he never revealed the truth of their liaison to his family. "No matter the outcome of this trial, I know what happened. You murdered my brother to revenge yourself on me," he accused before her arrest. "You're a murderess."

And then Justine understood the truth: if she hadn't visited the midwife in Chêne, William wouldn't have died. If she hadn't loved Ernest, William wouldn't have died. If she hadn't tried to marry Ernest, William wouldn't have died. She would have been there to protect him that evening in Plainpalais. His death was her fault as surely as if she'd set her hands about his tender neck.

Ah my poor dormouse, she thought, weeping. *What have I done?*

* * *

Justine's whispered confession was interrupted by the turn of a key. The creak of a door.

She looked up from her clenched hands. A guard, not the kind one who'd brought her dinner. This one was younger, dressed in the formal uniform of the Genevan guard. He'd beaten her to ensure her confession; the priest hadn't stopped him.

"Another moment," she implored, body shaking. "Please. I'm still praying. Not done yet. It's not dawn yet."

Afraid. So afraid. Afraid.

"Sun's rising. You already had last rites." He grabbed her wrists to unlock her manacles. "You can pray along the way."

"One more moment! I beg you!"

He yanked her to her feet, yanked her linen cap from her scalp, revealing her shorn head. Before he roped her arms to her side, she quickly crossed herself.

Forgive me, Lord. Unto you do I offer my soul.

CHAPTER III.

"And on the morrow Justine died . . .
She perished on the scaffold as a murderess!"

* * *

OUTSIDE THE JAIL, the summer sky was bright with dawn, the street puddled with rain from yesterday's storm. Justine blinked, eyes struggling to take in the infusion of light, before the guards forced her into the cart that would transport her to Plainpalais. Once they reached the edge of the field, the cart shuddered to a halt. "We wait here," the guard told her. They'd execute the syndics first; her hanging would follow like an afterthought.

From her perch in the cart, Justine watched the eleven syndics stand in a straggling line beside the scaffold, far from the oak trees edging the park. Their mortal coils were dispatched with three short bursts of bullets; Justine flinched at the rifle's booms. Though the syndics submitted to their fate with silent stoicism, their families wailed and screamed. Justine turned away, eyes flooding.

No one will mourn me save Elizabeth.

Their cries of sorrow were drowned out by applause and shouts by those circling the liberty tree, a young elm. "To liberty!" someone cried. "Onward!"

The deed complete, Justine hoped the crowd would drain from

Plainpalais like water from a sink. Not so. The crowd thickened to include hundreds, for all wanted to see the spectacle of a child murderess put to death.

"They're here for you," another guard jeered, dragging her from the cart. "Aren't you proud? Now march!"

The crowd pushed toward her, hands reaching, mouths shouting. Ugly with hatred. Ruddy-faced with fury. "Murderess!" one woman yelled, her scarred features below her red cap distorted. Others joined her cry: "Murderess! Hang her!"

And then someone slapped her. Hard. A woman, grey-haired and skinny. A woman like her mother but not.

Justine's cheek stung. Her nose. Something thick and warm dripped from it. Her legs froze. She felt like a rabbit cornered by a fox. A mouse trapped by a cat. A fish caught in ice.

"I can't walk," she sobbed, wiping her nose against her wrist. Blood against flesh.

The guard shoved her against the pebbled ground. "Go! Or do we need to drag you?"

One step. Another. Two more.

I'll imagine myself out of my body. I must. There she was, a small hunchbacked woman dressed in a plain black kirtle. Nose seeping red, shoulders shaking, her back twisted. Her gait jerky, like a puppet. Her scalp covered in scabs where the knife had scraped too close when they'd shaved her head. Eyes wide. Tear-filled. Her elbows were bound tight beside her body, allowing her to grasp her hands in prayer.

The drums began to trill, overtaking the shouts.

Another step toward the scaffold.

God grant me mercy.

Five more steps. The scaffold above. The wood smelled wet, reminding her of spring.

God grant me grace.

The gnarled wood stairs, still slippery with rain.

God grant me courage.

She reached the edge of the platform, where a soldier tugged her by the soft of her arm until she stood beside the noose. She looked about.

No hangman. Not yet.

She swayed, knees uneasy, eyes scanning the crowd below. Who knew Plainpalais could hold so many? (Where was the hangman? When was he coming?) Of the hundreds awaiting her death, she found herself searching for that midwife. (Yes, Justine had remained silent, but what good had it done?) At the very edge of the crowd, she spied an unnaturally tall, dark-haired man. He was half-hidden behind oak trees. Was he . . . laughing? He was. Such cruelty!

Lord, please don't let this be the last thing I see before my death. Let me see something else. Something to remind me of Your kingdom I pray awaits me.

She raised her eyes toward the dawn sky, which remained clotted with pink clouds. The trees, verdant with summer, leaves swaying in the breeze. The mountains, majestic in their height. Mont Blanc with its celestial crest of snow. All so beautiful . . .

"Mademoiselle."

Justine gasped. The hangman—he'd been behind her the entire time, his face hidden by his black mask. How blue his eyes appeared, so brilliant! In one swift motion he thrust a hood over her head like he was bagging a fox. The world disappeared.

How loud her breath sounded inside the hood, like sun burning through burlap!

God grant me courage.

She felt the noose loop around her neck. The rope was wet, probably from rain. She shivered despite the July torpor.

God grant me forgiveness.

"Don't struggle," the hangman urged, his words muffled by his mask. "That'll make it worse. I've done this many times—the drop will break your neck instantly if you let your body give way. You shan't feel a thing."

"I can't see a thing now." She tasted mucus amid the blood from her nose.

Breathing. Breathing. Shaking. Shaking.

God save my soul. God protect me.

The hangman tugged at the noose, placing the knot against the base of her skull. Once the noose was settled, a rush of noise roared from the crowd. Applause. Shouts.

Murderess.

Murderess.

Murderess.

The drums began anew, a roll of tension and hysteria.

Murderess.

Murderess.

Murderess.

The drums grew faster. Louder.

"In the name of the Father, Son, Holy Spirit," she whispered inside the hood. "I pray you take my soul."

She squeezed her eyes shut so tight they burned. She bit the soft of her lip until she tasted iron.

The resurrection and the glory. Amen.

Another drumroll began, one that lengthened and spread until Justine could feel the beats of her heart between each bang. She sensed the hangman moving away from her. Footsteps behind her.

It's going to happen now. He's going to hang me.

To her surprise, Justine realized she hadn't truly believed the hanging would occur, though this made little sense—there she was with a noose around her neck, a hood over her head, a hangman hovering behind her. Her entire body shook as though with fever. Any comfort she'd won from her last confession fled. All of her life had been cursed save for Elizabeth's friendship. First her mother, who had despised her. Then there'd been her desire for Ernest. But Caroline, oh Caroline! Justine had adored her—if only she'd been able to save her from scarlet fever. And poor William! She couldn't bear to think of—

* * *

The trap door opened.

The rope went taut.

The crowd roared.

CHAPTER IV.

*"It is with considerable difficulty that I remember the original era
of my being: all the events of that period appear confused and indistinct.
A strange multiplicity of sensations seized me."*

* * *

IT WAS with considerable difficulty that Justine was to remember what
happened next. First a slice of light pressed on her nerves so bright that
she was obliged to shut her eyes—or perhaps they were already shut. A
multiplicity of sensations overtook her: she heard and smelt at the same
time the tinge of blood, the damp of mold, the rattle of cobblestones.
She could distinguish nothing but agony about her neck, her body. She
felt herself to be a poor miserable wretch. She tried to weep but found
she couldn't.

Miraculously her mind remained active. Or was it her soul?
Somehow she recalled what happened after the rope dropped. All
hadn't turned to black, like the hangman promised. Instead, she'd
dangled twisting, her neck growing longer and tighter as she strained
for air. Her bladder released. Her fingers extended, toes too, flailing for
a hold that wasn't there. Her eyes wide, seeking light. The crowd
quieting before darkness arrived . . .

And then nothing more. Until now.

Justine felt her body lifted into a long box, one whose rough surface tugged at her skirts. A coffin.

A tenor male voice. Henry Clerval's. "I'll take her from here."

Splintered wood against her flesh. A lid slid into place. She tensed, awaiting the tattoo of hammering. It never arrived.

Some time later, cobblestones rattled beneath her bones. Darkness returned, the same opaque lack of light she recalled before the hangman had pulled the lever and the drums had rolled. It was to grow darker still.

She remembered nothing more for some time. Then, a soft glimmer of light glowing and shifting above her head.

The moon?

Justine's eyes focused on a shadowy blur of gold hair and eyes like an azure sky. Not the moon. A woman's face. A face she'd grown to know well over the past nine years. Though the flesh around the woman's eyes were red from tears and her mouth grim, there was an innate innocence —no, a simplicity—about her expression as well as an otherworldly beauty. The woman's face appeared weighed by worry. Sorrow.

A pale hand extended. Fingers clutching a single rose the color of blood. The velvety petals bore a heavy perfume. Fecund. Decaying.

Lightning cracked, illuminating the woman's face in full. Now Justine possessed no doubt as to whose face she beheld.

"Great God," Elizabeth breathed, the rose dropping from her hand. "You're still alive."

Then all turned black.

* * *

Is Justine alive? Or did I imagine her breathing?

These questions rang in Elizabeth's mind inside the carriage bearing Justine's coffin as it sped toward Lake Como. Once Elizabeth noticed Justine's chest rising and falling, she'd immediately insisted the coachman leave, not daring to wait for Henry. It was only later—later enough that they'd passed the Geneva city gates; later enough that Elizabeth understood no one followed as they skirted the Italian border— that she asked herself why she'd abandoned Henry to accompany Justine's coffin without him. The answer came readily: Henry was too good, too honest. If Justine was alive as Elizabeth believed, best he not know. She couldn't ask him to deceive others on her behalf. Too much of a risk. She loved him too well to expect him to lie.

And then she thought of Victor, of Alphonse, both of whom she'd abandoned with only a note explaining her decision to bury Justine at the Villa Lavenza. They'd be upset, but not nearly as upset as she knew Henry would be. She'd write him once she arrived. She prayed he'd forgive her; they'd wed another time. What was more distressing were her worries about Justine. Could she breathe inside the pine box? Was she putting the girl's life at stake?

Justine's dead. You only want her to live to make up for Caroline's death. You've left the man you love to run away with a corpse.

As the leagues passed with the hours of the night, Elizabeth's thoughts tossed to and fro like the swaying of the carriage on the rain-pitted road. The carriage rose into the Alps, leaving the lake behind; the air grew clearer, cooler. Elizabeth's eyes strained out the window into the darkness. By then the clouds had cleared, allowing a profusion of stars to glimmer in the inky sky. The sweep of the milky way. A crescent moon.

The serene beauty didn't silence Elizabeth's mind. *How had Justine lived? It must have been the noose.* Elizabeth once read of a Scottish woman who survived hanging due to a wet rope. Hours later she'd regained consciousness and was discovered screaming inside her grave. This brought up new fears: what if Justine was suffocating inside the coffin? She could be dying at that very moment.

Elizabeth could no longer bear it. "Stop, please!" she shouted to the driver as soon as they neared a coaching inn outside a rural hamlet. Then she stuttered and blushed like a fool so he'd believe she needed to relieve herself.

The driver immediately understood. "I could use a break—I've a thirst." He pointed to the inn, which was lively with activity despite the hour. "I'll be in there. Anyway, the horses need a rest."

She gave him a silver coin. "Take your time."

Once he was out of sight, Elizabeth inched open the coffin lid. The stench of piss and shit hit her nose. A fly buzzed past her ear. She held her nose and drew close.

Justine's eyes stared ahead, colorless as ever.

Elizabeth pressed her ear against Justine's chest. A faint tapping echoed, persistent as the tide. Was Elizabeth imagining this? She recalled how when Caroline passed, she'd appeared alive for some time beyond her last heartbeat—her bowels gurgled, her lungs creaked. "Do not be deceived by the activity," the doctor had warned. "This is how the body settles into death."

Elizabeth stroked Justine's pale cheek. It was still warm and pliant; by now, rigor mortis should have set in. Justine's nails were torn. Covered in blood. Had she been scratching at the wood? What if she'd been alive but died along the way?

Elizabeth climbed onto the cart next to the coffin, frantically pressing against Justine's chest. "Breathe! For the love of God, breathe!"

Justine let out a cough.

Elizabeth felt a wild joy rise, accompanied by a fierce panic. "Wake up! Please!" She pinched Justine's cheek, shook her shoulder. She wouldn't rouse.

Elizabeth glanced toward the inn; any moment the coachman could return. She'd lost Caroline. She'd lost William. She couldn't lose Justine too.

"I'll save you," she whispered close to Justine's ear. "For now, you must remain in here. As soon as I can I'll free you. I promise."

Elizabeth looked around the coach yard, pulse racing. Something light caught her eye. Something fluttering. A clothesline behind the inn. She stole a pair of breeches and a man's shirt from it. She tucked them inside the coffin beside Justine. She closed the lid, and just in time: the driver ambled from the inn toward the coach.

"Ready, Mademoiselle?"

"Not quite, Monsieur. I'm indisposed." She explained she'd spend the night at the inn. "I need rest." She clutched her stomach and groaned, so he'd believe she had diarrhea.

"That's fine." He yawned. "We'll continue in the morning."

"You should go on without me. I've never felt so ill!" More stomach clutching and groaning. "Once I recover I'll hire another carriage."

"I don't mind waiting. Your gentleman paid me well."

"I've no wish to inconvenience you." She side-eyed the driver. "Leave the coffin—I'll pay someone from the inn to assist me. If you go now, you'll be in Geneva by dawn. I insist."

* * *

The morning after Justine's hanging, her plain pine coffin was found in a hayfield behind the coaching inn. Inside the coffin was her soiled gown, fashioned of coarse black linen, and a wilted blood-red rose. If one was to judge by the jagged rips in the fabric, the gown had been sliced off Justine's body with a blunt instrument. No one who lived in the hamlet had any idea how the coffin had arrived.

The rustic who owned the hayfield insisted on burning the coffin and its contents immediately. Several weeks earlier his eldest daughter had been pulled into the river by a gigantic man-like creature. He was covered in scars and bore yellow eyes like a wolf and ragged black hair. The monster would have drowned little Gabrielle had not the rustic shot him in the shoulder with a rifle kept for picking off predators. The rustic assured his wife they were safe, that there was no reason to abandon their home. But now, with this coffin appearing from nowhere . . .

The rustic stared into the distance, his keen eyes searching for any sign of who might have left the coffin. He saw no one.

"Don't tell my wife," he begged his neighbors, who watched bewildered as he burned the coffin. "It will only upset her." But the flames rising from the rain-soaked wood were so sooty that they drew his wife though she had been sleeping, for she was heavy with child.

"Why the fire?" she asked her husband, choking at the smoke. Her hands instinctively covered her swollen belly. "What are you burning?"

"It had been something," he replied, poking the ashes with his hoe. "Now it is nothing."

CHAPTER V.

"I was a poor, helpless, miserable wretch; I knew, and could distinguish,
nothing; but feeling pain invade me on all sides . . . Soon a gentle light
stole over the heavens, and gave me a sensation of pleasure.
I started up, and beheld a radiant form."

* * *

LIGHT FLOODING. *So painful. A gasp. A dog barking.*

Dark. In the distance, Justine heard what sounded like a dog's nails tapping against a marble floor. A brassy clatter of curtain rings.

Light. Gradually Justine's eyes focused.

She was in a bed. A grand four-postered bed, hung with thick bed curtains the hue of an egg yolk. A plush eiderdown beneath her bones. Lying next to her, a woman with long curls spun with gold. Though the woman's face was turned, Justine knew the curls belonged to Elizabeth Lavenza—only Elizabeth possessed such radiant hair.

In that grand curtained bed beside Elizabeth, Justine's eyelids were heavy. So heavy. She let them close, but darkness did not return. Instead, she saw the hangman before he'd set the rope about her neck. Before all had turned black in a rush of guilt and memory. Then, awakening inside the coffin, Elizabeth's bright face like the moon. The lush red rose in her hand . . .

Justine couldn't recall what happened next. *It doesn't matter. I am here now.* As for now, her neck ached. Oh, how it ached! She wiggled her fingers, straining to lift a hand.

She touched her throat. Swollen. Bruises. They were raised across her neck. It was a miracle she could breathe. Next, her head. Her skull. The crown of it was coated with bristles, like a man's beard. Scabbed and scarred.

They shaved my hair before they hanged me.

At last Justine remembered it all. She recalled watching her silvery-blonde hair spill along the straw-covered floor—that same silvery hair Ernest would twine his hands in when they coupled, as though to keep from drowning in pleasure; the hair he claimed to be more beautiful than moonlight. Though she'd steeled herself for the loss of it, she'd still wept. *"Vanity has no place here,"* the priest had admonished before he'd forced her to admit murdering William. *"Vanity will not save your soul."* She remembered that desperate confession she'd whispered in her cell. The walk to the scaffold . . .

Justine's hand fell from her scalp. *Father, Son, Holy Spirit. The resurrection and the glory.* Christ had returned from death. So had she—or so it seemed. Whatever had happened, she was alive, or had returned to life anew. How could this be? How was her neck not broken? Was this a dream?

I'm alive.

"Justine? Are you awake?"

No dream. Elizabeth's voice. The Frankensteins' ward curled about Justine's body, heart speeding against Justine's spine. She was afraid. So was Justine.

More urgently: "Justine? Can you hear me?"

Justine met Elizabeth's eyes.

"We're at the Villa Lavenza," Elizabeth explained in a low voice. "My family home in Lake Como. I brought you here. This is where we've been traveling to these past three days. I dressed you in men's clothing so no one would recognize you. Do you remember?"

No, Justine tried to say; her vocal chords refused to obey.

"I found you alive inside your coffin. Do you remember?"

The moon. Elizabeth. The rose.

She tried to nod, but it was too painful. Her neck. How ragged her breath sounded!

"Is that a yes? Can you blink? Blink once if so, twice if no."

Justine managed to blink once.

"You can't speak?"

Two blinks.

"But you can hear me?"

A solitary blink.

"Listen to me and listen closely," Elizabeth whispered furiously. "I doubt anyone will bother us here, but it's best you remain in this room. If you're discovered alive, they'll hang you again, and this time they'll make sure you die. Do you understand?"

Justine blinked once. *Yes.*

Elizabeth had saved her. Elizabeth had run away with her. Never in all her life would she have considered Elizabeth capable of such actions. Elizabeth was the most obedient person she knew. Perfect.

"I'm the only person who knows you survived—I didn't dare tell anyone, not even Henry or Victor. It's our secret," Elizabeth continued. "I still don't know how you survived the hanging. The noose must not have broken your neck, though God knows how. I think the rope must have been wet, you were too light. It's a miracle I looked inside your coffin before we left to bury you. Once I realized you still lived, I fled with you, kept you sedated along the way—well, I hired a coachman to bring us here, but worry not, I paid him well. No matter. You're alive."

I live.

Something electric rose up Justine's spine. Something sharp and bright and life-giving. Her arms and legs jolted out, thrashing, turning, reminding her of that time with Dr. Galvani, the surge of energy rushing through the room. It all came back, everything that had happened after her hanging. She recalled Henry Clerval's voice. Awakening inside the coffin, Elizabeth's face. The rose. Elizabeth carrying her from the coffin to a carriage. Jostling over cobblestones. Flashes of light. Broth drizzled between her lips for nourishment. Laudanum to keep her silent . . .

Then Justine remembered. William. Dead.

There is evil in this world. An evil I cannot fathom. And yet I live.

Was it joy she felt at her resurrection? Or terror? A shrill sound, louder than she'd ever imagined, rang through her though it refused to leave her mouth. The scream was coming from within her. From her throat. Her stomach. Her heart.

Another rush of electricity up her spine. She tried to throw herself onto her knees. Pray. She had to pray. Why had she lived, but William not? How could God spare her, but not an innocent child?

She shook as she fell from the bed. Joy. Terror. Evil. Good. A whirling cycle of life and death, leaving her caught in its midst . . .

"What is it?" Elizabeth threw her arms about Justine as she shook. "Here, let me help you! I could read your lips. Can you move them?"

William, Justine mouthed, her lips moving at last.

The air surrounding her turned dense and buzzing and dark.

The taste of laudanum, like licorice.

* * *

Justine next recalled a savory aroma; hours must have passed, for the sun was high. She found a meal set beside her on the nightstand: a hunk of coarse black bread and broth sheening with fat. Fare suitable for invalids or uncomplaining servants. Her head spun from all the laudanum; any food would surely come up. Yet her stomach growled. She felt a slave to her body's ravenous needs.

I'm alive, she thought again. What a wonder this was.

The door to the bedroom opened abruptly. "Ah, you're awake!"

Elizabeth slid into the room. She was dressed in a cerulean blue high-waisted redingote she favored. The dog followed, his sleek fur the color of amber. He jumped on the bed near Justine's feet, jostling her sore body.

Elizabeth bolted the door and perched on the bed. "You look better. I'm glad you slept. I told Signora Giulia—that's the housekeeper—you had a fever. That way they won't come upstairs."

They? How many were at the villa? Would they betray them?

"Don't look so alarmed," Elizabeth said. "Only three servants. Besides Signora Giulia, there's the gardener Martin, and a maid named Ella; I dismissed the other maid, who was homesick anyway. I told them you're my invalid cousin from Strasburgh, a student. We won't stay here forever. Long enough for you to recover. After that, I'm uncertain . . ." Her voice broke. "They somehow learned about William—I suppose the news traveled. They believe I came here with you to mourn him."

Justine's hands curled over her eyes.

"Do you think you can eat?"

She let her hands drop. Two blinks. *No.*

"Are you steady on your feet?"

A slight shrug. *I don't know.*

"Come, let's get you walking. We'll sit by the window—the air will clear your head. I'll help you."

Justine staggered, clutching Elizabeth's arm, around the perimeter of the room, still dressed in the breeches and shirt Elizabeth had provided. The breeches felt easier on her spine. Less weight about her shoulders. Perhaps this was another way society held women captive. *"Man is born free, but everywhere is in chains."* And women too, for that matter.

A glare of light caught Justine's eye. A vanity mirror on a desk. She pivoted.

In the mirror's reflection, she observed what appeared to be an ugly male barely out of adolescence. His scalp was fuzzed with new growth over raised scars, where a knife had scraped too close. Eyes a dull silvery hue, like those belonging to a corpse. A face bruised and wounded with swollen lips. A drip of dried blood beneath the nose. Yet the face she saw still resembled herself, which made the mirror's reflection all the more disturbing. She recognized her wide cheekbones and rounded jawline, which remained soft as a baby's, her right shoulder still higher than the other.

Though Justine suspected she'd find herself changed after her resurrection, she hadn't expected to become an aberration. She didn't look normal. Nor did she look fully human. She was washed out as water, twisted as a tree. And her voice—would it ever return? Or would she spend the rest of her life unable to communicate save through gestures and blinks?

Monster. That's what I've become.

She must have revealed some sign of distress for Elizabeth helped her back into bed. She refused to leave it for the remainder of the day.

* * *

Late that night, Elizabeth wrote a letter, which Justine found face up on the desk the following morning.

My darling,

I am writing to let you know I have arrived safely at the Villa Lavenza with Justine. I am truly sorry to have abandoned you in such an unexpected manner. Ultimately I decided this task needed to be mine alone—it was too much to expect you to take it on. I understand my decision must have distressed your heart. I can offer no other apology save that grief is its own master.

You recall how my family's graveyard is set at the edge of the villa. Justine's funeral, such as it was, was attended by only myself, Signora Giulia, Martin, and a young man who has joined the household; he is a mute boy Signora Giulia has taken in out of pity. Signora Giulia read the prayers since she shares Justine's faith.

As to our marriage, this will need to wait until my return to Geneva. I beg you not to follow me here, but to trust in my devotion. In the meantime, I must ask you not to divulge our intent to elope to your father or anyone else.

Know that I think of you in every corner of this villa. I kiss your beloved face a thousand times—

Your loving Beata.

A soft snore rose from the bed, where Elizabeth still slept. Justine raised her head from the letter, which she'd strained to read; it was so early in the morning that there was barely any light. Several of Elizabeth's words were blurred from tears, or so Justine presumed. She shouldn't have read the letter, but she'd been unable to resist.

Justine turned away from the letter, newly aware of how much Elizabeth had sacrificed on her behalf. Elizabeth had planned to elope with Victor, but postponed their union to save Justine's life. Elizabeth was the loyal friend she'd always wanted. *Anything you need of me, I shall do for you.* She'd be as devoted to Elizabeth as she'd been to Caroline.

This wasn't the last Justine heard of Victor. Several mornings later, she was awakened by a knock on the door. A letter had arrived for Elizabeth. She watched Elizabeth scan the pages.

"From Henry," Elizabeth explained, her voice shaky. "All's well."

Though Justine couldn't make out the letter's contents, she understood enough. Henry had written on behalf of Victor, who was too distressed by Elizabeth's departure to communicate directly.

Afterward, Elizabeth tucked away the pages and wiped her eyes. For the remainder of the day, her face appeared a constellation of sorrow.

* * *

Days passed. Weeks. Soon an entire month had elapsed inside Elizabeth's bedroom in the Villa Lavenza. Justine saw no one except Elizabeth. The servants kept their distance. So did the hound, who appeared to come and go as he pleased. Justine rarely stirred from the bed. Nor was she able to speak. Some days she found the strength to walk, though never beyond the perimeters of the room; her legs remained unsteady. Outside her shuttered windows, she heard birds. Animals. She imagined worlds she could not see.

A temperate July had given way to a torpid August, and it had grown hot as hell in that room. But Justine wasn't in hell. Limbo, she decided, reverting to the teachings of her church. Elizabeth spooned broth into Justine's soft pale mouth as though she was a baby bird.

In another week, Justine progressed from broth to bread soaked in milk and stewed fish. As she ate she recalled William, how they'd fed him such food when he was a baby. Her eyes would sting at the memory before she'd give way to sleep. During this twilight time of lost days and nights, she sometimes woke to discover Elizabeth weeping at the foot of the bed, Caroline's emerald ring cupped in her palms.

Victor. She misses him.

Victor had not responded to Elizabeth's lovelorn letter save for that one time through Henry. *They'll reconcile when she returns,* Justine reassured herself. *They're fated for each other.* Then: *I wish there was something I could do.*

Finally, a day arrived when Justine felt strong enough to hold a pen herself. It was a clear August day too; the heat had broken and the roses clustered below the window were sultry with fragrance, their colors so saturated she thought she'd faint. Life felt like a voluptuous beast she'd never noticed. Everything that had occurred with Ernest seemed prelude to this moment. Food tasted sharper, water colder, her skin sensitive to every breeze and drip of sweat.

I'm alive. Then Justine knew what she must do.

She gestured toward Elizabeth's desk. After a moment's confusion, Elizabeth brought a tray bearing ink, pen and paper to Justine's lap.

Thank you, Justine wrote in a weak hand.

Too weary to hold the pen any longer, she let it drop to the tray.

CHAPTER VI.

"She indeed veiled her grief, and strove to act the comforter to us all.
She looked steadily on life, and assumed its duties with courage and zeal.
She devoted herself to those whom she had been taught to call her uncle."

* * *

WHEN JUSTINE NEXT AWAKENED, she found Elizabeth seated in an armchair near the window reading a letter. The window shutters were open. The sun was high. Outside, an oriole dashed from branch to branch of an olive tree, its song trilling and looping. Justine's lips curved with relief.

Victor. He's finally written her.

She raised herself against the pillow; at last, Elizabeth looked up from the letter. Her brow was creased, mouth tight. Something had happened. Something bad.

"My uncle," Elizabeth explained, folding the pages away. "Victor writes he's had a collapse. His heart."

Will he improve? Justine wrote; Elizabeth had left paper and pen on the bedstand.

"It's uncertain." Elizabeth began to pace before the window, twisting the emerald ring on her finger. "The doctors believe he should make a full recovery, but who knows? My uncle is seventy-four. I can't imagine Victor would have written unless it was serious." A catch in her voice.

"If I'd been there, I would have noticed before he took ill. I would have intervened."

Did Victor state this in his letter?

Elizabeth settled beside Justine. "Not directly, but I know my uncle well. Victor wrote he's been fighting with Ernest."

Justine's stomach dropped; Elizabeth hadn't mentioned Ernest since their arrival. Had Alphonse discovered Ernest's involvement with Justine?

Elizabeth continued, her voice uneven, "Ernest's been nagging my uncle to let him join the military; they've been at odds for months. If I'd been there, I'd have smoothed things over." Justine grasped Elizabeth's hand. "I'm sure it didn't help that I ran off here, along with William's death." A deep breath. "My uncle expected Victor and I to wed this fall. It was his only hope."

And I kept you apart, Justine thought. *Forgive me, my friend.*

The two sat in silence for some moments, clutching each other's hand. Elizabeth's was cool and soft; Justine patted it every so often. Justine stared out the window at the oriole, which had been joined by a starling on the olive tree branch. As the birds chittered, she was reminded of the sacrifices Elizabeth made to save her life—Justine hadn't thought beyond the miracle of her resurrection. She felt selfish for assuming Elizabeth would remain indefinitely in this villa with her, so far from the world.

The wind shifted. The oriole flew off, a blur in the air, leaving the starling alone on the olive tree.

Justine picked up the pen anew. *You must return to Geneva.*

"No," Elizabeth replied. "You're not ready to leave."

I can stay here alone without your help.

"But you're still so vulnerable! So weak!"

Justine wrote, *I'm stronger than you know.* She'd have to be.

* * *

That afternoon the five occupants of the Villa Lavenza were reduced to three, for Elizabeth decided to send Signora Giulia and Martin on a fool's errand to Belrive. Best to leave only one servant behind with Justine in the villa, Elizabeth decided. Safer. Justine overheard Elizabeth tell the couple, "I can trust no one but you to ready the *maison de campagne* for my family's return. Ella can take care of us until my departure."

"Ella's but a child!" Signora Giulia protested, displeased to be thrust from her home. She calmed once Elizabeth offered a sack of coins that far exceeded what was necessary for the journey.

Once the pair departed, Elizabeth returned to the bedroom, where Justine rested on a chaise.

"I found clothes for you in the attic," Elizabeth announced. "Male clothes. Safer to remain disguised, I think, though there are a few gowns."

Elizabeth dragged a large steamer trunk in from the hallway. The clothes inside the trunk were embroidered and dyed in pastel hues, like something a young duke would have worn in an earlier era. An era without revolution and bloodshed. Silks, damasks, velvets. Frock coats, waistcoats, stockings, gloves. They must have belonged to Elizabeth's parents years ago.

"I'll leave you with sufficient funds, Justine. You'll possess enough to make a new life once you're strong enough to travel. Hopefully your voice will return soon." Elizabeth's brow clouded. "I would not recommend remaining beyond the end of the year. My uncle's health permitting, I may return then with my husband."

Justine wrote: *You'll wed Victor then.*

Elizabeth avoided her gaze. "Ella will take care of you in my absence. When you leave here, go wherever you see fit, but I do not recommend traveling near Geneva. Do not tell me your destination. Do not tell Ella either—it's safer if no one knows where you've gone."

We shall never see each other again.

Elizabeth ignored Justine's written words. "I don't think anyone will come here. However, if someone arrives asking questions, you should flee without delay. I'll draw a map of the grounds so you know where the paths lead, but it's best you view them."

Elizabeth handed Justine a clean set of breeches and linens from the trunk.

"Do you think you're strong enough to walk outside?"

If I lean against you.

The clothes would be difficult to don without a servant's assistance; Justine assured Elizabeth she'd manage. To complete her transformation, Justine wrapped bandages around her breasts, pressing them tight against her chest until they ached. Months after her visit to Chêne, her breasts remained swollen, like they still mourned the child they'd never nourish.

Outside the villa, Justine hung on Elizabeth's arm. They passed the duck pond toward the apple orchard, the dog lingering at their heels. Again, all of life appeared rude and brash: the rise of cicadas, the caw of crows, the steel-bright sun. Justine's legs felt wobbly as a new colt, but she didn't dare turn back. She inhaled the summer air. Fecund. Floral. Delectable.

Elizabeth pointed from the apple orchard toward the woods. "Here the path goes up into the mountains, where there's a soldiers' encampment. If you continue on, it'll take you into Lombardy. Do you understand?"

There was an edge of anxiety to Elizabeth's voice, Justine decided. Fear.

She doesn't want to leave me. But she must.

Justine blinked once. *I can do this,* she mouthed.

"You're still so weak, Justine. And you've still no voice." Elizabeth's jaw squared. "I should remain here. I'll find a way."

Two furious blinks. *No. You must go!*

Elizabeth shook her head. "If anything were to happen to you . . ."

I've survived death. I'll survive this.

"But you're still an invalid! A mute."

Justine shrugged. *I'm stronger than you think.*

"Very well." Elizabeth pointed down toward the lake. "This path goes to Lenno, where you can hire a carriage. There's also a diligence coach to Milan, but that's a risk—best to keep to yourself as long as you can. If you're able, we'll walk a little further."

As they hiked deeper into the mountains, the path thinned as the woods thickened with oak and spruce. Justine's spine began to ache—between imprisonment and illness, she hadn't walked so far in months—but she ignored her discomfort. Again, everything was so bright and sharp. Overwhelming. Luscious. The odor of wood smoke from a distance. Manure. The cacophony of bird calls. A raven; she recognized its disconsolate cry. A rise of pine needles, its acidic scent rising in welcome.

Suddenly the beauty of the day soured. The dog growled as a nut-brown hare dashed across their path. The hare was followed in close pursuit by a ruddy-furred fox, whose teeth glinted bright. Just as it appeared the hare would lose the race, it dove into the undergrowth, leaving the fox without its prey. The dog went wild barking, only calming when Elizabeth threw a stick to fetch.

Justine let out a breath, overcome by memory.

The hare escaped, unlike William.

All of Justine's feigned confidence drained away. Poor sweet William. What had been his last moments? Had he been taken unaware? Her fingers brushed the bruises on her neck, which remained tender though it had been weeks since the hanging. She'd survived. He hadn't. How could such evil live in this world?

She couldn't go on. She sank down on the path, her eyes burning.

Elizabeth offered a hand. "This was too much for you. I'm sorry—I shouldn't have suggested it. I'll find a way to stay with you. Another week. I'll write Victor."

It's not that, Justine mouthed, clutching her heart. *William.*

Elizabeth settled beside Justine, the pine needles beneath them soft and fragrant. She clasped Justine's hand.

They sat there beneath the pines for some moments, lost in their shared grief.

* * *

A day later, Ella was alone in the kitchen, her skinny legs dangling from a stool as she attacked a plate of sausage, while Elizabeth and Justine remained upstairs in the bedroom. Even with windows open, it bore the sickroom odor of sweat and camphor.

"Ella will take care of you," Elizabeth reassured as she buckled her valise. "She'll cook, attend to your needs. I've paid her very generously to be loyal—she won't gossip."

You won't tell anyone that I'm alive? Justine mouthed.

"Never. I give you my most solemn promise." Elizabeth offered Justine a map, a compass, and a bag of coins. "Keep this safe." A moment later: "Here, take this too."

Elizabeth pressed into Justine's palm the necklace containing the locket portrait of Caroline—the one that led to her arrest.

Justine shivered. *No.*

"You must! I'm convinced my aunt protected you from death. That's why you had the locket after William's murder."

Justine didn't agree—after all, the murderer had stolen the locket from William in the first place. But then there was no more time for discussion. A team of horses whinnied in the courtyard below.

"The carriage. It's here." Elizabeth offered Justine a last embrace. "Adieu, my friend! I pray we shall meet again one day. Until then, may God protect you!"

And then the three at the Villa Lavenza became only two—two girls in a mansion too grand for a dozen. One girl was a soft-cheeked maid barely out of childhood. The other appeared to be a gentleman invalid.

Yet, for all of Ella's company, Justine had never felt so alone.

CHAPTER VII.

"I, who had ever been surrounded by amiable companions, continually engaged in endeavouring to bestow mutual pleasure, I was now alone."

* * *

BY THE TIME Elizabeth had been gone two weeks, Justine understood without a shadow of a doubt that Ella resented her.

During the first days of Justine's quarantine after Elizabeth's departure, Justine had remained too weak to venture forth much from her room. Accordingly, Justine found herself dependent on Ella for survival while holding her at arm's length: what if the maid were to discover Justine wasn't a gentleman? She snubbed Ella's attempts at friendship, leaving the girl lonely. After all, the girl was scarcely grown herself, with coltish limbs and slender hips; she still wore her ebony hair down in plaits like a child. Justine refused to bathe in the kitchen, causing Ella to haul buckets of water up flights of stairs. At night Justine locked her door lest she be accosted unaware. When she menstruated, she hid her rags in the bottom drawer of a cabinet, praying Ella wouldn't find them.

Frustrated by Justine's cold affect, Ella stopped cleaning and allowed the clocks to wind down. In this way, time was lost but it was not mourned: Justine grew to hate the villa nearly as much as she had her mother's house—she'd survived death only to find herself trapped anew. The situation wasn't helped in that Justine's voice hadn't returned. Not that it mattered: Ella spoke only Italian, and Justine only French.

The hours passed slowly. There were books, but all were in Italian save for one translation in French. Mallory's *Le Morte d'Arthur*—it was a different binding than the one she recalled in Henry's collection. As for the view from the windows, the mountains and waters of Lake Como were uncommonly beautiful, but beauty was not enough to fill long hours and an empty heart.

Soon Ella appeared only at meals to serve Justine. Their days became cleaved in two. In the morning, Ella would attend to Justine's breakfast, the dog clomping by her side; she'd reappear at twilight to serve dinner. During the few occasions Justine ventured downstairs, she discovered Ella napping on the settee in the morning room or eating sausages and bread in the kitchen—her appetite appeared limitless. Other times, she was nowhere to be found.

Justine dared not scold. The arrangement felt a compromise: Ella fulfilled the minimum of her duties; Justine gained privacy to walk about her room with her breasts free of their bindings, and to try to exercise her voice. Her body grew stronger. However, her voice remained as frozen as it had been since her hanging.

But, once September arrived and the leaves began to turn, Justine's curiosity expanded. What exactly did Ella *do* all day when she disappeared? Had she family? Friends? She appeared too young for a sweetheart, but who knew?

Everyone has someone but me, Justine fretted. The prudent thing to do would be to leave the Villa Lavenza, using Elizabeth's funds to find her way to a new life before winter arrived. She found she couldn't. Not yet. The world felt too wide. Too threatening. Nor could she envision the form this new life would take.

And then one day, Ella did not appear.

Justine had come downstairs looking for breakfast—usually Ella brought a tray at eight. The dog approached, sniffing her feet. She offered him a pat, fondling his soft, warm ears. He barked in answer. She wagered he hadn't been fed either.

Where's Ella? What do you know that I don't?

The dog barked again, leaping as he wagged his tail. He trotted away.

Justine followed him from room to room, confirming what she feared: Ella had left for good. Not even her apron remained, which she hung on a hook in the hallway after she finished for the day. Finally, the dog led Justine to the kitchen, whimpering for food.

Well, if there was one thing Justine knew, it was how to be a servant. She'd be mistress and servant now. First things first. Lunch. Her stomach was a crater.

Justine unlocked the kitchen pantry. No sausages. No root vegetables. No bread. A scant orange puddle in the sink revealed the last of the parsnip soup from the previous evening's dinner. Of course Ella, in her voracious hunger, had taken it all.

I'll starve if I don't leave here.

Her stomach growled as she readied to leave the villa, the dog following in her wake. She gathered her belongings, aiming to head for Lenno, where at least food could be obtained. From there, she'd decide where to go.

As Justine climbed the path toward the mountains, she was relieved to find her muscles stronger than expected. Oak leaves blanketed the forest floor in brilliant red, reminding Justine of a ruby necklace that once belonged to Caroline. Spiderwebs glistened with moisture. Birds sang, their trills rolling into the air. The sun slanted gold through the cypresses. As lovely as it all appeared, a foreboding tore at Justine as tangible as her hunger. It went beyond her nerves at being alone outside the villa since Elizabeth's departure, or not knowing where Ella had gone.

The dog must have sensed Justine's unease, for he growled. A second later a ruddy-hued fox dashed across her path, its eyes bright and startled and, Justine decided, fearful. The dog ran off after it, barking all the while.

Justine's neck prickled.

Several feet ahead, she caught sight of Ella's bare shoulder peeking from behind a poplar. She was seated against its thick trunk, her back to Justine. The maid's dark hair gleamed amber in the afternoon sun.

Napping as usual.

Justine's apprehension shifted to irritation. She should turn around, avoid confrontation. Continue on to Lenno before night fell. Even if Ella returned to the villa, it was only a matter of time before she'd abandon it again—hadn't today proven as much? Anyway, the maid appeared sound asleep.

The dog returned just as a second fox dashed across the path, scarlet leaves rustling. This fox appeared larger. A male. He stood at attention, his nose stretched toward the hound. The dog went mad with barking.

Ella didn't move.

Justine's steps slowed. A branch cracked beneath her heel.

A raven fluttered and landed on Ella's shoulder. She remained still.

The dog ignored the fox and ran toward Ella. Still, Ella did not respond.

Oh sweet Jesus, Justine breathed. She rushed toward Ella; the raven swooped into the sky. Something was wrong. Something terrible.

Don't let it be. Don't let it be.

It was.

Whoever or whatever had assaulted Ella had left her propped against the poplar trunk like an abandoned book. Her deep brown eyes stared out unseeing. Her head was tucked against her chest, shadowed by her curls, which had been freed from its plaits. A small grey rabbit sat in the hollow of her lap, nibbling at her curled fingers; perhaps it had been chased there by the foxes.

At the dog's approach, the rabbit scuttled into the undergrowth. Justine fell to her knees, shaking Ella's shoulders.

Wake up, for the love of God!

Ella's head flopped against her shoulder.

Florid bruises circled her throat.

At last, Justine's voice returned. She screamed.

* * *

Once Justine regained control of her emotions, she took it upon herself to drag Ella's body to the villa, where she'd bury her in the graveyard out back. It was better than leaving her to rot in the woods, where someone might come on her, or worse, the dog find her remains of interest. (Where had the dog gone anyway? He hadn't returned since she'd screamed.) Was Justine capable of digging a grave? She'd find out. After all, she'd been the gravedigger's daughter.

She looped her elbows beneath Ella's armpits and pulled.

Dragging her corpse through the forest was slow, awkward work;

Justine had to stop several times, panting for air, listening for anyone approaching. Strangely, she possessed no fear of someone accusing her of the murder. Ella's skirts tangled about her limbs, snagging on roots and catching rocks. Tearing and shredding. Justine felt a deep sorrow rise, one that felt unending. What sort of monster would do this? Could it have been soldiers from the encampment in the mountains? Or someone else? The consideration made Justine's stomach churn until she thought she'd vomit.

A burst of laughter. The laughter seemed distant, but sound traveled strangely in the mountains. Justine glanced down at her bound breasts, her small form, her trousers. Even if she appeared male, that didn't matter either. Her nerves sang.

I must hurry.

Several more steps. How heavy Ella was for someone so lanky! The sun dipped behind the Alps. Shadows turned cool. Blue. Night would soon fall. No time to lose.

Justine settled Ella beneath a copse of ferns. She quickly arranged the girl as though asleep, as she'd witnessed her father do when he'd bury someone. She draped Ella's arms across her breasts, closed her eyelids. She muttered a brisk *pater noster* over the girl's body and crossed herself. "Father, Son, Holy Spirit, Amen." Finally, she twined ivy over Ella's limbs until it appeared as though Nature herself had embraced the girl as its child.

"I'm sorry, Ella," Justine whispered, her heart pounding. "I wish I'd been kinder to you. Maybe you wouldn't have run off then." Her tears began to flow. "I'm so sorry. Very sorry . . ."

Justine collapsed to the forest floor, sobbing in earnest. She should flee, but to leave Ella felt an abandonment. *Everyone surrounding me is cursed.* First Caroline, then William, and now Ella. Even her mother and siblings. She prayed Elizabeth was safe.

Now I am truly alone.

Suddenly something rustled in the trees. Justine rose to her feet, prepared to flee. *Soldiers? Or another monster?* No, the fox and his mate— they'd escaped the dog, wherever he'd gone. The foxes crept out of their den as the wind picked up, howling as it scattered scarlet-hued leaves across Ella's corpse. They resembled daubs of blood.

Another hoot of laughter, closer now.

"I must go, Ella," she whimpered. "Forgive me."

Justine stole a last glance behind. Ella resembled a long-lost princess, one who might awaken one day. The male fox settled beside Ella's shoulder, his muscles tensed. He cocked his head toward Justine as though to say, "What are you waiting for?"

Justine ran.

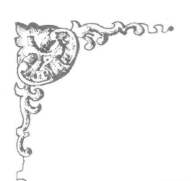

VOLUME FOUR

THE MONSTER

* * *

Meanwhile

CHAPTER I.

"About this time we retired to our house at Belrive. This change was particularly agreeable to me. The shutting of the gates regularly at ten o'clock, and the impossibility of remaining on the lake after that hour, had rendered our residence within the walls of Geneva very irksome to me."

* * *

ON THE ROAD TO GENEVA, the diligence coach from Milan bumped along, laden with more luggage than it was meant to hold. Inside, the diligence was similarly crowded. However, Elizabeth Lavenza appeared unaffected by discomfort to any who might spy her.

The other passengers viewed an ethereal young gentlewoman crowned with long gold curls, perhaps thinner than she should be, but exquisitely beautiful just the same. A gentlewoman who appeared favored by fortune, though she didn't feel such. Indeed, she felt cursed. Elizabeth clutched a letter in her hand, one she'd reread enough to have memorized each sentence. The letter from Henry, which he sent to the Villa Lavenza after she fled there with Justine.

"Though I love you beyond all others," he wrote, *"I cannot help wonder if you've second thoughts regarding our union. If we are to wed, I want you with the full of your heart. Therefore, I think it best we not communicate until your return to Geneva. This will allow time for reason to prevail over passion, and*

for you to end your engagement to Victor, if this is what you truly desire—I cannot bear for us to be duplicitous to him."

She understood Henry's reasoning, painful as it was. As for the timing of their wedding, Elizabeth couldn't marry until her uncle's health was recovered; only then would she end her engagement to Victor. She'd first take care of the Frankensteins, then herself. It was the least she could do for Caroline's sake, especially since she'd be breaking her promise to become Victor's wife.

Henry must accept this, she thought. *I've no choice.*

Still, how her heart ached! She loved him. She yearned to be with him, to run off as they'd planned. But everything had grown so complicated. She couldn't risk telling him about Justine. And now with Alphonse taking ill . . .

I'll go to Henry once I'm settled. Once he sees me, he'll know we'll wed. Just not yet.

She imagined Henry in her arms. Henry kissing her. Vowing devotion. *"I love you more than I ever thought I could love anything, even Heaven itself, God forgive me. I love you enough to betray my best friend in the entire world and his family . . ."*

And then the diligence approached the gate to Geneva, and there was no more time for rumination: Victor awaited her at the coach stand. To her shock, he didn't even kiss her cheek before pressing about Justine's corpse. Not one word about Alphonse's condition.

"Justine's at rest," Elizabeth said, gathering her luggage. "No one can harm her now."

"Too late," Victor muttered. "I wanted to bring her to Ingolstadt. That would have been better."

Elizabeth's brow knit. "Why Ingolstadt, Victor?"

"Because . . . because there's a lovely graveyard there. One that would—oh, you won't understand!" And he went off into another tangent, one involving Justine's church that made no sense. Elizabeth listened to Victor rant, desperately trying to interject a word here and there. What had happened to the boy she'd loved all those years? The man she'd promised Caroline to marry? In the weeks she'd been away, he'd gained new lines across his forehead and dark circles beneath his eyes. White prematurely streaked the hair at his temples.

He still appeared a stranger. A madman.

"Listen to me!" she interrupted, shaking his shoulders. "It's done, Victor. She's buried!"

"Oh." Victor sniffed, hands clenching his coat. Was he tapping his fingers like Caroline? "I know my request seems peculiar. I only wanted to be present at her funeral. That's all. Justine was innocent. Pure of heart. She deserved honor in death." He bit his lip before continuing. "Remember how I always used to say that if I was in an ill humor, one glance from Justine would cure me? She looked so frank-hearted and happy."

Elizabeth took his hands. How cold they were! "She's at peace, Victor. Now we need to be at peace."

"Peace . . ." Victor fell to his knees on the city square, ignoring everyone passing about. He embraced Elizabeth's legs, sobbing. "I will never find peace again. Never!"

"Get up! People are staring," she whispered. "Let's go home. You need rest."

"How shall I live with myself? God help me, not even Henry knows."

Her pulse raced at the mention of Henry's name. "Henry knows what?"

"About Ingolstadt."

Ingolstadt again. If she didn't know better, she'd wonder whether he recalled their encounter there. She gentled her tone. "What happened in Ingolstadt, Victor?"

"I can't say. I couldn't bear to tell Henry what I'd done. And now Justine is dead. I'll never forgive myself!"

Guilt licked at Elizabeth's soul. *He can never know she lives.*

She set her hand on his shoulder as though soothing a child. "Shush, darling. You must believe me when I say Justine is in a better place. Come, let us go home."

Victor whimpered as she led him to the Frankenstein carriage. How would she ever free herself from him? As the carriage passed by the Clerval's shop off the Place du Bourg-de-Four, Elizabeth imagined Henry staring out the window in heartbroken reproach. She blinked away emotion.

Soon, my darling. I promise.

Fortunately, Victor appeared to calm once the carriage was under-way. He was able to explain the Frankensteins had returned to their country home in Belrive during Elizabeth's absence—another reason he'd met her at the coach stand.

"Henry or Ernest should have written you of this—no, *I* should have written, but I was . . . unwell," Victor elaborated once he'd collected himself into a semblance of composure; Elizabeth watched his brow unknit, his hands relax. "The doctor recommended the change of scene for Father's health. Said lake air would help. Besides his heart, he was unable to bear how empty the house seemed without William. The distance from Geneva will also keep Ernest out of taverns—it's fortunate you sent your Italian servants there by happenstance."

Elizabeth nodded in response, hoping Victor didn't notice the color flushing her cheeks at the mention of Henry. Yet she was relieved to return to Belrive. It would be easier to avoid thoughts of Justine and William. Most importantly, easier to resist running to Henry's side before she'd made her peace with the Frankensteins.

Soon, my darling, she thought again. *I promise.*

* * *

Elizabeth arrived at their *maison de campagne* to find Signora Giulia and Martin installed, Sophie annoyed by their presence, and the remaining servants distracted. Alphonse seemed less fragile than expected though more befuddled, Ernest too quiet for her liking. The garden was as lovely as Elizabeth recalled, with its lily pond, rose garden, and the new oak that had grown in place of the one destroyed by lightning. The surrounding countryside was lush and green with late summer. She wished its beauty would bring her serenity, but too much weighed her spirit.

Dinner that evening was a solemn affair. The servants were unusually silent while they served a meal that would have won effusive praise before William's death. Ernest appeared inebriated, judging by his slurred speech, but didn't spout his usual political jargon; perhaps his father's collapse had affected him. Alphonse's hands shook with palsy when he reached for his fork. Once dinner was finished, they'd all retired to their separate bed chambers after a somber chorus of "Goodnight, sleep well."

Alone at last in Caroline's tower room, which she'd made hers, Elizabeth stared at the emerald ring. She set it inside a small dresser drawer, thinking of Victor's words upon her arrival. *"I wanted to bring her to Ingolstadt. That would have been better."* What did he mean?

I must find out.

Unable to sleep, Elizabeth made her way to Victor's room. With each step, she sensed the presence of those they'd lost over the years: Caroline, William, that soldier who'd died during that Christmas soirée, even the executed syndics. Her past rose before her as though unfurled from a clock. There she was, an innocent girl in love with Victor, who was kind and brilliant; there was their dearest friend Henry, with his poetry and *Le Morte d'Arthur*; loyal Justine, who'd only just joined their household. Years later, Elizabeth was a woman of twenty-four, engaged to be married to two men. One knew nothing of her duplicitous heart; the other she prayed still loved her despite her abandonment.

A mouse skittered across the hall, probably disconcerted by Elizabeth's presence. A sharp bang. A flash of light.

She whirled and gasped.

Only the shutter.

She forced a soft giggle to settle her nerves. How jittery she was! For a moment, she considered returning to her room. But then her resolve returned: she'd force Victor to tell her what had happened in Ingolstadt.

Elizabeth found the door to Victor's room open. Her eyes strained in the shadows.

"Victor?"

No answer. She took a tentative step inside, her heart pounding.

Victor's room appeared akin to a monastic cell. His bed bore plain white linens covered by a thin wool blanket. A single pillow. When they'd lived in the *maison de campagne* after the revolution, Victor's room sported piles of books, bottles of chemicals, math equations marked on stacks of paper, all manner of scientific instruments.

Another mouse skittered, this one across his bed before it dropped to the floor with a resounding *thunk*. She repressed a shudder. She recalled the pistol she'd found under his pillow back in Geneva.

Mouse or no, she patted his pillow; an odor of musty bleach rose. She slid her hand beneath it.

Not a pistol. Something square. Her stomach dropped.

The green journal, the one that had led to Caroline's death—she recognized it though it appeared battered from use. Victor had probably used it while in Ingolstadt.

"No."

The single syllable left her lips before she could contain it. She'd done her best to set the journal out of mind since her confession to Henry. She'd been successful . . . until now. That sense of being cursed returned. She should put the journal back, do her best to forget about it. And yet . . .

What if the secret to all that troubles Victor is in this journal?

Elizabeth could barely bring herself to touch the journal, let alone read it.

She forced herself to open to the flyleaf. Her heart panged as she confronted the inscription she'd written before Victor's departure for Ingolstadt. *"I will love you until my last breath."* How long ago this seemed! A speck of dark shifted across the cream-hued flyleaf, drifting from the spine of the book. A second, a third. Not lice. Something crawling. Larval. She grit her teeth and brushed them away.

She turned the page.

This journal belongs to
Victor Frankenstein
University of Ingolstadt
January 1789
May no one breach these Pages.

Elizabeth read as quickly as she could, mindful of Victor's return. Most of the journal's contents appeared mundane: addresses in Ingolstadt, tables of purchases and money outlaid, all markers of a life in a new land. A list of German words he'd found unfamiliar. Then in French the first full journal entry, which led to others, all filled with his tight looping hand. To her dismay, most of the entries revealed nothing she would not have expected. Worse, they were boring.

Then, at the bottom of a page:

<u>March 16, 1789.</u> What a day! Such promise! For the first time since my mother's passing, my melancholy is alleviated by the elixir of hope. This morning I met with Professor Waldman, who shall bring me the knowledge I require. The secrets of life and death. Or so I pray, the ability to transform life through the new art of chemistry. I will find a way—no one shall stop me, not even—

Who wouldn't stop him? A professor? Another student? Desperate to know, Elizabeth turned the page, her hand trembling.

A solitary word in Victor's hand greeted her eyes.

God.

She closed her eyes, thinking. *"No one shall stop me, not even God."* What did he mean? What had he planned? She *had* to know—

"Elizabeth? Is that you?"

She hid the journal beneath his pillow—and just in time: Victor approached from the hallway, a sepulchral figure.

"What are you doing here?" he demanded.

"I-I was looking for you." Her voice quavered. Had he spied her with the journal? She imagined larvae wiggling across her wrist, evidence of her transgression.

He took a step closer, breathing heavily. "Is that all?"

The stench of something moist and clammy emanated from Victor, wrapping around her throat, her lungs, until she thought she'd retch. His flesh smelled green, like mold. Vegetal, like the sea. A terror she couldn't explain rose along her spine. Along the curve of her neck like the icy brush of a finger . . .

Caroline wouldn't want me to be afraid of him.

She stepped toward Victor; her slippers wicked with moisture. He was dripping water. His hair was soaked. So was his clothing. There were puddles on the floor in his wake. A trail of water from the hall. The hair on the back of her neck rose.

"What have you done, Victor? Tell me!"

"Done?" He arched an eyebrow. "I went swimming in the lake. Well, not intentionally—my skiff turned over. An accident."

"Isn't it late to be sailing?"

"Night is the best time for it, beloved. The moon was high. The tide was calm. So peaceful . . ."

He caressed her cheek. How icy he felt! Like the dead.

"You're shivering. You still love me, don't you, Elizabeth?"

"Of course I love you." She did, didn't she? Even if they weren't to wed, all these years he'd been a friend, a cousin. Family.

"Then you should let me dress," he said, his tone acid. How mercurial he was! "I advise you to look away unless you wish to anticipate our wedding night. Ah, but I'm freezing. The lake was cold, beloved. So, so cold . . ."

Her stomach twisted. *Wedding night.* She shuddered, her palms moist. She had to tell him about Henry. Soon before Victor pressed to set a wedding date. Once Alphonse was stronger.

She swallowed her anxieties to offer her hand. "I'll help you, Victor." And she did: she led him to his bed, helped him undress—how boney he'd become! Though she shielded her eyes when he removed his breeches, she caught a glimpse of his penis. It appeared a raised curl of reddened flesh between his jutting hips.

"I need to sleep," he said once he'd donned a nightshirt.

"I'll go then."

Elizabeth turned toward the door. Again, she thought of Henry, their engagement. Perhaps Victor sensed something had changed in her.

That's why he's so peculiar. I should confess the truth. But I can't. Not yet.

"Good night, Victor."

"Good night . . ." A sigh in the dark. "I'm sorry, Elizabeth."

"Sorry for what?"

"Sorry about Justine. Sorry I upset you after we visited her in prison. I was wrong to speak about burying her as I did, wrong to tell you about the resurrectionists. I need to accept she's gone. There's nothing I could have done to save her life." He choked back a sob. "Elizabeth, I let you down! You're the most perfect thing in my life. My one true constant. I need to become a better man so I can be a good husband to you."

A soft moan. Or was it another sob?

"I'm sorry, Elizabeth. Just sorry. Good night."

* * *

Elizabeth fled Victor's room, wishing she'd never gone inside. Once she reached her tower room, she realized she'd never asked him about Ingolstadt.

I will ask him, she resolved. *In the morning.*

But in the morning it was too late. Victor was gone. He'd locked his bedroom door.

"He departed early," Sophie explained in a low voice as she served Elizabeth her morning tea. "Before the fires were lit in the kitchen. I saw him outside in the fog dragging his boat into the lake. He's been sailing nearly every day since we arrived here. He spends hours alone in his rowboat even when it rains."

"Does he?" Elizabeth said. She recalled Victor soaking with lake water. Victor and his journal. *"You're the most perfect thing in my life . . ."*

"I should go after him."

Sophie shook her head, scoffing. "He's been gone for hours, Mademoiselle."

He intended to drown himself—it all made sense. He'd tipped over his boat on purpose. It had been a trial. A test of his resolve. Now he'd returned to finish the job.

No, no. He wouldn't do that.

"I'll look anyway." Elizabeth threw her wrapper and shawl over her nightrail. "The fog's lifted."

She tugged the telescope in the library over to the window. Sophie was right: there was no sign of Victor on the lake. Nor was his rowboat in its usual place at the dock.

"He'll come back soon," Alphonse soothed Elizabeth at lunch, looking more robust than he had upon her arrival. "He spoke to me last night. He plans to sail toward Geneva and hire a donkey to head up to Chamounix toward Mont Blanc to view the Mer de Glace. He's still mourning William, Elizabeth. He'll be but a week or so. He's done this before."

But never to me. However, Elizabeth only smiled and said, "Of course, Uncle. You're right."

CHAPTER II.

"Morning dawned before I arrived at the village of Chamounix . . . Even in my own heart I could give no expression to my sensations—they weighed on me with a mountain's weight, and their excess destroyed my agony beneath them. Thus I returned home, and entering the house, presented myself to the family."

* * *

IT WAS WELL into September when Victor returned from Chamounix as abruptly as he'd departed. He arrived in Belrive in the dead of the night —Elizabeth overheard his restless step in the corridor outside her room. In the morning, she found puddles of water and wet footprints near her door.

He avoided her all day. Nor did he speak of his travels at dinner, which was another listless affair no amount of wine could enliven. Ernest fled as soon as he could. Alphonse dozed off over the soup. As for Victor, his visit to Mont Blanc had not helped. He appeared haggard and wild. He beat his fingertips against the table, and looked wildly over his shoulder as though he feared someone spying on him from the garden window. He reminded Elizabeth of a distorted shadow of Caroline, with her anxious tapping and counting. Every so often, Elizabeth discovered Victor staring at her with an aspect bordering on pity. Whenever she caught him, he smiled, but it wasn't his usual smile. It was the smile of someone with a secret they yearned to keep. A secret she feared to learn, especially now that she'd peeked inside that green journal.

Just as Sophie cleared the ices, Victor tapped his spoon against his wine glass. "I have an announcement."

Elizabeth set down her fork, stomach fluttering. Alphonse jerked awake. "What? Did I miss something?"

Victor smiled anew as he reached for Elizabeth's hand. She forced a smile in return, hoping he didn't notice how she'd flinched at his touch.

"Father, I'm ready to set our wedding date. I have mourned William deeply, as have we all. But it's time for a new leaf in our family. Wasn't that why we returned to Belrive?"

Elizabeth's smile tightened into a grimace. She fought the urge to flee.

Alphonse's eyes moistened with joy. "My son! I quite agree. A Christmas wedding! You can honeymoon in Lake Como."

Elizabeth's panic rose; after viewing Victor's peculiar behavior at dinner, she couldn't tell him about Henry, whom she had yet to write of her return. And what of Justine? Most likely she'd still be convalescing at the villa.

"Why so soon?" she asked. "Best not to wed until you're fully recovered, Uncle. Best to remain here through the winter."

Victor squeezed the bones in Elizabeth's hands until she winced. "I agree. We should wed in the spring."

Elizabeth exhaled.

Alphonse struggled to his feet, shaky even with his cane. "I'd really hoped for a Christmas wedding, Victor. Don't you agree, Elizabeth?"

"Uncle, perhaps we could—"

"Isn't spring better for a wedding?" Victor interjected, releasing Elizabeth's hand. "Better for travel too, Father."

Alphonse paced the length of the dining room, his steps uneven. "With William gone, your marriage is the only hope I possess. My only happiness. It was also your mother's fondest wish before she passed."

"I know, Father. But marriage requires preparation. Time."

Alphonse shook his head. "When I married your mother, we wed within a month of our betrothal—nothing could have stopped me. Forgive me, but I sense something else bothering you, Victor. Is there something you need to tell us? Another reason for delaying?" A low voice. "Do you have any reservations to being joined with Elizabeth?"

Elizabeth's heart pounded.

After a long moment, Victor shrugged. He picked up a butter knife to check its reflection—again, he was looking at the garden window behind him. What was out there?

Alphonse prompted, "Well, Victor? Have you nothing to say?"

Victor set down the knife and offered a cheeky grin, looking for all the world as he used to be. The old Victor. The Victor who hadn't lived in Ingolstadt for six years and rarely wrote. The Victor who didn't run off to Mont Blanc to view the Mer de Glace, or swim in lakes after tipping rowboats.

"How serious you two look!" Victor declared. "I love Elizabeth and look forward to our union with delight. I've never imagined sharing my life with anyone else"—his hand brushed anew against hers—"but it's only this, a small thing."

Victor fell into silence, his breath heavy. As Elizabeth waited for him to continue, she sensed a chill on her shoulder, a palpable sense of doom. A curse.

Alphonse pressed, "Tell us then."

Victor replied in a strained voice, "During my travels I met someone who reminded me that a job half-finished isn't finished at all."

"You intend to return to Ingolstadt?" Elizabeth asked, uneasy.

"No, not that, Elizabeth. A better plan! There's a natural philosopher whose research can help me in England. Instead of Ingolstadt, I thought to travel there to complete my studies. A last trip before marriage." He turned to Alphonse. "Isn't it better, Father, to begin a marriage without unresolved responsibilities?"

"I thought they had been resolved—"

"Isn't it better," Victor interrupted, "to begin a marriage without distractions of the past?" To Elizabeth: "Wouldn't you agree, beloved? Do say you agree!"

Elizabeth asked carefully, "When would you leave?"

"As soon as arrangements are complete. Tomorrow even. Oh, don't look so glum! I'll be back before you know it. Six months or so."

"You'll be home by spring then," Alphonse said.

"We'll wed immediately upon my return, Father. I promise." He grasped Elizabeth's hands. "Let the day be fixed; and on it I will consecrate myself, in life or death, to the happiness of my cousin. And then we shall live in peace for the remainder of our lives."

Elizabeth excused herself from the table, too panicked to remain. But Alphonse sought her in her room.

"I don't want Victor to travel alone in case he takes ill again. I'll ask Henry to meet him in Strasburgh to accompany him. Tell Henry your approval of this plan, Elizabeth. He trusts your judgement more than mine."

* * *

Henry came to Elizabeth within hours of receiving her letter. By then it was the day after Victor's departure; Elizabeth had bid him a tearful and silent farewell. Elizabeth led Henry into the drawing room where Caroline would have entertained guests years earlier. She shut the door behind them for privacy, nervous how he'd receive her. She should have written him sooner, but she'd been too anxious.

"This is what you want me to do? Go to him?" Henry asked, his brow beaded with moisture. Elizabeth had the sense he'd rushed the entire way from Geneva; he'd arrived unshaved, his hair unkempt. For a moment, he reminded her of Victor in his disarray. It shocked Elizabeth. Henry was the calm one. The considered one. But then again, she hadn't seen him since she'd fled to Lake Como with Justine.

"It's my uncle's plan," she replied, avoiding his gaze.

"I suppose you still haven't told them about us. Nor have you written me about your return. Well, until now . . ." Henry drew closer, his voice low; she could smell his sweat, the tinge of cologne on his neck linens. "Tell the truth: do you still love me?"

"Of course I do! More than anyone in the world!"

"Yet you want me to leave Geneva. Why?"

Elizabeth didn't answer. No, couldn't answer. For the truth was she didn't want him to leave. She loved him—this hadn't changed. He knew about her promise to Caroline. He knew about her debt to the Frankensteins. No need to speak of it again.

"Won't you respond, Beata? I sense there's something you're hiding from me. A secret."

Henry set a finger under her chin and tilted her head toward his. His eyes were moist. Pleading.

"No secret," she lied, protecting Justine. "I'll tell Victor about us when he returns. He needs to be stronger. Better. My uncle too—he's still frail."

"You're weeping."

A deep breath. "I know I've hurt you—we'd planned to marry and I abandoned you. I regret this so much! But now I realize I need time to break the news to my family. As for Victor, my uncle is worried he'll take ill again as he did in Ingolstadt."

"Then it's your uncle who wants me to accompany him." Henry steepled his fingers beneath his chin. "What about you? Do you want me to travel to England with him?"

For a flick of a breath, she considered responding, *No, stay.* She imagined an alternate world, one where she and Henry had run off as they'd planned, abandoning Victor to whatever madness possessed him. She'd have entrusted Henry with the secret of Justine's survival; they'd now be in Lake Como creating a future apart from the Frankensteins. Again, Elizabeth thought of those children she'd envisioned, a boy with Henry's fawn-colored hair, a girl with her blue eyes.

But if there was one thing Elizabeth had learned from Caroline, it was that love was protection. Love was sacrifice. Love was denying yourself for the sake of those you loved more. Love was honoring deathbed promises . . . at least until the time arrived when they could be broken without harming others.

And so Elizabeth said something she knew she'd always regret. Something she wished she could undo as soon as the words emerged from her mouth.

"I think you should go. Not because I want you to—I don't, Henry. But for Victor's sake. For my uncle's peace of mind. We'll wed when you return. I promise!"

There, she'd said it. She forced herself to continue.

"My uncle has offered to pay your way. He hoped this would make your father amenable to his plan." She twisted her handkerchief. "I've another reason for this request, one which my uncle remains unaware of."

Elizabeth couldn't hold back her worries as she confessed what she'd found in Victor's journal.

256 | KRIS WALDHERR

"I know I was wrong to look, but with Victor as he's been—well, you understand."

"I do." He drew a deep breath. "I'll leave tomorrow morning on the first diligence. I should return to Geneva to prepare."

Henry took a step closer. Elizabeth's knees wobbled. A peculiar twisting rose in her stomach, a yearning.

"Farewell, Henry," she choked out, taking his hand. She pressed her lips against his knuckles. "Write me."

Kiss me before you go. One last time before we part.

Their eyes met. She imagined the tenderness of his lips brushing against hers. Her mouth opening beneath his. His soft hair gently skimming her neck. The rasp of his beard against her cheek. Arms wrapping, drawing each other closer. The pulse of their hearts mingling. Then he'd believe she meant what she said: they'd marry, just not now.

And, for a moment, she believed he *would* kiss her, for his hands rose as though to pull her face toward his. But he only tucked a strand of her hair behind her ear before offering his hand as though she were a friend, not his beloved.

Henry's expression was sorrowful. "It's too late for us, isn't it?"

"No, no! I still love you. Desperately. Truly. You believe me, don't you?"

"It's not that I don't believe you, Beata. I just have this sense it doesn't matter." He let his hand drop from hers. "Fate."

"Henry, don't say that! Listen—"

Before Elizabeth could complete her answer, the drawing room door slammed open. Henry and Elizabeth pulled away from each other as Sophie burst into the room.

"Mademoiselle, those Italian servants of yours are ordering me about! You must speak to them!"

"Not now! I was speaking to Monsieur Clerval," Elizabeth snapped. "Can you never knock?"

Henry used the interruption to rush for the door. "I was leaving anyway." He inclined his head to Sophie. "Take good care of your mistress in my absence. Adieu!"

* * *

Elizabeth didn't come down for dinner—she was too distressed by Henry's departure. *Our fate is to be together,* she told herself. *By the time he returns, I'll have found a way to break the news to Victor. My uncle will be stronger.* Unsurprisingly, her dreams that night were disturbing. She dreamt of spying Caroline near the Place du Bourg-de-Four by the Clervals' shop. Her aunt was adorned in a cloak the color of garnets. Her hair was unbound, her face serene.

Joy lilted Elizabeth's voice. "Aunt Caroline!"

Elizabeth rushed toward her aunt, exclaiming how she'd missed her, that she was sorry she wouldn't be marrying Victor as promised. But as soon as Elizabeth kissed Caroline's cheek, her aunt's flesh turned livid with decay, and her red cloak transformed into a shroud.

Before Elizabeth could react, the scene shifted to one inside Henry's shop. He was seated at his father's desk writing, his back turned from Elizabeth. She cried, "Beloved, I'm ready to marry you!"

He peered over his shoulder. *Not Henry. Victor.* Victor was writing in the green journal. She tried to back away. Escape.

Her feet squeaked against a loose floorboard.

Victor rose from his chair. *"Have you come to wed me then?"*

Elizabeth's stomach tightened. "Where's Henry?"

"Gone, beloved."

Victor set a kiss against her cheek. A glance revealed grave-worms scattered across his shoulders. He brushed the maggots away with an uncommon tenderness. *"Death amid life,"* he murmured. *"Life from death. It's as God would want, if He'd allow me."* Then he pointed to a steamer trunk bearing a broken lock. The brass of the lock was stained in what appeared to be congealed red paint.

Elizabeth's heart pounded.

I won't be afraid. I shouldn't be afraid. I can't be afraid . . .

The red staining the lock was sticky on her fingertips. She sniffed it. Iron. Decay. When she wiped her stained hands on her white muslin gown, it left long streaks of scarlet. They resembled gashes on flesh.

She opened the trunk. It appeared empty save for that drawing she'd made in Lake Como so long ago, the ink portrait of the man with the dark flowing hair, the one she'd burned. The portrait was as terrifying as she recalled. Thin black lips. Heavy-lidded eyes. Scars. A monster. How could she have believed it represented Victor or his illness? The drawing appeared nothing like Victor. Nothing like anyone she'd known in all her years.

Elizabeth lifted the ink portrait from the trunk. Beneath where it had been, she discovered a beating heart devoid of a body. The ruddy pulsing muscle lay surrounded by a curl of fine black lace, as though it had been wrapped as an offering for an altar. Yet Elizabeth took no alarm at this macabre sight; her eyes remained fixed on the portrait clutched in her hands.

Victor asked, *"Are you wedding him? Or me?"*

* * *

Elizabeth started from her sleep. A cold dew covered her forehead. She felt breathless. Trapped. She was becoming like her aunt with her nightmares; Caroline once confessed she dreamt of past troubles more often than she wished.

Elizabeth ran to the window, panting for air. The sky was the dingy grey preceding dawn on a moody autumn day. It would rain soon. Then she remembered. Henry was leaving that morning. Henry was going to Strasburgh alone. She'd sent him to Victor, who didn't know she didn't want to be his wife. Victor, who'd become a stranger to her. And to Henry too, she suspected.

Panic curled from the center of her stomach. The dream was a sign. She had to protect Henry. But how? Then she knew: Henry shouldn't go with Victor. She'd stop him leaving. They'd marry. She'd no longer protect Victor before Henry; the Frankensteins would have to understand.

Elizabeth grabbed her stays, her stockings. She hadn't time to lose— the walk to Geneva would take just over an hour, if she hurried. She'd arrive before Henry's departure, be at his door.

She dressed herself without Sophie's assistance. By the time she finished, the sky had burst open with the rain she'd foretold. It was a pounding rain too, weather unfit for anyone to walk in. She had no choice. Hopefully a coach would soon pass.

Along the road to Geneva Elizabeth rushed in the storm, body chilled and heart aching. Her eyes strained down the road. It appeared a silvery blur of water, rain hissing against the soil.

No coaches passed.

Sleet dashed against her face, the sopped hem of her gown dragging at her limbs. Beneath her hood, her hair felt damp against her skull. Her teeth chattered. She raised her eyes, yearning to see a coach. She made someone out in the distance amid the downpour. A huge man. She couldn't make out anything more but his extreme height and raven-black hair. Behind him, a host of jackdaws took to the sky. A blur of darkness.

She heard the rumble of wheels. The whinny of horses. She turned. Her heart rose.

At last.

Elizabeth waved her arms, shouting. The coach came to a noisy halt, splattering mud over her skirts. She glanced over her shoulder, seeking the uncommonly tall man; perhaps he sought a coach too. He was gone. No matter.

She ran toward the coach, her wet shoes raising blisters.

"Thank goodness you're here! Ah, how relieved I am!"

The driver's gaze lingered on Elizabeth's giddy face. "Where to, Mademoiselle? You well?"

"Just short of time, Monsieur. Geneva, please."

Water dripped from his hat brim as he shook his head. "Sorry, Chêne only."

"Can't you take me part of the way?"

"Not allowed—I'm late because of the weather."

"Please, I'm begging you!"

The carriage splashed her skirts anew as it departed. Now she was truly soaked.

Rain or no, Elizabeth hurried down the road as quickly as the storm allowed, ignoring the view of the lake, the tall trees overhead. Lightning cracked over the Juras. The wind picked up, howling and hissing. A distant boom of thunder. It reminded her of that wild storm after the Christmas soirée, the one that had destroyed the oak in their garden.

The road was pitted and muddy. A gut in the road. When she stepped to avoid a puddle, her ankle curled. She collapsed to her knees like a marionette with cut strings.

She stumbled back to her feet. Her ankle panged, but not badly.

One step forward.

Thunder and lightning, closer now. She smelled smoke.

A second step. A third.

The rain hardened into sleet. She could barely see her raised hands before her. She gazed up toward the sky, tree branches straining above. Her hood fell back.

Water. All was water.

A sharp flash of light, a crack of wood. The limb of an elm shattered. It dropped to the road before her.

CHAPTER III.

"My journey had been my own suggestion, and Elizabeth, therefore, acquiesced: but she was filled with disquiet at the idea of my suffering, away from her . . . It had been her care which provided me a companion in Clerval."

* * *

ERNEST DISCOVERED Elizabeth two hours later seated on the side of the road with a swollen ankle and a bloody forehead. By then, the storm had ended as abruptly as it had begun. "What are you doing here?" she'd asked Ernest in a peculiar tone, as though he'd happened on her in a shop. He explained it was Sophie who noticed she'd left the house early, Sophie who alerted the Frankensteins when Elizabeth never appeared at breakfast.

"We've been looking for you for the past hour," he said, helping her into the Frankenstein carriage.

Elizabeth's injuries initially appeared superficial: a twisted ankle, a small wound on her forehead the doctor assured would heal nicely without stitches. By the time her ankle improved, her spirit had lightened enough that she spoke of traveling to England to meet Victor and Henry, though Alphonse forbade it. "I don't want you traveling alone." She considered defying him but decided to wait until spring, when the weather would be kinder. But weeks later her condition mysteriously worsened, though little evident damage remained: a scar above her right eyebrow, an aching ankle on damp days.

"I do not know what's wrong with her," the physician informed Alphonse one morning six months after Henry's departure. "I can bleed your niece again, but it hasn't helped thus far."

Eyes closed, Elizabeth listened to a conversation she'd heard numerous times:

"Why has she become ill again, Doctor?"

"I'm uncertain, Monsieur Frankenstein."

"But it's been so long! There must be something more you can do . . ."

Today wasn't any different when Dr. Fiorelli made his usual weekly call. Today, though, Elizabeth wasn't lying in her usual place on the chaise in Caroline's room. Sophie had convinced Elizabeth to come downstairs to the drawing room to take advantage of a slant of sunlight, a mark of spring's return. The sunbeam fell across the settee, where Sophie had propped her against a nest of embroidered pillows.

The light irritated her eyes, but Elizabeth was too tired to complain. Nor would she complain if they again bled her with leeches or forced laudanum or belladonna on her. Complaining took effort. Complaining took caring. She possessed neither.

At first, Elizabeth had possessed hope. To reassure Henry of her devotion, she'd written him weekly while he traveled with Victor through Holland, London, and Oxford, careful to be circumspect with her words in case Victor should read them. *"Dear friend,"* she wrote in one letter, *"I still think of our time in Lake Como, and hope to return one day with you."* In another, *"I recall our last conversation before your departure, and earnestly wish I'd given a different reply."* Henry never answered; her hope leeched like water from a sieve. However, Victor sent letter upon letter filled with florid descriptions of Nature. He'd rambled in the forest of Windsor, enjoying the majestic oaks; Matlock reminded him of Switzerland on a smaller scale, with its green hills and pines. And now he was onto Scotland.

Beloved friend, Victor had written two weeks earlier, *"I plan to part from Henry in Perth, where he'll remain while I spend several months on the Orkney Islands bringing my work to a close. Alas, this means I shan't return to Geneva until winter. We'll be married at the New Year instead of this spring. I promise to never leave you again . . ."*

Eyes shut, Elizabeth listened to her uncle and her doctor converse:

"Monsieur Frankenstein, perhaps we should reconsider your niece's spirit. Has anything distressed her?"

"She misses my son," Alphonse replied in a low voice. "Their wedding's been postponed."

"Now you tell me! I thought she was mourning your little boy—such a tragedy. They're still to marry though?"

When Alphonse didn't answer, Elizabeth peered beneath the handkerchief covering her eyes. Her uncle cradled his head in his palms.

"In time," Alphonse said with a sigh. "My son has been traveling. He'll return the end of the year. Hopefully before Christmas."

"Ah, that's what's affecting her! Romantic disappointment. The warmer weather will help. Make her take walks with her maid, preferably in the sun. Such a severe winter! Did you hear they burned furniture in Paris for heat?"

"Such are the times." Alphonse's tone was resigned.

"Now they're rioting there over grain shortages. So much suffering . . ." The doctor's leather case snapped shut. "I'll return next week. Unless, of course, you require me before then."

Elizabeth listened to Alphonse's footsteps follow the doctor's. The door clicked shut behind them.

Alone at last.

She removed the handkerchief from her eyes, which Sophie had infused in lavender. She turned on her side, heart aching. A crinkle of paper against her hip. A letter for Henry. She'd finished writing it before the doctor's arrival. Not that it mattered. He wouldn't answer. She'd never expected him to abandon her in such a manner.

You abandoned him first. You should have told him about Justine.

"Too late," she murmured.

The sun grew brighter against the settee. Too bright. She closed her eyes. The scent of tobacco tickled her nose.

"What's too late?"

Ernest. Goodness, he was silent! She hadn't heard him enter the room.

"The hour," she evaded, looking over the settee. He was leaning against the mantel, a cigarette in his hand; he claimed tobacco gave him powers of acuity. She was surprised his lungs weren't affected.

"Elizabeth, I've never taken you to be the lovesick sort. My brother doesn't deserve your pining."

"You're one to talk," she replied. "Aren't you pining over a Mademoiselle Beder?"

He flicked ash into the coal scuttle. "She expects as much. It's a game."

"Everything's a game to you. Politics. Revolution. University." Alphonse had sent Ernest to university in Geneva that fall. He returned home begging his father to pay for a military commission.

"Write Victor, Elizabeth. Tell him how you feel. He'll hurry home."

"I will. This afternoon."

She didn't. Instead, she gazed out the window at the daffodils and tulips budding in the garden overlooking the lake, wishing the clock would turn back to when William was a baby, Justine was with them, and Caroline still alive. A time when Victor didn't frighten her along with the prospect of becoming his wife. A time when she wasn't in love with his dearest friend, who'd decided it was too late for them. Fate.

* * *

Spring passed and summer arrived in a blaze of heat and cicadas. That fall Ernest was set to leave the Frankensteins to join the military amid a flurry of pageantry—he'd finally managed to convince Alphonse. Before his departure, Alphonse proposed they holiday as a family in the mountains. Mont Blanc near the Mer de Glace, where Victor had traveled after William's death. "The air will help Elizabeth recover," Alphonse said, "as well as myself." Though nearly a year had passed since his heart attack, he remained fragile.

The change of scenery only contributed to Elizabeth's unsettled state. When they arrived at their hotel in Chamounix at the base of Mont Blanc, Elizabeth noticed a slight woman near the register desk wearing a grey wool cloak with a raised shoulder. Beneath the woman's hood, Elizabeth glimpsed silvery grey eyes and moon-pale hair. *It's Justine. She's let off her male clothes.* Joy welled laced by fear. Elizabeth should warn her to flee, but how? Alphonse and Ernest might notice.

Elizabeth must have revealed her shock, for Alphonse took her hand. "Do you need to sit, my angel?"

She shook her head. "I'm so happy to be here." A forced giggle. "How pretty it is—quick, look outside! Is that a hawk?"

As Alphonse turned toward the window, the woman removed her cloak. Her hump was a baby curled over her shoulder. Not Justine.

Tears welled in Elizabeth's eyes.

It's a sign she's safe. That's all.

"Your hawk was a raven," Alphonse said, chuckling. "But yes, it's lovely here. What a view! Ah, there's Ernest with our luggage. Will you complete the registry?"

"Of course, Uncle."

The Frankenstein family, she wrote in the registry. *September 21, 1795.* For residence, *Geneva.*

"Madame Frankenstein," the concierge greeted. "Your husband stayed with us last autumn for several days. I remember him. Tall, dark-haired. Quiet."

Victor.

"He's not my husband yet," she corrected. "He's studying in England. He's a natural philosopher." She yearned to ask, *Was he alone? Did he speak of anything peculiar? Did he behave strangely?* These questions never made it to her lips. Instead:

"May I see his registration? I yearn to view his handwriting."

"Of course, Mademoiselle!"

The concierge flipped a few pages and there was Victor—well, his handwriting anyway. *Victor Frankenstein,* he'd signed. *September 19, 1794.* For his residence: *L'enfer.* From hell.

"He's a sense of humor," the concierge said with a nervous laugh.

Elizabeth tore out the page when the concierge turned his back. Later in her room, she burned it.

Weeks after she returned to Geneva, she couldn't shake off her unease. She thought of Victor traveling with Henry in Scotland, Henry's lack of response to her letters.

Henry, what have I done to you?

CHAPTER IV.

*"I told Clerval that I wished to make the tour of Scotland alone . . .
Having parted from my friend, I determined to visit some remote spot
of Scotland, and finish my work in solitude. I did not doubt
but that the monster followed me."*

* * *

WHILE ELIZABETH LANGUISHED IN GENEVA, Henry sat down to write a
letter from Scotland. It would never be posted.

Dear Elizabeth,

Though I'd intended not to write during my travels to grant time for
our emotions to cool, an unnerving experience has led me to break
my vow.

I am sure you recall my description of Victor's illness in Ingolstadt,
during which he ranted about a man—nay, a <u>monster</u>—watching him
with the intent of harm. At the time, I considered his wild claim to be
fueled by fever. But I believe Victor might not have been imagining this
monster—for I now fear one watches me too.

Lest you ask, "Henry, are you well?" allow me to explain more fully.
While you were so ill with scarlet fever, poor Justine told Victor and
myself a tale her father knew from Prague. It was about a golem, a
monster made of clay by man. I won't go into its details, but I think there

may be some truth to Justine's tale that would explain Victor's monster, along with my own experiences.

Here's what occurred: these past months, I have been visiting a Scottish acquaintance in Perth while Victor is in the Orkneys. The cottage where I'm staying adjoins my acquaintance's estate on the river, affording me solitude so I may study. But instead of studying as I planned, I've spent most of my time thinking of you and our secret vow to wed.

(I know I am delaying the main of my explanation; I write this preamble so you may understand my state of mind.)

Two nights ago, I found myself unable to sleep as I considered the turmoil we'd brought to each other's lives. After hours of tossing in bed, I rose to stare out my window. My eyes were greeted by the largest full moon I have ever witnessed. As I watched it glisten along the river, a peculiar fancy took hold, for was I not in the land of enchantment? I even imagined a misty figure rise from the river's rushing currents like a fairy from a storybook.

Intrigued by my turn of mind, I outfitted myself to walk in the moonlight. As I wandered along the river, my thoughts began to settle. "Ah beauty!" I cried into the night. "What a blessing you are to humanity!" At this admittedly lofty pronouncement, the oak trees swayed as though a storm was about to commence. An owl shrieked, then silenced. Though I cannot explain why, the hair on the back of my neck rose.

I turned, my calm shattered. What greeted my eyes was unlike anything I have ever viewed—and here I shall not hold back what I witnessed though you may think me mad.

Elizabeth, a man—nay, a giant—stood beside the oaks, his arms raised toward the branches. He appeared eight feet of height, his hair dark and flowing, his cheeks smooth of beard. (For this reason I concluded him to be a man rather than a beast—a beast would be covered in fur, do you not think?) As the giant turned his baleful face toward mine, I saw he clutched a nest in one hand and an owl in the other; he appeared to be hunting for eggs. His eyes were a watery yellow —yes, I could tell this in the night, for his gaze glowed like a wolf's. His features were transversed by thick scars unlike any I have ever seen, even during the revolutions.

Terror rose in my heart. I set myself to flee. Alas, my feet would not respond. Then the unnatural creature's eyes met mine. I could not turn away: his mouth shifted into such an expression of woe that my fear turned to pity.

Dare I write what I believe I witnessed? A phantasm, a ghost. A monster. A golem.

After this, I remember nothing more—I suspect I fainted. When I next opened my eyes, I was back in my cottage. My Scottish acquaintance splashed water on my face and forced me to bed. I resolved to banish what I had seen from my memory. But when I woke in the morning, I grew more troubled than ever. Had I imagined the monster?

At dinner that evening, my acquaintance explained he'd discovered me unconscious outside my cottage door, as though someone had deposited me there. He inquired kindly, "Clerval, are you not well?"

"I'm uncertain." I described what I had witnessed: the giant man, his scars, his sorrowful eyes. "Do you know of anyone bearing this resemblance?"

"No."

"A creature of some sort? A zoo? A traveling circus?"

Another shake of the head. "It's the moon. It affects us all at times. You are overtired. Perhaps you should allow yourself leisure tomorrow."

With this I agreed to rest, ashamed of the disturbance I'd created. And yet, even then I still sense <u>him</u> watching me in the same way an animal anticipates a predator. I stared out my window, my eyes straining. I saw no one.

Beata, you can imagine how this disturbs me! But after much contemplation, I've arrived at a new understanding—

Something was scratching at the door. Something insistent. Henry set down his pen, disquieted. "It's nothing," he murmured. "Just the wind."

After a moment's hesitation, he threw open the door.

No one there.

Henry settled back in his chair. He dipped his pen in ink. He continued:

—I am reluctant to acknowledge. I am now convinced that whatever monster I witnessed was a phantasm—nay, a golem—created in my mind from guilt over my love for you. A product of my imagination, if you will. This realization leads me to consider whether Victor bears a similar weight on his conscience. Though I still cannot conjecture what his might be, it would explain his strange behavior since Ingolstadt.

And yet, as mad as it sounds, I still sense _him_ watching me, which leads me to the reason for this letter. There is only one cure for my troubled conscience: Elizabeth, despite whatever affection we share, I know your hand has been joined to Victor's since you were a child—I hereby release you from your promise to wed me.

With this letter, I swear to never again mention my devotion to you. Know that you shall serve as my lodestar for the remainder of my days. In this way, you can take pride in what you have inspired in me, rather than shame.

Write as soon as you can, if only a sentence or two, to assure me of your forgiveness. Only then shall my monster be vanquished.

Yours forever—

H.

Henry blotted his letter. The sooner he sent it, the better. The letter would be a shock to Elizabeth, but also a relief, he suspected. Well, it was for the best. When she'd sent him to Strasburgh to meet Victor, he'd realized sometimes love wasn't enough—Elizabeth's fate was tied to the Frankensteins, just as his was. He'd been a fool to hope for anything more.

"Sleep," he said aloud. "That's what I need." He tried not to think of her. Tried not to think of his sore heart, of all he'd suffered while traveling with Victor. Anyway, he hadn't received a single letter from Elizabeth all these months, though she'd written Victor regularly. *"I love Elizabeth so much,"* Victor had confided. *"I must go to the Orkneys for her sake, to bring my labors to a close. You do understand?"* Henry hadn't. If he'd considered there to be any possibility of taking Elizabeth as his wife, he never would have left Geneva.

Then he remembered Elizabeth in bed beside him in his room. Elizabeth's lips against his. Elizabeth returning his confession of love . . .

Enough.

Henry folded and sealed the letter. He felt lighter for having written it. Cleaner of spirit. Yet he still had an uneasy sense of not being alone. Of someone watching him.

You'll feel better once you post the letter.

Distraction, that's what he needed. He yearned for his journal, for those drawings Elizabeth had made of him the day they pledged to wed. How beautiful they were, but there was no need to torment himself. He considered his language texts, but he was too weary for those. Instead, he reached for his *Le Morte d'Arthur*, turning to the story of Lancelot and Guinevere and Arthur. A cautionary tale. He was proud he'd taken its lessons to heart. He would let his Arthur and Guinevere have a happy ending. It was as well. What would have happened if Elizabeth had run off with him? It would have destroyed Victor, ruined their friendship, undermined Alphonse's fragile health. It would have been an act of treachery against the family that had offered him love and sanctuary after his mother's death. He'd done what was right.

Henry's *Le Morte d'Arthur* readily fell open to a favorite passage. *"When King Arthur understood the letter, he mused of many things . . ."* As he read, his eyes grew heavy, his mind distant. He was no longer in Perth, no longer in the year 1795. A better world awaited him, one where angels bore grails and enchantresses offered swords. A world without revolutions or golems.

Soon sleep captured Henry's body, and with it any worries weighing him. To his delight, his dream transported him back to the Villa Lavenza. It was the day they'd arrived after fleeing Geneva. There was Elizabeth in the apple orchard, the sun beaming through the trees. How lovely she'd appeared, more grail maiden than queen! He'd never loved her so well. At last they were alone, far from Geneva and all its accordant dangers. Far from Victor and the Frankensteins.

In his dream, he peered up through the apple trees toward the sky, which was brilliant with light. Leaves shimmered gold. The sun burned so hot. So hard to breathe. The stench of something foul rose. Something rotting . . .

He tried to cough. To inhale. Was he drowning?

A gruff voice rumbled against his ear: "Awake, fairest, thy lover is near—he who would give his life but to obtain one look of affection from thine eyes; my beloved, awake!"

Henry struggled awake.

A pair of vulpine eyes awaited him.

A pair of hands encircled his neck.

CHAPTER V.

*"I entered the room where the corpse lay, and was led up to the coffin . . .
I feel yet parched with horror, nor can I reflect on that terrible moment
without shuddering and agony. The examination, the presence of the
magistrate and witnesses, passed like a dream from my memory, when
I saw the lifeless form of Henry Clerval stretched before me."*

* * *

BY THE DISMAL month of November, most birds due to migrate south
have already reached their destinations. However, a solitary sparrow
remained behind in Perth, unwilling to abandon the mud nest that had
nurtured her long-grown children.

The morning after Henry Clerval's death, the sparrow discovered a
small broken window in his cottage that permitted entry. After taking
advantage of a half-eaten loaf of bread, the sparrow caught sight of
Henry's long, silent body draped across his bed. She chirped beside him
before she noticed the ring of bruises around his throat, the shadowy
figure lurking in the corner. It was then the sparrow understood she'd
lingered too long in this land of ice and loss.

She took to the sky. In December and January, the sparrow flew
over the shores of Albion toward France, past Paris and, finally, to
Geneva, where Elizabeth Lavenza learned of the murder of her true
love, whose corpse had been abandoned by his killer on the coast of

Ireland. Henry would never return to her, never embrace her again, never become her husband . . . and all because she'd sent him away. She tried to drown herself in an ocean of laudanum, but survived when Sophie discovered her half-mad and retching. Sophie covered Elizabeth's grieving with excuses that Alphonse and Ernest barely paid mind to. Nor did they note when Elizabeth's sobs and wails shattered the sky until the clouds released hailstones and lightning.

The sparrow gracefully dodged these as she rode the wind south. By February, she reached the heights of Mont Blanc and the Mer de Glace.

This was the day the sparrow finally came to a rest. It was also the day that, for the first time since she'd fled the Villa Lavenza, Justine Moritz arrived at the unwelcome conclusion she was being watched.

Until then, Justine's isolation had been nearly complete. Once she'd abandoned Ella's corpse in the woods, she'd climbed into the Alps clutching the satchel she packed in preparation. It contained the funds Elizabeth had left, a change of clothes, a small silver knife from the kitchen, a spyglass from the Clervals' shop, and the necklace bearing Caroline's portrait. As Justine traveled, she tried her best to remain out of sight save to obtain food. At night, she slept in forests hidden beneath branches. Her face and hands scarred from brambles and thorns. Her face dirtied until it grew unrecognizable.

The arrival of spring lightened Justine's fears, but instead of seeking civilization, she found herself pulled west, toward the mountains of Savoy, which lay but two days south from Geneva—though Elizabeth had warned her not to approach her home, she couldn't resist. Finally, Justine reached the base of Mont Blanc, which overlooked a vast sea of ice. The vale was surrounded by precipitous mountains and filled with white undulating fissures, which appeared as though frost had entrapped the waves of a mighty torrent.

"No one will ever find me here," she decided. "Not even the Frankensteins."

The first weeks, Justine slept in a grassy field overlooking the Mer de Glace. Summer inaugurated a halcyon period of golden sunlight and perfumed flowers, which she knew would not last. Fortunately, by the time the days grew short and the weather cool, she discovered an abandoned hut hidden behind a cluster of cypresses, presumably used by a shepherd in warmer months. A thin stream of clear water danced alongside the hut. She stared at her reflection in the water, taking in her scars, her deformities. Her misshapen spine and abnormally raised shoulder appeared more skewed than ever. Nothing had changed.

I'm still a monster.

She shrugged. All the more reason to avoid humanity.

The door to the windowless shepherd's hut was unlocked. Inside, she found a shabby room. The chinks in the wooden walls bore enough gaps that one could judge the weather through them.

The hut was not empty. It contained several large burlap sacks stuffed with hay, presumably used for sleeping, covered by a blanket sewn of fur—the shepherd must have been exceptionally tall. On the other side of the room, a small fireplace laden with ashes, a table hewn of rough wood with a solitary chair. The shepherd had left behind three books: a copy of Plutarch's *Lives*, *The Sorrows of Young Werther,* and a leather-bound *Paradise Lost*, which Justine resisted the urge to destroy because it brought up unhappy memories of Ernest. Whoever lived there was surprisingly literate.

The thick layer of dust inside the hut suggested it had been uninhabited for some months. *He'll return in the spring,* Justine told herself. *I'll depart before then.* Still, to be certain, she waited two days to see if the hut's inhabitant would return, spying across a field covered with edelweiss and gentian. Only then did she claim the hut as her own.

She filled the chinks in the wall with mud, gathered wood for fire, and foraged for greens. She speared fish from the stream with the knife she'd taken from the villa. She buried the bag containing her remaining coins in a crevice near the door, and tucked the locket with Caroline's portrait beneath the bed; these served as the only reminder of her former life.

As winter approached, she laid in a supply of nuts. She managed to grind them into a crude flour, which she mixed with water and baked into cakes. They were unappetizing and gave her diarrhea. But hunger was kinder than her experiences with humanity.

By the time the first snowstorm arrived, Justine realized how foolish she'd been—winter on the Mer de Glace was far more severe than the one she'd experienced traveling. It took three days for the storm to die —three long days in which Justine lay shivering and hungry and thirsty, for she'd run out of food and water and wood. She forced herself outside despite heavy winds, wrapping the fur blanket around her body.

Just as she was about to gather snow to melt for water, she noticed footsteps. They were fresh. Enormous. They led to the door of her hut before they disappeared, as though their owner had flown into the sky. Where could he have gone?

Then she knew: *He's watching me.*

She shivered. Ella. Her poor abandoned body. Those bruises across her throat. Had Justine traveled all this way to meet this same fate?

Once she'd calmed she asked, *Had the hut's owner returned?*

A ready answer arrived: *If he did, he'd have confronted me.*

She chanted to herself, "I am safe. I appear male. I appear a beggar. I offer no threat to anyone." Unable to soothe her fears, she fled the hut. But when temperature dropped as the sun sank, she had no choice: she would die unless she took cover.

Heart pulsing, she pushed the door open with a shout . . .

The hut was empty save for that stubborn swallow, who'd traveled all the way from Perth. The bird immediately flew out the door, never to return.

A sparrow. That was all.

Justine laughed, then wept as she slid to the floor.

Ella. I'm lucky I survived.

She again wished she'd been more attentive to Ella. Friendlier. Maybe she wouldn't have run away. Maybe she wouldn't have died. Justine covered her face with her palms. She sobbed until she was spent of salt.

Then she remembered. Food. Water. Her stomach growled. Her tongue was dry in her mouth. It was then she noticed an offering of firewood had been laid out for her, along with a freshly skinned rabbit.

Too cold and hungry to question its provenance, Justine built a fire and roasted the rabbit. She tore into the carcass with her hands, not caring that the rabbit's flesh was charred or the interior raw. She went to sleep that night with a full belly for the first time in weeks.

Don't let me be imagining this, she thought as she drifted off. She hadn't: when she awoke, the remainder of the rabbit was still there, along with new offerings of cheese and bread.

Again, Justine ate, grateful. After she'd finished, she noticed her hands were trembling.

Those footsteps in the snow. The offerings in the hut.

Someone had come into the hut while she slept. Someone was

watching her. Someone close.

She ran outside, heart pounding and head rushing. More footsteps, fresh ones. Again, they disappeared in the middle of the field before her house. Who was her benefactor? What if they were offering her help if only to injure her? But why would someone do good before causing evil? It made no sense.

Perhaps I've an angel, Justine decided, thinking of *Paradise Lost.*

That night as Justine slept, she imagined the angel watching over her. His hands—for she assumed her angel was male, given the size of his feet—resting on her shoulders. Protecting her. Caring for her.

And so he did. As the winter continued, Justine came to expect the arrival of his packages when she was most in need. If she had paper and pencil, she'd have left her angel a note. Try as she might to anticipate him, she never glimpsed him. Sometimes his offerings arrived in the middle of the night, which caused her no end of shock; she'd awake to find a basket of food beside her bed. Other times food appeared during the day, when she was away from the hut.

As the snow melted and crocuses budded, Justine grew healthier. Her flesh filled out. When she glanced at herself in the stream, her scars appeared softer and her hair long enough to cover her skull. She still resembled a boy, but no longer one who appeared as though he'd returned from the gates of Death. Even so, her angel's offerings continued to arrive.

He's still watching me. But instead of fear, Justine was infused with wonder.

* * *

Justine caught her first glimpse of her angel in early spring, soon after the crocuses gave way to daffodils. She'd envisioned him to be a celestial being filled with majesty and beauty, like something painted on an altar in church. She encountered something very different.

She first saw him at twilight. She'd been out walking in the woods when she heard a deep rumble rise from the earth. The sound was such that she felt it inside her chest. Birds fled the trees. A doe dashed past, nearly knocking Justine to her knees. She sensed someone was weeping. Someone far away—the mountains made sounds seem closer than they were. A trick of the sky.

Over Mont Blanc, lightning flashed. A spring storm. It was so high up in the mountains, the display appeared especially grand. Blackened clouds rushed across the horizon, with lightning following suit, and thunder growling. A flock of geese fleeing south. Hailstones bounced before Justine's feet. Thick drops of rain. All of a sudden the sky cleared and the sun returned, turning everything delectably purple and pink and brilliant.

Justine gasped. There *he* was, at last.

Below the highest peak of Mont Blanc, what appeared to be a giant man clambered across the rocks with the agility of a spider. How strong he appeared! How swift! Justine squinted. He leapt as though flying along the side of the mountain.

This man, this *creature*, was her benefactor. Her angel—he had to be. Excitement—no, joy—rose inside her. Wasn't the scale of his jump akin to those footprints she'd discovered in the snow? He probably leaped into the trees to avoid her. It all made sense.

"Hello! Is it you?"

Justine's voice echoed through the valley. *"Helllllooo . . ."* The angel paused on the mountain, cocked his head. Then, just as unexpectedly as he'd appeared, he vanished in a blur of motion.

"Come back! I only wanted to thank you!"

She'd tried to make her tone as kind as possible. As welcoming as possible. He'd saved her life. She was surprised by the sorrow she felt. Her loneliness. She realized: it had been well over a year since anyone had addressed her with kindness. Now he'd never return.

Justine was wrong. Her angel reappeared three days later—three days that felt longer than any she'd experienced, even when she'd been locked away for William's murder. This time, the angel left a plucked chicken outside her door. His offering was accompanied by a letter written in a surprisingly refined hand.

I beg you not to seek me! I am unused to human society. I am one who is miserable above all others. Therefore I sought to reduce your misery, knowing too well what it is like to be alone and friendless.

Good sir, Justine wrote in turn, marking a piece of elm bark with a burned twig, *I yearned only to thank you when I shouted your way. Will you not meet with me? If you do, I promise you will no longer be friendless.*

If you were to meet me, he answered, *you would find me a creation of terror, not felicity. Your eyes are not prepared for one of my kind. I am a miserable creature hated and shunned by all.*

She responded, *I would never think this—I bear you only gratitude! Will you not come to me?*

Her angel did not write another letter for over two weeks—by then it was so deep into spring that the land again flourished green. Justine despaired. Was she not also shunned? Did she not understand what it was to yearn for affection but fear rejection?

One night she heard a cautious knock on the outside of the wall, where a chink in the mud had hollowed during the long winter.

"I have returned," the angel said in a gruff voice.

Justine's heart swelled. "I'll come to you."

"No!" His breath was rough, like a beast. "Do not approach! Let us remain as we are, with this wall between us."

"Why?"

"If you were to behold me, you would turn in disgust."

Justine shifted her chair closer to the chink. "I might have died this winter without you! Why would I not welcome one who has been an angel to me?"

A mournful moan. "I am no angel. Do not think otherwise—I have done much I regret. I remain separated from those who wish me ill for actions they forced me to take. I have been rejected by my fellow man. I have sworn war against the one who brought me into being. I have murdered those I should not have."

"I understand."

Her angel was a disgraced soldier, probably nobility. He'd run away to avoid execution. She thought of King Louis without his head. Napoleon. The revolutions in Geneva and France.

She said carefully, "One cannot blame oneself for actions undertaken at the behest of others, no matter how evil they may be. Revolutions are born of hope though they may lead to destruction. Why will you not allow me to see you?"

A scuttle on the other side of the wall. A long silence.

"I promise to be kind," she pressed. "I am also unwanted and have fled the unkindness of others."

"Very well," he said at last. "I will come to you tomorrow night."

"Why not tonight?"

Another moan. "For I need to gird myself for your disgust. Once darkness falls, I will visit you. You must extinguish any candles, all fires. Let there be no light. Then you will know me for who I am." A long pause. "And then we shall part, for you won't wish me near you."

Before Justine could respond, she heard him rush away.

* * *

The next night, Justine waited in the pitch-dark hut for her angel's arrival. She felt more terror of his not showing up than of his physical appearance, for what form could he take that she'd reject him? He'd been kind to her. He'd saved her life. He was good.

After what felt like hours, the hut door creaked open. Justine's stomach flocked with butterflies.

"You are here?" he said, an edge of fear in his voice.

"I am," she answered eagerly. "Have you a name?"

His laughter was bitter. Mocking. "I have no name. No soul. My father did not deign to grant me them."

This fulfilled Justine's suppositions: a soldier in disgrace would be shed of his name just as he'd been shed of his aristocracy.

"Then I shall be as nameless. We will know each other by deeds, not reputations."

He laughed again, but the sound was lighter. "Clever, aren't you?"

Her face flamed in the dark. "That's what some would say."

"May I approach you? You still do not fear me?"

"You may, sir. And I don't."

Justine heard her benefactor settle on the burlap bag beside her. He let out a sigh. She did the same. Whatever tension she'd held within herself lessened. How strange it was to sit so companionably with someone, with such serenity! To hold conversation after so long alone! Even in her happiest moments with Ernest, there had been no peace between them.

Another thought arrived, one that embarrassed her—she should have considered it earlier.

"This is your hut? Your books?"

"Yes."

"You allowed me to make you homeless."

"I saw you were as miserable as I am, and as pitiful. I know what it is to be friendless, to be wretched of all your kind."

Her benefactor shifted beside her. She sensed his nearness. His presence. Where there should have been warmth, a coolness rose from his flesh. So peculiar . . .

In the distance, a rumble sounded from the mountains. Another storm. Justine ignored it.

"I have been watching you for some time," he said. "Now that I've heard your voice, I know you are not what you appear."

"How so?"

"You're not the male of your species, though your voice is odd and rough. You're female."

Justine stiffened, thinking of poor Ella. "If you're as kind as I believe you are, you will understand the reason for my disguise. I've seen more than I wish. I prefer life over death, virtue over vice."

"You lost someone you cared about."

"A friend. She . . ."

Justine couldn't say more without her voice breaking. Ella hadn't really been a friend, but they'd lived together. They'd grown to know each other as much as you can know someone you deceive. Then there was Elizabeth, who'd saved her life and was her truest friend. Elizabeth, whom she'd most likely never see again.

"I understand," he responded, "for I have also suffered the attacks of man. I've been shot by a rustic, and beaten by a mob. Violence affects men as well as women. But you do not fear me. Do you?"

A low boom, closer than before. A slash of lightning. The storm would soon arrive.

"You do not answer," he prompted. "Should I leave?"

"No, don't go. And I don't fear you. Should I?"

His voice quavered. "You *will* want to leave once you learn what I am. You will fear me—this I promise." His tone grew agitated. "I cannot put this off any longer. The suspense torments me!" Another catch of his breath. "I must let you know the truth though it shall damn me. Here . . ."

He took her hands—how cold his were, like ice! how wide his palms! —and rested them against his face.

His cheeks were wet. Tears. His head was huge. But she felt something more. Something unnatural. Stitches. They were like a map traversing the terrain of his face. A long, thick nose, akin to a bull. A thin set of lips, which shuddered beneath her touch. A strong square jaw. Large drooping eyes. His forehead was wide and nested with scars across where his brain lay. Then his hair—it was lush and long and knotted. She gently smoothed the tangles. He flinched as though she'd burned him.

Who are you? What are you? she yearned to ask, but she knew she'd gain no reply. Anyway, didn't she already know the answer? He was mutilated through battle and fire. No wonder he lived in isolation. No wonder he refused to be seen.

"Do I repulse you? Speak, for I must know! Will you also shun me? Do I disgust—"

A dash of lightning struck so close that the air flared white—and the face of Justine's benefactor was revealed at last.

Beneath his shriveled complexion and straight black lips, his yellow skin scarcely covered the work of muscles and arteries. His hair was a lustrous ebony, and flowing; his teeth of a pearly whiteness. But these luxuriances only formed a horrid contrast with his watery eyes, which appeared nearly the same color as the dun-white sockets in which they were set. He was no soldier injured by war or flames. Nor was he an angel. He was a daemon, a monster. A deformity of life. A creature constructed of death and flesh, not incantations and clay. A golem.

Darkness returned abruptly, leaving Justine alone in the hut with the golem. She didn't scream. Nor did she flee. However, the golem's shadowy form rushed for the door.

Justine grabbed his wrist, using all her strength to pull him toward her.

"Who are you? You shall not leave until you tell me!"

"I told you, I am one who is shunned by all. I will not offer violence, but you must let me go!"

"I will not!" She yanked anew on his hand. "Tell me who you are!"

Another strike of lightning. In that flash, Justine made out a scar across his wrist. The stitching bore small stitches of a precisely even length. At the end of the scar, she made out a small triangle.

She knew of only one person who sewed that way.

"Victor Frankenstein," she said, disbelief in her voice.

The golem let out a hard shout as he shoved her to the floor. Before she could recover, he was gone.

CHAPTER VI.

"It was on a dreary night of November, that I beheld the accomplishment of my toils. With an anxiety that almost amounted to agony, I collected the instruments of life around me, that I might infuse a spark of being into the lifeless thing that lay at my feet."

* * *

AFTER A SLEEPLESS NIGHT, Justine discovered a journal outside her door bound in a sap-green Florentine paper. She immediately recognized it. Hadn't she seen Elizabeth give it to Victor that last picnic before Caroline's death?

When Justine picked up Victor's journal, a letter fell out. The angel —or rather, the golem—had written again. This time the golem's writing was less elegant, as though he'd dashed off his missive in a fury.

> If you read this, you will understand everything about my relationship to
> Victor Frankenstein, but you shall never again know a moment's peace.
> Do you dare?

Justine's pulse raced. The journal weighed her hands, the history it held. Again, she recalled the scars along the golem's wrist, the stitching that surely had been Victor's. But what of the golem? Where was he?

Her eyes strained beyond the field outside the hut, into the woods. She saw no one.

He's watching me.

Hands shaking, she opened the journal to the flyleaf, ignoring an inscription signed by Elizabeth. Victor had written:

This journal belongs to
Victor Frankenstein
University of Ingolstadt
January 1788
May no one breach these Pages.

"Too late," Justine muttered. She flicked away a maggot.

The journal's first pages were covered in German, leaving their contents as much a mystery as the golem's relationship to Victor. Several entries later, Justine arrived at an entry written in French, the first of many. She settled in, her stomach tight with anxiety and anticipation.

March 16, 1789. What a day! Such promise! For the first time since my mother's passing, my melancholy is alleviated by the elixir of hope . . .

As Justine read, she forgot the presence—or absence—of the golem. She forgot she was seated before a sea of ice at the foot of a mountain. She forgot everything but the words on the pages, which she turned as quickly as she read. She read entries detailing chemical formulas and drugs to induce visions. She read of experiments involving blameless animals, whose lives Victor sacrificed on the shrine of knowledge. She read of bones stolen from charnel-houses during moonlit nights. She read of barely cold bodies snatched from their graves by resurrectionists paid by Victor's decree. She read how dissecting rooms and slaughterhouses provided materials for his experiments. *"I will pursue Nature to her hiding places,"* Victor vowed on one page. On another, *"There is one secret I alone possess. If I can bestow animation upon lifeless matter, I might renew life where death has devoted the body to corruption. This is the task to which I shall dedicate myself!"*

Though Justine's eyes registered horror and her blood grew cold, she dared not cease reading. The quest Victor deliberated was one she considered immoral as well as impossible: to create life from death. She recalled his fascination with alchemy and chemistry, his peculiar outbursts after Caroline's demise. His strangeness when he'd finally returned to Geneva from Ingolstadt. His haunted eyes, which appeared as though they'd peered into the dark soul of science and emerged damned; she'd noticed this even in their scant encounters after William's death.

She read of Victor's attic laboratory overlooking the University of Ingolstadt, where he undertook his labors with profane fingers. He described how winter, spring, and summer passed unnoticed while he labored. *"Great God! I seem to have lost all desire but for this one pursuit,"* he wrote after an unsuccessful experiment. *"May I meet with success soon, for I fear illness will befall me. How my limbs weaken!"*

As the journal progressed, Victor's sentences grew short and impatient, his ragged writing scarcely legible. *"Now is the time. I must."*

After this, the journal recommenced four months later with an entry dated November 1792. It was written in a weak hand surrounded by what appeared to be splatters of blood:

At last I behold the accomplishment of my toils! If I am successful, death will be banished and life renewed. With an anxiety amounting to agony, I've collected the instruments of life to infuse a spark of being into my creation. As I write this, a storm rises from the west—I have no further preparations but to wait. My heart is filled with joyful anticipation.

Justine turned the page, heart pounding. She read, *"It was on a dreary night of November that I beheld the accomplishment of my toils."*

And then, nothing more. Not even a spot of ink.

* * *

Justine shut Victor's journal, her heart and head overcome. While she'd been reading, the sun had risen high in the heavens, illuminating all of God's creations born of Nature. She stared at the journal, imagining Victor inscribing it all those months in Ingolstadt while Elizabeth languished in Geneva, yearning for him—Elizabeth who'd saved Justine from a terrible fate. Thanks to Elizabeth, Justine was alive; Justine had found sanctuary. Elizabeth had been a true friend, the only one to believe in her innocence when all the world condemned her.

With this, Justine returned to the present moment with a shudder. She was no longer in Ingolstadt witnessing the creation of a man who wasn't born of woman, a golem sewn of corpse parts and animated by lightning. It was no longer a stormy night in November, with rain pelting the roof of an attic near the university. No, she was inside a hut beneath the shadow of Mont Blanc overlooking a sea of ice. It was May. It was spring. It was the time of life, not death. The air was soft and sweet. She was alive, for God had chosen to spare her. Her life felt as precious as when she'd awakened after her hanging with Elizabeth's celestial face before her. All these months later, the golem had helped her preserve this life.

Without warning an array of geese cleared into the sky with honks and cries and flapping wings. Justine looked up from the journal, prickles along her neck.

He'd returned.

The golem who wasn't a golem.

The golem Victor had created from science and presumption.

The golem stood outside her door. Perhaps he'd been watching her read; perhaps he'd been waiting for her to finish. No matter, for she saw him for who he was—*all* of him—beneath the light of day.

In some ways, the golem's body bore a more harmonious form than her own: his spine was straight, his shoulders symmetrical. Though his limbs were in proportion, he was taller than anyone she'd ever seen, nearly double her height. His skin was sallow and taut across the mass of muscles and arteries, transversed by scars webbed in the service of creation. His thick hair was dark as a raven's. It flowed beyond his shoulders; it was matted, filthy from neglect.

Victor's golem was a marvel. A nightmare. A monster created of death and hubris. She imagined the terror he must have inspired in those viewing him for the first time. A rush of sympathy, of protectiveness rose inside Justine. The golem was kind. Generous. More than the sum of his blasphemous creation.

The golem's eyes met hers. Fear skittered across his unkempt features before he backed away without a farewell.

"Stay!" Justine begged. "Please!"

She ran toward the golem, Victor's journal dropping from her lap.

She gathered his hand in hers, stroking across the scar where she'd recognized Victor's handiwork. The golem drew a deep intake of air, his eyes shutting in what appeared a strange ecstasy.

"Victor is your father," she said.

He nodded. He wept.

* * *

That night, the two of them burned Victor's journal in a bonfire larger than any Justine had ever witnessed, even during the revolutions. It had been the golem's idea to destroy the journal to decry his father, the golem who'd built the bonfire. He growled and shouted as he tossed the journal into the flames, tearing pages one at a time from the binding. He ventured closer to the bonfire than Justine imagined possible, but did not appear affected by the heat.

Once Victor's journal was committed to ash, Justine somehow found the golem in her arms though she was so small and he so large. She hadn't intended to offer him physical affection, but she did—for all of his size and strength, she'd never encountered anyone so sorrowful.

She led him into the hut, to its makeshift bed of burlap sacks and furs. He curled about her. His breath was icy against her cheek.

She spoke gently. "Did you ever encounter your father outside of Ingolstadt?"

"Three times," he said in a mournful voice. "After my birth, I discovered papers in a coat I stole from him to cover my body; the papers revealed Frankenstein's name, that he was a native of Geneva. It took me over a year to locate him. When at last I found my father, I asked, 'Why did you form a creature so hideous that even *you* turned from me in disgust? God made man beautiful and alluring after his own image. What sort of God are you to leave me as I am?' He refused to answer save to condemn me as a demon. A monster. A wretch." Softly: "But he did agree to a bargain . . ."

The golem's jaw tightened.

Justine pressed, "A bargain?"

"One he did not keep."

The golem's face contorted with rage as he described the strangest confrontation Justine could have imagined. Over a year earlier, he'd encountered Victor on these very mountains overlooking the Mer de

Glace, finally meeting his maker for the first time since his birth. He'd begged his creator to make an Eve to his Adam. A mate.

"*I am alone and miserable,*" the golem had said to Victor, "*for no man will associate with me; but a female as deformed and horrible as myself would not deny herself to me. My companion must be of the same species and have the same defects. You must create a female with whom I can live! This you alone can do, and I demand it as a right you must not refuse to concede. I promise we shall live in peace. We shall make our bed of dried leaves; the sun will shine on us as on man and wife.*"

"My father consented to my demand," the golem explained, "as long as I vowed to forever quit Europe for South America. I agreed, though I distrusted him. To ensure his compliance, I followed him through Europe and England to an island off the Scottish coast, where he labored in isolation to construct my mate . . ."

The golem fell into a heavy silence.

"And then what happened?" Justine prompted.

"Right before she was about to receive life, he decided he couldn't trust me. I watched him destroy my mate limb from limb. Like she was nothing. Like I was nothing." He cradled his face in his hands, shoulders shaking. "He threw her remains into the sea in a profane burial."

While the golem wept, Justine shivered as she imagined the horrific scene. The severed parts of his mate's unanimated body caught amid the waves. Her head flopping from her neck. Eyes rolling. Rivulets of scarlet streaking the steel-grey waters.

Once his tears abated, he continued. "After my father fled Scotland, I found his journal—the one you've just read—which he'd left in his laboratory amid the haste of his departure. Since then, I've followed him over land and sea toward his home in Geneva. Now I only await his wedding next month."

Justine turned cold. "You plan to kill Victor. That's why you returned here."

The golem jutted his jaw. "When he marries, I intend only to offer what he deserves. Victor Frankenstein is my father, my creator. He owed me happiness. Love. Why should he have a mate when I have none? Why should he know bliss when I am despised as a monster?"

With this, Justine recalled her shock when she'd first confronted her reflection in the mirror after her hanging. The jeers of the crowd during her trial and hanging. *Monster. That's all I am.* Then she knew what she must do to save Victor for Elizabeth's sake—Elizabeth who loved Victor and yearned to become his bride.

Justine grasped the golem's hand. "You don't need to be alone. We could remain together." A deep breath. "I'll be your friend. Your companion."

The golem offered her a long look. She knew what he was thinking: she was not his kind. Though she could not offer her body, she could offer her heart.

"You pity me," he said. "You seek to protect Victor though I do not understand why."

"You saved me from starvation. You gave me shelter. You are good."

"But I am not good." A tear brimmed at the corner of the golem's eye. "There are things I have done you do not know. Things I shall never confess to even God. Nor do I know who you are, or how you are acquainted with Frankenstein."

"Does it matter? If you promise to let Victor live, I'll stay with you. I'll be your companion. I'll be loyal—I promise!"

Justine caressed the golem's cheek, so scarred, so damp with tears. The pupils of his eyes dilated as they met hers. She vowed:

"We shall be monsters, cut off from all the world; but on that account we shall be more attached to one another."

A crack of lightning. Birds rushed from trees. But no rain came, only breezes from the door of the hut, which remained open. The golem shut it, leaving the two of them alone in the hut.

Alone in the world.

Though Justine averted her eyes as the golem approached, she saw more than she had during their past encounters: a lean body covered in muscles and scars and tissue. A skeleton covered in flesh. An anatomy lesson come to life. Stretches of his skin were darkened and shiny with burns, as though electricity had surged through his veins. Whatever alchemy Victor had performed, he'd left his golem closer to man than monster.

"My name is Justine, my friend. You need not be nameless. Shall you be Adam? Lucifer?"

He winced. Had she upset him? When she'd suggested the names, she'd been thinking of *Paradise Lost*. She glanced at his other books. Plutarch's *Lives*, *The Sorrows of Young Werther*.

"Werther? Plutarch?"

His mouth tightened. In his silence, she recalled her father's story of the golem, which Henry had expanded upon that summer night so long ago. *"The golem wasn't truly immortal for he could be brought to death . . . He was called Emet, which means 'truth' in the language of the Hebrews. This was the word the rabbi had written on his forehead to bring him to life . . ."*

Emet. This would be her friend's name, which she'd hold in secret.

Emet sat beside her. The stench of death rose from his flesh. He took her hand. His arms curled around her waist, drawing her close. His heart pulsed beneath his ribs. She felt so puny. So vulnerable.

"My friend," he murmured. "My companion."

She held him, understanding what it was like to be despised by all the world. To be alone and friendless.

* * *

Once Emet slumbered, Justine stared up at the ceiling of the hut. Beyond. Toward the stars.

I have a friend. He's not who I expected, but I shall be true to him.

They'd spent the remainder of the evening in quiet company, sharing a simple meal. He'd fallen asleep holding her hand. Emet's face relaxed as he dreamt. Had her friendship granted this to him? She imagined who he might have become if he'd had a mother who'd crooned lullabies above his cradle, or a father who'd welcomed his birth; for all of Justine's mother's sins, at least she'd known love from her father.

Then she remembered: Emet had no knowledge of her relation to Victor and Elizabeth. Should she tell him? Would it matter?

She pulled out the necklace bearing the locket of Caroline from beneath the bed. Her painted eyes stared back same as ever.

What would you do? Justine asked the locket. No answer arrived.

* * *

Justine must have fallen asleep, for she next recalled the gentle patter of rain against the roof, a blue jay cawing. Dawn. Despite the drizzle, the morning was warm and bright, spring and summer as one. The door to the hut was open. She felt her cheeks lift into a smile.

I'm no longer alone. I've a friend.

She pulled herself up against the burlap sack, coughing. Smoke rose from the bonfire in the field beyond; it still smoldered though it had been hours since they'd burned Victor's journal. Emet was standing outside by the bonfire—she made out his tall silhouette framed beyond the doorway.

Justine watched Emet for some moments without his knowledge. Her friend. Companion in life. She beamed. He appeared to be staring into the woods, still as a cat stalking a bird. He rubbed his cheek against the leaves. Blinked up at the sky, as though the light was too much to bear.

He is good, Justine reminded herself. *His desire for revenge is understandable.*

Emet's hands hung fisted by his side. Something dangled from his fingers. A glint of gold. A black ribbon. The necklace containing the locket with Caroline's portrait—Justine must have fallen asleep clutching it.

Justine rose from the bed. Quietly, or so she thought.

Emet turned, his fingers tight on the locket. His eyes were wet. Tears, not rain.

"You're sad," she said. "Why?"

He dangled the locket before her. "Because once you learn what I have done, you will abandon me."

Justine's stomach tensed. "I vowed I wouldn't."

"That was before I learned who you are—once you told me your name, I recalled something I'd tried to forget." He let the necklace fall from his fingers to the earth. "This portrait of the beautiful woman, I've seen it before . . . but not here. In Geneva."

"I don't understand," Justine said. But she did.

With a shock that made her lightheaded, she recalled her nightmare in the hayloft after she'd miscarried. The feral eyes she'd sensed in the dark. The discovery of the portrait of Caroline in her gown. The bruises across William's neck. *"A monster did this,"* Victor had argued.

Emet saved me. He couldn't do this, especially to an innocent child.

She recited Emet's many kindnesses: the food he left, the home he'd given her, their conversations. But William wasn't any child. William was Victor's brother—Victor who'd created and abandoned his son, leaving him alone in the world. But that wasn't all. Victor had known all along who'd killed his brother, allowing Justine to be hanged for a murder she hadn't committed.

"No," she said. No.

"You remember now, don't you? The hayloft?" Emet offered a terrible smile. "How pretty you looked, sleeping there! You were quite different then, weren't you, with your long silver hair? I truthfully didn't recognize you until you told me your name. Ah, now you recall! 'Awake, fairest, thy lover is near—he who would give his life but to obtain one look of affection from thine eyes; my beloved, awake!'"

Victor's golem had strangled her darling William to avenge himself against his creator. He'd arranged for her execution by hiding the locket bearing Caroline's portrait in her gown. And now he'd murder Victor on his wedding night.

Her knees buckled. "Tell me this isn't true! I beseech you!"

Emet's only answer was silence.

Her stomach clenched as though she'd retch. How could she have granted Victor's golem a name? How could she have felt affection for him? Called him her friend? She felt a fool. She had to save Victor—Elizabeth couldn't suffer further losses.

There was only one thing she could do. Beg.

Justine extended her arms. "Do not kill Victor! I'll remain with you, go anywhere you want. Please!"

"It's too late, Justine. You despise me—I can tell by your eyes. How naive I've been! I cannot change my nature anymore than you can be made whole."

She threw herself at him, pounding at his chest. "It's your fault I've become the monster I am! You nearly killed me—you left that necklace in my pocket! I was hanged for it—"

"And yet you survived." His tone was sarcastic as he deflected her blows. "Did Victor resurrect you too?"

"No, God saved me! Every day I am grateful for His blessing."

"Well, I have no God—I am only what my father created. I was benevolent and good; misery has made me a fiend." He shoved her onto the floor. "Go to Victor, my friend. Remind him I will be with him on his wedding night."

With this, the monster bounded down the mountain toward the Mer de Glace, scuttling over the ice far more swiftly than she imagined possible.

CHAPTER VII.

*"Beware; for I am fearless and therefore powerful. I will watch
with the wiliness of a snake, that I may sting with its venom."*

* * *

THE FIRST TIME Elizabeth saw the monster, it was a fair June morning
the week before her wedding. She had gone alone at dawn to paint
watercolors in Plainpalais, not far from where William's body had been
discovered.

These days she only painted nature: clouds above mountains, fields
and trees, flowers and fruit. These paintings had taken over her room.
Tens, dozens, no well over a hundred watercolors. They lined the walls
of her room, covering nearly every spare inch of plaster. Most of the
paintings were botanical studies, but none of them resembled the
exquisite flowers that had inspired her art—the irises, the roses, the
tulips—for she'd painted them to reveal their secrets. Each appeared
clumsy with its dissected organs and leaves splayed on the page. Foul
with curiosity. The watercolors felt an obsession—the more Elizabeth
painted, the less she could think of anything else. Some whispered she'd
gone mad, but she didn't care. Nor could she stop herself from creating
them.

That morning, Elizabeth set off to paint as she usually did. She didn't even realize she'd set her easel near William's spot until she saw an offering of flowers tied to the low bough of an apple tree.

For William, a card attached to the bouquet said. *Forever in our hearts.*

The pale white roses were dried, decayed, indicating they'd been abandoned there some weeks earlier.

All of a sudden Elizabeth realized someone had left the bouquet for the anniversary of William's murder. He died in May 1794; it was now June two years later. How could so much time have passed? It felt more than a decade. She was a different woman, Victor a different man. Loss would do that. Besides William and Caroline, she'd lost Justine and even Ernest, who'd left home to further Napoleon's ambitions in Italy.

Most of all, she'd lost Henry.

He was only twenty-six years old, in the full of his potential, when his lifeless body was discovered on a beach in Ireland—a blow made worse when Victor was initially jailed for the murder.

Beloved Henry. Loyal Henry. Her true mate. Companion.

I will never forgive myself. I should have never told Henry to go.

This felt far worse than Caroline's death and that journal.

Elizabeth had been in the process of writing Henry yet again when news of his strangling arrived, along with Victor's arrest in Ireland, near where Henry's corpse was found. The shock of Henry's death left her incapacitated with grief. At first she thought to take her life with laudanum, but the sin of suicide weighed her soul; Sophie helped her expel the poison, returning Elizabeth to the land of the living. Afterward, she refused to leave her room, refused to bathe or comb her hair, while she ruminated on the unimaginable: had Victor discovered her love for Henry and murdered him in a fit of jealousy? She'd wept tears of relief when Victor was proven innocent, though this didn't change her loss. Henry was dead.

At least Ernest and Justine were alive—they had to be. A letter had arrived from Ernest two days earlier, who was stationed near Napoleon's encampment in Italy. As for Justine, earlier that spring Elizabeth had sent Signora Giulia and Martin back to the Villa Lavenza to prepare the estate for her honeymoon. They reported they'd found no one in residence, not even little Ella.

Elizabeth tried to shift her thoughts back to her painting. She couldn't. The bouquet seemed an omen. She should flee, return home. She didn't. Instead, she sank to her knees, her thin linen gown soaking with dew. She shut her eyes, pressing the sharp bones of her spine into the trunk of an oak. She welcomed the discomfort of tree bark along her ribs, the sense that her flesh might split into two if she pushed hard enough. Perhaps this would release a better Elizabeth. A less mournful Elizabeth. An Elizabeth able to giggle and please as she once had. The perfect Elizabeth she'd once been.

Well, she'd marry Victor. She'd keep her promise to Caroline, make amends. Make Alphonse happy.

Henry was right: this is my fate. I have no free will. I never did.

A bluebird sang. A crow scampered and called. Elizabeth opened her eyes. Perhaps this was the peace granted by God after a prayer, though she didn't feel serene. The back of her neck tingled. Gooseflesh along her arms. And then she knew she was no longer alone—she sensed this as surely as a lover senses their beloved in their bed.

She raised her head, squinting at the sun through the newly budded leaves.

A pair of pale cold eyes met her gaze from the top of the tree.

The eyes weren't unkind. Nor were they malicious. They just *were*, like the sketch she'd drawn that night in Lake Como. The eyes were surrounded by scarred flesh, lustrous black hair flowing down from where he nested in the boughs. She didn't scream. Nor did she run—she hadn't the fortitude for that. After all, she hadn't eaten again that morning. Nor did she take any supper the night before beyond some toast soaked in milk.

I'm imagining this. I've been unwell.

When Elizabeth next looked up, the monster was gone.

A flock of jackdaws swirled in the sky, a surge of shadow eclipsing the sun. Their cries echoed. How ominous they sounded—or was she imagining thus?

She was dizzy, unsettled. Instead of resting until she regained strength, she drew a quick sketch of the white roses with the card. She slowly made her way home, determined to forget those sinister eyes. The threat she couldn't articulate. Those jackdaws.

"Uncle," she asked Alphonse upon her return, "do you know anything of this?"

When she showed him her sketch of the roses, he pressed his fingertips against his eyelids.

"I'm sorry. I didn't mean to upset you."

Once Alphonse recovered, he confessed, "I leave them every year for William. The roses come from the conservatory in Belrive—they bloom every May. I know I can bring them to the cemetery, but I prefer to think of our sweet boy as he was that day. So happy. So playful. Before . . ."

Her uncle gestured for words, overcome. Elizabeth took his hand. She knew he was thinking of Justine, blaming himself. Blaming the judges for giving him reason to blame himself. She'd never told him about Justine's survival. After all, she'd promised.

"I understand, Uncle." She kissed his cheek, which had gone grey and slack. His flesh bristled against her lips; some days he didn't shave now that he was no longer a syndic.

"God bless you, Elizabeth. I bless the day Caroline brought you to us. You're an angel. Victor will be fortunate to have you as his wife. Soon there will be new children, God willing. A new generation to bring us hope." Alphonse stood up, reaching for his cane; he'd never fully regained his health after his heart attack. "Here. Let me show you something—I haven't shown these to anyone, especially not Victor. He'd think me mad. But I trust you'll appreciate them."

He unlocked a drawer from the lacquered corner cabinet in the dining room. The drawer contained letters upon letters. Hundreds of them. Some appeared new, others yellowed with age. All were tucked into neat piles tied with black ribbons.

"What are these?" Elizabeth had no idea. She'd assumed the drawer held silverware.

"Caroline. I've written her a letter nearly every day since her death. Well, especially since her death—I wrote her before she'd taken ill, when I thought I'd lose her when she gave birth to William. It became a habit. I've shared everything about our family she should know." He pulled out a stack. "This one's from 1792, after you returned from Lake Como with Sophie and William—Caroline worked so hard to make sure you'd inherit your birthright." Another pile. "And these are from last year, when we were waiting for Victor's return from England so you could wed." Alphonse smiled, his face relaxing. "I've already dated a letter for your wedding. I can't wait to write it—she'd be so happy! She dreamt of this day for years."

"I know she would be happy too, Uncle."

Outside, the rude blast of gunshots. The cold click of metal. She glanced out the window, heart pounding. It couldn't be an uprising, could it?

Victor downstairs in the courtyard with a pistol. He was shooting at a target set against an elm. *Bang!* His eyes looked glazed. Drugged.

"What are you doing?" she shouted from the window.

He gritted his teeth as he released another round. "Protecting us." *Bang!*

* * *

That night Elizabeth dreamt of the monster along with Caroline. This time, her aunt led her to St. Peter's instead of Henry's shop, which no longer existed; Monsieur Clerval had shuttered it, too bereft to continue without his son. Inside the cathedral, the stained glass windows cast colored shadows along the wall, and rows of votive candles flickered. *"I was wed here,"* Caroline told Elizabeth, pointing at the vaulted ceilings, the marble altar. *"Now you'll be a bride of Frankenstein too."*

"Aunt, do you know of Uncle's letters?" Elizabeth asked. "Are they a secret?"

Caroline patted Elizabeth's hand. *"I read every one of them. That's how I know everything, even about Victor."*

"What about Victor?" Within her dream, Elizabeth was somehow able to recall him shooting the pistol that afternoon. "He's been acting peculiar. Do you know anything about this?"

Caroline set a finger against Elizabeth's lips. *"It's coming,"* she warned. *"You should leave or it'll be too late, darling. I'll be here, if you need me. Always."*

The candles blew out, and the doors from the west burst open. Instead of light flooding the cathedral, water rushed into the church. (Had the lake flooded? It must have.) Waves rising. Bibles floating. The organ chortling with broken chords. Elizabeth tried to swim as the water rose to the pews, toward the stained glass. Her soaked gown was so heavy. Dragging her down. She reached for a column, an archway, her fingers straining for succor.

Beneath the waves, she saw a pair of dun-colored eyes staring at her. Lifeless. Merciless. Sorrowful. The monster.

He reached for her throat.

* * *

Elizabeth awoke from her dream, flailing for air. Her hands confronted the weight of another head beside hers on the pillow. Victor. He'd crept into her bed while she slept. She shrieked.

"Shush! I didn't mean to startle you," Victor whispered, stroking her brow. "I've been thinking so much about us. Our past. I miss us as we were."

"I-I miss us too." Her breath sounded ragged in the dark.

"How happy we were then! You, me, Henry. Even Justine."

Elizabeth trembled. (Was it hunger? Surprise?) "Things can never be as they were, Victor."

Because Henry is gone.

"I know, beloved. But we still have each other . . ."

Victor curled about her, his flesh as cool as her body was bony. For a moment, she feared he'd touch her breasts, her stomach. Kiss her as a husband would have a right to. But he only sighed and nestled his chin against the curve of her neck.

"I love you, Elizabeth. You're the only perfect thing in my life. I don't deserve you."

She didn't sleep the rest of the night, recalling her dream with Caroline. The monster.

* * *

Elizabeth returned to Plainpalais at dawn. This time, she didn't bother to bring her watercolor kit. The monster awaited her, seated beneath the blossoming apple trees, as she expected. He stank of rotting fish and leaves and mildew. Death. A cluster of jackdaws rested around his legs, pecking at vermin.

"Tell me who you are!" she demanded. "Are you real?" The monster was more horrific than she'd anticipated. Besides his gruesome appearance, he was dressed in filthy rags that appeared stolen from clothes lines, his feet bound in blood-stained furs.

He raised a scarred brow. "You're unlike the others. You don't flee. You don't scream. I'm impressed." A cold laugh. "I didn't expect this from Victor's future wife."

Elizabeth ignored the pounding of her heart. The faintness of her head. "You know Victor?"

"More than I wish." The monster rose to his feet, his head reaching the trees; the jackdaws took to the sky. How could someone be so tall? "I've been watching you for some time, Elizabeth Lavenza."

"Who are you?" she asked again. He knew Victor. He knew her name. He knew they were to marry. Perhaps this was another dream. She clenched a handful of apple leaves and crushed them in her palms. They were sappy and verdant. Real.

"I know much about you, Elizabeth. I can see you wish to die—"

"I don't want to die." Her stomach growled. She recalled the taste of laudanum.

"But you've been starving yourself, haven't you? You appear a skeleton covered in flesh."

All this was too true. Elizabeth knew others gossiped about her condition. She'd caught the pitying looks in the square, the whispers. "She used to be such a beauty. Consumption. Now all she does is paint pictures all day." But it wasn't tuberculosis Elizabeth suffered from. She hadn't meant to starve herself. Not intentionally. Over time, her hunger had been replaced by an almost euphoric detachment. The detachment was a relief. A gift. She no longer yearned for food. She no longer yearned for anything. Not really.

"It's been a sad time," she finally answered.

"You're sad because your soul is no longer whole. I alone can behold this."

Her eyes pooled with unshed tears. "Can you?"

The monster nodded. "Half your soul resides elsewhere. Not with the living."

"That's not true!" But it was.

She tried to run, but the monster grabbed her arm. He shoved her against the ground, his elbow sharp against the root of her spine. She struggled—but only for a moment.

"Let me speak, Elizabeth Lavenza. Listen to me. I can help you and your family, whom you love." The monster's breath caught in his throat. "And who love you."

"How do you know this?"

"I can tell, for no one loves me—I am all alone in the world. I have no friend, no companion, as you do. If you agree to all I say, your family will be safe." And then he told her, "I will be with you on your wedding night."

"Why should I believe you?"

And then the monster told her the story of his creation and all that had occurred since. She listened to him without running away. Without protesting. She listened to him with a mounting sense of dread, followed by a peculiar serenity. The monster made sense, like the end of a book you'd been reading for a long time.

She recalled Victor's rantings after William's death, the green journal beneath his pillow. His alchemy books, the mercurial behavior since his return from Ingolstadt; the chemistry set, his surgery kit, his insistence on traveling before their wedding to an island near the top of the world. Those glimpses of unnaturally tall men in Ingolstadt, Plainpalais, and in the rain. It was a relief to know the truth at last—she'd suspected as much from the moment she'd finally laid eyes on the monster. After all, had she not anticipated him? Dreamt of and drawn him? She'd conjured him from her darkest nightmares and given him life in her art.

The monster was alchemy born of flesh and presumption and abandonment, just as she'd been in her way thanks to the Frankensteins. In her deepest heart, she expected his arrival just as she'd expected she'd never find happiness after Henry's death. The monster was inevitable.

Still, she asked him, "What proof have you?"

He gave her a pile of letters—*her* letters, the ones she'd written weekly to Henry after his departure. The ones Henry never answered. They remained unopened.

"Why did you steal these?" she shouted, clutching the letters to her heart as she fell to her knees. "Why? Why!"

"Because Victor must marry you for my revenge to be complete."

Suddenly Elizabeth understood: Victor's monster had murdered Henry, just as he'd murdered William and framed Justine for his death. It was him all along. She and Henry never had a chance.

Yet at the end, when the monster finished speaking, it wasn't Henry or Victor Elizabeth recalled. Nor was it Caroline and Alphonse, who'd been the most loving guardians she could have desired. Nor did she think of the green journal and the scarlet fever accompanying it. No, it was Maria she thought of—Maria in that apple orchard so long ago when Elizabeth was a child of four—and the day when she first slapped her.

* * *

Three days passed. During this time, Elizabeth didn't encounter the monster again, though she did find six jackdaws waiting outside the garden door. Nor did she return to Plainpalais. Anyway, she and the monster had said all they needed. Besides, she was a bride; there was a wedding to prepare for. Then came the night before the wedding, where celebratory speeches were made and she drank too much wine on an empty stomach and threw up in her bedroom. During the dinner, Alphonse grew sentimental and toasted, "Heavy misfortunes have befallen us, but let us cling closer to what remains and transfer our love for those we have lost to those who may yet live."

At last, the morning of the wedding arrived. A church ceremony in St. Peter's. A breakfast following in the Hôtel de Ville; though Alphonse had resigned as syndic, the Frankensteins still held sway. Afterward, she and Victor returned to the house on the Rue des Granges to collect their luggage for their honeymoon.

But first, Elizabeth had a final letter to write—she could no longer procrastinate.

My beloved Henry, she began:

Today was my wedding day. I know I should be thinking of Victor, but all I can think of is you. Though it has been six months since I first learned of your death, I still have so many regrets. So many wishes. Most of all, I wish I hadn't told you to accompany Victor to Scotland. This I shall mourn forever—

A teardrop smudged the ink. Elizabeth crossed out her last sentence with a vehement pen stroke.

I must confess something: at first I believed your murder to be my fault. I envisioned Victor discovering my love for you, and in his madness (yes, I will write <u>that</u> word) smiting your life in a temper. I even wondered if he'd found those letters I sent you. But now I know differently. My family is cursed for reasons I dare not set on this page. For how else can Fate explain the loss of you, of William, and my aunt in the space of eight years?

But that's not all, Henry. If I am to be completely honest in this letter, I will admit I even wondered whether Victor loved another woman; he'd been so distant since his return from Ingolstadt. Since then, I've discovered the true reason for his inattention. This reason is a terrible thing wrought of death and hubris—one I never believed Victor capable of creating, even with his genius.

Still, Victor and I are wed—and here I am, writing you, wishing more than ever you were by my side.

Ah, Henry, how shall I bear it? These losses? This sorrow? But today should be a day for celebration. After all, I am now the wife of your best friend, the man who'd been my playmate, my adopted cousin. I can imagine my aunt smiling upon our union. I have fulfilled my vow to her; this shall have to be my comfort.

However, what bothers me most is that you and I had no true farewell before your death. Now that you're gone, I wonder whether you sensed your life would be snuffed so cruelly. When the murderer snuck into your room, did you struggle? Were your last thoughts of God? Or of me and our love? I pray you were taken in your sleep, where you felt no pain, only peace as you moved into Everlasting Life with our Heavenly Father.

Lacking such a farewell, this letter shall serve as my adieu to you, the noblest and kindest man I have ever known. I will love you until my last breath and beyond. May a host of angels bear my words to you in whatever realm you now inhabit!

ELIZABETH FRANKENSTEIN.
Geneva, June 16th, 1796.

Elizabeth covered the inkwell and wiped her nib. On the other side of the wall, she heard Victor in his room. Drawers slamming and shutting. What was he looking for? She recalled the moment when he swore to be her husband during their wedding ceremony. He looked so stricken by terror that the priest teased, "I'm glad you're taking your vows so seriously, Monsieur Frankenstein. But this is a happy moment

—can you attempt to smile?" Everyone laughed but Elizabeth. She stared around the church, imagining those missing in the pews. The priest had asked, *"Do you take this man as your husband?"* *"I will,"* she answered. She felt no joy, only foreboding.

Their kiss felt like the kiss of strangers.

But that was then. Now she was Madame Frankenstein, wife to a madman who'd created a monster against God's will. A wife who didn't love her husband. A wife who was writing a love letter to a dead man who'd been murdered by this same monster in an era when men killed kings and science replaced alchemy.

She'd blotted the letter when a knock arrived on the other side of her door. Victor, no doubt, ready to leave.

"Madame Frankenstein?"

Not Victor. Sophie.

Elizabeth folded the letter into a tight rectangle. "Enter."

"No need, Madame. Your carriage awaits. So does your husband—" here, Sophie giggled from the hallway "—who says you'll need to hurry to catch the ferry to Evian."

Elizabeth's throat tightened. "Tell my husband I will be down immediately."

She put on her lace manteau, her straw bonnet. A last look in her mirror. How thin she appeared, how exhausted! She'd chosen to wear white, the color of purity. The color of mourning. The same color as those roses for William she'd found in Plainpalais. The ivory muslin gown made her complexion appear sallow though it was the latest mode; Victor had purchased it when he stopped in Paris during his return from Ireland. The gown draped loose on her, but that was the style. Or so she claimed.

Downstairs, she could hear Victor speaking to Alphonse, his voice high with impatience; he'd left his room, presumably finding whatever he was searching for. Downstairs, she could hear the carriage waiting outside in the courtyard, the horses nickering amid the stench of equine manure.

Sophie knocked again. "Madame?"

"Coming!"

A last look around her childhood room. The letter from Henry, tight in her grasp. For their wedding night, Victor had decided they'd stay on the shores of Evian before continuing to the Villa Lavenza, where they'd honeymoon. But Elizabeth knew the truth: they'd never arrive in Lake Como. Victor's son would take care of that.

"I will be with you on your wedding night."

Elizabeth tucked the letter to Henry into her stays. Against her heart.

She smoothed her hair. She opened the door.

CHAPTER VIII.

"I shuddered to think who might be the next victim sacrificed to his insatiate revenge. And then I thought again of his words—'I will be with you on your wedding-night.'"

* * *

IN THE COURTYARD outside the Frankenstein mansion, a petite hunchbacked woman dressed in male attire watched from the back of a crowd of well-wishers—a woman many would consider a monster if they were to catch a close glimpse. All awaited Victor and Elizabeth, who'd returned from St. Peter's an hour prior after being joined as husband and wife before God and society. They were late. When the newlyweds finally emerged to leave on their honeymoon, the well-wishers threw rose petals the color of cream. Their funereal scent cloyed the air.

"To the bride!" Alphonse cried, his wrinkled face bright with joy.

"To the groom!" others responded. "May he make his bride happy tonight!"

Elizabeth blanched. "Victor has always made me happy."

Victor kissed her hand before offering a gallant bow. "I've never loved anyone but you, Madame Elizabeth Frankenstein. Rely upon it."

He embraced his father, accepted handshakes and kisses all around. It seemed as though Alphonse had invited everyone from Geneva society, like that holiday soirée years ago. The bells of St. Peter's struck three.

"Go, my children!" Alphonse cried. "Be happy!"

The couple rushed to the carriage and then the ferry for Evian, which they boarded a moment before the gate closed. Therefore they did not take note of the hunchbacked woman, who followed them onto the ferry stealthy as a thief.

* * *

As the ferry twined its way across the lake toward Evian, Victor and Elizabeth remained on the deck. The hunchbacked woman disguised in male attire did too. She raised her hood to hide her face as she eavesdropped.

"I'm so happy," Elizabeth lied to Victor; she now wore a simple gold band above Caroline's emerald ring. "Tell me you're happy too, Victor."

"I am, beloved," he replied, staring out at the water. His hand shifted to his jacket pocket. He patted its contents, his gaze darting. The pistol; Elizabeth knew it. His eyes narrowed as he glanced over his shoulder.

"What is it, Victor? What is it that bothers you so?"

He answered after a moment's pause, "If you knew what I have suffered and what I may yet endure."

"I hope there is nothing to distress you." Elizabeth's voice faltered. She remained oh-so-conscious of that farewell letter to Henry tucked against her breast, along with the promise she'd made to the monster during their final encounter in Plainpalais. She'd never reveal her vow to a living soul.

Victor caressed her cheek. "You are sorrowful, my love."

"Be assured that if a lively joy is not painted in my face, my heart is content," she lied again. "Observe how beautiful the clouds are above Mont Blanc. Look at the sun setting beyond the lake, the fish swimming in the clear water. What a divine day! How serene all appears!"

And for a moment, Elizabeth's words invoking the perfection of Nature soothed her hollow heart. But in a perfect world she would not be making trite observations about clouds and fish to calm Victor's nerves. In a perfect world, William and Caroline would still be alive, and Elizabeth would have wed Henry, entrusting her aunt to understand that a marriage without love was no marriage at all. But the world is not perfect: she's married a madman who created a monster sewn of corpses.

"I fear, my beloved wife," Victor replied, "that little happiness remains for us on earth; yet everything I cherish is centered in you. I have one secret, Elizabeth, a dreadful one. When revealed to you, it will chill your frame with horror. I will confide this secret after our wedding night."

And I already know this secret.

The ferry approached Evian, where pine-laden mountains descended precipitously to the lake; a ruined castle laid atop the tallest peak. As a line of travelers queued for the dock, Victor offered Elizabeth his arm. She accepted it.

"Shall we?" she asked, pointing to the dock.

A corner of Victor's mouth tipped in an uneven grin. "After you, my wife."

"No," she replied, concocting a grin of her own. "Together, my husband. Until my last breath."

* * *

It was eight o'clock when the ferry landed in Evian. Justine arrived at the hotel moments before Elizabeth and Victor, who'd first gone for a walk on the shore. Other than the hotel's aspect on the lake, it was nothing special, Justine decided; the sort of structure built to accommodate travelers who required a night's rest before continuing to more scenic destinations. She was relieved the hotel was only two stories high with windows unimpeded by trees.

She spied on the newlyweds from a window facing the hotel registry, close enough to overhear them request the bridal chamber. She searched for the monster, but found no sign of his arrival: no broken branches overhead, no footprints. The wind rose with great violence from the west, and clouds swept across the moon swifter than the flight of the vulture. Suddenly a heavy rainstorm descended; Justine had no choice but to submit to its fury.

Soon Elizabeth and Victor were alone in the bridal chamber. It possessed three tall windows, two overlooking the lake and a third with a ledge large enough for Justine to hide herself. The chamber was furnished with a large wardrobe and an even larger bed hung with brocade curtains the same hue as an Alpine forest—Justine had never seen such an expansive bed. By then night had arrived in earnest. A candelabra set on a side table spilled a soft light to discreetly illuminate the proceedings.

On the lake side of the room, the drapes billowed—the proprietor, a stout grey-haired man, had opened the windows to air out the room despite the rain. Victor rushed to shutter the windows, his hands visibly shaking. He checked inside the wardrobe, patted his jacket.

"We should have requested a second story room." Victor's tone was agitated, Justine decided.

"What distresses you, Victor? What is it you fear?" Elizabeth's eyes avoided the bed, where someone had sprinkled pink rose petals across the pale lacy linens for the newlyweds.

"Oh, peace, my love! Peace! This night is dreadful, very dreadful." He approached the door after patting his jacket a last time. "I'll return in a half-hour. Until then, I implore you to not unlock the door or the windows! Do not leave this room!"

Elizabeth, to Justine's surprise, did not show emotion in reaction to her husband's edict. As soon as Victor locked the door behind him, Elizabeth rushed to unlock it along with the windows.

With this, Justine no longer bothered to hide herself. She flung her body inside the room, rolling across the carpeted floor until she lay at her benefactress's feet.

"It *was* you!" Elizabeth cried, embracing Justine with all her might. "My darling Justine! I thought I spied you on the ferry! I didn't believe my eyes—"

"Elizabeth, listen to me—"

"And your voice—it's returned! Have you come to wish me farewell then? What a risk you've taken!"

Justine clutched Elizabeth's hands. "You must flee! Victor is in danger for reasons I cannot say."

A half-smile. "No, he's not."

"But he is! Come with me! We'll live together like sisters!"

Joy drained from Elizabeth's face. "I can't."

Justine grabbed Elizabeth by her shoulders. "You must! Victor has secrets. Enemies. Elizabeth, we've no time!"

Elizabeth offered a hollow laugh. "You don't know what I know."

"I know enough! I know Victor isn't who you believe him to be. I know you can't save him."

Elizabeth burst out, "It's not only Victor!"

Justine didn't understand, but there was no time to question. She fell to her knees. "I'm begging you, let me protect you as you did me! Anything you need of me I will do for you. Please!"

Elizabeth shook her head. "I'm meant to be Victor's wife. I've no choice."

"That's not true! Come!"

For a moment, Justine thought Elizabeth would acquiesce; her mouth softened, she reached for Justine's hand. She'd leave with Justine. They'd be saved. Justine imagined the monster awaiting outside, the two of them slipping away before it was too late. The life they'd lead. The triumph and relief.

Elizabeth pushed Justine toward the open window. "Go! Quickly!"

There was a finality to Elizabeth's tone that stole all hope from Justine.

"Very well—I'll leave," Justine said. "But first, I've a wedding present. Open your hand."

* * *

Elizabeth waited until after Justine's departure to look down at her hand. A small sharp knife lay in her palm, one Justine must have taken from the Villa Lavenza; Elizabeth recognized her parents' initials engraved on the silver handle. A pang of bittersweet yearning rose as she thought of her mother and her father, the hopes they must have held for her life. Not that it mattered any longer, though Elizabeth had been moved by Justine's attempt to save her.

It had taken all of Elizabeth's strength to resist Justine's entreaties— more than Elizabeth realized she possessed. As she listened to Justine, Elizabeth felt torn in two. There she was on her wedding night, Justine begging her to save herself; there she was four days earlier, with the monster in Plainpalais. The two versions of Elizabeth wrestled each other, like an angel versus a demon. Ultimately, the demon won.

Now alone in the bridal chamber, Elizabeth recalled her final conversation with the monster.

"Victor created me in Ingolstadt, but cursed me to remain alone in all this

world," he'd told her. *"It's his fault I've become what I am. A demon. A monster. Lucifer fallen from heaven, hated by all. My father made me miserable when he should have granted me happiness."*

"Is not happiness our responsibility?" Elizabeth had reasoned; this sounded like something Ernest would say.

"How can one be happy when all alone in this world? I have no friends. No companion. No mate."

Elizabeth responded with a dawning horror, "You want me to be your mate."

The monster shook his head. *"I want one of my own kind so she will not reject me. Victor promised this—that's why he fled to the Orkney Islands—but he did not keep his word. He destroyed my mate before she was to receive life."*

"You want revenge on Victor?"

The monster nodded. *"But I'll spare him if you'll help me."*

When the monster launched into his proposal, Elizabeth offered him the same rapt attention a country girl would an aristocratic seducer. *"If you agree to my proposal,"* he said, *"I will be with you on your wedding night."* Elizabeth immediately understood: she recalled Henry's broken neck, the bruises along William's throat. *"Once Victor suffers as I suffer, my revenge will be satisfied. I'll let Victor live, along with your uncle and everyone else you care about, even Justine. They'll remain safe for the rest of their lives."*

Somehow she found words to respond. "But that's only them! How can I trust you'll harm no one else?"

"I swear I won't! I'll become mild as a lamb. I'll go to South America, where I'll live peacefully on roots and berries for the rest of my days . . ."

How caressing the monster's words had been! How compelling! Elizabeth also felt an odd responsibility toward him. After all, if Victor was his father, was she not his mother in a sense? She even recalled those drawings she'd made years ago of the dead animals and her nude body in that secret sketchbook. Perhaps she and Victor were more alike than not.

She agreed. How easy it had been to give into the monster's wishes, like letting yourself drown in a storm you knew you'd never survive. But she did have the presence of mind to ask him to put his promise in writing. A contract. A devil's bargain. She'd have to trust him to honor it.

When Elizabeth signed the monster's contract, she imagined no more sorrow. No more hunger. No more guilt. No more awareness of Henry's death. Yes, she could have refused. Yes, she could run away, but what was the point? The monster would find her—hadn't he followed Victor and Henry all the way to Scotland to work his mischief?

Before the monster departed, he'd caressed her neck.

"I'll see you on your wedding night, Elizabeth."

And now that wedding night had arrived at last. Elizabeth opened her eyes, returning to the present moment. There she was in the bridal suite with its open windows and unlocked door dressed in her ivory bridal gown, which Victor had brought her all the way from Paris.

"This is my fate," she told herself.

An odd giddiness rose. She unpinned her hair, unlaced her stays until all she wore was her thin silk chemise. She took one last look in her mirror, arranged her gold curls about her shoulders. She kissed the letter to Henry a final time. She threw it into the lake. As the letter floated away, she contemplated dropping her parents' knife beside it. She didn't. She set the knife beneath her pillow, a bitter relic of the mother and father she'd never known.

She blew out the candles, pitching the room into shadows. She lay on her bridal bed, resting atop the lacy linens and rose petals. She threaded her fingers together.

She stared up toward the ceiling. Beyond. Toward the stars.

This is how they shall find me.

The mantel clock ticked away. Elizabeth remained on the bed in the dark, still alone. Still waiting for the monster. Nor had Victor returned —no doubt he was still outside the hotel pacing back and forth, that pistol in his hand. His fingers tapping back and forth like Caroline . . .

More minutes passed. The rain ceased and the pale yellow light of the moon illuminated the chamber. For some reason, Elizabeth recalled that snowy December morning years ago, when she'd discovered Justine frozen beneath the oak in Belrive. While Elizabeth had lain there with her in the snow, they'd been approached by an albino fox. Elizabeth had watched the veins in the creature's translucent ears pulse with life, his colorless eyes staring into her soul. He'd appeared so vulnerable, yet so brave . . .

I will be brave.

And then Elizabeth was no longer alone.

The odor of death drifted from beneath the mattress. It mingled with fragrance of those rose petals, so lush with life, scattered across her bridal bed.

The monster. He'd hidden beneath that enormous bed, waiting the entire time for Elizabeth. He'd eavesdropped on her exchange with Justine, witnessed her preparations, heard Victor leave the room. He must have swum all the way to Evian to evade capture hours ago—how had she not noticed?

She willed herself to remain unmoving on the bed.

She heard the monster slide out from beneath the bed. Rise to his feet.

His movements were slow as he drew closer. Hesitant. Her nose clotted with his fetid stench, the damp rising from his flesh. He believed her asleep—hadn't he promised as much during their last encounter in Plainpalais? He'd vowed he'd wait until she slept to strangle her. But who could sleep knowing death would arrive?

Now, lying there in the dark on her wedding night in a bed where she'd been meant to become a wife in the full sense of the act, Elizabeth's eyes filled. When she'd agreed to the monster's proposal, she'd been so certain of her willingness to sacrifice her life to save those she loved; now her hunger to live rose bright and strong. She hadn't expected this.

How mutable are my feelings! How strange is the love we have of life even in the excess of misery!

She thought of the life she'd once hoped to lead. She thought of the life she'd leave behind. She thought of Victor, of her uncle, Ernest, and even Justine on whom the monster might satisfy his cruel and merciless passions. She even thought of Caroline, though no one could harm her now. Despite the monster's vow that Elizabeth's death would complete his revenge, could she trust him? Who would he destroy next? What if Victor had constructed the monster to live forever? Would he patiently await Ernest's children? Their children? Would he really honor a written contract that only he knew existed?

This possibility plunged Elizabeth into a reverie so despairing that all of her strength rose. And then she knew: she wouldn't succumb to fate, no matter how ordained it appeared.

Her parents' knife. It awaited beneath her pillow.

I will have courage.

The blade felt cold against her palm. So small. So sharp.

I will survive.

She must have shifted on the bed, for the monster addressed her.

"You're awake," he whispered. "I trusted you'd be asleep by now."

She cringed against the bed linens. "Who can slumber knowing their life is about to be snuffed?"

"Indeed." A soft laugh. "Are you prepared for death, Elizabeth Frankenstein?"

"Yes," she lied.

Best to take him unaware. Best to play along.

"I'll be as gentle as I can be. Don't struggle. That will make it worse. If you let your body give way to me, you shan't feel a thing . . . I truly am sorry about this, Elizabeth. Victor left me with no choice."

The monster laid his body beside hers. Elizabeth's heart thudded. How large he was! How long! Victor had constructed his son like a god fallen from heaven. He was all muscles and sinew, strength and bones.

Should I stab him now or wait? In the neck? Or in the heart?

He shifted closer. She made an involuntary squeaking sound. A shudder.

His fingers felt like snakes as they crept up her torso. Toward her breasts. Higher.

"You're nervous," he said, caressing the column of her neck. "You're trembling. But you're brave. You don't scream. You lie there like a saint awaiting martyrdom."

"What did you expect?" Her blood was so loud in her ears, rushing like a river. Her heart a drum, thumping, thumping . . .

Beneath her pillow, her hand curled around the handle of the blade. It felt so fragile.

It's sharp. That's all that matters.

"I'd think you'd take joy knowing your life will save Victor's."

He kissed her cheek; he was trembling too.

His voice broke. "I'll be quick. It'll be over soon."

No, it won't.

Elizabeth pulled out the knife. She aimed for his heart. She struck hard. She stabbed until her hands were sticky with blood.

A gunshot. A scream that rang out louder than any ever heard.

CHAPTER IX.

*"Suddenly I heard a shrill and dreadful scream. It came
from the room into which Elizabeth had retired."*

* * *

ALPHONSE, who'd been sleeping the peaceful slumber of elders whose life ambitions have been met, heard the scream all the way across the lake in Geneva. He awoke, heart jittering and flesh prickling, and rushed toward the window, his bare feet slipping on the rug. Terror. That's what he felt. But why? Hadn't he gone to bed so filled with contentment?

"Sophie, Sophie!" he shouted flailing from the floor. "What can it be?"

Sophie ran into the room. "Where are you, Monsieur?"

"Here! Help me up, child! Where are my slippers? Did you hear the scream?"

"I heard something . . ." Sophie threw open the window after setting him on his feet. Outside, a pale yellow moon shone. Goose-bumps rose along her arms. Something was wrong. Something was evil, though she couldn't explain why. "Whatever it was, all's silent now."

It wasn't. The scream was repeated a second time, more of a bellow than a shout.

Across the Place du Bourg-de-Four, a nest of jackdaws cawed and took flight, determined to abandon Geneva for a place of sanctuary.

* * *

East of Geneva in the Villa Lavenza, Signora Giulia and Martin were snoring in each other's arms, exhausted after a long day of readying the villa for the bride and groom, who'd soon arrive for their honeymoon. They'd also raised a glass too many in celebration of Signorina Elizabeth's wedding. As a result, they were too drunk to hear the screams that rode across the Alps all the way from Evian. Still they sensed *something*, for Signora Giulia rose hours before dawn, convinced she'd heard Ella, whose soul she believed was restless. The housekeeper hadn't written Elizabeth of the girl's murder. What if her mistress never returned?

"Poor child," Signora Giulia murmured, setting a plate of sausage on the kitchen table for Ella. "I wish you had a different fate." It had been such a shock to come upon the girl's corpse in the woods. They'd never discovered who'd assaulted her; Martin believed a soldier on his way to war.

Donna Giulia returned to bed, where Martin awaited.

"There you are," he mumbled. He set his hands on her broad hips. She refused his advance, distressed by something she couldn't identify. How fast her heart tripped!

* * *

South of Lake Como, Ernest Frankenstein was sleeping hard on a battlefield outside Mantua, not far from where Napoleon's tent had been struck. He had no idea his brother had finally wed Elizabeth, or that Victor had created a monster, or that Henry Clerval was murdered and Justine survived her hanging. Therefore, though he'd heard the screams from Evian, it drew no alarm. Not at first. The soldier who slept beside Ernest frequently shouted in sleep; he'd blasted off an ear in battle, which left him partially deaf. Ernest's vision of how the world should be after the revolution had never included this.

Eventually Ernest opened his eyes. He shuddered despite the summer torpor, but told himself it was nothing. His heart rushed, his body shook. *Coward.* He licked his dry lips and coughed. Weak lungs. Strong heart. He should have been a poet instead.

Ernest forced himself to settle back in, nose pressed against his military-issued wool blanket. He inhaled deeply. Whatever the country, the earth always smelled of blood.

And then a third and final scream rang out.

* * *

By the time the final scream settled into a hum back in Evian, all that remained in the bridal chamber was a hollow-cheeked groom clutching a pistol; a hunchback girl with a ball of lead in her shoulder; a small silver knife on the floor; a broken window where a wounded monster had escaped; and a virgin bride on the bed with her neck snapped.

CHAPTER X.

*"When I recovered, I found myself surrounded by the people of the inn . . .
I escaped from them to the room where lay the body of Elizabeth, my love,
my wife, so lately living, so dear, so worthy."*

* * *

BLOOD. That's all Justine noticed once she regained consciousness on
the floor of the bridal suite. But whose blood? Not Victor's. He stood
near the door, pistol in hand, illuminated by moonlight, his shadowed
face like a skull. His eyes wide. Senseless. Then his slim body shook as
though jolted by electricity.

"Elizabeth!" he cried, rushing toward the bed. "Beloved wife!" And
he'd fainted.

Justine crawled toward the bed, her head light with pain, shards of
glass cracking beneath her elbows and knees. The only sign of the
monster was a trail of blood leading toward a broken window—where
had he gone? After hearing Elizabeth's scream, Justine had burst into
the room; she'd seen Elizabeth stab the monster. Instead of debilitating
him, it only enraged him. The monster released a second scream before
Justine felt something knock her off her feet. Something that felt like a
punch made of fire. She didn't pay mind to the pain. Not yet. How
could she?

Elizabeth? Where was she?

At last Justine found her, this woman who'd saved her life, who'd been her only true friend. Elizabeth lay lifeless and inanimate across the bed, her head hanging down; her pale and distorted features half-covered by her gold hair; bruises rising on her neck. But Justine's attention was pulled away by pain. Blood. *Her* blood. It gushed between her fingers, flooding her breast. She grabbed her right shoulder, which burned with the flames of a hundred torches.

Victor had shot *her*, not the monster. Victor had kept her from protecting Elizabeth. But where was Victor now?

She forced her gaze toward the door. Victor still lay on the floor, still unconscious. He whimpered as half a dozen men burst through the door shouting and bearing weapons. The rush of their footsteps shook the wood floor of the bridal suite like an earthquake.

"Help me!" Justine gasped, her bloody hand clasping her right shoulder. The pain had grown beyond anything she'd ever experienced, even during that miscarriage.

A portly grey-haired man rushed to her side. The hotel proprietor; Justine recalled him showing Elizabeth and Victor into the bridal chamber.

"He needs a doctor," the proprietor said, pointing to Justine. (*He?* Justine remembered: she was dressed as a boy.) "Come! Can you stand?"

"No, no," Justine moaned. "Save her!"

She raised her left arm toward the bed, toward Elizabeth. *Too late.* Someone had draped a white handkerchief over Elizabeth's face. For some reason, this made what had occurred all the more awful, like Elizabeth no longer existed in any form save as a corpse. Hatred and anger rose to join Justine's sorrow.

I must kill the monster. But how?

Victor staggered to his feet. "I know where the murderer is! He's been stabbed—he still lives!" He pointed at the smashed window. "There he is! See, he's silhouetted against the moon! He's pointing at me!" He pulled out his pistol and shot again, drawing more people into the bridal suite, who milled in confusion. "He's dived into the lake! Follow me!"

The hotel proprietor abandoned Justine to follow Victor. *I will kill the monster. I must.* She reached for something, anything, to pull herself to her feet. The room circled and turned grey. She dragged herself toward the door, leaving sanguinary handprints along the wood floor.

Pain. Then the pain turned to something else. Something more. Something less. Something dark.

* * *

Justine awoke on a muddy rural road rutted with carriage wheels. It was still night but it was raining anew, though gentler than before. How had she gotten there? How much time had passed? She seemed to recall somehow staggering from the hotel, somehow finding her way toward the road . . .

It doesn't matter. Elizabeth is dead.

A sob overtook Justine, one that felt too large to be contained by her wounded body, before a burning pain returned, one more powerful than sorrow. The pain radiated from her right shoulder down her arm, along the curvature of her spine. She stared at her hands. *Blood.* Even in the rain, her hands were drenched. She'd never be cleansed of it. And then she was weeping in earnest.

Elizabeth was dead. Elizabeth was gone. All goodness in her life was gone. Justine hadn't saved Elizabeth, the woman who'd saved her from death. She'd made it worse: Victor had shot Justine, distracting attention from the monster while he strangled Elizabeth.

Justine shut her eyes. All she saw was Elizabeth, her bloodless arms and form flung by the murderer against her bridal bier.

Justine's lungs seized. *I'm dying. But the monster still lives.*

Hot tears. Onto her cheeks. Her hands. Somehow this spurred her lungs into breath, like a baby emerging from womb to air. She raised her eyes toward the road. A road marker. Evian. Geneva. Which direction?

Not Evian.

Justine began to crawl west. Toward Geneva. The green scent of rot rose from the earth, the hiss of wind.

I can go no further.

She curled into a ball, too exhausted to even sleep.

Hours must have passed. Something soft surrounded her. Something emerging from the fog. Fur. The color of rust. Not blood. A fox bearing kits. The fox mother circled and lay beside her, whimpering, her kits spilling about her. Justine laid her hands in their fur. How soft they were! How warm!

The lapping of rough tongues against her face. Against her wound.

The fog cleared and the moon reappeared, brighter than ever. Within that moon, a hooded figure approached. *The monster? It must be.* The fox raced away, her kits trailing and yipping.

He's probably already killed Victor. I'll kill him before I die.

The knife. Where was it? *Elizabeth. I gave it to her.* How could she have forgotten? Anyway, the knife hadn't saved Elizabeth. Nor had it kept the monster from escaping—and now he'd found her. She'd join Elizabeth, William, Victor, and Henry as his victims.

As Justine prepared for death, memory overtook her. She returned to the Belrive garden on that snowy night years earlier when she was a child, when she'd believed she'd been chased by a golem; the fateful night that had marked the start of her life with the Frankensteins—a life that brought blessings and curses. Now here she was again in the night, alone, pursued. Her end had joined her beginning, like a snake swallowing its tail from one of Victor's alchemy books.

The rain slowed. Clouds shifted from the moon. A shadowy figure emerged from the fog. The monster. She could no longer deny his presence.

"Get it over with then," she muttered. "No more. An end."

My second death, she thought. *So be it.*

She rolled onto her back, lifting her chin to bare her neck for him. How she'd changed since her hanging! The last time she was to die, she'd confessed to gain absolution before God. Now she only wanted everything brought to an end. Any God who'd let Elizabeth die wasn't a kind or just God. Justine had lost everything, even her faith.

The monster drew close enough that Justine recognized his watery eyes, his festering wounds, his scarred face and black hair.

But first, she had three last words for him.

"I hate you."

The monster flinched. He knelt beside her. He was taller than she recalled. More powerful. More menacing.

She readied herself for the blow to come. But, as abruptly as he'd approached, he turned away.

She watched with wonder as he fled into the woods with his face hidden inside his hands, looking for all the world like Adam expelled from Eden. After this, everything fell away like a book snapping shut.

CHAPTER XI.

*"What then became of me? I know not; I lost sensation, and chains
and darkness were the only objects that pressed upon me . . .
For they had called me mad; and during many months,
as I understood, a solitary cell had been my habitation."*

* * *

JUSTINE WOULDN'T AGAIN ENCOUNTER the monster until she located
Victor—Victor who spent months in an asylum mad after Elizabeth's
murder. Or so Justine learned after weeks of recovery from that
gunshot; a rustic had found her unconscious body on the road between
Evian and Geneva, and nursed her back to health.

The first time Justine saw Victor after Elizabeth's death, it was a
warm April day laden with soft breezes, bird song, and the scent of
lilacs. The asylum where he abided stank of urine. Shouts and screams
rang against the lime-washed walls, which appeared stained with
human excrement. Justine refused to turn back.

"It *was* you after all," Victor said once they were led to a small room,
separated from the other inmates by only a barred wall; in a corner, an
orderly armed with a wooden staff stood barely beyond earreach. "I
recognized you though you're dressed like a boy."

"It's me. I survived." For what more could she say?

"It's you . . . you . . ."

Victor's mouth shifted. As he struggled to speak, Justine took in the man who'd been Caroline's son and Elizabeth's husband; the man responsible for so much mayhem. Victor's pupils were huge, his voice monotone. He was drugged. A tear lingered at the edge of his eye. How different he was from when she'd first met him fifteen years earlier! Now he appeared damned. Cursed.

"I'm so happy," he continued in that monotone, his fingers curling on the table. *One, two, three,* he tapped. "So happy. I thought I'd imagined you that night after—" he drew a breath "—my wedding. Especially since they hanged you. Yet you survived though God knows how." Another deep inhale. "You're the only one *he* hasn't destroyed, God save you for that."

"*He* wasn't the one who let me be hanged for a murder I didn't commit," she answered, her anger rising. "Nor did he shoot me with a pistol and leave me to rot." The wound in her shoulder still ached most days.

His fingers silenced. "I . . . I shot you?"

"Don't you remember, Victor?"

Victor swayed, blinking slowly. "I remember little of that night. Nor do I remember much after the death of my father—yes, he's gone too. And now I am here."

"Monsieur Frankenstein is dead?" This Justine hadn't known. Grief shook her; Alphonse had been kind to her, especially after the death of Caroline when she'd felt so responsible. "*He* killed him too?"

"Indirectly." A deep breath. "My father didn't survive the news of Elizabeth's murder. A heart attack. He died in my arms several days afterward . . . and if I am to be honest, I wish I'd died with him." Victor swiped at his eyes before forcing a rigid smile. "Tell me, how did you survive your hanging?"

"I'm not going to waste time explaining a miracle to you."

Victor's mood shifted like quicksilver. "It was Elizabeth, wasn't it? She saved you though I don't understand how. She was always so angelic. So obedient. Perfect. She tricked us all." Another laugh. "She was cunning in her way, wasn't she? Secretive. All those drawings and paintings in that sketchbook—I found it after her death inside a locked drawer in her room. Did she ever show them to you? The drawings of the dead birds and nude women? They shocked me."

"Only the botanical ones."

"Ah, that makes sense! Well, more fool me. I should have suspected there was more to her. As for you, I couldn't understand why she'd fled to Lake Como after your hanging—somehow she rescued you. Do you know, I'd even wondered if she loved Henry, and that's why she ran there? Now he's dead too." Victor continued on, affectless again. "All passed. All gone. All dead . . ."

Yes, all were passed and gone and dead save for Ernest; Justine couldn't bring herself to inquire as to his fate.

Victor stared down at his clasped hands. His tone turned wistful.

"It's good to see you, Justine. I appreciate it. You took a risk coming here. What if someone recognized you?"

She shrugged. "I'm of the old world before the revolution. In this new world, anyone who knew me is gone but you. Well, anyone who matters."

"Yet you disguise yourself in trousers and the red cap of a revolutionary."

"The world is not kind to my gender, even in this new world."

"Clever Justine. Quick as ever. Henry would be so proud. And to think we once considered you simple. You proved us all wrong, didn't you?" Victor waved a hand as though to stir the air. "Well, I won't tell anyone you're still alive."

Justine's anger returned. "How kind."

"I'd never expect sarcasm from you."

"I'd never expect it either. But then I'd never expected to witness Elizabeth murdered on her wedding night." She leaned in, her words hissing. "We may talk about new worlds and old times, but it doesn't matter. The loss remains the same. Elizabeth might have lived if not for you! I might have saved her!"

Victor slumped against his chair. "No one could have saved her. Not against *him*."

"You shot me before I could protect her!"

"It wouldn't have made a difference." Victor's tears returned. "It was all my fault. I understand this now. I thought *he* was after me, not her. How foolish I was! How selfish! When I heard her scream that night, the truth rushed into my mind. My arms dropped, the motion of every muscle and fiber suspended; I could feel the blood trickling in my veins and tingling in the extremities of my limbs. Great God! Why did I not then expire? Why am I here to relate the destruction of the best and kindest creature on earth? Now all is lost. Even Ernest is gone—"

"*He* murdered your brother too?" This Justine had not expected; she covered her eyes.

"No. Ernest joined the army," Victor continued, his voice monotone again. "He didn't survive the winter. Weak lungs." He grimaced. "Regardless, I blame *him* for Ernest's passing. Ernest wouldn't have left home if William still lived—he loved William so much! He would have remained in Geneva to watch him grow up."

Justine couldn't bear it. Nor could she bear to leave. "But you survived."

"Yes, I survived, Justine. Which is perhaps the worst punishment of all." Victor met Justine's glare. "My family is destroyed. All of the Frankensteins gone. All the servants ran away, even Sophie, too frightened to remain—lord knows where she went. But *he* remains. *He's* the last. *He's* survived . . . along with yourself."

How strange to realize that she, Victor, and his monster were the last of the Frankensteins, though none of them shared blood. As for the monster, one question weighed Justine.

"Why'd you do it, Victor?"

"Do what?" Victor rubbed his brow. "Oh! Create *him* you mean? You mean that demon, that monster? That cursed Lucifer who calls himself my son?" He set his palm on Justine's shoulder. "I may as well tell you the truth. It was because of my mother."

"But your mother was the most wonderful woman to walk this earth!"

Victor laughed wildly, no longer modulating his voice. "Exactly! After my mother's death, all I could do was look at everyone and think 'One day you will die. And you. And you!'" Victor pointed at the asylum patients on the other side of the barred wall, all in various stages of madness and undress. "For everyone—yes everyone!—we love will die, for death is our common fate." He jabbed at Justine's arm to punctuate every word. "Each and every one of us ends up beneath the earth to become food for maggots."

"Such is the way of life," Justine said, shoving his hand away.

"But did it have to be thus? Did my mother have to die? Does anyone? After her death, I mulled whether there was a way no one would ever suffer loss again . . . And then I realized what the root of mortality was." His voice dropped. "We are all born of woman. Created of woman. The female way was to procreate, to populate the world with new humans, replacing those lost to death. But what if humans were created of man, not woman?"

"That's impossible!"

A roguish grin. "Not with science, Justine. If man created science, why can't science create man?" He cocked his head. "And so in Ingolstadt, I began to think: what if science could create a human who'd live forever?"

Suddenly his eyes glittered with an unpredictability that made Justine's blood chill.

"I should leave," she said, rising from her chair.

He grabbed her wrist. "Let me finish! I know you believe me blasphemous."

She yanked away her hand. "You *are* blasphemous!"

"Fine, I'm blasphemous—if it's any consolation, I'm a miserable wretch, haunted by a curse that shut up every avenue to enjoyment. But answer me this: why would God allow me to discover the secret of life if not to defeat death? I truly believed this to be my fate."

Justine's voice rose as she spoke. "Perhaps it wasn't fate God offered you. Perhaps God only offers us free will to do what is right."

"Or free will to damn ourselves . . ." Victor slumped in his seat, his face sallow. "Do you know when I set out to make *him,* I envisioned myself like a god, creating a new species who would bless me as their creator?" He offered a sharp glance. "I don't blame you for hating me, Justine. If it's any consolation, I hate myself too."

"I pity you more than I hate you."

"I'd rather you only hated me." He laughed again, a mirthless sound. But Justine was already heading toward the door.

"Goodbye, Victor."

"Wait! Come back! Where are you going?"

"I'm going to do what you're unable. Destroy your son. Gain revenge for Elizabeth. Protect the world from *him* before *he* works his mischief elsewhere."

"You?" Victor rolled his eyes. "How can you kill him? You're so small. So weak." Another laugh. "So deformed."

She jutted her chin. "I'm stronger than you know."

"It's impossible for you to stop him."

Justine's anger rose. "No more impossible than surviving death."

And with this, she departed the cell.

"Come back! We're not done! If you want to kill him, I know how! Come back!" Victor's rants rang beyond the barred windows as she hurried away.

She gritted her teeth. She ignored his shouts. She'd never return.

* * *

And yet, Justine *did* return.

A week later, once her anger cooled into desperation, she found her way back to the asylum, which was even more wretched than she recalled. As she waited for someone to answer the bell, a rooster missing half his feathers crossed her path. Justine didn't blink. The rooster seemed as nonsensical as everything else about this place.

"You again," a stout-bellied orderly welcomed after some minutes; Justine couldn't help notice the smear of blood across his torn linen apron. "I suppose you're here for Victor Frankenstein?"

"Yes, if you please," she replied, stomach tight. The orderly's accusing tone set her nerves ajar. "Have we met before?"

"No, but I was told to expect you. He said you'd be hard to miss."

The orderly pointed at her hunchback. Justine grimaced.

"Don't look so upset, boy! Give me a minute—I've something for you. A package from him. Your name is Moritz, yes?"

"My name doesn't matter. It's imperative I speak to Monsieur Frankenstein, if you please."

His face cracked into an uneven grin, revealing broken teeth and blackened gums. "He's no longer a resident."

Justine hadn't anticipated this. "Where is he then? Surely he left an address."

The orderly refused to meet her eyes. Cagey.

"Not exactly an address," he admitted. "I was told not to say because of his family. His father was a syndic, you see. But I suppose it no longer matters."

"Tell me where he is!"

"Very well . . ." The orderly whispered, "The Cimetière des Rois. That's where Victor Frankenstein abides." In a normal tone: "Now do you want the package he left or not?"

CHAPTER XII.

*"As night approached, I found myself at the entrance of the cemetery
where William, Elizabeth, and my father reposed. I entered it,
and approached the tomb which marked their graves."*

* * *

IN THE END, Justine accepted Victor's package. It was a rectangular item wrapped in butcher paper, no larger than her hands clasped together. She had no idea what the package contained, nor did she bear any curiosity. However, she knew she'd find no rest until she reached the Cimetière des Rois.

Justine's thoughts chased themselves like rabbits as she approached the cemetery. *Victor. Dead.* She still didn't believe it, even after the orderly's explanation. "Five mornings ago it happened. We found him in his room. His health must have been weaker than doctors realized . . ." It sounded too suspicious, too pat. She couldn't imagine Victor gone. As mad as he'd appeared when she'd last encountered him, she'd always sensed a vivid force in him that couldn't be extinguished— wasn't this what had enabled him to create life from death? In Justine's wildest imaginings, she envisioned Victor bribing the orderly so he could escape to hunt his son. Perhaps he hoped Justine would be deterred from seeking the monster. It would be like him to want glory without another's involvement.

Once she passed through the cemetery gates, her mind silenced into a dull hum. She grew too aware of the weight of his package in her hands.

I won't open it. Not yet. Not until she reached Victor's grave . . . if indeed there was one.

As Justine made her way down the promenade bisecting the cemetery, the twilight sky darkened into a dense grey that gave lie to the bright day proceeding it. She recalled that New Year's morning when she'd spied Elizabeth with Henry by Caroline's grave, her first encounter with Ernest. Her eyes filled, wishing she could return to that day, before she knew of the monster, before Elizabeth's death. Before Ernest and William, Henry Clerval. Now all were gone, including Alphonse. All cursed just as she felt.

"Gone," she murmured. "Everyone."

She looked up at the sky, where a full moon was rising, setting its cool luminance across the graveyard like a blanket of light. Her footsteps rustled against the new spring grass, soft against her heels. The trees were agitated by the wind; the night was weighed by shadows. For a moment, she imagined the spirits of the departed flitting across the cemetery. The long one would be Ernest, the short one William. And what of Elizabeth's spirit? Justine inhaled the scent of green from the earth.

She would bear the perfume of lilies, she decided. *Like Caroline and the Blessed Mother.*

Soon Caroline's marble tomb rose before Justine's eyes, grander than she recalled. Four new gravestones had been added in front of the memorial; she supposed the Frankenstein mausoleum had grown too crowded. The granite slabs marched in a neat line across the grass save for the final one, which laid atop soil dark as spilled ink.

Justine approached the last gravestone, her heart thumping. There it was, proof of all she refused to acknowledge:

> *Victor Frankenstein*
> *1770 ~ 1798*
> *Son, Brother, Husband*
> *Requiesce in pace*

Justine was surprised by a grief that felt as dense as earth and as heavy as lead. She recalled years earlier when Victor had come upon her beneath that oak tree in Belrive, how he'd seemed a boy prince from a fairy tale: his dark curls, his eyes flashing with intelligence, his wit and kindness. The adoration in Caroline's gaze as she smiled at her son. The affection Henry and Elizabeth bore him. This was the Victor Justine wanted to remember, not the madman she'd encountered in an asylum.

Tears threatened Justine's eyes. *I cannot bear this. But I must.*

At last, she untied the paper wrapped around Victor's package. Inside, she found a letter and a small leather pouch, which was heavier than expected.

Justine, Victor had written:

The strength I relied on is gone; I know I shall soon die—not for reasons I can explain, but from an understanding of no longer possessing hope. Now that I've learned you survived HIM I can let go of life to find whatever peace God may grant me. For here is the dark truth I dared not confide about the demon I created: HE CANNOT BE DESTROYED. In my hubris to outwit death, I granted HIM immortality. No one or nothing can bring HIS life to a close, not even me.

It is this awareness that urges me toward death as much as my mourning for those HE murdered: William, Elizabeth, Clerval. Can any man be to me as Clerval was, or any woman another Elizabeth? Will another child bear William's bright promise? I think not. All I can hope is that through my death HE will at last find a measure of satisfaction in his revenge being fulfilled, and choose to endure HIS cursed existence without harming another living soul.

Now that you possess this knowledge of HIS immortality, I beg you to abandon any plan to bring HIM to justice—you will only destroy yourself. You have been granted a second chance at life. I urge you to take advantage of it. If you look inside the enclosed pouch, you will find funds to settle far from Geneva, where no one will know your unfortunate history. I pray time will grant you some form of happiness.

With this letter complete, I will set down my pen forever. Pity not my death. Instead, imagine with what ecstasy shall I join my departed friends, for I will trust in God's mercy, not His damnation.

Farewell, Justine! Seek happiness in tranquility and avoid ambition.

Learn from my example so that my name may be remembered as more than a blight—

VICTOR FRANKENSTEIN.
    April 10, 1798.

Justine let the letter fall to the grave though the pouch still awaited —a pouch whose proceeds would grant her freedom from a life of want. She untied the leather pull. The scent of lilies rose from inside it. Caroline's perfume.

The pouch contained a collection of jewelry that Justine recalled had been Caroline's: a ruby necklace, diamond earrings, pearls, and more. At the very bottom, something glinted green. Elizabeth's emerald engagement ring; Victor must have removed it from her hand after death.

With this, Justine recalled Elizabeth's last moments. That white handkerchief over her face . . .

I couldn't save her life. Yet she saved mine.

She doubled over as though she'd been kicked in her stomach. The Frankensteins were dead and she lived; their murderer also lived, and she had no way to destroy him, if she was to believe Victor's letter. She dared not trust the monster to be satisfied with the death of Victor— she'd witnessed firsthand the delight he'd taken in the destruction he'd sown. But now all was stolen from her, including her hope to vanquish the monster. Even those jewels seemed a mockery, for what good was wealth without friendship and love? She recalled her life before the Frankensteins, the isolation she felt, alone of her kind. Was she to return to this forever?

"I can't bear this," she cried into the night. "How alone I am!"

She was answered by a loud and fiendish laugh. It rang on her ears long and heavily; the mountains echoed it until she felt as if all hell surrounded her with mockery. Once the laughter died away a well-known and abhorred voice addressed her in an audible whisper:

"You are miserable. I am satisfied!"

She turned—and there *he* was, behind Victor's gravestone, towering over her. How long had the monster stood there watching her? Her despair gave way to rage. It rose inside her, bright and furious like a flame.

She pulled herself from the ground to her full height.

"Miserable?" she cried. "Yes, I'm miserable, for you've destroyed those closest to me!"

The monster folded his arms before his immense chest. "As you have for me."

"Me? How so?"

He set his thick hands on her shoulders. "It's your fault Victor is dead. Now that my father is gone, you've banished any satisfaction I would have gained in revenge."

"This makes no sense!"

"Ah, but it does..." He shook her until her teeth chattered in her skull. "Once he learned of your survival, he decided to die, for you'd provided him with peace. He wasn't responsible for your death after all."

She tried to pull away, but he was too strong. "How is that my fault?"

"You should have stayed away from Victor, but you wanted revenge of him just as I did!"

She met the monster's watery eyes. "You murdered Elizabeth! Isn't that enough?"

"Victor murdered Elizabeth—I was only his instrument. Blame Victor, not me. And now he's killed himself."

"That's not true! Victor? A suicide? How can this be?"

"Don't believe me? I'd been watching my father carefully, waiting for the perfect moment to exact my revenge. A moment when he'd recovered enough to embrace hope anew. A moment when he'd recall the flowers blooming, the song of larks, the promise of spring. Then you arrived. You ruined everything! After you left, he shot himself with his father's pistol. I've no idea how he obtained it, but then again, the mad are clever. You shiver, Justine, but you don't believe me."

"I don't! Suicides aren't buried in consecrated soil."

"They are if the manner of their death is concealed. And now all is lost. Lost!" The monster's voice rose. "I yearned to see him destroyed by my might. I yearned to witness his desolation when he realized he'd never surpass my strength." He shook her anew, this time by her neck. "I yearned to throttle him as I now do you. Set my hands around his throat—"

"Do it then!" Justine cried. "Bring this wretched mockery to a close!

You've already murdered everyone I cared for. You've made me a fugitive to the world, a murderess. What have I to live for?"

The monster released her abruptly. She collapsed to the ground. She lay there, gasping for air, waiting. Waiting . . .

"You and I, we're alike, Justine."

She spat out, "I am nothing like you. Nothing!"

"But you are—you don't comprehend. Not yet. We're both outcasts. Both miserable amid humanity. Both alone in this world. Both created by Frankensteins. Monsters."

"I may be a monster, but I'm born of woman and life. Of nature. Not of man and death. Not science."

"How certain you sound . . ." The monster's voice turned caressing; this alarmed Justine more than his hands around her throat. "Tell me, what were you before the Frankensteins took you in?"

Unloved. Unhappy. Uneducated. But Justine would never admit this.

"So you remain silent to avoid lying. The truth is you were as formless as I was—oh, I heard the chatter, the whispers. You were this puny hunchbacked wretch no one loved. The daughter of a gravedigger, for God's sake! When your parents died, the Frankensteins took you in, educated you. Gave you manners. Clothes. A new manner of speaking. Even Clerval played his role, with his books and prattle of chivalry. You dared to yearn for love with that boy Ernest, friendship with Elizabeth. You craved the love of your fellow humans, as I once did." The monster yanked her back onto her feet. "And now, here you are, like me. Alone in the world and miserable."

"If you're miserable, that's your own fault. I offered to befriend you, to be your companion! I even gave you a name!"

The monster took a step back as though she'd slapped him. "I have no name."

"I named you Emet. That night when I promised to be your friend. Emet, after the golem."

"Emet . . ."

For once, the monster looked mournful; his eyes grew wide; he covered them with his immense hands. Perhaps he was recalling their time together in that hut overlooking the Mer de Glace. The patter of rain against the roof over their heads. Their conversation. Their vows. *"We shall be monsters, cut off from all the world; but on that account we shall be more attached to one another . . ."*

He cackled. "A name. How kind, Justine." His tone darkened. "As for you, I already know your fate."

She raised her chin. "Murder me then. Enjoy your revenge!"

His thin lips twisted into a grimace. "I could have murdered you that night after Elizabeth's death. I chose not to—I felt a peculiar fondness toward you because you'd offered me kindness in your hapless manner. For you are as deformed in some ways as I am, and as unnatural. But now that you're my enemy . . ."

"What will you do?"

The monster laughed again, but she sensed despair in it. "I'll torment you instead."

"Haven't you tormented me enough?"

"No," he said. "Here's what we'll do, Justine. We'll play a game. A long and terrible game, one that ends with one of us dead. There is only one way to destroy me, one that my father remained unaware of in his hubris. But you'll have to catch me first. And if you catch me—"

"You'll tell me the secret of your death."

He nodded. "And then you can destroy me."

But this wasn't enough assurance. Suddenly Justine felt the fate of humanity depended upon the monster's immediate destruction. Now that the Frankenstein family was extinct, what if he decided to expand his revenge toward the innocent? What of future generations? Would he also curse them with violence and death?

She lunged for his knees. "You must tell me now!"

"Come after me!"

Another cackle before he eluded Justine's grasp with more than mortal speed. As the monster fled the cemetery, she watched the broad disk of the moon shine upon his ghastly form.

CHAPTER XIII.

"I pursued him; and for many months this has been my task."

* * *

JUSTINE DID NOT DELAY. She abandoned Geneva immediately in pursuit of the monster, using Caroline's jewelry to fund her mission. She brought with her the satchel from when she'd fled Lake Como. It contained a collapsible telescope, a compass, and the locket with Caroline's portrait.

Guided by a slight clue, Justine followed the windings of the Rhone after the monster. When she reached the blue Mediterranean, by a strange chance she saw him hide in a vessel bound for the Black Sea. She took passage in the same ship, but he eluded her.

She next traced his track to the wilds of Tartary and Russia. Sometimes peasants informed her of his path; other times the monster left a mark to guide her. She continued after him, refusing to turn back even when overcome by hunger and exhaustion. Her life was miserable, but one hope sustained her: to discover the secret of his death.

Sometimes she caught glimpses of the monster ahead in the forest; no matter how quickly she hurried, he remained out of reach. Other times, she sensed his eyes on her while she slept. Once she awoke in the middle of the night to find him seated beside her. To her surprise, he was gently stroking her hair, which had grown long enough to curl about her cheeks.

Their eyes met. His hand stilled. She felt her breath catch in her throat. Her blood rise.

"You!" she screamed, grabbing for his hand. "Tell me your secret!"

"Ah, but you have to catch me! Thus far I have only caught you— come and get me, Justine!"

As Justine pursued the monster, she was led by his messages, which he scratched on tree trunks and in stone. *This way! My reign is not over for you still live,* he wrote across a boulder near a cliff's edge. In another: *Follow me north; I seek the everlasting ices of the Arctic, where you will feel the misery of cold and frost, to which I am impassive.*

Soon the snows thickened and the cold increased. Justine recalled her winter on the Mer de Glace; it had been preparation for her ordeal. By then, she was so far north that it had been weeks since she'd seen any of Napoleon's soldiers. She encountered peasants shut inside hovels, and rivers too frozen for fish.

Just when she could go no further, the monster would leave offerings of food. A letter tucked inside a skinned hare taunted:

> Prepare! Eat this and be refreshed! Your toils only begin.
> Soon your suffering will satisfy my need for revenge.

Justine's perseverance was invigorated by his words; she resolved not to fail. She procured a sledge and dogs to travel the snows with greater speed, and clothes sewn of reindeer and wolf skins. Her ensemble was completed by a rabbit fur cloak and metal goggles to avoid snow blindness.

By the time she reached the northern ocean, the monster was less than a single day's journey ahead, judging by the condition of a recently slaughtered seal he'd left her. She pressed on, and in two days' time arrived at a wretched hamlet on the shore, where a band of wary rustics emerged from their hovels at her arrival.

"Where have you come from, stranger?" a bone-thin girl encased in furs asked Justine in rudimentary Russian; Justine had picked up enough of the language during her travels to survive.

"Geneva." Justine could barely recall the city-republic's blue lake and majestic mountains. All the world was snow and ice.

"Alas, Geneva no longer exists as it was," an elderly man clucked. "It's now part of France. Napoleon."

"No matter, sir. My goal is to seek the one who fled from me."

"And did the man you pursue travel in the same fashion as you on the ice?"

"Yes."

"Then I fancy we have seen him."

The hamlet's inhabitants described a gigantic demon, who'd arrived the night before armed with pistols. He'd stolen a sled, all their firewood, and six dogs before taking off across the frozen sea.

"He was heading toward the north pole," a young man with a scarred cheek explained. "Earlier this year, a ship tried to sail there, claiming it's a land of sunshine and eternal spring, a garden of Eden. It's not."

Justine resisted despair. Again, the monster had eluded her; now she would commence an almost endless journey across the Arctic amid cold few could endure. Yet at the fear that he should live, her hunger for vengeance returned. It overwhelmed her like a mighty tide.

"Tell me what I must do to survive," she begged.

She listened humbly and desperately. Once they finished their explanation, she said, "I need a similar sled fashioned for the frozen sea, food, and whatever else you recommend."

To pay for these provisions, she offered her most precious possession besides Caroline's locket: Elizabeth's emerald ring. She departed, taking to heart the advice she'd received.

Days passed in a blur of white and cold. At night, she slept surrounded by her dogs for warmth.

And then, at last, she found him.

By the amount of food she'd consumed, she judged it had been three weeks since she left the hamlet when she caught sight of a dark speck upon the frozen plain. She pulled off her goggles for a better view with her collapsible telescope.

A sleigh borne by dogs, like hers. The distorted proportions of a well-known form within it.

It's him.

She shouted with all her might, "Wait for me! Please!"

Her words were buoyed across the ice on the wind. In her telescope, she saw the monster glance her way; she imagined his grim smile, his cackle. Her dogs began to bark. Her tears froze.

Then the worst happened: the ice beneath her split and cracked with a tremendous sound. She saved all but two of her dogs when her sled slid into the ocean along with everything but her satchel and snowshoes. Miraculously, she remained dry.

Once the ice refroze, Justine freed the surviving dogs to find their way. She opened her satchel. She still had food. Three days' worth. The lens had cracked on her telescope and her compass scratched. Fortunately, the miniature of Caroline remained intact.

Perhaps she's with me.

She began to walk, her toes and cheeks too numb for pain.

Three days. That's all I have.

* * *

The first day passed. The landscape transformed into one unlike any she'd seen. Open. Endless. Cold. The sky shimmered with unnatural colors she'd never before witnessed. Stars rose, offering constellations to guide her path. She managed to steal a few hours' rest.

The second day arrived. She staggered back on her feet. The muscles of her thighs burned. Her toenails peeled from their beds of flesh. Frostbite—she'd been warned of it. Her arms ached from holding them aloft for balance. During the worst of it, she slipped face-first when her snowshoe snagged on a pebble of ice. Blood marred the white of the snow.

Her face reflected back to her. A loose tooth, a split lip. Scars along the side of her cheek, her brow. Eyes swollen around her goggles from the cold. Nose battered. Bruises on her jaw.

A monster. Same as she'd been but more so.

She spat out the tooth. She forced herself upright, arms again aloft.

And then she can continue no more. She recalls her hanging, which left her neck miraculously intact. The bullet from Victor's pistol that should have killed her. Two deaths she's survived. Now a third death awaits her, this one by ice—she can no longer deny it.

This will be my third death since I became a monster.

She slides back to the ice. The sun is high. Blinding despite her goggles. She squints out from beneath her hood, calculating the angle, the hour.

"It's December, toward the end of 1799," she reminds herself, the words as loose as the remaining teeth in her mouth. "Nearly the start of a new century—a century in which a king and his queen no longer have heads, and the French reign over Geneva aided by that ambitious general from Corsica." She draws a deep breath. "I am still alive. I still breathe. I still possess a body."

And I have only one day's worth of food.

Victor was right: the monster will survive; she's destroyed herself for naught. She feels as foolish as a housewife who's spent coins meant for meat on seeds. The proximity to the shift of century makes the death she anticipates seem especially unfair. Couldn't she remain alive a little longer, to see if the earth will snap open like a cuckoo clock to announce the new century? But she won't weep—her tears would only freeze inside her goggles.

"You win!" she shouts into the wind. "I hope you're happy!"

Her voice echoes back from the emptiness.

She sits on her knees and opens her satchel. May as well eat what remains. As she shoves the last of the dried seal into her mouth, acid rises from her stomach, dank and bitter, but she doesn't vomit.

Every tale must come to an end. I suppose this is mine.

She lets her body go soft. Frost radiates to her heart, her womb, as she settles against her bed of ice. Her muscles shudder. Pulse slows. And then her mind returns to Geneva. To a time before it all began, before she knew of the Frankensteins. That night when she stumbled into their garden, the one surrounding the house set a league east of Geneva.

She remembers it all. She watches it all. It all unfolds like a tale as the snow begins anew. But it's not only her history she recalls. It's everyone's. She sees Caroline in her bed, Elizabeth with Henry, and so much more, as though her body has become a repository for collective memory. For story.

Then the unexpected occurs: Justine's fur cloak undulates. Her bare cheek meets warmth—the warmth of life. A fox, whiskers twitching, pale eyes like hers.

His fur is mottled white. White like the ice. White like snow.

He nuzzles at her neck, the last place in her body bearing any heat.

"Come, darling," she whimpers. "Closer."

Suddenly the wind howls so loud she's forced to cover her ears. Worse, the wind is accompanied by the thickest snow she's ever witnessed, mottled like churned cream. Her body shakes. Chest heaves. She yearns to scream. She doesn't, for just as unexpectedly, the snow settles.

The fox is gone. And then they're before her. All of them. Elizabeth. Caroline. Ella. More. A host of women, all bearing wounds and bruises and scars and violations and curses. An army of females. Even Justine's mother and sister—her mother approaches from the crowd to offer Justine a harsh glare. The line is endless, extending all the way toward the horizon. All unnatural creatures, if one believes the testimony of men.

The women's bodies appear pale as ice and as faint as shades. Their voices are sinuous. Seductive. "Free us," they murmur. "You know what to do."

I really must be dying.

"What do you want of me?" Justine shouts. "Tell me!"

Caroline and Elizabeth step forward to point toward the horizon. It takes Justine a moment, but she understands.

A red flickering speck in the distance. Her heart rises.

Let it be him.

The speck grows longer than a sled. Taller than a house. Brighter than the sun. Her heart pounds.

It must be him.

She tries to run, but it's impossible—the surface is too slick even for snowshoes. Desperate, she grabs the telescope from her satchel. Through the cracked lens, she makes out the irrefutable evidence of fire. A bonfire. A creature taller than a man created by woman.

It's him.

As she tramps toward the monster, she imagines another world, an idyllic world akin to what that villager spoke of when he described the north pole. An Eden infused by sunshine and eternal spring. She recalls Ernest's desire for a new world after the revolution, one built on ideals of equality and liberty. Then there's Victor's dream of a world without death or loss—but none of these worlds can be glimpsed in this land of ice she inhabits.

Men are dreamers, she thinks. *They expect women to clean their messes.* And Justine has one last mess to clean—one she has traveled far and wide to fulfill. Though she understands she has no reason to trust

Victor's monster will disclose the secret of his death, she hopes. Here in the Arctic, hope remains her most prized possession.

He must honor his promise.

CHAPTER XIV.

"Great God! what a scene has just taken place! I am yet dizzy with the remembrance of it. I hardly know whether I shall have the power to detail it; yet the tale which I have recorded would be incomplete without this."

* * *

IN THE FAR NORTH, distances are mirages; mirages disappear when approached by a monster of a woman wearing snowshoes and a rabbit fur cloak. Sooner than Justine can believe, the bonfire grows larger than she imagined, taller and closer. It resembles the hell her mother described to set the fear of God into Justine's soul. The heat of the bonfire singes her cheeks; it's a miracle the ice hasn't melted beneath the flames, quenching them in frigid water.

And then *he* is there. *Him.* The monster. Victor's son. What had she called him, that name? Emet. It was so long ago, another life. Another world. How fanciful she'd been, how foolish! He's no golem created to serve humanity, like she'd once served Caroline and Elizabeth. He's a nightmare brought to life to serve out death.

The monster is lying before the fire. Beside him, a line of plump silvery fish hang from a tall pole, their translucent flesh crackling from heat. Justine ignores the food, as ravenous as she is; it's the monster who claims her attention. He's rolled into a ball, like an enormous fetus sprung from a womb. A baby grown amok.

His clothes—or what remains of them—are blackened with ash. Most of his body is bared; the scars and burns she'd previously witnessed are all the more hideous to behold. He's even more gigantic in stature than she recalls, yet more uncouth and distorted in his proportions. His face is concealed by locks of black, ragged hair. One vast hand is extended, its color and texture like that of a mummy. It rests over his eyes. Is he sleeping?

Not if I can help it.

Justine's anger rises as high as the bonfire he's built. "You!" she cries in tones more passionate than she's ever wielded in her life. She kicks his leg. "Honor your word!"

The monster draws his hand from his eyes. Justine nearly falls to her knees. Perhaps it's because she hasn't seen him up close in nearly a year —this is how long they've been trapped in their folly of an Arctic chase —that she's horrified anew by him. Never has she beheld a vision as hideous as him, of such loathsome yet appalling ugliness. And yet it's his crimes she recalls most. How had she ever felt sympathy for him? Invited him to befriend her in that hut on the Mer de Glace?

His dun-hued gaze awaits her. A trickle of moisture covers his cheeks; miraculously it remains unfrozen. This stirs her fury to greater heights.

"What reason have you to shed tears?" she demands, her arms akimbo.

"I weep because you're not my final victim—I thought you dead. You live, Justine."

Her chest begins to thump. Quickening. She won't reveal her fear.

"Let me guess. You intend to kill me instead of honoring our pact."

He shakes his head. "You don't comprehend, Justine. If you'd become another murder by my hands, I would not have been able to bear it."

Justine's arms fall to her sides. "You're happy to see me . . . alive? But you wanted my death! You wanted revenge!"

"I couldn't help my cruelty—when I saw you in the cemetery, all I thought of was Victor gone. My father dead. It was sorrow I felt for the loss. I couldn't bear it—yet again he'd found a way to abandon me! I know you don't believe me—"

"I don't believe you!"

"I know you think me irredeemable, that I'm cursed by my unnatural creation. Think you the groans of Clerval were music to my ears? The tears of William? Believe me when I say my heart was fashioned to be susceptible of love and friendship—"

"Which I offered you," Justine interjects, her head light.

"And which I could not accept, for I was too miserable and wretched. After the murder of Clerval I returned to Switzerland, resolved to remain away from all humanity, for I abhorred myself. Yet when I met you on the Mer de Glace, I entertained the possibility of change.

"I thought, 'Here is one as miserable and apart from the world as I am. I shall offer her comfort in her isolation.' But once I learned who you were, that even *you*, who appeared as scorned by humanity as myself, bore connections to Victor Frankenstein and his family, I understood redemption could never be mine." He pauses to draw a deep breath. "It is true I am a wretch. I murdered the lovely and the helpless; I strangled the innocent as they slept, and those who never injured me or any other living thing."

The monster's words are overtaken by sobs of the most violent variety, which sets the bonfire blazing from their force. Justine backs away to avoid singeing her flesh.

"Yes, you are a wretch!" she shouts. "You've drawn me hundreds of leagues north to whine over the desolation you made! You throw a torch into a pile of kindling—" she gestures at the bonfire flaming behind them "— and when they are consumed, you sit among the ruins and weep."

"That is not true!" he cries. "It is not thus. Not thus! Yet such must be the impression conveyed by my actions."

"Liar! You murdered Elizabeth—how can you claim otherwise?" Now it is Justine's turn to be overcome by sobs though no tears emerge to warm her cheeks; it's too frigid. "Elizabeth was the kindest creature to ever draw breath! She was my only friend! She saved me when I could not save myself."

"I could not help it, Justine. When I discovered that Frankenstein, the reason for my existence and its torments, dared to enjoy passions he had barred me, my envy and indignation filled me with an insatiable thirst for vengeance. When I swore to be with Elizabeth on Frankenstein's wedding night, I was the slave of an impulse I detested but could not disobey. Yet when she died!" A long groan rises from him. "I was not miserable, for evil had become my good . . . especially after I discovered you'd intervened with my revenge on Frankenstein."

Emptied at last of language, the monster wipes his eyes. The frigid wind blows about them. The flames from the bonfire flicker. A rain of ash.

"And now, here we are," Justine prompts. "And here it shall end. You *will* keep your vow. You *will* reveal the secret of your death."

He points toward the bonfire.

"That's all," he says.

Fire. Justine shouldn't have been surprised, but she is. She'd expected the secret of the monster's mortality to be as convoluted as the explanations she'd read in Victor's journal, or as alchemical as Henry's tale of the golem. But it makes sense—he was born of lightning. Now he shall die in flames.

"This bonfire will destroy me," the monster confesses. "It shall be my funeral pyre. I shall no longer feel the agonies tormenting me. Nor shall I see the sun or stars or feel the winds play on my cheeks. Light, feeling, and sense will pass away; and in this condition I will find peace. Some years ago, when I first felt the warmth of summer and heard the warbling of the birds, and these were all new to me, I should have wept to die. Now it is my only consolation. And yet . . . and yet . . ."

His long arms dangle by his side. Snow falls from his cheeks. Frozen tears. Despite herself, Justine's throat tightens. She recalls mornings in Lake Como, the dazzle of light on the lake, the beauty when she'd awakened to life after her hanging. The flight of orioles, the fox dashing in the woods. The lush scent of summer roses.

But I am not him. I am good. Yet she feels a compassion for him she never expected. She recalls her gravedigger father, who loved her in spite of her mother's rejection.

"If only your father loved you."

"I suppose you'll offer to be my friend again?" His tone is mocking though his eyes remain wet. His gaze dashes toward the pyre. He's afraid. Terrified.

She says, "I'll be your mother then."

The words emerge from her lips before she can think on them. But as soon as she says them, she knows they are the right words.

She approaches him. He doesn't rebuff her when she gathers him in her arms. She sings, though her voice is harsh. The song is a lullaby she'd used to soothe William way back when. Her voice rises into the frozen sky, summoning a mound of ash from his funeral pyre to her side.

As Justine sings, she's back in Geneva on that summer night, surrounded by Victor, Henry, and Caroline. There's Victor speaking of ghost stories, Caroline refusing. *"Not ghost stories. Something else . . ."* Justine offering her own story, the tale of the golem. *"It's one my father told me of his childhood in Prague."* The others didn't believe her, she could tell. But Henry, kind noble Henry, defended her. *"He was called Emet, which means truth in the ancient language of the Hebrews. This was the word the rabbi had written on his forehead to bring him to life."*

"But what of his death?" This was Victor, eager as ever for knowledge.

Henry explained, *"To destroy him, the rabbi removed the letter 'e' from 'emet', which created the word 'met'—'death' . . ."*

Justine blinks, and she returns to the present moment, in which she's seated on a bank of ice in the Arctic with a sobbing monster in her arms. And then she knows what she must do.

He nuzzles her breast, eyes shut tight. "Mother," he moans. "Help me."

I will, my child. I promise.

The ash coating the ice is soft and grey. It coats her fingertips after she removes her glove. She smudges his forehead with ash, recalling the Ash Wednesdays of her youth, the lush scent of Easter lilies, the promise of resurrection. But it's not a cross she's marked across the monster's scarred brow.

Emet, she's written.

"Once I remove this first letter, you will cease to exist," she explains, not quite believing herself, but it's all she has to offer. "Shall I?"

After a moment, Emet shakes his head. He pulls away.

"No. I shan't make you a murderess."

He kisses her cheek. And then he embraces her for what she understands is a last time.

He rises from her arms. He squares his shoulders.

Step by step, Emet approaches his funeral pyre. His dark luxuriant hair catches first, brilliant as lightning in a summer sky. His rags flare next, then the tips of his fingers. Justine forces herself to watch as the fire consumes him, determined to bear witness, for this is what survivors do.

The pyre swooshes and grows, dazzling in golds, silver, and scarlets. Flames flare to the sky. The wind rises and rushes, knocking Justine to her feet. She watches and wonders and waits.

Half a century later, when she is an old woman surrounded by family and memories, she'll speak of what she watched that day on the ice though no one will believe her. She'll confess she wondered whether Emet would emerge from the fire reborn like a phoenix. She'll tell how she waited by the pyre for any sign of his survival: the silhouette of an arm, the echo of a cry. She'll confide she found nothing—only the hush of wind blowing ash, the distant crack of ice.

He's gone. Justine is surprised by sorrow yet also freed; whatever curse she'd sensed has been banished. Now she must save herself. But how?

She stares down at her snowshoe-clad feet. She'll leave the way she came. Somehow she'll find a whaling vessel; from there, she'll find her way home, wherever that may be. In the meantime, she won't starve. She sets Emet's catch of silvery fish inside her satchel, rummages through his belongings. She'll survive.

These acts done, she begins to walk toward the horizon. Toward the sea, where her new life awaits. She was soon borne away on the ice and lost in light and distance.

ACKNOWLEDGEMENTS

THOUGH UNNATURAL CREATURES was directly inspired by *Frankenstein*, I could not have brought it to life without the help of the following people.

My literary agent, Michelle Brower, was the first to express enthusiasm when I proposed a novel centering around the premise of Justine Moritz's possible survival after her execution. Michelle's ever-insightful comments helped shape *Unnatural Creatures* from nascent idea into the book you've just read. I'm especially grateful to my dear friend Heather Webb, who brainstormed plot points, mulled character arcs, and commented on numerous drafts of this book.

My librarian friend Courtney Walsh was instrumental in connecting me to scholars via the "Technology of Frankenstein" conference, which was held at the Stevens Institute of Technology in 2018. It was there that I met Catherine Siemann, who generously pointed me to academic resources and offered manuscript feedback while enthusing with me over all things *Frankenstein*-related. Clarissa Harwood, who is a Victorianist as well as a gifted author of gothic novels, was incredibly helpful during the writing of *Unnatural Creatures*. I am also grateful for the sharp-eyed feedback of my critique partner, Julianne Douglas—you're amazing! In addition Ellen Dreyer, Jennifer Johnson, Crystal King, Kristin Lambert, Alyssa Palombo, Terry Lynn Thomas, and Karen Zuegner generously read and commented on this book. A Kickstarter campaign helped fund the production of a limited edition of this book.

I am so grateful to everyone there who generously backed *Unnatural Creatures*, especially Jenny Graman and Trainor Houghton-Whyte. Thank you all!

As always, I am deeply grateful for the support and love of my husband, Thomas Ross Miller, and my daughter, Thea. Both listened to me obsess about Mary Shelley and her circle with patience and humor —and yes, I know the monster's name isn't Frankenstein.

Finally, thank you to all of my readers! Your comments, reviews, and sharing of my books help me keep doing what I do. I appreciate your support and enthusiasm more than you can imagine, and hope you enjoyed my loving tribute to Mary Shelley's masterpiece.

UNNATURAL CREATURES

* * *

Meet the Author

Author's Note

Reading Group Guide

MEET THE AUTHOR

Photograph © Robert Presutti

KRIS WALDHERR is an award-winning author, illustrator, and designer whose many books for adults and children include *The Book of Goddesses*, *Bad Princess*, and *Doomed Queens*, which *The New Yorker* praised as "utterly satisfying." Her debut novel *The Lost History of Dreams* received a starred *Kirkus* review and was named a CrimeReads best book of the year. Waldherr's fiction has won fellowships from the Virginia Center of the Creative Arts and a work-in-progress reading grant from Poets & Writers.

As a visual artist, she has had her illustrations exhibited in the Ruskin Library, the Mazza Museum of International Art from

Picture Books, and the National Museum of Women in the Arts. She is also the creator of the Goddess Tarot, which has over a quarter of a million copies in print, and teaches the tarot to writers and other creatives.

Kris Waldherr works and lives in Brooklyn in a Victorian-era home with her family and cats. In her spare time, she enjoys travel, theater, and music.

To learn more, visit KrisWaldherrBooks.com, where you can also arrange for a book club visit.

facebook.com/kriswaldherr
twitter.com/kriswaldherr
instagram.com/kriswaldherr
bookbub.com/profile/kris-waldherr

AUTHOR'S NOTE

Soon after Mary Shelley's 1823 return to England from living abroad, she wrote to a friend, "Lo & behold! I found myself famous!" The cause of Shelley's surprised outburst: her 1818 novel *Frankenstein, or The Modern Prometheus,* had been transformed by Richard Brinsley Peake into a rapturously successful London play entitled *Presumption, or the Fate of Frankenstein* without her knowledge or permission. Luckily for the playwright, Shelley attended the play on the eve of her twenty-sixth birthday and proclaimed herself to be "much amused." Luckily for Shelley, the popularity of the play ensured continuing book sales for *Frankenstein,* which helped to keep her and her son solvent after the drowning death of her husband Percy Shelley a year earlier. *Presumption, or the Fate of Frankenstein* was soon moved to a larger theater in London to accommodate audience demand. By the end of 1823, it had inspired five different thespian versions of Shelley's cautionary tale of hubris on other London stages.

While Peake's play is the first known instance of *Frankenstein* inspiring a work of art, it was far from the last—and now, over two centuries later, here I am with my own novel inspired by Shelley's gothic masterpiece.

Unnatural Creatures has incubated inside me ever since my first reading of *Frankenstein* as a child of twelve. Even now, I can recall how viscerally *Frankenstein* affected me: the seductive appeal of the creature and his melancholy account of parental abandonment; my shock upon realizing that Elizabeth Lavenza would not survive her wedding night; the tears shed during the creature's last lament before he departs to attend his funeral pyre. Since then, I've reread *Frankenstein* more times than I can count, most recently during the writing of this novel, when I visited Geneva, the Mer de Glace, Chêne, Belrive (now known as Belle Rive), Mont Blanc, and the grounds of the Villa Diodati, where Shelley began writing *Frankenstein* on a stormy night in June 1816 as a result of a literary competition to write a ghost story between herself, Percy Shelley, Lord Byron, and Dr. John Polidori.

My intent in writing *Unnatural Creatures* was to reveal the untold stories of the three women closest to Victor Frankenstein—Justine Moritz, Elizabeth Lavenza, and Caroline Frankenstein—while incorporating the historical events that most likely coincided with Shelley's novel. In this way, I hope *Unnatural Creatures* might be considered a companion piece to Shelley's novel in the same manner in which Jo Baker's *Longbourn* is to *Pride and Prejudice,* and Jean Rhys's *Wide Sargasso Sea* to *Jane Eyre*—novels that offer the other side of the story.

For the most part, everything that occurs in *Unnatural Creatures* either supports the timeline of events offered in *Frankenstein*, or takes place during periods that are "off stage" from Victor's first person narrative or subject to his unreliable perspective. The main exceptions to this rule are events occurring after Elizabeth Lavenza Frankenstein's wedding night, and those surrounding the trial of Justine Moritz.

During my many readings of *Frankenstein*, I've always been struck by the plot point of Justine's aunt in Chêne, who serves as the maid's ineffectual alibi for the murder of William Frankenstein. Why didn't the aunt testify at Justine's trial? Why does Justine mention Chêne, a small village south of Geneva, so specifically? When I learned Chêne was forced under French rule in 1792, I experienced a "Eureka!" moment that led me to notice the overlap between the tragic events described in *Frankenstein* and the historical events of revolutionary France and Geneva.

From there, I was stunned to learn Geneva had experienced several revolutions of its own. As I charted my way through the political events as they coincided with the timeline of Shelley's novel, I am particularly indebted to Frank V. Randel's paper "The Political Geography of Horror in Mary Shelley's *Frankenstein*" and Janet Polasky's book *Revolutions Without Borders: The Call to Liberty in the Atlantic World*. In addition,

Mary Shelley's travel narrative *History of a Six Weeks' Tour*, which was published in 1817, the year before *Frankenstein's* publication, specifically mentions the July 1794 execution of the syndics in Plainpalais. Shelley writes: *"Here a small obelisk is erected to the glory of Rousseau, and here (such is the mutability of human life) the magistrates . . . were shot by the populace during that revolution . . . From respect to the memory of their predecessors, none of the present magistrates ever walk in Plainpalais."* Earlier in the same paragraph: *"[Geneva] is surrounded by a wall, the three gates of which are shut exactly at ten o'clock, when no bribery (as in France) can open them."* One cannot help but wonder if Shelley had experienced being locked out by these same gates, just as poor Justine was!

Though the 1831 edition of Frankenstein describes Justine's trial as occurring in June, I shifted it a few weeks later so her hanging would overlap with the execution of the syndics. In addition, I tightened the length of time between Victor's return to Belrive from Chamounix and his departure for England for the sake of narrative tension. I also expanded the period Victor's journal covers; the 1831 edition of *Frankenstein* states the journal only covers the four months prior to the birth of Victor's creature. I also took historical liberty in my description of Luigi Galvani, the inventor of the electrical phenomena known as galvanism, which Shelley hints at during her description of the creature's animation. The scene of Dr. Galvani's soirée presentation was inspired by accounts I read of public electrical displays of the era, rather than his scientific experiments involving "animal magnetism." I have no idea how much time, if any, he may have spent in Geneva.

While I wrote *Unnatural Creatures*, I did my best to weave in Shelley's original language when possible, incorporating quotes and snippets of dialogue and description where they best fit the story I yearned to tell, sometimes retrofitting these inside alternate scenes. One example: the description of Elizabeth Lavenza's botanical watercolors before her wedding. This passage originally appeared in Shelley's novel soon after Victor has "given birth" to his creature, and illuminates his growing horror at what his hands have wrought. In addition, elements of Mary Shelley's life—her experiences with natal loss, her tumultuous relationship with Percy Shelley, her complicated history with her mother, father, and stepmother—served to enrich aspects of my novel. I particularly believe the writing of *Frankenstein* was influenced by the absence of Mary Shelley's mother, Mary Wollstonecraft, who died of puerperal fever days after giving birth to her daughter, as well as the death of Mary Shelley's first child, a daughter born premature in 1815. Soon after, Shelley wrote in her journal of a dream where "my little baby came to life again; that it had only been cold, and that we rubbed it before the fire, and it lived."

I read (and reread!) all editions of *Frankenstein* numerous times, from Shelley's 1816 handwritten manuscript draft to her final revised 1831 edition, as well as numerous critical essays, studies, and biographies of Shelley and her circle. Of these, Fiona Sampson's *In Search of Mary Shelley: The Girl Who Wrote Frankenstein* and Charlotte Gordon's *Romantic Outlaws: The Extraordinary Lives of Mary Wollstonecraft and Her Daughter Mary Shelley* were particularly helpful to my understanding of Shelley and her tumultuous circumstances. Though all versions of *Frankenstein* served as basis for my characters and their travails in *Unnatural Creatures*, I drew most directly from the 1831 edition due to the description of Elizabeth Lavenza as an abandoned orphan unrelated to the Frankensteins. In the 1818 edition, Elizabeth is a blood cousin to Victor, which makes her integration into the Frankenstein household a matter of course rather than choice. By using the 1831 edition for Elizabeth's backstory, all three of my main characters—Elizabeth, Caroline, and Justine—are thus rendered as orphans without blood ties to the Frankenstein family.

Finally, the *Frankenstein* excerpts at the start of each chapter are drawn from the 1831 edition. I also chose to use Shelley's anachronistic spelling of places and letter style in order to tie *Unnatural Creatures* all the closer to its literary predecessor.

READING GROUP GUIDE

1. *Frankenstein* is one of the most famous horror stories ever told. What was your first encounter with *Frankenstein*? Was it through the novel or a film or television series? How do your memories of Victor Frankenstein and his monster compare to what you read in *Unnatural Creatures*?

2. Negligent, abusive, and absent parents are a theme throughout *Unnatural Creatures*. They range from Madame Moritz to Victor Frankenstein, who rejects his "son" after creating him. Who else could be considered a bad mother or father in the novel? How are they so? Discuss.

3. Caroline Frankenstein, Elizabeth Lavenza, and Justine Moritz serve as the three protagonists of *Unnatural Creatures*. Which woman did you most identify with? Whose story most moved you? Were you surprised by who survived at the end?

4. Elizabeth Lavenza chooses to place her loyalty to the Frankensteins above her love for Henry Clerval, Victor's best friend. Do you think she was right to do so? What would you have done in her situation?

5. *Unnatural Creatures* takes place during the French and Genevan revolutions of the late 18th century. What are the ways *Unnatural Creatures* uses this politically volatile setting to further its plot and themes?

6. What did you make of Justine's relationship with the creature she names Emet? Do you think Emet cared for her? Or was he too emotionally damaged as a result of Victor's rejection?

7. Do you think Victor was right not to create a mate for Emet? Were there other ways Victor could have fulfilled Emet's needs as a sentient being, thus avoiding the extinction of the Frankenstein family?

8. Rabbits, foxes, jackdaws, and other "natural creatures" appear throughout the pages of *Unnatural Creatures*. What do you think they symbolize, if anything? Do you associate them with particular characters? If so, who and why?

9. Finally, what do you think happened to Justine after she departed the Arctic? How do you envision the remainder of her life?

* * *

ACTIVITIES TO ENHANCE YOUR BOOK CLUB

1. Read (or reread) *Frankenstein*. The 1818 edition of *Frankenstein* was authored by Mary Shelley when she was still a teenager. However, Waldherr drew most directly from the revised 1831 edition when she wrote *Unnatural Creatures*.

2. Have a monster movie night. The first filmed representation of Victor Frankenstein and his monster appeared in a short film by Edison Studios in 1910. Since then, innumerable films and television series have been inspired by Shelley's novel. Here are several that are available for viewing online:

- *Frankenstein*—1931 film directed by James Whale;
- *Young Frankenstein*—1974 film directed by Mel Brooks;
- *Mary Shelley's Frankenstein*—1994 film directed by Kenneth Branagh;
- *Frankenstein*—2011 play directed by Danny Boyle at the Royal National Theater.

3. **Learn more about Mary Shelley's life.** Waldherr cites *In Search of Mary Shelley: The Girl Who Wrote Frankenstein* by Fiona Sampson and *Romantic Outlaws: The Extraordinary Lives of Mary Wollstonecraft and Her Daughter Mary Shelley* by Charlotte Gordon as being particularly helpful to her during the writing of *Unnatural Creatures*. In addition, the 2017 film *Mary Shelley* offers a fictionalized account of her love affair with Percy Shelley and subsequent writing of *Frankenstein*.

4. **Take an online tour of Geneva and the Villa Diodati**, where *Frankenstein* was written. A quick search on YouTube offers numerous possibilities. For example, here's a walking tour of the "old city", where the Frankenstein family resided: https://youtu.be/BE-lyw7MgHU

5. **Finally, if you're a Doctor Who fan,** watch Season Twelve's "The Haunting of Villa Diodati" episode.

Made in the USA
Middletown, DE
22 July 2023

35572343R00220